"Hello," she called. "Any

Her footsteps echoed on of the center hall. To her left was a formal sitting room with a marble fireplace and a crystal chandelier, then a smaller room and the library. There had to be someone around. Nobody would leave the door open with the place empty.

"Louis? Are you here? It's me, Carine."

He could be upstairs, she thought, slinging her camera bag over her shoulder. As she turned to head back to the front entry, something caught her eye in the library. She wasn't sure what—something out of place. Wrong.

She took a shallow breath, and it was as if a force stronger than she was compelled her to take a step forward and peer through the double doorway. Carine touched the wood molding, telling herself she must have simply seen a shadow or a stray drop cloth. Then she jumped back, inhaling sharply, even as her mind struggled to take in what she was seeing—a man facedown on the wood floor. Louis. She recognized the dark suit, his scrub-brush hair. She lunged forward, but stopped abruptly, almost instinctively.

A pool of something dark, a liquid, oozed toward her. She stood motionless, refusing to absorb what she was seeing.

Blood.

It seeped into the cracks in the narrow-board floor. It covered Louis's outstretched hand.

Help…

CARLA NEGGERS

COLD RIDGE

MIRA®

ISBN 1-55166-684-7

COLD RIDGE

Copyright © 2003 by Carla Neggers.

Visit us at www.mirabooks.com

Printed in U.S.A.

ACKNOWLEDGMENTS

A very special thank-you to Merline Lovelace, a retired air force colonel, a terrific writer and a friend, and to Monty Fleck, an air force pararescueman (PJ), for answering my many questions about the air force and pararescue. I'm also grateful to Monty, R. B. Gustavson, Patty Otto and Dr. Carla Patton for sharing their medical expertise with me, and to Lynn Camp for her insight into nature photography. Thanks also to Lieutenant Kevin Burns, Nancy Geary, Robyn and Jim Carr, my brother Jeffrey Neggers—and to my teenage son, Zack Jewell, for his technical know-how.

Finally, I'd like to thank the incredible team at MIRA Books—Amy Moore-Benson, Dianne Moggy, Tania Charzewski and all the rest of the "gang"—as well as my tireless agent, Meg Ruley, and my talented Webmaster, Sally Shoeneweiss, for all your hard work on my behalf.

Enjoy!

Carla Neggers
P.O. Box 826
Quechee, Vermont 05059

To Fran Garfunkel

Prologue

Carine Winter loaded her day pack with hiking essentials and her new digital camera and headed into the woods, a rolling tract of land northeast of town that had once been dairy farms. She didn't go up the ridge. It was a bright, clear November day in the valley with little wind and highs in the fifties, but on Cold Ridge, the temperature had dipped below freezing, wind gusts were up to fifty miles an hour and its exposed, knife-edged granite backbone was already covered in snow and ice.

Her parents had hiked Cold Ridge in November and died up there when she was three. Thirty years ago that week, but Carine still remembered.

Gus, her uncle, had been a member of the search party that found his older brother and sister-in-law. He was just twenty himself, not a year home from Vietnam, but he'd taken on the responsibility of raising Carine and her older brother and sister. Antonia was just five at the time, Nate seven.

Yes, Carine thought as she climbed over a stone wall, she remembered so much of those terrible days, although she had been too young to really understand what had happened. Gus had taken her and her brother and sister up the ridge the spring after the tragedy. Cold Ridge loomed over their northern New Hampshire valley and their small hometown of the same name. Gus said they couldn't be afraid of it. His brother had been a firefighter, his sister-in-law a biology teacher, both avid hikers. They weren't reckless or inexperienced. People in the valley still talked about their deaths. Never mind that weather reports were now more accurate, hiking clothes and equipment more high-tech—if Cold Ridge could kill Harry and Jill Winter, it could kill anyone.

Carine waited until she was deep into the woods before she took out her digital camera. She wasn't yet sure she liked it. But she wouldn't be able to concentrate on any serious photography today. Her mind kept drifting back to fleeting memories, half-formed images of her parents, anything she could grasp.

Gus, who'd become one of the most respected outfitters and guides in the White Mountains, would object to her hiking alone. It was the one risk she allowed herself to take, the one safety rule she allowed herself to break.

She'd climbed all forty-eight peaks in the White Mountains over four thousand feet. Seven were over five thousand feet: Washington, Adams, Jefferson, Monroe, Madison, Lafayette and Lincoln. At 6288 feet, Mt. Washington was the highest, and the most famous, notorious for its extreme conditions, some of the worst in the world. At any time of the year, hikers could find themselves facing hurricane-force winds on its bald granite summit—Carine had herself. Because of the conditions the treeline was lower in the White Mountains than out west, generally at around 4500 feet.

It was said the Abenakis considered the tall peaks sacred and never climbed them. Carine didn't know if that was true, but she could believe it.

Most of the main Cold Ridge trail was above four thousand feet, exposing hikers to above-treeline conditions for a longer period than if they just went up and down a single peak.

But today, Carine was content with her mixed hardwood forest of former farmland. Gus had warned her to stay away from Bobby Poulet, a survivalist who had a homestead on a few acres on the northeast edge of the woods. He was a legendary crank who'd threatened to shoot anyone who stepped foot on his property.

She took pictures of rocks and burgundy-colored oak leaves, water trickling over rocks in a narrow stream, a hemlock, a fallen, rotting elm and an abandoned hunting shack with a crooked metal chimney. The land was owned by a lumber company that, fortunately, had a laissez-faire attitude toward hikers.

She almost missed the owl.

It was a huge barred owl, as still as a stone sculpture, its neutral coloring blending in with the mostly gray November landscape as it perched on a branch high in a naked beech tree.

Before Carine could raise her camera, the owl swooped off its branch and flapped up over the low ridge above her, out of sight.

She sighed. She'd won awards for her photography of raptors—she'd have loved to have had a good shot of the owl. On the other hand, she wasn't sure her digital camera was up to the task.

A loud boom shattered the silence of the isolated ravine.

Carine dropped flat to the ground, facedown, before she could absorb what the sound was.

A gunshot.

Her camera had flown out of her hand and landed in the dried leaves two feet above her outstretched arm. Her day pack ground into her back. And her heart was pounding, her throat tight.

Damn, she thought. How close was that?

It had to be hunters. Not responsible hunters. *Insane* hunters—yahoos who didn't know what they were doing. Shooting that close to her. What were they thinking? Didn't they see her? She'd slipped a bright-orange vest over her fleece jacket. She knew it was deer-hunting season, but this was the first time a hunter had fired anywhere *near* her.

"Hey!" She lifted her head to yell but otherwise remained prone on the damp ground, in the decaying fallen leaves. "Knock it off! There's someone up here!"

As if in answer, three quick, earsplitting shots

cracked over her head, whirring, almost whistling. One hit the oak tree a few yards to her right.

Were these guys total idiots?

She should have hiked in the White Mountain National Forest or one of the state parks where hunting was prohibited.

Just two yards to her left was a six-foot freestanding boulder. If these guys weren't going to stop shooting, she needed to take cover. Staying low, she picked up her camera then scrambled behind the boulder, ducking down, her back against the jagged granite. The ground was wetter here, and her knees and seat were already damp. Cold, wet conditions killed. More hikers in the White Mountains died of hypothermia than any other cause. It was what had killed her parents thirty years ago. They were caught in unexpected freezing rain and poor visibility. They fell. Injured, unable to move, unable to stay warm—they didn't stand a chance.

Carine reminded herself she had a change of clothes in her pack. Food. Water. A first-aid kit. A jackknife, flashlight, map, compass, waterproof matches. Her clothes were made of a water-wicking material that would help insulate her even when wet.

Her boulder would protect her from gunshots.

The woods settled into silence. Maybe the shooters had realized their mistake. For all she knew, they— or he, since there might only be one—were on their way up her side of the ravine to apologize and make sure she was all right. More likely, they were clearing out and hoping she hadn't seen them.

Three more shots in rapid succession ricocheted off her boulder, ripping off chunks and shards of granite. Carine screamed, startled, frustrated, angry. And scared now.

A rock shard from her boulder struck her in the forehead, and her mouth snapped shut.

Good God, were they *aiming* at her?

Were they trying to kill her?

She curled up in a ball, knees tucked, arms wrapped around her ankles. Blood dripped from her forehead onto her wrist. She felt no pain from her injury, but her heart raced and her ears hurt from the blasts. She couldn't think.

Once again, silence followed the rapid burst of shots.

Were they reloading? Coming after her? *What?*

She tried to control her breathing, hoping the shooters wouldn't hear her. But what was the point? They had to know now, after she'd screamed, that she was behind the boulder.

They'd known it before they'd shot at it.

She couldn't stay where she was.

The low ridge crested fifteen feet above her. If she could get up the hill, she could slip down the other side and hide among the trees and boulders, make her way back to her car, call the police.

If the shooters tried to follow her, she'd at least see them up on the ridge.

See them and do what?

She pushed back the thought. She'd figure that out later. Should she stand up and run? Crouch? Or should she crawl? Scoot up the hill on her stomach? No scooting. She'd be like a giant fluorescent worm in her orange vest. Take it off? No—no time.

She'd take her day pack. It might stop or impede a bullet.

Or should she stay put? Hope they hadn't seen her after all?

Every fiber in her body—every survival instinct she had—told her that she'd be killed if she stayed where she was.

She picked out the largest trees, a mix of evergreens and hardwoods, their leaves shed for the season, between her boulder and the ridgeline. The hillside was strewn with glacial boulders. It was New Hampshire. The Granite State.

Inhaling, visualizing her exact route, she crouched down racer-style, and, on an exhale, bolted up the hill. She ducked behind a hemlock straight up from her boulder, then ran diagonally to a maple, zigzagged to another hemlock, then hurled herself over the ridge crest. She scrambled downhill through a patch of switchlike bare saplings as three more quick shots boomed in the ravine on the other side of the ridge.

A whir, a cracking sound over her head.

Jesus!

They *were* shooting at her.

A crouched figure jumped out from behind a gnarled pine tree to her left, catching her around the middle with a thick arm, covering her mouth with a bare hand, then lunging with her back behind the tree.

"Carine—babe, it's me. Tyler North. Don't scream."

He removed his hand, settling in next to her on the ground, and she jerked herself away, although not entirely out of his grasp. "Was that you shooting at me? You *jackass*."

"Shh. It wasn't me."

She blinked, as if he might not be real, but she was sprawled against him, his body warm, solid. Tyler…Tyler North. He was at his most intense and focused. Combat ready, she thought, feeling a fresh jolt of fear. He was a PJ, an air force pararescueman. PJs were search-and-rescue specialists, the ones who went after pilots downed behind enemy lines. Carine had known Ty since they were tots. She'd heard he was home in Cold Ridge on leave—maybe the shooters were firing at *him*.

She tried to push back her fear and confusion. She'd been taking pictures, minding her own business. Then someone started shooting at her. Now she was here, behind a tree with Ty North. "Where—where did you come from?"

"I'm hiking with a couple of buddies. We saw your car and thought we'd join you for lunch. Figured you'd have better food." He frowned at her, peeling hair off her forehead to reveal her cut, and she remembered his search-and-rescue skills included medical training above the level of a paramedic. "Piece of flying rock hit you?"

"I think so. Ty, I don't know if they were aiming at you—"

"Let's not worry about that right now. The cut doesn't look too bad. Want to get out of here?"

She nodded, thinking she had to look like a maniac. Bloodied, twigs in her hair. Pant legs soaked and muddy. She was cold, but a long way from hypothermia.

Ty eased her day pack off and slung it over his shoulder. "We're going to zigzag down the hill, just like you came up. That was good work. Hank Callahan and Manny Carrera are out here, so don't panic if you see them."

Hank Callahan was a retired air force pilot, and Manny Carrera was another pararescueman, a master sergeant like North. Carine knew them from their previous visits to Cold Ridge. "Okay."

"All right. You got everything? If you're woozy, I can carry you—"

"I'll keep up."

North grinned at her suddenly. "You've got the prettiest eyes. Why haven't we ever dated?"

"What?"

As much as his question surprised her, he'd managed to penetrate the fear that seemed to saturate her, and when he took her hand, she ran with him without hesitation, using trees and boulders as cover, zigzagging down the hill, up another small, rounded hill. They ducked behind a stone wall above the leaf-covered stream she'd photographed earlier. Carine was breathing hard, her head pounding from fear and pain, the cut on her forehead bothering her now. They were getting closer to the main road. Her car. A place where she could call the police. She had a cell phone in her pack, but there was no service out here.

Leaves crunched nearby, and Hank Callahan joined them, exchanging a quick smile with Carine. He was square-jawed and blue-eyed, distinguished-looking, his dark hair streaked with gray. He had none of the compact, pitbull scrappiness of tawny-haired Tyler North.

"Christ, Ty," Hank said in a low voice, "she's hurt—"

"She's fine."

"I'm scared shitless! Those bastards were *shooting* at me!" Carine didn't raise her voice, but she wasn't calm. "Yahoos. Hunters—"

Hank shook his head, and Ty said, "Not hunters. A hunter doesn't take a three-shot burst into a boulder, even if he's using a semiautomatic rifle. These assholes knew you were there, Carine."

"Me? But I didn't do anything—"

"Did you see anyone?" Hank asked. "Any idea how many are out there?"

"No, no idea." Her teeth were chattering, but she blamed the cold, not what Ty had said. "There's an old hunting shack not far from where the bullets started flying. It looked abandoned to me. I took pictures of it. Maybe somebody didn't like that."

"I thought you took pictures of birds," North said with a wry smile.

"I'm just most known for birds." As a child, she'd believed she could see her parents as angels, soaring above Cold Ridge with a lone hawk or eagle. Ty used to tease her for it. "I was just trying out my digital camera."

But she was breathing rapidly—too rapidly—and Ty put his hand over her mouth briefly. "Stop. Hold your breath a second before you hyperventilate."

Already feeling a little light-headed, she did as he suggested. She noticed the green color of his eyes. That wasn't a good sign. She'd never noticed anything about him before. She couldn't remember when she'd seen him last. Fourth of July fireworks? They were neighbors, but seldom saw each other. His mother had moved to the valley just before Ty was born and bought the 1817 brick house that Abraham Winter, the first of the Cold Ridge Winters, had built as a tavern. She'd called herself Saskia, but no one believed that was her real name. If she had a husband, she'd never said. She was a weaver and a painter, but not the most attentive of mothers. Ty had pretty much grown up on his own. Even as a little boy, he'd wander up on the ridge trail for hours before his mother would even realize he was gone. She died four years ago, leaving him the house and fifty acres of woods and meadow. Everyone expected him to sell it, but he didn't, although, given the demands of his military career, he wasn't around much.

Hank Callahan shifted. "I don't know about you, but I'd like to put some serious mileage between me and the guys with guns."

Carine steadied her breathing. "What about your other friend Manny—"

"Don't worry about Carrera," Ty said. "He can

take care of himself. What's the best route out of here?''

"We could follow the stone wall. There's an old logging road not far from the shack—''

He shook his head. "If the shooters are using the shack, that's the road they'd take. They'll have vehicles.''

She thought a moment. "Then we should follow the stream. It's not as direct, but it'll take us to where we parked.''

"How exposed will we be?''

"From a shooter's perspective? I can't make that judgment. I just know it's the fastest route out of here.''

"Fast is good,'' Callahan said.

Ty nodded, then winked at Carine. "Okay, babe, we'll go your way.''

She didn't remember him ever having called her "babe'' before today.

Thirty minutes later, as they came to the gravel parking area, they heard an explosion back in the woods, from the direction of the shack and the shooters. Black smoke rose up over the trees.

Hank whistled. "I wonder who the hell these guys are.''

Manny Carrera emerged from behind a half-dead white pine. He couldn't have been that far behind them, but Carine hadn't heard a thing. He was another PJ, a dark-haired, dark-eyed bull of a Texan.

"Good,'' Ty said. "That wasn't you blowing up. The shack?''

"That's my guess." Manny spoke calmly, explosions and shots fired in the woods apparently not enough to ruffle him—or North and Callahan. "There are two shooters, at least one back at the shack. I couldn't get close enough to any of them for a good description."

"I have binoculars you could have borrowed," Carine said.

He grinned at her. "But they were shooting at you, kiddo."

"Not necessarily *at* me—"

"Yes. At you. They just didn't want you dead. Scared, paralyzed, maybe. Otherwise, they wouldn't have missed, not that many times. They were using scoped, semiautomatic rifles." His tone was objective, just stating the facts, but his eyes settled on her, his gaze softening slightly. "Sorry. It wasn't an accident. It wasn't target practice gone awry. They didn't mistake you for a deer."

"I get it." She tried to be as clinical about her near-death experience as the three men were, but she kept seeing herself crouched behind the boulder, hearing the shots, feeling the rock shard hit her head. The bullets had been flying at her, not them. "Maybe they saw me taking pictures, but—" she took a breath "—to me it was just a hunting shack."

"That's enough for now," Ty said. "We can speculate later. You have a cell phone on you?"

Carine nodded. "I doubt there's any coverage out here."

She took her day pack from him and dug out her

phone, but she was totally spent from dodging bullets, diving behind trees and boulders, charging through the woods with two military types, all after tramping around on her own with her camera. She hit the wrong button and almost threw the phone onto the ground.

North quietly took it and shook his head. "No service. Hank and Manny, you take my truck. I'll go with Carine." He turned to her, eyeing her pragmatically. "Can you drive, or do you want me to?"

"I can do it."

There was no cell coverage—there were no houses—until they came to a small lake on the notch road north of the village of Cold Ridge. Even then, Ty barely got the words out to the dispatcher before service dropped out on him.

He clicked off the phone and looked over at Carine. "I'm serious," he said. "Why haven't we ever dated?"

She managed a smile. "Because I've always hated you."

He grinned at her. "No, you haven't."

And she was lost. Then and there.

By the time state and local police arrived on scene, the shack was burned to the ground and the shooters were gone. According to various law enforcement officers, Carine had likely stumbled on to a smuggling operation they'd had their eye on but couldn't pinpoint. They smuggled drugs, weapons and people into and out of Canada and were, without a doubt, very dangerous.

Everyone agreed she was lucky indeed she hadn't been killed.

Even if the pictures she took of the shack were the reason the shooters came after her, they didn't tell her anything. She'd printed them out in her tiny log cabin while she and her military trio had waited for the police to get there. They'd been and gone, taking the memory disk with them. She still had the prints. A shack in the woods with a crooked metal chimney. It looked innocent enough to her.

Ty cleaned and treated the cut on her forehead. She kept avoiding his eye, aware of her reaction to him, aware that, somehow, everything had changed between them. She'd known him forever. He'd always been a thorn in her side. He'd pushed her out of trees. He'd cut the rope on her tire swing. Now, he was making her tingle. It had to be adrenaline—a post-traumatic reaction of some sort, she decided.

Hank and Manny built a fire in her woodstove. Hank, she learned, was a newly announced, dark horse candidate to become the junior U.S. senator from Massachusetts. He was a former air force rescue helicopter pilot, a retired major who'd received national attention on his last mission a year ago to recover fishermen whose boat had capsized.

As unflappable as he'd been in the woods, Hank Callahan was rendered virtually speechless when Antonia Winter walked into her sister's cabin. It made Carine smile. Her sister was a trauma physician in

Boston, but she'd been drawn to Cold Ridge for the thirtieth anniversary of the deaths of their parents. She was a couple of inches shorter than Carine, her auburn hair a tone lighter, but Gus said both his nieces had their mother's blue eyes.

Antonia inspected Ty's medical handiwork, pronouncing it satisfactory. Ty just rolled his eyes. She was focused, hardworking and brilliant, but if she noticed Hank's reaction to her, she gave no indication of it.

Gus arrived a few minutes later and shooed out all the air force guys, glowering when North winked at Carine and promised he'd see her later. Gus let Antonia stay.

Their uncle was fifty, his dark hair mostly gray now, but he was as rangy and fit as ever. In addition to outfitting and leading hiking trips into the White Mountains, he conducted workshops in mountaineering, winter camping and mountain rescue. His goal, Carine knew, was to reduce the chances that anyone would ever again die the way his brother and sister-in-law had. But they did. People died in the mountains almost every year.

He brought in more wood for the woodstove and insisted Carine sit in front of the fire and tell him and her sister everything.

She did, except for the part about Ty saying she had pretty eyes.

Gus wanted her to head back to town with him, but Antonia offered to stay with Carine in her small cabin. Their brother, a U.S. marshal in New York, called and agreed with the general assessment that the shooters hadn't "missed" her. If they'd wanted her dead, she'd be dead. "Lay low for a few days, will you?"

Out of Antonia's earshot, Carine asked Nate what he'd think if she dated Tyler North.

"Has he asked you out?"

"No."

"Thank God for small favors."

The next day, Ty and his friends ended up rescuing a Massachusetts couple who got trapped on Cold Ridge. Sterling and Jodie Rancourt had recently bought a house off the notch road and set out on their first hike on the ridge, for what they'd intended to be a simple afternoon excursion. Instead, they encountered higher winds, colder temperatures and rougher terrain than they'd anticipated. Ty, Hank and Manny, prepared for the conditions, helped transport them below the treeline, where they were met by a local volunteer rescue team.

Jodie Rancourt had sprained her ankle, and both she and her husband were in the early stages of hypothermia, in danger of spending the night on the ridge. Given their lack of experience and the harsh conditions, they could easily have died if the three air force guys hadn't come along when they had.

An eventful weekend in the White Mountains.

After Manny went back to his air force base and Hank to his senate campaign, Ty and Carine were alone on their quiet road in the shadows of Cold Ridge.

Gus sensed what was happening and stopped by to tell Carine she'd be out of her damn mind to get involved with Tyler North.

She didn't listen.

Her uncle's warning was too late. Way too late. She was in love.

She and Ty set their wedding date for Valentine's Day.

A week before she was to walk down the aisle, he showed up at her cabin and called it off.

He couldn't go through with it.

Enter Tyler North into her life.

Exit Tyler North.

As quick as that.

One

For the first time in weeks, Carine didn't spend her lunch hour thinking about photographing wild turkeys in the meadow outside her log cabin in Cold Ridge. She wandered through Boston Public Garden, eating the tuna sandwich she'd made and packed that morning. Every dime was critical to her ability to afford both her cabin in New Hampshire and her apartment in the city. Not that it was much of an apartment. Not that she could ever live in her cabin again.

The last of the leaves, even in Boston, had changed color, and many had fallen to the ground, a temptation on a sunny, mild November afternoon. Carine remembered raking huge piles of leaves as a kid with her brother and sister—and Tyler North—and diving into them, hiding, wrestling.

Ty almost suffocated her once. Unfortunately, she hadn't thought of it as a premonition. It was just Ty being Ty, pushing the limits.

But the nine months since their canceled wedding

had taught her not to dwell on thoughts of her one-time fiancé and what might have been. She dashed across busy Arlington Street to a French café, splurging on a latte that she took back outside with her. Of course, it was true that she *could* be photographing wild turkeys in Cold Ridge—or red-tailed hawks, mountain sunsets, waterfalls, rock formations, alpine grasses. She was still a nature photographer, never mind that she'd been in Boston for six months and had just accepted a long-term assignment photographing house renovations.

Not just *any* house renovations, she thought. Sterling and Jodie Rancourt had hired her to photograph the painstaking restoration and renovation of their historic Victorian mansion on Commonwealth Avenue.

Carine sighed, sipping her latte as she peered in the display windows of the upscale shops and salons on trendy Newbury Street. But Ty kept creeping into her thoughts. Even when she'd chased him with a rake at six, spitting bits of leaves out of her mouth, she'd known not to get involved with him, ever. The six-year-old inside her, who knew better than to trust anything he said, must have been screaming bloody murder when she'd fallen in love with him last winter.

The man could jump out of a helicopter to rescue a downed aircrew—it didn't matter where. Behind enemy lines, on a mountaintop, in a desert or a jungle or an ocean, in snow or heat or rain. In combat or peacetime. He had a job to do. Getting cold feet wasn't an option.

Not so when it'd come to marrying her.

Carine hadn't spoken to him since he'd knocked on her cabin door and said he couldn't go through with their wedding. He'd disappeared into the mountains for a few days of solo winter camping, lived through it, then returned to his base. She'd heard he'd been deployed overseas and participated in dangerous combat search and rescues. CSARs. He'd also performed humanitarian missions, one to treat injured women and children in an isolated area. Carine appreciated the work he did, and gradually, her anger at him had worn off, along with her shock. They were easy emotions to deal with in comparison to the hurt and embarrassment that had followed him walking out on her, the palpable grief of losing a man she'd come to regard in those few short months, maybe over her lifetime, as her soul mate.

Even when he was away, there were reminders of him everywhere in Cold Ridge. And, of course, when he was on leave, when he could get away for a couple of days, *he* was there.

By early summer, Carine knew she had to pick up the pieces of her life and make some changes, explore new options, expand her horizons—not that it always felt that way. Sometimes, even now, it felt as if she were still licking her wounds, still running from herself and the life she wanted to lead.

But not today—today was a gorgeous late autumn day, perfect for *not* thinking about Cold Ridge and Tyler North. As far as she was concerned, he was back to being the thorn in her side he'd always been.

She'd trust him with her life—who wouldn't? But she'd never again make the mistake of trusting him with her heart.

That was what Gus had tried to tell her after the shooting incident in the woods last November. "You can trust him with your life, Carine, but—damn it, he'll break your heart in the end."

She'd thought her uncle was just worrying about her. People tended to worry about her. She wasn't a tough U.S. marshal like her brother or a physician who'd seen everything like her sister—people saw her as the sensitive soul of her family, a nature photographer who'd never really left home.

Well, now she had.

She finished her latte and decided to head back to Commonwealth Avenue and the Rancourt house, although she wasn't under any time constraints. The Rancourts hadn't just hired her out of the blue. They weren't part of her horizon-expanding. They'd hired her, Carine knew, because she was from Cold Ridge, friends with the three men who rescued them the year before. Hank Callahan and Antonia had started dating in Boston after that first meeting in Carine's cabin. He was now her brother-in-law. As of a week ago, the voters of the Commonwealth of Massachusetts had made him their junior senator-elect. Since he was friends with Ty and Antonia was a fiercely loyal sister, their relationship had suffered after Carine's aborted wedding. Then Antonia found herself trapped on an island off Cape Cod with a violent stalker and with a hurricane about to blow on shore; Hank had come after her, ending any doubts either of them had. The media—and voters—lapped up the story. But it was clear to everyone that Hank hadn't been thinking about their opinion when he'd headed to the Shelter Island.

No, Carine thought, she had no illusions. As much as she liked them, Sterling and Jodie Rancourt had their own reasons for asking her to do the job.

She walked slowly, in no hurry. Her hair was pulled back neatly, and she wore jeans, a black turtleneck, her barn coat and waterproof ankle boots, comfortable clothes that permitted her to go up and down ladders, trek over drop cloths and stacks of building supplies and tools, do whatever she had to do to get the particular picture she wanted. She was used to climbing mountains and edging across rock ledges to get the right light, the right color, the right composition. Negotiating house renovations didn't seem that daunting to her. It had been a quiet morning—she hadn't even taken her camera out of its bag and had left it at the Rancourt house while she was at lunch. She was using her digital camera today, at Jodie Rancourt's request—Jodie wanted to get a better idea of the technical differences between digital and film.

A shiny black sports car pulled alongside her, and Louis Sanborn, also newly employed by the Rancourts, rolled down his window and flashed his killer smile at her. "Hey, Ms. Photographer, need a ride over to the big house?"

Carine laughed. "Thanks for the offer, Mr. Security Man.'' Louis was tall and, despite his prematurely gray, scrub-brush hair, younger than he looked, probably just a year or two older than she was. The Rancourts had hired him two weeks ago as the assistant to their chief of security. ''I don't mind walking. We won't get many more days like today. It's beautiful out.''

''Only according to you granite-head types.''

''It's in the fifties!''

''That's what I'm saying. Having a good lunch hour?''

''An excellent lunch hour.''

''Me, too. See you over on Comm. Ave.''

His car merged back into the Newbury Street traffic. Carine continued on up to Exeter Street, then cut down it to Commonwealth Avenue. With its center mall and stately Victorian buildings, it was the quintessential street of Boston's Back Bay, all of which was on reclaimed land that used to be under water—hence its name.

Still in no hurry, she sat on a bench on the mall, famous for its early springtime pink magnolias, now long gone. A toddler ran after a flutter of pigeons, and Carine tried not to think about the babies she'd meant to have with Ty, but, nonetheless, felt a momentary pang of regret. The toddler's mother scooped him up and swung him in the brisk November air, then set him back in his stroller. He was ticked off and started to kick and scream. He wanted to chase more pigeons. Two months ago—a month ago—the scene would have made Carine cry, but now she smiled. Progress, she thought.

She walked across the westbound lane to the historic brick-front mansion the Rancourts had snapped up when it came onto the market eighteen months ago. It was a rare find. Its longtime owner, now dead, had never carved it up into apartments, in fact, had done few renovations—many of the house's original features were still intact. Hardwood floors, ornate moldings, marble fireplaces, chandeliers, wainscoting, fixtures. It had taken most of the past eighteen months for the team of architects, preservationists, designers and contractors just to come up with the right plans for what to do.

Carine's job photographing the renovations could easily take her through the winter, while still leaving room for her to pursue other projects. She'd been at it for six weeks. Work would happen in a frenzy for a few days, the place crawling with people. Then everyone would vanish, and nothing would happen for a morning, an afternoon, even a week. That left her with spurts of time she could put to use doing something more productive than drinking lattes and window shopping.

She noticed Louis Sanborn's car parked out front and smiled, shaking her head. Leave Louis to find a convenient parking space—she never could, and almost always walked or took public transportation in the city.

Since she'd left for lunch, someone had set out a pot of yellow mums on the front stoop; the wrought-iron rail was cool to the touch as she mounted the steps to the massive dark wood door. It was open a crack, and she pushed it with her shoulder and went in, immediately tossing her latte cup into an ugly green plastic trash bin just inside the door. Sweeping, graceful stairs rose up to the second floor of the five-story house. She'd never been in any place like it. Not one inch of it reminded her of her little log cabin with its rustic ladder up to the loft.

"Hello?" she called. "Anyone here?"

Her footsteps echoed on the age-darkened cherry floor of the center hall. To her left was a formal draw-ing room with a marble fireplace and a crystal chan-delier, then a smaller room and the library. There was even an elegant ballroom on the second floor. The Rancourts had promised to invite Carine the first time they used it, teasing her that they wanted to see her in sequins.

She retrieved her camera from a cold, old-fashioned radiator in the hall. There had to be some-one around. Nobody would leave the door open with the place empty.

"Louis? Are you here? It's me, Carine."

He could be upstairs, she thought, slinging her camera bag over her shoulder. She'd assumed work-ers would be in this afternoon, but she didn't keep close track of their comings and goings. As she turned to head back to the front entry, something caught her eye in the library. She wasn't sure what—something out of place. Wrong.

She took a shallow breath, and it was as if a force

stronger than she was compelled her to take a step forward and peer through the double doorway. Restoration work hadn't started yet in the library. Intense discussions were still under way over whether it was worth the expense to have its yellowed wallpaper, possibly original to the house, copied.

Carine touched the wood molding, telling herself she must have simply seen a shadow or a stray drop cloth. Then she jumped back, inhaling sharply, even as her mind struggled to take in what she was seeing—a man facedown on the wood floor. Louis. She recognized his dark suit, his scrub-brush hair. She lunged forward, but stopped abruptly, almost instinctively.

A pool of something dark, a liquid, oozed toward her. She stood motionless, refusing to absorb what she was seeing.

Blood.

It seeped into the cracks in the narrow-board floor. It covered Louis's outstretched hand.

Help...

She couldn't speak. Her mouth opened, but no sound came out.

His hair...his hand...in the blood...

"Oh, God, oh, God—Louis!" Carine leaped forward, yelling back over her shoulder. "Help! Help, someone's hurt!"

She avoided stepping in the blood. It wasn't easy—there was so much of it. *Louis...he can't be dead. I just saw him!*

She had only rudimentary first aid skills. She

wasn't an ER doctor like her sister or a highly trained combat paramedic like North and Manny Carrera. But they weren't here, and she forced herself to kneel beside Louis Sanborn and control her horror and fear as she touched two fingers to his carotid artery. That was it, wasn't it? Arteries beat with the heart. Veins didn't. To see if he had a pulse, she had to find an artery.

There was no pulse, not with that much blood.

"Louis. Oh, God."

She looked around the empty room, her voice echoing as she yelled again for help. Had he fallen and landed on a sharp object—a stray chisel or a saw, or something? The back of his suit was unmarred. No blood, no torn fabric. Whatever injury he had must have been in front. But she didn't dare turn him over, touch him further.

She rose shakily. No one had come in answer to her yells for help. Louis Sanborn was dead. She was alone. She absorbed the reality of her situation in short bursts of awareness, as if she couldn't take it all in at once.

Hey, Ms. Photographer, need a ride over to the big house?

What if she'd said yes? Could she have saved his life? Or would she be dead, too?

How had he died?

What if it wasn't an accident?

It wasn't. She knew it wasn't.

She ran into the hall, her camera bag bouncing on her hip. Where was her cell phone? She needed to call the police, an ambulance. She dug in the pocket of her barn coat, finding her phone, but she couldn't hang on to it and dropped it on the hardwood floor, startling herself. She scooped it up, hardly pausing as she came to the front hall.

The front door stood wide open. She thought she'd shut it when she got back from lunch. Was someone else here?

She could feel the cool November air.

"Help!"

She looked down at her cell phone, realized it wasn't on. She hit the Power button and ran onto the front stoop, knocking over the pot of mums, hoping someone on the street would hear her. She charged down the steps to the wide sidewalk. She'd call the police, stop a passing car.

Suddenly Manny Carrera was there, as if she'd conjured him up herself. He'd danced with her at Hank and Antonia's wedding a month ago and cheerfully offered to cut off Ty's balls the next time he saw him.

"It's Louis...he..." She couldn't get out the words. "He's—oh, God—"

Manny swept her into his embrace. "I know," he said. "I know."

Two

Tyler North pulled two beers out of his refrigerator and brought them to the long pine table where his mother used to sit in front of the fire with her paints. Gus Winter was in her spot now, lean, scarred and irritable—and tired, although he'd never admit to it. He took one of the beers and shook his head in disgust. "You always have to allow for the moron factor."

"People make mistakes."

Gus drank some of his beer. It had been a brutal day, but one with a happy ending. "Forgetting your suncreen's a mistake. These assholes didn't bother to check the weather conditions. They didn't take enough food or water. You saw how they were dressed—jeans and sneakers. It's November. Any goddamn thing can happen on the ridge in November. They're lucky to be alive."

No one knew better than Gus Winter that what he

said was true. Ty didn't argue with him. He sat with his beer and stared at the fire in the old center-chimney stone fireplace. Three seventeen-year-old boys from the local prep school decided to skip classes and hike the ridge trail. If they'd stayed on it, they might have been okay, but they didn't. By early afternoon, they were cold, lost, battered by high winds and terrified of spending the night above the treeline.

"If Fish and Game determines these guys were reckless, they'll have to cough up the bucks for the rescue," Ty said.

"They're complaining because we didn't send a helicopter! Can you imagine? They figured they'd dial 911 on their cell phones if they got into trouble—"

"That's what they did."

Gus snorted. "Yeah. And we came. What's with this picture? We should have waited, let them get good and scared." He drank more of his beer. "I'm telling you, North. The moron factor."

Ty expected the three boys they'd just rescued were the sort of hikers the New Hampshire Department of Fish and Game had in mind when they came up with their protocol for charging expenses for search and rescues in cases of out-and-out recklessness. Rescues could be difficult and dangerous—and expensive. Lucky for the boys, they hadn't encountered moisture. Even a light rain would have soaked their cotton clothing, a poor insulator when wet. As it was, they'd suffered mild hypothermia. And intense, warranted fear for their lives.

"I did dumb-ass things at that age," Ty said.

"You do dumb-ass things now. But do you expect people to come to your rescue?" Gus shook his head, not waiting for an answer. "Not you, North. You've never expected anyone to come to your rescue in your entire life, not with your mother, may she rest in peace. Lovely woman, but in her own world. It's the arrogance of these jackasses—"

"Let it go, Gus. We did our job. The rest isn't up to us."

Reckless or not, the boys today weren't the first people he or Gus had pulled off Cold Ridge. It was unlikely they'd be the last.

But Gus wasn't willing to let it go. "Cell phones give people a false sense of security. They should be banned."

Without a cell phone, the kids undoubtedly wouldn't have been missed before nightfall. They'd have ended up spending the night on the ridge—a dangerous situation that might not have had a happy ending. On the other hand, without a cell phone, they might have taken fewer risks or even gone to their classes instead of sneaking off on an illicit hike. Other hikers had made the mistake of thinking their cell phones worked anywhere and didn't discover there were gaps in coverage until they were ass-deep in trouble and had no way to call for help. Even if they did get through, help wasn't necessarily around the damn corner.

Either way, it was North's job to rescue people. He did it for a living in the military, and he did it as a volunteer when he was home on leave.

Gus set his beer bottle down hard on the table. "People think because the White Mountains aren't as high as the Rockies or the Himalayas, they're not dangerous. The reason the treeline's lower in the northeast than it is out west is because we've got such shitty weather here. Three major storm tracks meet right over us—ah, hell." He gave a grunt of disgust. "I'm preaching to the converted. You know these mountains as well as I do."

"I've been away a lot."

That was an understatement. His career as a pararescueman had taken him on search-and-rescue missions all over the world. The pararescue motto— These Things We Do That Others May Live— underscored everything he did as a PJ in both combat and peacetime. A pararescueman's primary mission was to go after downed aircrews. Anytime, anywhere. In any kind of terrain, under permissive or hostile conditions. If there were injuries, they treated them. If they came under fire, they took up security positions and fired back.

The job required a wide range of skills. When he enlisted and decided to become a pararescueman, Ty had only a limited understanding of what it entailed. For starters, two years of training and instruction—

the "pipeline." It began with ten weeks of PJ indoc-trination at Lackland Air Force Base in San Antonio. Running, swimming, calisthenics, drownproofing. Se-rious sleep deprivation, or at least so it seemed at the time. Of the hundred guys who showed up for indoc with him, twenty-four were still there after four weeks. He was one of them.

Then it was on to a series of specialized schools. He went through the Army Special Forces Under-water Operations Course and Navy Underwater Egress Training—navigation swims, ditching and donning of equipment underwater, underwater search patterns, getting out of a sinking aircraft. He made it through the Army Airborne School, where he had to make five static-line jumps before he could move on to freefall school, which took him through jumps at high altitude, with oxygen, at night, during the day, with and without equipment.

Fun stuff, he thought, remembering how he'd steel himself into not quitting, just sticking with it, one day—sometimes one minute—at a time.

At Air Force Survival School he learned basic sur-vival skills, evasion-and-escape techniques, what to do if he was captured by the enemy. Then it was on to the Special Operations Combat Medic Course and, finally, to the Pararescue Recovery Specialist Course, where, over a year or more, all the previous training got put together and more was added—advance EMT-paramedic training, advance parachute skills, tactical maneuvers, weapons handling, mountain climbing and aircrew recovery procedures. They worked through various scenarios that tied in all the different skills they'd learned, seeing their practical application for the job that lay ahead.

Then came graduation, the PJ's distinctive maroon beret, assignment to a team—then Ty thought, the real training began.

PJs had been called SEALs with stethoscopes, ninja brain surgeons, superman paramedics—if people knew what they did at all, since so many of their missions had to be done quietly. It wasn't a job for someone looking for money and glory. Ty cringed at all the nicknames. He thought of himself as an average guy who did a job he was trained to do to the best of his ability. He'd become a PJ because he wanted an action-oriented career where he could save lives, a chance to "search and rescue" instead of "search and destroy."

But he could "destroy" if he had to. PJs were direct combatants, and, as such, pararescue was a career field that remained closed to women.

Ty was currently assigned to the 16th Special Operations Wing out of Hurlburt Field in the Florida panhandle. As the leader of a special tactics team, he had performed a full range of combat search-and-rescue missions in recent years, but it was seeing Carine Winter under fire last fall that had all but done him in.

The "incident" was still under investigation.

The only positive outcome of the whole mess was

that Hank Callahan and Antonia Winter had met and fallen in love. Ty had missed their wedding a month ago. Antonia was too damn polite not to invite him. His behavior toward her younger sister had put a crimp in the budding romance between his friend the ER doctor and his friend the helicopter-pilot-turned-senate-candidate—fortunately, they'd worked it out.

Senator Hank Callahan.

Ty shook his head, grinning to himself. He and Hank had damn near become brothers-in-law. They would have, if Ty had gone ahead and married Carine in February. Instead, he'd cut and run.

It was the only time in his life he'd ever cut and run.

"Have you decided whether or not you're selling the house?" Gus asked him.

Ty pulled himself from his darkening thoughts. "No. I haven't decided, I mean."

He'd been on assignment overseas when his mother took a walk in the meadow and died of a massive stroke. Carine had found her and tracked him down to make sure he got the news, to tell him his mother had painted that morning and died in the lupine she'd so loved. But Saskia North had never really fit in with the locals, and few in Cold Ridge knew much about her, beyond her skills as a painter and a weaver—and her failings as a mother.

"You should sell it," Gus said. "There's nothing for you here, not anymore. What do you want with this place? You're never here long enough to fix it up. Basic maintenance isn't enough. It'll fall down around your ears before too long."

Now that Ty had broken Carine's heart, Gus wanted him to clear out of Cold Ridge altogether. The man made no secret of it. It hadn't always been that way, but Ty knew that was before and this was now. To Gus, Carine was still the little girl he'd loved and protected since she was three years old—the little girl whose parents he'd helped carry off Cold Ridge.

People make mistakes.

It was the way life was. You make mistakes, you try to correct them.

North frowned at a strange ringing sound, then watched Gus grimace and pull a cell phone out of his back pocket. He pointed the cell phone at North. "Just shut the hell up. I've never used it to call for someone to come rescue me." Then he clicked the receive button and said, "Yeah, Gus here." His face lost color, and he got to his feet. "Slow down, honey. Slow down. What—" He listened some more, pacing, obviously trying to stay calm. "Do you want me to come down there? Are you okay? Carine—" He all but threw the phone into the fire. *"Goddamn it!"*

Ty fell back on his training and experience to stay calm. "Service kick out on you?" He kept his voice neutral, careful not to say anything that would further provoke Gus, further upset him. "It does that. The mountains."

Gus raked a hand through his gray, brittle hair. "That was Carine."

Ty felt a tightening in his throat. "I thought so."

"She—" He sucked in a sharp, angry breath. "Damn it, North, I hate it that she's in Boston. With Antonia and Hank married, she's alone there now for the most part. And, goddamn it, she doesn't belong there."

North didn't argue. "You're right, Gus. What happened?"

Tears rose in the older man's eyes, a reminder of the years he'd invested in his brother's three children. His own parents couldn't take them on—they were shattered by the untimely deaths of their older son and daughter-in-law and had chronic health problems. It was Gus who'd made the emotional commitment at age twenty to raise his nieces and nephew. Ty thought of the sacrifices, the physical toll, it all had taken. For thirty years, Gus Winter had put the needs of Nate, Antonia and Carine ahead of his own. He was the only one who didn't know it.

"Gus?"

"There was a shooting. A murder. She found the body. Christ, after last fall—"

"Where was she?"

"At work. She's photographing the renovations on that old house the Rancourts bought on Commonwealth Avenue. She went out for a latte—Christ. That's what she just said. *Gus, I went out for a latte.* When she got back, she found a man dead on the library floor." Gus snatched up his beer bottle and dumped the balance out in the sink. "She didn't want me to hear about it on the news."

"Did she say who the victim was?"

He shook his head. "She didn't have a chance. I'll go home and call her." He grabbed his coat off the back of the chair, and when North started to his feet, Gus, refusing to look at him, added abruptly, "It's not your problem."

"All right. Sure, Gus. If you need me for any-thing—"

"I won't."

Ty didn't follow him out, but he was tempted. He pulled his chair over to the fire and let the hot flames warm his feet. He still had on his hiking socks. It felt good to get out of his boots. One of the prep-school boys needed to be carried off the ridge in a litter. The other two responded to on-site treatment, warm duds and warm liquids, and were able to walk down on their own. Gus didn't think they were contrite enough. But Gus had been in a bad mood for months. For good reason. Antonia's wedding had temporarily lifted his spirits, but North's return to Cold Ridge had plunged him back into a black mood.

The old house seemed huge and empty around him, the late afternoon wind rattling the windows. It got dark early now. November. No more daylight savings. North put a log on the fire. The fireplace supposedly was made from stone that Abraham Winter had pulled off the ridge when he carved the main ridge trail, still almost intact, almost two hundred years ago.

Ty felt the flames hot on his face. His mother had never minded living out here, even after he'd gone into the air force and she lived in the big house all alone. She said she was proud of him, but he doubted she really knew what the hell a PJ did.

"I understand you," she used to say. "I understand you completely."

Whether she did or didn't, Ty had no idea, but he had never come close to understanding her. When she died, she'd left him the house and fifty acres, which he'd expected.

A trust fund. He used to make fun of people with trust funds.

For five years, he hadn't touched a dime of it except what he needed to hang on to the house.

He lifted his gaze to the oil painting his mother had done in those solitary years here. It depicted the house and the meadow on an early summer day, daises in bloom. She hadn't put Cold Ridge in it. She'd never said why. As far as he knew, she'd never climbed any of the hundreds of trails in the White Mountains.

He wanted to call Carine. He wanted to be in Boston. Now.

His telephone rang. His hard line. He thought it might be Gus, changing his mind about wanting to shut him out. He got up from the fire and picked up the extension on the wall next to the refrigerator.

"North? It's Carrera." Manny Carrera's normally steady, unflappable voice sounded stressed, tightly controlled. "I've got a problem. I need you here."

"D.C.?"

"Boston."

North didn't let himself react. "Why Boston?"

"I flew up here last night to talk to Sterling Rancourt about Louis Sanborn, his new security hire. By the time I got to Sanborn, he was dead."

"Manny—"

He took a breath. "You've heard."

"Carine just called Gus. I don't have the details. She found this guy shot to death? What happened? Where the hell were you?"

"There. I don't want to get into it now. We both gave statements to the police. They want me to stick around in case they have more questions. Which they will. I figure I don't have long before they slap on the cuffs."

"Cuffs? Manny, you didn't kill this guy—"

"It's not that simple."

North stared out the kitchen window into the darkness. The fire crackled behind him. Manny Carrera had surprised everyone when he retired from active duty in August, but North didn't fault him. Manny had done his bit, and he had different priorities nowadays: a son who'd almost died and a wife who was on edge.

But North wasn't going to coddle him. Manny would hate that. "What's not simple? You either killed him or you didn't kill him."

"I'm not going there with you."

"Then what about Carine?"

"She doesn't know the police have their eye on me. When she finds out—"

"She'll want to spring you."

Carine had always liked Manny Carrera. Everyone did. He'd show up in Cold Ridge from time to time for a little hiking, fishing and snowshoeing. Even Gus liked Manny. The air force tried to tap him as a PJ instructor, but he was determined to retire and go into business for himself. He was in the process of getting a Washington-based outfit off the ground, which trained individuals and companies in a broad range of emergency skills and procedures—not just self-defense and how to treat the injured, but how to think, how to respond in a crisis, *before* a crisis. He wanted his clients trained, prepared, able to help themselves and others if something happened. Ty didn't know how it was going or what kind of businessman Manny would make. Manny Carrera was a hard-ass, but he was fair, scrupulous and, at heart, a natural optimist.

He also had the skills and worldwide connections to disappear before the police got to him—just melt away. If he put his mind to it, he could probably even gnaw his way out of a jail cell.

Except he had a fourteen-year-old son with severe asthma and allergies at the prep school just outside the picturesque village of Cold Ridge.

"What do you want me to do?" Ty asked.

"Make sure Carine doesn't pursue this thing. She knew Louis Sanborn. She liked him. She found him dead. Plus," Manny added pointedly, "she had her life pulled out from under her not that long ago. She's ripe for trouble.''

"She's a Winter, Manny. She's always ripe for trouble.'' What Manny didn't say—what he didn't need to say—was that Ty was the one who'd pulled her life out from under her. "Is she in danger?''

"Five minutes sooner, she'd have walked in on a murder. Anything could have happened. For all I know, it still could. Just keep an eye on her, North. That's all I'm asking.''

Ty was silent a moment. "You're not telling me everything.''

Manny almost laughed. "Hell, North, I'm not telling you anything.'' But any humor faded, and he asked seriously, "You'll do it?''

As if there was a question. "If Gus doesn't let all the air out of my tires before I can get there. If Carine doesn't kill me when I do. I haven't seen her since I left her at the altar.'' North sighed heavily, feeling the fatigue from his long day. He hadn't quite left her at the altar. At least he'd come to his senses and called off their wedding a full week in advance. It could have been worse, not that anyone else saw it that way. "Manny, Jesus. Murder—what the hell's going on?''

"Looks like Carine and I are shit magnets these days. Jesus. Look, Ty. She found a dead man this afternoon. I should have made sure that didn't happen. I didn't, so now I'm asking you to do what you can to make it right.'' He groaned to himself. "Ah, screw it. You're on a need-to-know basis. It's the best I can do. Just get down here."

"I'll be there tonight."

Manny hesitated. "I saw the story about the rescue you did today on the news. My son—"

"Eric wasn't involved. He's only a freshman. These guys are seniors."

"Geniuses, from the sounds of it."

"Ivy League material. They've got their applications in. Watch. They'll all be running the show when we're in the home."

"Scary thought. Ty—"

"Forget it. It's okay."

But Manny Carrera said it, anyway. "I know I'm asking a lot. Thanks."

Three

After throwing up for a third time, Carine staggered into her kitchen. She hoped that was the last of it. Nerves, she thought. Fear, disgust, grief, horror. Poor Louis. Dead. Murdered. *Why?*

She found the little bag of oyster crackers the Boston Police Department detective had given her when she'd almost passed out on him. He'd said she looked green. At least she hadn't thrown up then. She'd given her statement, read it, signed it and, when told she could leave, got a cab and came straight back to her apartment. She didn't know what else to do. The Rancourts were with the police. Manny was with the police. And Louis Sanborn was dead, his body transported to wherever the medical examiners performed autopsies.

Her hands trembled, and she couldn't get a good hold on the package of crackers to pull it open. Finally, she grabbed a fork from the strainer and stabbed the cellophane, and little round crackers popped out all over her counter and floor.

"Damn it!"

She picked one up off the floor and nibbled on it, making herself fill her kettle with water and set it on the stove for tea. It wasn't much of a stove—it wasn't much of an apartment. It was a one-bedroom unit on a narrow, crooked street off Inman Square in Cambridge, an eclectic neighborhood of working-class families, students and professionals. She'd painted the walls and her flea-market furnishings with a mix of mango, lime green, raspberry, various shades of blue and violet, whatever she thought would be cheerful and not remind her of the rich, woodsy colors of her log cabin in Cold Ridge.

The tiny cracker didn't sit well in her stomach. Her mouth was dry. She was wrung out. She'd cried, she'd screamed, she'd barfed. Yep. What a rock she was. But she didn't care. She wasn't embarrassed by her reaction—she didn't ever want to get used to coming upon a murder.

Manny Carrera had called the police by the time she got out to the street. He wouldn't tell her a thing—why he was there, what he saw, nothing. Just that he was consulting for the Rancourts, whatever that meant. Then the police arrived, as well as Sterling and Jodie, their security chief, the media, onlookers. Carine and Manny were separated. He was as self-contained as ever. Definitely a rock.

"Think of it," he'd said in the minutes before the

police got there, "if you'd married North, you could be in flea-infested military housing right now."

"Manny...I knew Louis. He—he was shot, wasn't he? Murdered?"

"Carine, something you need to keep in mind."

He hesitated, but she prodded him. "What?"

"Louis Sanborn wasn't a nice man."

He didn't have a chance to elaborate, and she'd repeated his words to the detective when he asked her what she and Manny had talked about.

Louis Sanborn wasn't a nice man.

Manny could have meant anything. It didn't have to be ominous.

She switched off her kettle. Even tea wasn't going to stay down. She wished she hadn't called Gus. Talking to him was comforting on one level, because he was unconditionally on her side, but, on another level, it added to her tension—because he'd wanted to head to Boston. It'd been a near thing to keep him up north. She'd called him for moral support. She needed time to pull herself together. Gus would hover. He'd scowl at her living accommodations. He'd tell her she didn't belong in the city.

He'd make her soup. He'd listen to her for as long as she wanted to talk.

Her doorbell rang, the noise sprouting an instant headache. Carine knew she was dehydrated, her reserves exhausted, but her first-floor apartment didn't have an intercom or buzzer, which meant she had to stagger out to the front hall. Her old tenement building had three floors, with two apartments on each floor and a main door that creaked and stuck half the time, making it easy for people to just walk in.

Her sister gave her an encouraging smile and wave through the smudged glass panel. When Carine pulled open the heavy door, Antonia grimaced and shook her head. "Good God, you look awful."

"Is that what you say to all your ER patients? I've been throwing up."

Antonia felt her sister's forehead, then grabbed her wrist. "No fever. Your pulse is a bit fast. Are you keeping anything down?"

"I just ate an oyster cracker."

"Try a little flat Coke."

"I don't have any."

Carine led her sister back to her apartment, but Antonia's tight frown only worsened when she looked around at the kitchen and the spilled crackers. "Half the rats in Boston live better than you do."

"What? It's a great apartment."

Antonia sighed. She was dressed elegantly in a black top and pants and a pumpkin-colored coat that brought out the softer tones of her auburn hair. It was shorter than Carine's, not as dark. "You can only do so much with paint," she said. "Why don't you go home? Let Gus fuss over you."

"I live here now. Don't you remember your hand-to-mouth years in medical school?"

"That's the point. I was in medical school. You're just—I don't know what you're doing. Marking time." She squatted down and scooped up a handful of the crackers, dumping them in the trash. "You weren't going to eat them off the floor, were you?"

"Antonia—"

Tears welled in her sister's eyes. "I'm sorry. I'm not being very sensitive or helpful. Oh, Carine, I'm so sorry about what happened. I'm supposed to take the shuttle down to Washington tonight. There's some function tomorrow for freshman senators—Hank left this afternoon, before he heard about the murder."

Carine nodded without comment.

"He's tried several times to reach Manny. No luck." Antonia tore open the refrigerator with more force than was required. "Do you have any ginger ale? Carine, what on earth is *that?* It's blue!"

"Oh, that's my Gatorade. I've been trying to do more exercise. It's good for restoring electrolytes, isn't it?"

"I wonder how they get it that shade of blue. Well, drink it if you can keep it down. It'll help with any dehydration. Is there someone who can spend the night here with you? I hate the idea of leaving you alone—"

"I'll be fine." Carine manufactured a weak smile. "Go on and catch your plane, Antonia. I just want to crawl into bed. It wasn't a great day for me, but I'm not the one who was killed. Poor Louis."

"Did you know him well?"

She shook her head. "Just to say hi to."

"What a nightmare. What *is* it about you and the month of November? Well, at least last year no one was killed. Look, if you need me to stay—"

"No! Go be the smart doctor wife to your handsome senator-elect husband. Wow Washington. Thanks for stopping by."

Antonia smiled, but she didn't look reassured. "You really won't eat any crackers off the floor, right?"

"Promise."

"Call my cell phone anytime, day or night. Okay? I can be on the next shuttle back here. Just say the word."

Five minutes after Antonia left, Nate called from New York. He didn't want to hear about crackers and blue Gatorade—he wanted to make sure Carine had told the police absolutely everything and wasn't going to get involved any more than she had to be. She assured him she was being the good soldier.

"Good," he said. "Keep it that way."

Her brother, too wanted her to go back to Cold Ridge. He'd left their hometown, and Antonia had left, but they both still considered it home, their refuge. Carine, who'd never left, wasn't as nostalgic about it, and she didn't like the idea that she might run into Tyler North.

She promised Nate she'd take care of herself and hung up, pouring herself a glass of Gatorade. She hoped she kept it down, because damned if she wanted to throw up anything blue.

Ty made the three-hour trip to Boston in under two-and-a-half hours, but lost time in Inman Square and the tangle of five million streets that radiated out from it. He went past a fancy bakery, a hardware store, a lesbian bookstore, several churches, a mosque, service stations, a Portuguese restaurant, a Mexican restaurant, a Moroccan restaurant, a Jewish deli, a Tibetan rug shop and an Irish bar with a shamrock on its sign. He went down the same one-way street twice. Maybe three times. Where the hell was his GPS when he needed it? Never mind satellite navigation—he could have used a damn map.

Finally, he found his way to a crowded street of multifamily homes with pumpkins and mums on their front steps and foldout paper turkeys and Pilgrim hats in their windows. There were a few fake cobwebs strung to fences, left over from Halloween. A couple of strings of orange lights in the shape of little plastic pumpkins. Hank Callahan and Manny Carrera, who'd both been inside Carine's apartment, reported that it was a solid, working-class neighborhood, but her building needed a little work.

Her building was a dump. The porch roof sagged. The steps had holes in them. The whole place needed paint. Outdoor lighting was nonexistent. Tall, frostbitten hollyhocks bent over the walkway—Carine's doing, no doubt. She'd always loved hollyhocks. The neighborhood dogs probably loved them, too.

A pack of boys careered down the dark street on scooters and skateboards. One kid, who couldn't have been more than thirteen, had a cigarette dangling from his mouth. It was just shy of ten o'clock on a school night. North mentally picked out which ones he'd liked to see go through PJ indoc. Pass or fail, they'd get in shape, learn a little something about themselves.

"Live free or die," the boy with the cigarette yelled as he sailed past North's truck with its New Hampshire plates and their Live Free or Die logo. "Yeah, go for it, woodchuck."

That one, he thought. That one he'd liked to see tossed in a pool with his hands and feet tied.

On the other hand, maybe the kid would make a good pararescueman. Stick with it, don't give up, don't drown—it wasn't always easy to tell who'd make it and who'd wash out.

Antonia Winter Callahan, wife of senator-elect Hank Callahan, lifted a swooning hollyhock out of her path, stood on the main sidewalk a moment, then frowned and marched up to Ty's truck. He kept a truck in Florida, too. This was his at-home truck. Rusted, nicely broken in. Recognizable to someone who'd known him most of his life.

He rolled down his window. "Nice night. Warmer down here in the big city."

"I don't believe you, Ty. Gus didn't send you, did he? No, of course he didn't. What was I thinking?" She groaned, her hands clenched at her sides. "God, Ty, you're not what Carine needs right now. She's been sick to her stomach."

"She's never come upon a murder before."

Antonia nodded reluctantly, calmer. "It's awful. She knew the victim, Louis Sanborn. He worked for the Rancourts. Did you know him?"

"No."

Her eyes narrowed. "You heard Manny Carrera was on the scene? He's had a rough year. He—" She broke off, giving a little hiss between clenched teeth. "Ty, don't tell me—did Manny send you? Is that why you're here?"

"Sorry, Dr. Callahan, I'm in the dark as much as you are." He thought that was a diplomatic way to stonewall her. "You looked like you were in a hurry a minute ago."

"I am. I have a plane to catch—damn, I hate this. She says she's fine. You know Carine. She's resilient, but she's also proud and stubborn, sensitive about being sensitive. Ty, I swear to you, if you do anything, and I mean *anything,* to make matters worse for her, I will find you and inject you with something that'll sting parts that you don't want stinging. Do I make myself clear?"

He leaned back in his seat. "You bet, Doc."

She hissed again, disgusted with him. "The jackass fairy must have visited you every night when you were a kid," she snapped. "Some days I don't know how you stand yourself."

"I'm a disciplined military man."

She straightened, glancing back at her sister's apartment. No foldout turkeys. No Pilgrim hats. Carine's life here seemed temporary, something she was trying on for size. An escape. When Antonia turned back to him, Ty thought she looked strained and worried. "Promise me," she said seriously, in an exhausted near whisper. "You'll be good?"

"Relax, Antonia." He smiled at her. "I'll be very good."

"You're not going in there tonight, are you?"

He shook his head. "I'll give her some time. Besides, I hate barf."

"Yeah, right, with all you've seen in your career?" She started to say something, then just heaved a long sigh. "I'm trusting you."

It was progress, Ty thought. A Winter hadn't trusted him in months.

Antonia climbed into a taxi that had been idling farther down the street, and Ty watched it negotiate the crooked street, the oversize cars parked in too-small spaces, the potholes, the kids on skateboards.

He'd never had a thing for Antonia. It was always Carine.

Always and forever.

Four

Val Carrera learned about Louis Sanborn's murder when she flipped through the *Washington Post* over her morning coffee, and it pissed her off. A man was dead, and her husband hadn't bothered to tell her he was involved. He was in Boston. It wasn't like he was on a secret military mission. He could have called her.

But here she was, once again, on a need-to-know basis, with Manny Carrera deciding what she needed to know and her having to live with it.

Bastard.

The details in the article were sketchy. It said photographer Carine Winter found the body when she got back from her lunch break. It said the Rancourts had hired Manny to analyze their personal security needs and make recommendations, and, most important, to train them and their employees—of which Louis Sanborn was one—in the basics of emergency medicine and survival in various types of environments and conditions. After their scare in the White Mountains last fall, the Rancourts said, they wanted to be more self-reliant.

"What a crock," Val muttered over her paper. "Damn phonies."

She hadn't liked the Rancourts since Manny had pulled them off Cold Ridge on a weekend he was supposed to be resting, having a good time. Sterling—who'd name a kid Sterling?—and Jodie Rancourt had donned expensive parkas and boots and trekked up the ridge, never mind that they didn't know what in hell they were doing. They got a dose of high winds, cold temperatures and slippery rocks and damn near died up there.

"They should be Popsicles," Val grumbled.

Instead it was Hank Callahan and the PJs to the rescue, although Val was of the opinion that someone else could have done the job. But that wasn't the way it was with Manny, North or Callahan, not when they were right there and could do something.

Now the Rancourts were returning the favor, helping Manny establish his credentials in their world. And the big dope fell for it. He didn't see that they were ingratiating themselves—he didn't see that he should have stayed in the air force, teaching a new generation of young men how to be pararescuemen.

But Manny hadn't listened to her in months, and, depending on her mood, Val didn't blame him.

She sank back in her chair at her small, round table in what passed for an eating area. The kitchen wasn't much bigger than a closet, and the bedroom was just big enough for a double bed and a bureau. She hadn't slept *that* close to Manny in years. Fortunately, she was a petite woman herself—black-haired, brown-eyed and, at thirty-eight, still with a good future ahead of her. If she stopped screwing up her life.

The living room was kind of cute—it had a large paned window shaded by a gorgeous oak tree, its leaves a rich burgundy color now that it was November. A one-bedroom apartment on a noisy street in Arlington was the best she and Manny could find—and afford—on short notice. At least it was clean and bug-free. If he made a go of his business and they decided to stay in the Washington area, they'd start looking for a house.

Their son was doing well, and she was off anti-depressants.

Remember your priorities, she told herself.

She folded up the paper and called Manny on his cell phone, getting his voice mail. "Hi, it's me. I heard about what happened. Sounds hideous. Call me when you can and let me know you're all right."

There. That was nice. She hadn't yelled anything about being his wife and having a goddamned *right* to know. For all she knew, he could be in jail.

She doubted he'd call back. He'd given her six months to get her shit together. He'd stick it out with her until then. If she stayed on her current track, he was gone. That was five months ago, and she was doing better. Manny was the same. He was a bossy, stubborn SOB and refused to recognize his own stress reaction to the utterly crappy time they'd had of it lately, but Val couldn't control what he did—she'd finally figured that one out after months in psychotherapy. Twenty years of sleeping with him hadn't quite done it.

But Manny wasn't responsible for the allergies and asthma that had come so close—so very close—to taking their son's life. Neither was she, but that had taken more months of therapy to sort out, because she'd wanted someone to blame. Otherwise—why? What was the point of a thirteen-year-old boy almost dying from eating a damn peanut? Coughing and choking just trying to breathe?

She didn't want her son having to struggle for the rest of his life with a chronic illness. She wanted her son to have a chance to be a PJ like his dad if that was what he chose.

She wanted the Manny Carrera she'd married back—smart, funny, sexy, self-aware.

And she wanted herself back, the tough Val, the Val who didn't take shit from anyone.

But Manny was struggling, although he wouldn't admit it, and she was struggling, and Eric would never be a PJ, his choices limited by asthma and allergies so severe he had to wear a Medic Alert bracelet and carry an inhaler and a dose of epinephrine wherever he went. He was on daily doses of four different medications. Even with the promise of new treatments and desensitization shots, he'd never be accepted into PJ indoc—it just wasn't going to happen.

None of it was anyone's fault. It just was.

And Eric was doing fine, with a long, good life ahead of him. He would say to her—"Mom, Dad could never be a ballet dancer or a calculus teacher. That's okay, right? Then it's okay that I can't be a PJ."

Val debated calling him at his prep school in Cold Ridge, but decided Manny should be the one to talk to their son about whatever had gone on in Boston. Whatever was still going on. It wasn't easy having Eric away at school, but it was what he wanted—and, after weeks fighting it, she could see it was what he needed at least right now. Between a scholarship and scraping together what they had, she and Manny were managing the tuition. *Just* managing.

She'd been such a trooper through those early days of diagnosis and treatment. Supermom. She'd done it all. Manny's work was demanding, his paycheck not optional. When Eric went into anaphylactic shock the first time, last spring, Manny's paramedic skills had saved his life. But he wasn't around for all the late-night asthma attacks, the trips to the emergency room, the ups and downs as Eric's illness got sorted out and brought under control. Val quit her job as a bookstore manager and devoted herself one-hundred percent to restoring her son's health.

But even when Eric was on his feet, she didn't back off and return to her job at the bookstore near the base where Manny was stationed. She became a total nutcase, a control freak, suffocating Eric—suffocating herself. And Manny. He was caught in the cross fire.

Not that he'd done anything to help the situation.

He was oblivious, content to let her handle all the details, the doctors, Eric's volatile emotions—do it all, until it started affecting him.

Last fall in Cold Ridge hadn't helped matters. Manny had put everything on the line to sneak around in the woods after Carine Winter was shot at, then traipsed after a couple of rich people in trouble—Val knew he was just doing what he did, but what about her? Why the hell couldn't he be there for her?

That was when she'd started on antidepressants. Manny dug in, finally threatening to kick her butt out the door if she didn't get her act together.

She smiled ruefully to herself and folded up the newspaper. Well, that was her version of events, anyway.

Manny would say he'd been at his wit's end with her inability to rebound and had enough to cope with himself. He'd say he understood perfectly well that depression was an illness—that wasn't what bugged him. He'd say he'd done the best he could. She supposed it was true—they'd all done their best. Anger, blame, fear and exhaustion weren't a good mix. On a good day, sparks tended to fly between the two of them. They liked it that way—it worked for them. But they hadn't had very many good days since their son had nearly died.

Now the *ass* had retired and moved her to Washington, D.C., so he could play around with rich guys like Sterling Rancourt, and what did he get for his trouble? A dead guy at his feet, the police on his case.

Val groaned to herself, heading to the bedroom to

get dressed. "No wonder Eric wanted to go to school in New Hampshire. Get away from his parents."

Ten minutes later, she was standing on the sidewalk in front of her building as Hank Callahan pulled up. She jumped into his pricey rented car and grinned at him. "What, no police escort? I expected something a little fancier now that you're a senator."

"Senator-elect," he corrected. He was in a subdued gray suit with a pale blue tie, as handsome as ever. "Thanks for getting up early to join us. Antonia'll meet us at the restaurant."

"Are you *sure* you want to hire me, Major Callahan?"

He smiled. "Just Hank is fine, Val. When did you ever stand on ceremony?"

"Senators scare me even more than majors do. All that pomp and circumstance."

"You've never been intimidated by anyone or anything."

She tried to smile but couldn't. "I should have been an astronaut like my mother wanted." Both her parents had worked for NASA; they were retired now in Houston. "I got to pick what I wanted to be. I'm lucky that way. Hank—I don't know. I've worked in bookstores for the last ten years. For most of the past year, I've been a nutcase."

"I haven't changed my mind. Neither has Antonia. The job's still yours, if you want it."

Joining the staff of a United States senator—Val loved the idea, although maybe not as much as having her own bookstore. "I didn't vote for you. I'm not a Massachusetts resident. I didn't even know the Callahans were a hot-shit Massachusetts family until your wedding last month.''

Hank pulled out onto the street, and two stoplights later, Val realized he wasn't going to mention Manny's situation. He was too polite. She'd have to do it. "Hank, you know about Carine and Manny, don't you? What happened yesterday at the Rancourts' house in Boston? And Antonia? She knows, right?''

He nodded but kept his gaze pinned on the road. "Antonia almost stayed in Boston last night. She stopped by to see Carine. I gather she's in rough shape.''

Val winced. "I can imagine.''

"Have you talked to Manny?''

"Are you kidding? I had to read about his goings-on in the morning paper. Do you know anything about this Louis Sanborn, the man who was killed?''

"Just what you know from the paper.''

"I don't understand why the Rancourts hired Manny if they already had this guy Sanborn and the other guy, the one who hired him—''

"Gary Turner,'' Hank supplied.

"Right. So, what, are the Rancourts paranoid? Are they afraid of something? I don't get it. Why do they need Manny to teach them how to tie off a bleeder? Jesus, call 911 like the rest of us.'' Val tried to stifle a sudden pang of fear, recognized it as her habitual anxiety reaction to everything these days—fear, foreboding, a palpable sense of gloom. "Hank, do you think something's going on with the Rancourts that

Manny doesn't know about? What if they're holding something back?''

Hank shrugged, no sign he was experiencing the same kind of apprehension she was. ''I haven't heard of anything. I think they just like hanging around people who do this kind of work.''

''Manny's not hired muscle. He—''

''I know, Val. Manny's one of the best at what he does.''

''He's demeaning himself, working for those phonies. He should be training new PJs,'' she said half under her breath, then sighed. ''Just what Manny needed, a couple of wannabe types sucking him in. What the hell's the matter with him?''

''Val.''

She glanced over at the pilot-turned-senator, the man whose skill and quick thinking as a Pave Hawk pilot had saved more than one life in his air force career. He said he wanted to work toward the common good as a senator. Hank Callahan had steel nerves and a kind heart, but right now, Val could sense his uneasiness. ''What is it, Hank?''

''Manny should call you—''

''Manny's not going to call me. He won't want me to worry.''

Hank sighed. ''Val, the police think he's their man. You need to prepare yourself if he's arrested.''

She couldn't take in his words. ''What?''

Hank said nothing.

She absorbed what he'd said, then made herself stop, breathe and think, not let her first physical reaction get out of control, suck her in to the point where she couldn't function. It was as if all her nerve endings had been rubbed raw by the months of stress over Eric, how close she'd come to losing her son—and now that he was okay, she could let her emotions run wild. She had to work to keep them in bounds.

There was no way Manny had committed murder. He was a lot of things, but not a murderer. If the police thought they had their man, they were wrong.

It was that simple.

She glanced over at Hank. "Are you reading the tea leaves, or do you know?"

"I know."

He was a senator, and he was a Callahan. He knew everyone, had contacts everywhere. If he said he knew, he knew. "Carine Winter?"

"Innocent bystander."

"Manny—should he get a lawyer?"

"He has one."

Val sank back in her seat, her coffee crawling up her throat. Manny Carrera was her husband. He was in Boston facing a possible murder charge. So much had happened, and all she knew, she'd learned from the newspaper and her friend the senator-elect from Massachusetts.

That *bastard*.

She cleared her throat, summoning her last shreds of dignity. "Thank you for telling me."

"Val—"

"Manny's a big boy. He can take care of himself. If he needs me, he'll be in touch." She stared out her window and saw that they were on one of the prettier streets of Arlington now, the last of the autumn leaves glowing yellow in the morning sun. "Let's go see your beautiful bride and have breakfast. I'm starving."

Five

Carine tried sleeping late, but that didn't work, and she finally got up and made herself a bowl of instant oatmeal that tasted more like instant slime. She downed a few spoonfuls, then drank a mug of heavily sugared tea while she pulled on her running clothes. When she didn't pass out doing her warm-up routine, she decided she might be good for her run.

She did a quarter mile of her one-and-a-half-mile route before she collapsed against a lamppost, kicking it with her heel in disgust. A quarter mile? Pathetic. She was determined to do one-and-a-half miles in under ten minutes and thirty seconds. It wasn't the distance that got to her—she could run ten miles—it was the time, the speed. But running a mile and a half in ten-and-a-half minutes or less was one of the fitness requirements for the PJ Physical Abilities and Stamina Test, which, if passed, led to a shot at indoctrination. She'd pulled the PAST off the Internet.

Of course, she was a woman, and women didn't

get to be pararescuemen. But she didn't want to be a PJ—she just wanted to pass the initial fitness test. It was the challenge that drove her. The test included the run, plus swimming twenty-five meters underwater on one breath—she'd damn near drowned the first time she tried that one. Then there was swimming one thousand meters in twenty-six minutes…doing eight chin-ups in a minute…fifty sit-ups in two minutes… fifty push-ups in two minutes…fifty flutter kicks in two minutes. Technically, she was supposed to do the exercises one after another, all within three hours, but she had to cut herself some slack. She was thirty-three, not twenty.

Normally, it was the swimming that killed her. And she hated flutter kicks. Who'd invented flutter kicks? They were torture. But this morning, after yesterday's shock, she suspected everything on the list would do her in.

She decided to be satisfied she'd been able to keep down her oatmeal.

She trudged back to her apartment, pausing to do a few calf stretches on her porch before heading inside to shower and change clothes. She made short work of it—jeans, sweater, barn coat, ankle boots, camera bag. She doubted she'd be taking any pictures today, but she wanted to go back to the Rancourt house. Provided the police no longer had it marked off as a crime scene, she thought it might help her to see the library again, although it wouldn't, she knew, erase the memory of Louis. After the incident last fall, she'd returned to the boulder on the hillside and touched the places where the bullets had hit. *Real* bullets. No wonder she'd been scared. Going back had helped her incorporate what had happened into her experience, accept the reality of it and find a place for it in her memories so it didn't float around, popping up unexpectedly, inappropriately.

But she'd had Ty with her that day.

She'd parked her car, an ancient Subaru Outback sedan, down the street. She'd gone to the trouble of changing her plates from New Hampshire to Massachusetts and getting a new license, just so she could get a Cambridge resident's sticker—otherwise, parking was a nightmare. But she didn't like driving into Boston and took public transportation whenever she could, picking up the Red Line in Central Square, which was a fifteen-minute walk from her apartment. It could be her exercise for the day.

She stopped at a bakery for a cranberry scone and more tea. Her mind was racing with questions and images, but she pushed them back and tried to focus on her scone, her tea, the brisk morning and the other people on the streets. Kids, workers, bag ladies, students. She passed a nursery school class of three- and four-year-olds hanging on to a rope to keep them together, their young teacher skipping along in front of them like the Pied Piper. The kids were laughing, making Carine smile.

She got a seat on a subway car and shut her eyes briefly, letting the rhythms of the rapid-transit line soothe her as the train sped over the Charles River, then back underground. She got off at the Charles

Street stop and walked, peeking in the shop windows on the pretty street at the base of Beacon Hill, giving a wistful glance at the corn stalks and pumpkins in front of an upscale flower shop. They reminded her of home.

When she turned down Beacon Street and her cell phone rang, she almost didn't answer it, then decided if it was Gus and she ignored him, she risked having him send in the National Guard. She hit the receive button and made herself smile, hoping that'd take any lingering strain out of her voice when she said hello.

Gus grunted. "Where are you?"

"Just past the corner of Beacon and Charles."

"Boston?"

"That's right," she said. "What's up, Gus? How's the weather in Cold Ridge?"

"Gray. Why aren't you home with your feet up?"

"I'm on my way to the Rancourt house. I want to see—"

"Carine, for chrissake, they can't possibly need you today. Why don't you drive up here for the weekend? Or jump on the train and go visit your brother or your sister for a couple days. They'd love to have you."

"I'm fine, Gus. I've been thinking about it, and I just need to go back there."

"For what, closure? Give me a break." But he sighed, and Carine could almost see him in his rustic village shop, amid his canoes and kayaks, his snowshoes and cross-country skis, his trail maps and compasses and high-end hiking clothes and equipment.

"The police haven't arrested anyone for this guy's murder. You know what that means, don't you? It means whoever did it is still on the streets."

"I'll be careful. Besides, the police and reporters are still bound to be there—and if not them, the Rancourts, their security chief—it'll be okay."

"You thought it'd be okay yesterday before you walked into the library, didn't you?"

"Gus—"

"Yeah. Yeah, I know. Nothing I can do. But I don't have to like it."

She heard something in his voice and slowed her pace. "Gus? What?"

"Nothing. Take care of yourself. You even *think* something's wrong, you call the police, okay?"

"Believe me, I will."

She clicked off, feeling vaguely uneasy. Gus was holding back on her. It wasn't like him. Normally he was a straight shooter. He had warned her about getting mixed up with Tyler North, when it was obvious their long tolerance for each other had sparked into something else. Her uncle said his piece, then shut up about it. When Ty dumped her a week before the wedding, Gus'd had the moderate grace not to actually say the words "I told you so." But he didn't need to—he *had* told her so, in no uncertain terms.

What wasn't he telling her now?

When she reached the stately mansion on Commonwealth Avenue, Carine could feel her scone and tea churning in her stomach. The police cars and yellow crime-scene tape were gone, and she didn't see any obvious sign of reporters. She mounted the steps and noticed the yellow mums were gone, too.

Sterling Rancourt opened the front door before she knocked. He was a tall, silver-haired man in his early fifties, and even the day after a man was murdered on his property, he radiated wealth and confidence. He was raised on the South Shore, where he and his wife owned their main home, and had gone to Dartmouth and Wharton, taking over his family's holdings in business and real estate twenty years ago. He was dressed casually and looked only slightly tired, perhaps a little pale—and awkward at seeing her. Carine thought she understood. He'd tried to do her a good deed by hiring her to photograph his house renovations, and she'd ended up discovering a dead body.

She mumbled a good morning, feeling somewhat awkward herself.

"How are you doing, Carine?" he asked. "Yesterday was a nightmare for all of us, but for you, especially."

"I'm doing okay, thanks." Suddenly she wondered if she should have come at all. "I guess I didn't know what to do with myself this morning."

He acknowledged her words with a small nod. "I expect we all feel that way. We won't get back to work here until next week at the earliest. Why don't you take a few days off? Go for walks, visit museums, take pictures of pumpkins—anything to get your mind off what happened yesterday."

Carine leaned against the wrought-iron rail. He hadn't invited her in, but she thought it would seem ghoulish and intrusive to ask outright if she could see the library, even if it was the reason she was here. "That's probably a good idea. I thought—look at me. I brought my digital camera. I don't know what I was thinking."

"It's all right. We're all struggling today. I'm not quite sure what I'm doing here myself. You're a photographer. Having your camera must help you feel like it's a normal day."

"Louis—his family—"

"Everything's being handled, Carine."

She suddenly felt nosy, as if she'd overstepped her bounds. "Have you talked to Manny Carrera? Do you know where he is?"

"Carine—perhaps it's best if you go home." Sterling's voice was gentle, concerned, but there was no mistaking that he wanted to be rid of her. "The police know how to get in touch with you if they want to speak with you again, don't they?"

"Of course—"

Gary Turner, Sterling's security chief, appeared in the doorway next to his boss. He nodded at her. "Good morning, Carine," he said politely. "It's nice to see you, as always. The two lead detectives will be back later this morning. I'll tell them you stopped by."

Dismissed, Carine thought, but without rancor. Sterling was just as on edge as she was, neither of them accustomed to dealing with this sort of emergency. But Gary Turner radiated calm and competence, a steady efficiency, that she found reassuring.

He was a strange guy. The Rancourts hired him in the spring, and she'd met him in Cold Ridge a few times before she went to work for them herself. She didn't understand exactly what he did, or what Manny Carrera was supposed to be doing, for that matter.

She was aware of Turner studying her, an unsettling experience, not just because he was so focused—he looked as if he'd lived most of his life underwater, or maybe in an attic. He had close-cropped, very thin white hair. He might have been in his eighties instead of, at most, his forties. His skin was an odd-looking pinkish-white, its paleness exaggerated by his habitual all-black attire. He had no eyebrows to speak of, and his eyes were a watery, almost colorless gray. He was missing his middle and ring fingers on his left hand. Carine knew he carried a concealed nine-millimeter pistol and assumed he could fire it, but she'd never asked.

"How are you doing?" Turner asked softly. "I'm sorry I didn't get a chance to talk to you yesterday."

"You were busy, and I'm doing fine. Thanks for asking. Look, I'm sure you both have a lot to do. I won't keep you—"

Turner stepped out onto the stoop with her. "You've experienced a trauma. Finding Louis yesterday was a physical and mental shock, a blow on multiple levels to your well-being. Perhaps you'd like for me to arrange for you to talk to someone?"

She shook her head politely. "There's no need to go to any trouble. I can always ask my sister for a recommendation, if it comes to it."

"Give yourself some time. It'll be hard for a while, but if after a few weeks you experience flashbacks, nightmares, sleeplessness, feelings of panic or emotional numbness—then don't wait, okay? Go see someone."

"I will. Manny Carrera—I'm worried about him—"

"That's understandable," Turner said mildly, then glanced back at Rancourt, who seemed paralyzed in the doorway. "I'll walk with Carine a minute."

"Of course. I'll see you back here later." Rancourt rallied, taking a breath. "Carine? If there's anything Jodie and I can do, please don't hesitate to let us know. I mean that. I'm so very sorry it had to be you yesterday."

"Thanks," she said. "I'm just sorry about Louis."

"The media—" Sterling paused and leaned forward to glance down the street, as if he expected someone to pop up out of nowhere. "I'd like you not to speak to any reporters. It's quiet at the moment, but they'll be back. Be polite, but be firm."

"Not a problem. The last thing I want to do is talk to a reporter."

He withdrew without further comment, the heavy door shutting with a loud thud behind him.

Gary Turner walked down to the sidewalk without a word, and Carine followed him, her knees steadier, her stomach still rebelling. "I shouldn't have come," she blurted. "I have no business being here. There's nothing for me to do, and you and the Rancourts must have your plates full."

"You thought it would help you to revisit the scene," Turner said.

"I suppose I did." They crossed Commonwealth to the mall, where a half-dozen pigeons had gathered on dried, fallen leaves. There was no toddler today. Carine felt none of yesterday's sense of peace with her life in Boston. "I'm not sure I really know what I was thinking."

"You're fighting for some sense of normalcy." Turner spoke with assurance, as if he knew, then fastened his colorless eyes on her. "Did you drive?"

"I took the T to Charles Street and walked."

"Walking's good. Keep it up. And eat right. Don't overdo anything. It's good to try to follow your normal routines as much as possible, even if you're not working." He smiled at her, seeming to want to help her relax. "Fortunately, your work lends itself to an erratic schedule—you're used to switching from one job to another. It's not like you've been getting up every day for the seven-to-three shift at the factory and suddenly there's no factory."

"That's true. I appreciate the advice, but please don't worry about me."

He paused, folding his hands behind his back as he walked smoothly, steadily. "But people do worry about you, Carine," he said finally. "I expect they can't help it, and you might benefit from their attention. Don't try to control what other people are feeling. Right now, just focus on what you need. The rest of us will manage."

"Mr. Turner—"

"Gary." He laughed, shaking his head. "You call Sterling Rancourt by his first name, but me—"

She tried to return his laugh. "I think it's because you carry a gun."

"Ah. Well, for you, Carine, I'd take it off, if it would make you feel more at ease."

"That's not necessary." She picked up her pace, feeling a fresh surge of awkwardness. She never knew what to say to him. She changed the subject. "I've known Manny Carrera for a long time. Do the police suspect him of being involved in Louis's death? Because it's not possible—"

"The police don't tell me what they think. One step at a time, Carine. Keep your focus on the here and now. Don't think back, don't think ahead. It's the best advice I can give you. Mr. Carrera is perfectly capable of taking care of himself." Turner stood back a moment, then frowned at her in a way she found faintly patronizing. "You aren't thinking of playing amateur detective, are you?"

"No! It's just that Manny's a friend. Do you know where he's staying?"

"If I did, I wouldn't tell you." There was no hint of condemnation in Turner's tone. "Take yourself out to lunch, Carine. Treat yourself to dessert. Browse the galleries on Newbury Street. Do you have a friend who can join you?"

"Most of my friends are working, but—"

"Your sister?"

"She's in Washington. She'd come if I called her."

He looked at her. "But you won't. You're a strong

woman, Carine. Stronger, I think, than people often realize at first.''

Hey, Ms. Photographer.

Poor Louis. Dead. She still could see the blood on his fingers.

Louis Sanborn was not a nice man.

Manny, clear-eyed and uncompromising. What did he know about Louis?

Carine swallowed hard, pushing back the memories of yesterday. Turner was right—she needed to stay focused on the present. ''To be honest, I don't worry about whether or not people think I'm strong. Louis stopped me on my way back from lunch and asked if I wanted a ride. If—''

''Don't. No ifs. They'll drive you crazy.'' Turner squeezed her upper arm. ''Take it easy on yourself, okay? Go take some pretty pictures. You didn't do anything wrong yesterday. Remember that.''

She blinked back sudden tears, feeling light-headed, her stomach not so much nauseated as hurting. ''Thanks.'' Her voice faltered, and she cleared her throat, annoyed with herself. ''I just need some time, I guess.''

''Newbury Street. Art galleries.'' He started across Commonwealth, pausing halfway into the lane of on-coming traffic and shaking his head at her. ''You might want to hold off on the dessert. You're looking a little green.''

She managed a smile. ''It wouldn't be a good idea to get sick on Newbury Street, would it?''

He chuckled. ''You'd be banned for life.''

* * *

Sterling Rancourt stared into the library, its wood floor still marred by crime-scene chalk and dried blood. The police forensics team had done its work, and a cleaning crew that specialized in ridding all trace of this sort of mess was due in that afternoon. Gary Turner had arranged for it. He'd been incredibly helpful—steady, knowledgeable, even kind.

Gary was in his office in the Rancourt building in Copley Square at the time of the shooting, while Sterling was enduring an interminable business lunch a few blocks over at the Ritz-Carlton Hotel. After-ward, he'd planned to meet his wife at a designer showroom on Newbury Street, so she could model an evening gown she wanted to wear to a charity ball over the holidays. She liked having his approval. Ten years ago, she'd bought a dress he didn't like, and he'd been stupid enough to say so—now she insisted on these modeling sessions for anything that cost more than a thousand dollars.

But he'd received the news about Louis at lunch and excused himself, heading straight over to Com-monwealth Avenue, calling first Jodie, who was on Newbury Street, then Turner. They all met at the house, where police and reporters were already swarming. Detectives quickly pulled aside Carine Winter, white-faced but functioning, and Manny Car-rera, as stalwart as ever. Sterling was unable to speak to either of them alone.

Jodie had remained at their South Shore home this morning. She said she didn't want to see or speak to anyone unless she had to—as far as she was concerned, if the police wanted to interview her again, they could drive down to Hingham and find her.

She knew nothing, Sterling thought. None of them did. Louis Sanborn had been in their lives for two weeks. That was it.

Manny Carrera couldn't have killed him. Manny saved lives. He only took a life when he came under enemy fire and had no other choice. Sterling had read up on PJs and their heroic work, although Manny and Tyler North would be the last to call what they did heroic. It wasn't false humility—Sterling would have recognized it if it were.

He and Jodie owed Manny Carrera *their* lives. But if the police wanted to waste their time pursuing him, that was their choice. There was nothing Sterling or anyone else could do.

"Mr. Rancourt?"

Gary Turner walked down the hall, his nearly colorless eyes and extremely pale skin disconcerting, off-putting even before anyone had gotten to the point of noticing the missing fingers. But he was quiet and supremely competent, and Sterling knew better than to underestimate him because of his strange appearance. Jodie said she found him fascinating, even sexy in a weird way. He wasn't ex-military or ex-law enforcement—Sterling suspected he was ex-CIA. Whatever the case, his credentials in private and corporate security had checked out. He hadn't said a word when Sterling hired Manny Carrera as a consultant. Either he was too self-disciplined to criticize his employer's decision, or he approved. Sterling hadn't asked him his opinion.

"Carine's on her way?"

Turner nodded. "She doesn't know what to do with herself."

"A shock reaction. She'll rally. It just might take a little more time than she wants it to. I've met her brother and sister—and her uncle—and they're all strong, resilient people."

But he could tell concern over Carine Winter wasn't why Turner was here. The man shifted slightly, lowering his voice although there was no one within earshot. "There's been a new development. Tyler North is in town. I just saw his truck on Comm. Ave."

"Tyler? Interesting." Sterling didn't share Turner's sense of drama over this news. Of course Tyler would be here if was able to. He'd known Carine since childhood and had almost married her in February, and Manny was a friend. They'd gone on missions together. "He must be on leave—he'll have heard about Manny's predicament. Word like that travels like wildfire."

"I don't think he's here because of Mr. Carrera. Not directly."

Sterling nodded, sighing. "Of course. Carine." He pictured Tyler North, a compact, rugged man, incredibly loyal despite being something of a loner himself. "Well, she won't like it, but I suppose having him here will be a distraction for her."

"What do you want me to do?" Turner asked.

"About Tyler?"

Sterling thought a moment. He hated the situation he was in, how out of control it felt. Boston's best homicide detectives were on the case, but he wasn't involved—they didn't answer to him. A man, an employee, had been found murdered in a house he owned. Everything about him and his life was fair game. Yet the murderer was probably a drifter, a petty thief or a drug addict, who'd wandered in after Louis stupidly left the door open and, for reasons that might never be known, decided to shoot him.

The police had no motive, no murder weapon, no suspect in custody. Until they did, Sterling thought, he and Jodie, Gary Turner, Carine Winter, Manny Carrera—none of them would have much room to maneuver.

"Tyler's a friend," he told Turner. "Do nothing."

Six

❧❧

Boston Public Garden, which dated back to 1859, was one of Carine's favorite places in the city. Its curving Victorian paths, lawns, gardens, statues, benches and more than six hundred trees were enclosed within arched, wrought-iron fences, making it feel like a retreat, as if she'd stepped back in time.

If only she could step back to yesterday morning, she thought. She could warn Louis not to go back to the Rancourt house alone—delay him, get in the car with him, talk him into watching the pigeons with her.

She crossed the small bridge over the shallow pond where the famed Swan Boats, a century-plus tradition, would cruise during warmer months. They were put away for the season, and now just fallen leaves floated on the water. But she didn't linger, instead took a walkway over to Tremont Street and the Four Seasons Hotel. When the Rancourts had people in town on business, they tended to put them up at the Four Seasons. Manny Carrera couldn't afford it on his own.

Neither could she, but if she wasn't paying the tab, she'd stay there. Maybe Manny would, too.

She entered the elegant lobby and wandered over to a seating area that looked across Tremont to the Public Garden, its soft sofas and high-backed chairs occupied by a handful of well-dressed men and women in business attire. Carine felt out of place in her barn coat but didn't worry about it—she didn't plan to stay.

She spotted Manny on a love seat in front of a window as he drank coffee from a delicate china cup. He wore a dark suit with a blue tie and motioned for her to join him, shaking his head as she sat on a chair opposite him. "I saw you beating a path across the park. Got a brainstorm I was here?"

"It's not a park. You're not supposed to walk on the grass."

"Then what is it?"

"A public botanical garden. It was designed by Frederick Olmsted. He did Central Park, too, which *is* a park."

"Ah."

She leaned forward. "Manny—"

"I'm stuck here, Carine. You're not. Why don't you go home?"

"I am home. I live in Boston now."

"*For* now, you mean."

"Why are you stuck here? Did the police say you can't leave? You're not under arrest or you wouldn't be here."

He shrugged, not answering. He had broad shoulders, a thick neck—his suit was tight around his upper arms and thighs. He was six feet tall and strongly built. Carine doubted the PJ Physical Abilities and Stamina Test had given him any trouble. He and Ty both insisted a pararescueman didn't have to be big, but Manny was one who was.

"Manny, I'm not trying to interfere in your business. I just—" She sighed, uncertain how she could explain why she was here. "We both were there yesterday. I guess I just wanted to see you. I'm not having an easy time of it, and I thought—I don't know what I thought."

His dark eyes warmed slightly. "The police want to talk to me again today. I'm cooperating. If I don't, they'll probably find a reason to throw me in jail sooner rather than later."

"Why at all?"

"They have to do their thing." He leaned over to refill his coffee cup from a silver service set on the low table in front of him. "You know what's good about staying at a fancy place? You can pick out the cops. They fit in about as well as I do."

"There's a police officer here?"

"I'm under surveillance. I think it's supposed to be covert."

"Manny!" Carine found herself glancing around at the occupied seats, noticing an older couple, a middle-aged man reading a *Wall Street Journal,* a young woman tapping at a PalmPilot. "The woman?"

"Uh-huh."

"Manny, doesn't this bother you? Having the police waste their time on you, when you know you had nothing to do with Louis's death?''

He sipped his coffee. ''Getting bothered isn't going to change anything.''

''So, what're you going to do, sit here and do *nothing?*''

''Sure, why not? Enjoy the fancy digs while I can. Rancourt hasn't told me to clear out yet. So long as he's footing the bill, I can—''

''You can what, drink coffee out of a silver pot?''

His eyes didn't leave her. ''I have to tell you, drinking coffee out of a silver pot suits me just fine.''

She immediately regretted her words. Manny wouldn't bring it up, but he and North had been in Afghanistan and Iraq. Manny's last mission before he retired was to recover an aircrew killed in a training accident. ''I'm sorry. I didn't mean—''

''Actually,'' he added with a hint of a smile, lifting his pinkie finger from the too-small handle of his cup, ''I'm drinking out of a china cup, not a silver pot.''

Carine didn't know what to say. She could feel tension and frustration eating away at any calm she'd found during her walk in the Public Garden. ''What can I do to help?''

''Nothing. Go back to Cold Ridge.'' He looked at her over the rim of his cup, his dark eyes unrelenting. ''For all you know, I could be guilty. I could have killed Louis Sanborn.''

''You had no motive.''

He was motionless for a split second. ''I had motive.''

''What?'' She lowered her voice, aware of the cop

and her PalmPilot. "Manny, what are you talking about?"

"Why do you suppose the police have me under surveillance but not you? Come on, Carine. You don't know what I was doing at the Rancourt house yesterday."

She sat back, irritated with him for playing games with her. "I don't care. I don't care if you didn't think Louis was a nice guy or what you're doing in Boston, it's impossible—Manny, I'm your friend. I know you didn't kill him."

"You're my friend's ex-fiancée. That's a little different."

Carine's mouth snapped shut, and she stared at him. He'd obviously meant to sting her, and he'd succeeded. "All right. Why tell me Louis wasn't a nice man?"

"Because he wasn't."

"That's not an answer."

"I thought it'd be enough to scare you into going home. A minute ago I thought telling you I'm under police surveillance would scare you into going home. Now I'm telling you I had a motive—"

"Stop saying that!"

"Listen to me, Carine." He set down his cup again. "I don't need your help."

"You're being an ass just to get rid of me."

He smiled faintly. "It's not working very well, is it?"

"What about Ty? Have you talked to him? He'd help you. You know he would."

"Ty's on a mission, not that I'd ask him for his

help. He's still on active duty. He doesn't need to get mixed up in a murder investigation.'' Manny sat back, studying her for a moment. ''That's what this is, Carine. A murder investigation. A man was killed yesterday. You need to back off.''

''Yes,'' she said, ''I'm well aware a man was killed.''

His expression softened. ''I'm sorry. I haven't forgotten you were the one who found him. How're you doing?''

''Okay.''

''Sleep last night?''

''Not much.''

He winked at her. ''Now you're looking for trouble to distract yourself, aren't you? I know it's hard to figure what to do after something like yesterday.''

''It was hard enough getting shot at last year. This—''

''Give yourself some time. And don't worry about me, will you? I'll be fine. If I need help...'' He shrugged, deliberately not finishing.

''If you need help, you won't turn to a nature photographer, not with all the tough types you know.'' She gave him a quick smile and got to her feet. ''Just stating the facts, not putting myself down. You're not going to tell me anything, are you?''

''The police asked me not to talk to anyone.''

''Right. Like you needed their say-so to keep your mouth shut.''

He rose, and she could see the lines at the corners of his eyes, the strain. He'd just gotten his son back on his feet, and now he was in the wrong place at the wrong time when a murder was committed—but he didn't let any of that show. He kissed her lightly on the cheek and admonished her one more time. "You don't have a dog in this fight, Carine. Stay out of it."

When she got back out onto the street, she made herself take three deep cleansing breaths before she decided what to do next. Her hands were shaking. Her stomach muscles were tight to the point of soreness, but at least she didn't feel as if she'd throw up— minor progress, but progress nonetheless.

She fished out her cell phone and dialed Gus's number. "Gus? It's me. The police have Manny under surveillance. Can you believe it? They think he killed Louis. Why don't they think *I* killed him?"

"What the hell were you doing talking to Manny Carrera?"

"Relax. He's at the Four Seasons having coffee." She sighed, starting down Tremont Street toward the intersection of Arlington Street, the Public Garden across from her, people passing her on their normal routines. "Manny's in trouble, Gus. He won't admit it, of course. He's going to have ulcers and heart disease in a few years from keeping it all under such tight control."

"Carine—"

"I'm thinking about calling Ty. Do you know where he is?"

"Why do you want to call him? Manny can take care of himself."

"Manny's *not* taking care of himself. You should see him. Maybe Ty can talk to him. He must have heard about what happened."

Gus hesitated. "He heard."

Carine stopped abruptly, a man in a suit nearly crashing into her as he rushed past. Gus was being evasive, and that wasn't his nature. He'd been evasive earlier, and she'd let it go. Normally he was the most straightforward person she'd ever encountered. "Gus?"

"What, honey? You sound stressed out—"

"Gus, where is Tyler? Is he on leave? Manny said he was on a mission."

"You haven't seen the news, have you? Well, you'll find out sooner or later—North and I pulled three prep school seniors off the ridge yesterday."

"So, he's there. I'll call him at home."

"Try his cell phone."

She frowned. "Gus? Gus, what is it you're not telling me?"

"Ah, shit, honey, I'm losing the connection. I can't hear you. Can you hear me?"

"I can hear you fine."

"What? Carine? Are you there? These goddamn cell phones."

"Gus—"

He disconnected.

And she knew. Ty was en route to Boston or already there. The fact that Gus didn't want to tell her meant North had come because of her. Gus wouldn't like it either way—Ty in Boston, her there on her own.

"Mission, my ass."

Manny had to know. He must have contacted Ty and put him up to keeping an eye on her—probably to take her back to Cold Ridge, since that seemed to be the general consensus of what she should do with herself. Go home. Stay out of trouble. Don't *cause* any trouble.

She didn't feel warm and safe and less isolated, less vulnerable, as if her family and friends were trying to do right by her after she'd had a shock.

"Ha," she muttered. "I know better."

She'd been conspired against by her own uncle, by Manny Carrera—and North. They'd obviously believed she couldn't resist meddling.

She could see herself standing in the library door yesterday and relived the jolt of awareness that had warned her something was wrong. She saw the blood. Louis's hand. She felt herself running in panic out of the house, into Manny Carrera's arms.

If she hadn't been there, would Manny have slipped away before the police arrived?

Was it her fault he was under suspicion?

Louis Sanborn was not a nice man.

Maybe not. But Manny hadn't shot him in cold blood.

She dialed Gus's number. "When did Ty leave for Boston?" she asked him.

"Can't hear you," her uncle said, and hung up.

Seven

Antonia had already tracked Ty down on his cell phone and given him an earful about leaving her sister on the loose in Boston, and now he was getting it from Manny Carrera. Ty just listened. They didn't realize what it was like to watch Carine do calf stretches on her porch—watch her as she sipped tea and tried to eat a scone on her way to a murder scene.

He'd lost her on the subway, picked her up again on Beacon Street. It wasn't as if he didn't know where she was going. He'd reminded Antonia of the promise she'd extracted from him last night not to make things worse for her sister. Hell, he was trying.

But as a practical matter, Antonia wanted Carine back in Cold Ridge, out of harm's way. Everyone did. It was the only reason Gus had let him out of town alive—because he figured Ty would come back with Carine, one way or another. She didn't like it that people worried about her, but they did. And not without cause. A year ago, she unwittingly disturbed a smuggling operation and came under fire while she was off taking pictures. Then she'd gone and fallen in love with him. Now it was out-and-out murder that had her life in an uproar, her family wanting to keep her safe.

She'd surprised him, sneaking into the Four Seasons and tracking down Manny. As usual, Manny's instincts were right on target—she wasn't going to back off. But that was Carine. She never backed off. Ty had seen her lie in wait for the perfect shot of a spruce grouse. She had focus, commitment, inner reserves. He remembered her making a break for it from behind her boulder last fall, zigzagging from tree to tree, launching herself down the hill, out of the line of fire. She might have made it out of there just fine if he hadn't been around.

Manny exhaled, looking out at the busy street. "I hope I put the fear of God in her. She was all set to jump in headfirst and prove my innocence."

"She likes you."

"Big deal. And that's not it. She has this strong moral compass. You know, this acute sense of right and wrong—as in, it was wrong for you to skip out on her a week before your wedding."

Ty didn't squirm. Nobody had liked what he'd done. "It was wrong for someone to murder this man, Louis Sanborn. If she wants to do the right thing, she should back off and let the police do their job."

"Not if she's not convinced they're going after the real killer. She'll feel it's her duty not to walk away."

"Because she found Louis," North said.

"Because she thinks she could have saved his life. He offered her a ride, and she refused. If she hadn't—"

"Then we'd have two dead bodies instead of one."

"Carine doesn't see it that way. And," Manny added, with obvious reluctance, "she thinks it's her fault the police are sniffing my trail."

"Is it?"

"Not really. She went screaming out of the house, and I was there. That put me on the scene, but—" He shrugged. "The police have more than that to go on."

North didn't ask what that was. If Manny intended to tell him, he'd already have done it. "Carine sees things the way she wants them to be, not necessarily the way they are. She has a rosy-eyed view of the world. You don't ever see her taking a picture of an osprey ripping apart a baby duck, do you?"

"Christ, North. I just had breakfast."

"You're making too much of her reasoning. She's just bored."

"Maybe. I don't know." Manny leaned back against the soft cushions of the couch and frowned at his longtime friend. "Why haven't you gotten her out of here by now?"

"Timing. She had to go back to the scene. Maybe she had to see you, too, but I should have prevented that. By the time I realized what was going on, she was sitting across from you."

"I should have told you where I was staying."

Ty didn't comment. "If I grabbed her too soon,

she'd be impossible to keep still. She'd be back down here in a flash. Now—'' He sighed, picturing her as she'd left the hotel. He knew her so well, her body language, the way she thought. "There's a chance."

"You're not giving yourself enough credit. Toss her butt in the back of your truck and beat a path to New Hampshire. You know how to hold a prisoner if you have to."

It had been a long night in his truck, Ty thought. He'd had to move it several times, and he was stiff. "I'm still an outsider in Cold Ridge."

"You've lived there your whole life—"

"Doesn't matter. The Winters have been there since 1800. Figure it out, Manny. I live in their old house."

"Your mother bought the place from a Winter?"

"No. A Winter built it. Last one moved out in 1878. Doesn't matter. I'd be holding a prisoner in enemy territory."

"You mean the bad-ass uncle wants you to go easy on her."

Ty shrugged. "I'm on death row with Gus as it is."

Manny leaned over and poured the last drops of coffee into his cup, not because he wanted more, North thought, but because he needed something to do. "You're sure you're not dragging your heels because you're afraid to face her?"

"I'd be afraid to face her if I'd done something I shouldn't have done. I didn't."

"Right," Manny said with open sarcasm. "Bet Carine looks at it that way, too."

North got to his feet. "I should head out before she gets too big a lead on me. You know what you're doing, Carrera?"

His friend relaxed his guard, his dark eyes showing his tension—his fear. "I came up here to recommend the Rancourts fire Louis Sanborn."

"That's reason for him to kill you, not the other way around."

"Suppose I got to him first, before he could kill me?"

"I'm not speculating, Manny. You want to tell me the whole story, fine. Tell it. Otherwise—"

"I've told you what I can. I don't have the whole story. There are gaps I need to fill in."

"Can you do it from here?" But Manny wasn't going to answer, and Ty didn't push him. "You know how to get in touch with me. Stay safe, okay?"

"If something happens to me and I can't—" He paused, searching for the right words, then went on, "If I can't function, remember I love Val. All right?"

"Yeah, Manny. Sure. She knows—"

"Just remember. I've got computer files—" He broke off. "That's all I'm saying. You'll remember."

North turned to cross the plush carpet, noting a woman with a PalmPilot, making no bones about watching him. A cop. She must have realized she'd been made. It wouldn't be easy to conduct covert surveillance on a man with Manny Carrera's training and experience. Maybe she was the reason for Manny's cryptic comment about loving his wife and computer files.

"One more favor," he said quietly.

Ty glanced back at him, not knowing what to expect.

"Eric—could you look in on my kid if you get the chance? I don't know if Val's talked to him. I haven't talked to either one of them. I don't like the idea of having to explain to the police why I called my family."

"What do you want me to tell him?"

"Not to worry."

Ty nodded without argument, because there was no way to tell Manny Carrera that a fourteen-year-old boy was going to think what he wanted to think, worry if he wanted to worry.

When North got back out to Tremont Street, he noticed the smell of exhaust fumes and the noise of the traffic speeding past him. He was used to making quick switches in his environment, but he'd never liked cities. Carine had been out of his sight for less than fifteen minutes, but he didn't think it'd be difficult to pick up her trail. She was on foot, and she was aimless, restless, ripe for doing something she shouldn't. The Winters were all risk-takers at heart. Even Carine, except none of them saw it.

She was a nature photographer. She had a camera with her. Maybe she'd slipped back into Boston Public Garden to take pictures of the trees.

Ty waited at a red light at the corner of Arlington and Tremont, debating his next move. Head to Copley

Square? Turn onto Arlington and check Newbury Street? Or go back to the Rancourt house, or to Inman Square and her apartment—or chuck it and head back to New Hampshire without her. Mind his own damn business.

He hadn't made up his mind when she swooped up from the steps of the subway station on the corner, diving at him as if he'd just tried to mug her. She damn near knocked him on his ass.

He caught her around the middle. "Hey—babe, there are cops all over the place."

"You've been following me. For how long?"

He kept a tight hold on her, taking due note of her strong abdominal muscles and overall increased level of fitness. He'd followed her on her halfhearted run this morning—from the shape she was in, he'd guess she'd had better mornings.

"Not that long," he said. "Take it easy."

"Why should I?"

Good point. He held her arms down, but she kicked him. He had on khakis and his brown leather jacket, too warm for the city temperatures. He'd be working up a sweat with too much more of this. He grabbed her camera bag in self-defense. "Want me to throw this under a car? Come on. Get a grip. I have tender shins."

"You don't have tender anything. When did you get here?"

"Last night."

"You've been following me since *last night?*"

He dodged her next kick. People passed by, eyeing

them nervously, and one guy pulled out his cell phone. North smiled, trying to look nonthreatening, and Carine, apparently realizing the scene she was making, backed off. Strands of hair had pulled out of her loose ponytail. She grabbed her camera bag back and adjusted it on her shoulder, breathing hard, a little wild-eyed.

"Manny sicced you on me, didn't he?" she demanded.

"I had a feeling you wouldn't thank me. Does it feel better to go on the offensive?"

She sighed, shaking her head. "I wish it did. At least I didn't push you out into traffic." She seemed calmer, but Ty could see the effects of the past twenty-four hours in the puffy, dark circles under her eyes, the paleness of her skin, the rigid hold she had on her camera bag. Her eyes, so damn blue, narrowed on him. "Are you on leave? I don't want you wasting any more of it on me. You can turn around and drive back to New Hampshire. There's a deli on Arlington. I'll buy you a sandwich for the road."

"Carine…hell, babe, you look like you're in tough shape. Let me—"

"Good. I'd hate to look great the day after I discovered a dead body." She looked up at the traffic light, apparently waiting for a walk sign. "And don't call me babe."

"Why'd you attack me?"

"I thought about throwing a rock through your windshield, but I couldn't find your truck. Or a rock."

North shrugged. "Makes sense, I guess."

"It *was* Manny who sent you, right? Gus wouldn't. He'd stonewall me if he knew you were on your way, but he would never ask you to keep an eye on me." She still didn't look around at North. "Does Manny think I'm in danger from the real murderer, or does he just not trust me to mind my own business?"

"Nobody trusts a Winter to mind their own business." He resisted touching her. "Damn it, I'm not going to stand out here talking murder with you. Let's go."

"The deli's just up Arlington—"

"You're not buying me a sandwich and sending me on my way."

A bit of color rose in her cheeks, and she refused to look at him, her shoulders hunched as she continued to wait for the walk signal. It came, but she didn't move. Ty remembered why he'd fallen in love with her—why, ultimately, he'd walked away from her. She was sensitive, loyal, artistic, a fighter and a dreamer. He was loyal and a fighter, but sensitive? Artistic? A dreamer? No way. Although she was the youngest of the Winter siblings and remembered their parents the least, she was also the one who seemed most affected by their deaths. She deserved a man who led a safer life than he did.

"This was a bad idea," Ty said, half under his breath. "All right, suit yourself. You're on your own."

She stood up straight and whipped around at him. "I am?"

"You bet. Go on. Scoot. I won't strong-arm you."

"You'll follow me," she said. "You're an expert in evading pursuit."

"I'd be doing the pursuing. That's a different skill."

"You'd manage."

"Not around here. I like the desert. Caves. Bugs to eat. A jungle's good, too. I could manage in a jungle."

She almost smiled. "You're totally impossible, Tyler. I don't know why I ever wanted to marry you." She thought a moment, then sighed. "But, seeing how you're listening to reason, I suppose I could let you drive me back to my apartment. I don't have the oomph to walk, and I don't think I could handle the subway again right now."

"Better me than the subway?" He grinned at her. "It's a start."

"You won't try to take me to New Hampshire against my will?"

"No, ma'am."

She looked faintly skeptical, but she was, at her core, the most trusting person he'd ever known. She wasn't naïve—she knew more than most about what life could throw at people, without rhyme nor reason. But she was an optimist, a glass-is-half-full type, a believer in truth and justice, all of which, in Ty's view, guaranteed she'd be a pain in the ass with Manny and this murder investigation. No wonder Manny had enlisted him to get rid of her.

Carine spotted his truck on Boylston and shot ahead of him, leaning against the passenger door until he got there to unlock it. She had her arms crossed, and more hairs had pulled out of her ponytail. ''I know you're trained to resist the enemy,'' she said. ''I probably could shove burning bamboo sticks under your fingernails, and you wouldn't talk.''

''You're not the enemy.'' He unlocked her door and pulled it open. ''And you wouldn't have the heart to torture me.''

''I'd have the heart. There's just no point if it's not going to work.''

She climbed into the truck, and when North got behind the wheel, he saw the tears in her eyes. But she turned away quickly and gazed out the passenger window. He started the engine. ''Carine...ah, hell...''

''Feel like a heel, do you? Good.'' She sniffled, not looking at him. ''Just don't get the idea that I'm not over you, because I am. I just need protein, that's all. I'm having a sugar low.''

''You might be over me, but you're not neutral—''

''I've never been neutral about you. I wasn't neutral when I was six years old and you cut the tire-swing rope on me. It doesn't mean anything.''

He let the engine idle a moment. ''I'm sorry I hurt you.''

''You didn't hurt me, Ty. You did me a favor.'' She glanced at him sideways, her tears gone. ''Isn't that what all the men who get cold feet say?''

''It wasn't cold feet.''

''No, not you. You're way too tough for cold feet.'' She wasn't going to give him an inch. He didn't blame her—she'd given him her heart, and he'd broken it.

He shifted his truck into gear. "Just for the record," he said, "I've never been neutral about you, either."

Eight

When they reached her apartment, Carine climbed out of the truck, thanked Ty for the ride and told him to have a safe trip home. She gave him a parting smile, shut the door and mounted her porch steps at a half run, not so much, he thought, because she wanted to get there fast but because she wanted to prove to him she could do it. Maybe to herself, too. She'd had a shock, and she was back on her feet, up and running.

He wondered how long before she figured out he wasn't going anywhere.

Hauling her back to Cold Ridge against her will was out, but Manny had his reasons—however close-mouthed he was being about them—for asking Ty to keep an eye on her. She'd found Louis Sanborn dead. She'd worked with him. A murderer was on the loose. Something was up.

And Ty couldn't abandon her again. Gus would pitch him off the ridge for sure. When he wasn't looking, just when he let his guard down—off a ledge he'd go.

But it was more than Gus, more than Manny, more than murder that was keeping him in Boston—it was Carine, seeing her again after all these months. He had to do right by her, somehow make up for what he'd done.

She seemed to be having trouble with the front door.

That wasn't it. Her keys were in her hand. She hadn't touched the door. She glanced back at him, her eyes wide, her mouth partly open, and Ty was out of his truck in an instant. "What's wrong?"

"I don't know. Nothing, probably." She took a breath, pushed back more hair that had escaped from her ponytail. "The door sticks. I'm sure that's all it is. People leave it open all the time."

"Let's take a look."

Ty took the sagging steps onto the porch. The door to her building had dirty glass and peeling white paint that had grayed with neglect and the onslaught of city soot and grime. It was open slightly, about six inches.

"I don't want to overreact," Carine said.

"It's okay, Carine. Anyone would be on edge after what happened to you yesterday. Why don't I check your apartment, make sure everything's okay?"

She hesitated, long enough for him to push the door open the rest of the way and enter the outer hall. It was poorly lit and smelled like cat litter. Dirty steps led up to the second floor. Carine fell in behind him, then gasped and lunged forward, but Ty grabbed her wrist, keeping her from shooting past him. He saw what she obviously had already seen—the door to her apartment was also open.

There was no sign of forced entry—no ripped wood, no broken locks.

"I locked up this morning," she whispered. "I know I did."

Ty released her. "It was a rough morning for you. You were off your routines. Anything's possible."

"Anything's *not* possible. I locked my door. It's not something I even think about anymore. It's routine—"

"All right. You locked your door. Do you want to call 911 and let the police check it out?"

She grimaced, then sighed heavily. "Not yet. I'd feel ridiculous if they're just going to tell me I forgot to lock up. I'll have a look first." She glanced at him. "It's my apartment, so it's my responsibility."

"Suppose someone's in there?"

"I'll yell."

Ty rolled his eyes. "Right."

"Don't argue with me. It's not like you came down here with an M16 strapped to your back." She lowered her camera bag. "Hang on. I'll get out my cell phone—"

"If someone hits me over the head, you'll call 911?"

"I might," she said, but her smile didn't quite make it.

While she dug out her cell phone, North slipped inside her apartment, moving quickly down a short hallway into the kitchen. The other rooms all connected to it. Bathroom, living room, bedroom. The doors were open, the apartment was quiet, still and, he thought, very bright. Yellow, citrus green, lavender blue, dashes of raspberry. Some white, but not much. Not enough.

He snatched a paring knife out of the dish drainer, Carine behind him, her cell phone in hand. She got her own knife and followed him as he entered each room and looked around, seeing no sign of a rigorous search or any obvious missing valuables. Television, laptop and stereo were all intact. What else there was to take, he didn't know. Carine had never been into jewelry. He remembered she'd wanted a simple engagement ring. When he pulled the plug on their wedding, she'd offered to feed it to him.

She led the way back into the kitchen and sank against the sink and its citrus-green cabinets, her arms crossed, the last of her ponytail gone. She chewed on the inside corner of her mouth. "Maybe you had a point and I did forget to lock up."

"Is that what you think?"

"I don't know that I *can* think. I'm a damn wreck. I keep expecting any minute I'll just put it all out of my head and be fine—" She broke off with another sigh. "It doesn't look as if anyone got at the door with a crowbar—I suppose it could have popped open on its own. This place is old, and the landlord doesn't fix anything until it's absolutely necessary. But why would it pop open *today*?"

"Who else has a key?"

"Antonia. When she started spending more time in D.C. I gave one to the Rancourts in case I ever lose mine. And Gus. He has one."

Ty returned the knife to the dish drainer and stood back from her, taking in her pale skin, her tensed muscles, her shallow breathing. A thick covered rubber band clung to the ends of a small clump of hair. He pulled it out and handed it to her. She'd had enough. She'd reached her saturation point. Time for him to break through. "Ten minutes," he said.

"What do you mean, ten minutes?"

"You've got ten minutes to pack up. We're leaving."

She straightened. "Says who? What about the police?"

"You're not even sure there's been a break-in."

"You don't want to explain why you're here to them, do you? You'd have to tell them about Manny—"

"You're under nine minutes. Keep talking." He settled back against the sink next to her, noticed the photograph of a red-tailed hawk above her table. It was one she'd taken—he remembered she'd had to lie on her stomach and hang off a ledge to get the angle she wanted. "If you don't have time to pack, I can always run into Wal-Mart with you for new undies."

She didn't budge. "What if I tell you to go to hell?"

He smiled, leaning in close to her. "Eight minutes."

Her arms dropped down to her sides, and she scowled at him. "You're serious, aren't you?"

"Yes, ma'am. You need to get out of here and clear your head. Anyone in your position would, so don't take it as a knock on you. You just can't see it. I can." He glanced at his sports watch. "I'm counting."

She disappeared into her bedroom without further argument. His head was pounding. Maybe it was all the cheerful, bright colors, so different from the warm, dark colors of her log cabin in Cold Ridge. It wasn't the same, not having her across the meadow, waking up to the smell of smoke from her woodstove on cold mornings. She was down here, finding dead people and painting things lavender.

A wave of nostalgia and regret washed over him, and he wondered if they could ever go back to the easy friendship they'd had before he'd decided he was in love with her, or recognized that he was, had been for a long time. Whatever it was.

He walked over to her bedroom doorway and watched her load things into a soft, worn tapestry bag opened on her bed. "Need some help?"

"No, thanks."

Cool. A hint of irritation. She womped a pair of jeans into her bag. North smiled. "Give it up, Carine. If you didn't want to go with me, you'd make me hit you over the head and carry you out of here."

She fixed her blue eyes on him. "Being an experienced combat medic, you'd know just where to hit me so it wouldn't inflict permanent damage, wouldn't you?''

"Actually, I would. But you want to go home. Admit it. You don't want to stay here by yourself—"

"Fine. You're right. So let's do it. Let's go home."

She zipped up her bag, slung it over her shoulder and marched across the shaggy blue rug to him, but when she started past him, he caught one arm around her waist. "Are you going to be mad the whole trip?"

"I knew I'd have to face you again one of these days," she said. "I just didn't think it'd be under these circumstances. No. I won't be mad the whole trip. I can't stay here. I know that."

She let her bag fall to the floor, didn't move away from him. He didn't know why, unless she was remembering, as he was, what it was like when they'd made love. "Ty—" She broke off, a warmth in her tone that hadn't been there before. "I don't know anyone else who'd do what you've done, come down here, follow me around, let me come close to shoving you into oncoming traffic."

"It wasn't that close."

But she was serious, sincere, and didn't respond to his stab at humor. "Here you are, trying to look after me, whether I want you or need you to or not, even when you know—well, never mind what you know. Thank you."

"You were going to say even when I know what I did to you."

"I guess what I should say is even when we know what we did to each other."

"Damn it, Carine." He could hear the pain in his own voice, wished it had stayed buried. "I can't undo what I did. If I could…"

"It's okay."

She touched her fingertips to the side of his face and, without any other warning than that, kissed him, lightly, gently, but not, he thought, chastely. It was like being mule-kicked, like setting a match to super-dry kindling. All the clichés. There'd been no other woman since her. He kept thinking there should be, that he ought to get on with his life, but the weeks had ticked by, now the months.

He fought an urge to carry her to bed, but she pulled away from him, smiled at him, her skin less pale, less cool to the touch. "A lot's changed in a year, hasn't it?"

He smiled back at her. "Not some things."

She gave him a pointed look. "Sex isn't everything, Sergeant North. You said so yourself when you gave me my marching papers."

"Did I say that?"

"Not in as many words—"

"Yeah, no kidding." He held her more closely, suddenly not wanting to let go. "The reason I didn't marry you was because of me, not because of you."

"Semantics. You ready?"

"Not quite."

And he kissed her this time, felt her arms tighten around his middle, her shirt riding up—he touched the bare skin of her midriff, and when she inhaled, he deepened the kiss. She responded, sliding her hands around to his belt buckle, her fingertips drifting lower, outlining his obvious arousal. She took his hand and eased it over her breasts.

"Carine—"

"Just this once." Her eyes were wide, alert, nothing about her anywhere but here, right now. "It's been such an awful twenty-four hours. Ty—please, I know what I'm doing."

She touched him again, erotically, and he was lost. He swept her up and carried her to the bed, laying her on top of her down comforter. He paused, looking at her for any indication she'd changed her mind, giving her the chance to send him back to the kitchen. Ty told himself he should put a stop to this insanity, but he didn't. Neither did she. She scooted out of her clothes, and in five seconds, he was out of his, on top of her, stroking her smooth hips, her breasts—but she was in a hurry.

"Make love to me," she whispered. "Now."

She pulled him into her, shutting her eyes, no hesitation now. He kept his eyes open, watching her as he made love to her, the flush on her face, the way she bit her lower lip when she came, seconds before he did. It was then he shut his eyes, savoring his release, the feel of her body all around him.

Making love to her was natural. Perfect. And it couldn't happen again.

He kissed her forehead and rolled off the bed, grabbing his clothes. "No regrets?"

She shook her head. "Not this soon. Later, maybe."

"Carine—"

"Just turn your head when I get my clothes back on."

He did as she asked.

He had regrets. About a thousand of them. He couldn't seem to keep his head glued on straight when he was around her. He'd almost sent her an old-fashioned telegram to call off their engagement, just to make sure he got the message delivered, that she understood it—he couldn't marry her. Not that next week, not ever.

As if to prove his point, here he was. One minute, he was checking for intruders with a sharp knife, the next minute, making love to a woman who'd pretty much had him by the short hairs all her life. She deserved someone more like her, someone more attuned to her sensibilities. He wasn't as creative or perceptive or optimistic as she was. He was restless, an adrenaline junkie for as long as he could remember. He needed the kind of physical and mental challenges his work as a PJ provided. Even his mother would have had less trouble with a quieter kind of kid—he'd see her eyes glaze over many times as she became so absorbed in her work she was unaware of what was going on around her, and he'd clear out, head up the ridge. It wasn't like he'd sat there and played quietly by the fire.

Carine cleared her throat. "I'm ready. You can turn your head now."

North didn't feel self-conscious about his own absence of clothing. He supposed he should, but this wasn't the first time he and Carine had made love—the first time was almost a year ago, a few days after the shooting in the woods, less than twenty-four hours after he got rid of Hank and Manny. It was in the loft in her log cabin, with the fire crackling in her wood-stove, and it hadn't seemed sudden at all. It had seemed natural, as if they should have been making love for years.

He pulled on his pants, noting that she didn't turn her head away, but when he grinned at her, she made a face, blushing slightly. "Regrets?" he asked.

She shook her head.

But that was now, he thought. Give her a couple of hours in his truck and see what she thought.

She swore under her breath and grabbed her tapestry bag and her cameras, not asking him to carry a thing as she pushed past him into the kitchen.

He had a feeling it was going to be a long drive back to New Hampshire.

Nine

The lead homicide detective had Sterling take him through the entire house after lunch, describe each room and explain its status in terms of renovation. Sterling tried not to let his impatience show, but he could see no relevance in having the detective inspect the fifth-floor maid's quarters. But the man insisted, and Sterling cooperated. Afterward, the detective thanked him, and Sterling returned to his office in a deceptively plain building that his company owned in Copley Square.

He was exhausted and uneasy, and try as he did, he couldn't summon much sympathy for Louis Sanborn. Why the hell hadn't he taken more care not to get himself killed? Or at least, if it had to happen, why not somewhere else? Why on Rancourt property?

Sterling stood in front of the tall, spotless windows in his office and looked across Boylston at Trinity Church and the mirrored tower of the Hancock building. He could see a corner of the original wing of the

Boston Public Library, the oldest public library in the country. So much history all around him. It was something he loved about Boston. He thought of it as his city. He and Jodie had such great plans for the house on Commonwealth Avenue. They wanted to entertain there, open it up to charitable events, allow for people outside their immediate circle of family and friends to enjoy it.

Now it was tainted by murder.

If not Louis, why hadn't Gary Turner done something to prevent this nightmare? Sterling would give anything for yesterday never to have happened. At this point, the best he could hope for was a quick arrest, preferably of someone who had no connection to him. A drug dealer or a drifter who'd followed Louis into the house and shot him in an attempted robbery, or just for the hell of it.

But that didn't look likely. The detectives had refused to tip their hand, but Sterling knew Manny Carrera was in their sites. A consultant *he'd* hired. A man he'd trusted.

He had to be patient and let the investigation play itself out.

His wife, however, didn't have a drop of patience in her character. She didn't last long at their home on the South Shore and stormed into his office, dropping onto a butter-soft leather couch she'd picked out herself. She was his partner, always at his side. Whenever he felt his energy and drive flag, Jodie would be there, reinvigorating him, urging him on. She was forty-eight, trim, independent—and a little remote.

Even after fifteen years of marriage, Sterling couldn't help but feel an important part of her lay beyond his reach. He wondered if it would have been different if they'd had children, but that had never been in their stars.

She was ash-blond, elegant in every way, yet buying their place in Cold Ridge had been her idea. Venturing onto the ridge last November—again, her idea. She continued to insist they'd have survived, even if they'd had to spend the night on the ridge. Sterling knew better. They'd have been lucky if they'd managed to set up their tent in the high wind, and if they'd succeeded, there was a real possibility they'd have suffocated inside it with the amount of snow that fell by first light. Simply put, they were out of their element. But the situation was made less galling, at least to her, because it was Tyler North, Manny Carrera and Hank Callahan who got to them first. If Jodie had to be rescued, better by a hero-pilot-turned-senate candidate and a pair of air force pararescuemen.

It came as a surprise to people that she enjoyed their home in Cold Ridge as much as her husband did. Sterling liked that. He liked having people not quite able to figure them out.

"I can't stand the tension, Sterling." She jumped back to her feet, her restlessness palpable. "I really can't."

He went around his desk and sat in his tall-backed leather chair, giving her room to pace. "I know. It's getting to all of us. I think today will be the worst day. Once we know what we're dealing with, we can adjust. It'll get better, Jodie. You know that.''

She didn't seem to hear him. ''I thought Louis was this smart security type. How did he manage to get himself killed? He should have been able to save himself—'' She stopped, waving a hand at him as if to forestall the criticism she knew was coming. ''I'm sorry. That's a terrible thing to say.''

Sterling made no comment. Sometimes his wife's lack of compassion, her inability—or her unwillingness—to connect with other people, startled him. But usually it was momentary, and he never gave up hope that there wasn't a window into her soul.

She seemed slightly calmer. ''Gary wants me to go up to Cold Ridge at least until the police make an arrest. I don't know what I'd do up there all alone. Go crazy, probably. And I don't want to leave you down here—''

''Gary's already told me he thinks I should go with you. I don't feel I can right now, but perhaps it's a good idea for you—''

''Why can't you? The police haven't said you can't leave town. If they need anything, they can call you in New Hampshire.'' She flounced onto the couch once more, stubborn more than upset. ''We've done nothing wrong. I can't believe our lives are so turned upside down just because a murder was committed on our property.''

''Jodie,'' Sterling said quietly, hearing the admonishment in his tone, ''a man who worked for us is dead.''

"I know. Oh, God, I *know!*" She groaned, shaking her head in frustration, fighting tears. "My reactions are all over the place. I can't believe—" She swallowed, looking down at her feet, her voice lowering to almost a whisper. "Who'd have thought something as small as a bullet could kill Louis Sanborn? He was so alive, wasn't he?"

Sterling felt a sudden sense of loss, although he hadn't known Louis that well. But he was so young, and now he was gone. "I know what you mean."

"I feel sorry for Carine." Jodie shook her head, displaying one of her rare tugs of real compassion. "Of all the people to find him. I hope she's gone back to Cold Ridge. She should just sit in front of the fire in that little log cabin of hers and relax for a few days."

"Manny Carrera is a friend."

"I know he is. There's just nothing good to be found in this situation, is there? I thought we were doing Carine a favor when we hired her. Now look. It's hard to believe Manny could murder someone, but I suppose we have to keep an open mind."

Sterling shook his head. "I can't do it, can you? Manny's no murderer. I refuse even to consider that he might be guilty."

"That's because you're fascinated by him," Jodie said. "Speaking of doing people favors—"

"Don't, Jodie. I won't take responsibility for Manny's situation. I didn't ask him to show up at the house when he did."

"Why was he there?"

"I have no idea. He's a good man, and I'm sorry he's under even the slightest cloud of suspicion. That doesn't make it my fault."

"No, of course not." She smiled abruptly, unfolding her legs and sliding to her feet. "But who are you trying to convince, hmm? Keep in mind that normal people don't jump out of helicopters to rescue people."

"Manny helped save our lives, Jodie."

"And how many times have he and Hank Callahan and Tyler North said we don't owe them a thing? They *like* what they do. They didn't rescue us because it was us—they rescued us because we were in a tight spot and they were in a position to help."

"Still—"

"Don't let your gratitude and respect affect your judgment."

He watched her walk across his office, her impatience less visible as she came behind his desk and kissed him on the top of the head. He grabbed her hand and squeezed it gently. "We'll get through this," he said.

"We just need to remember to take care of ourselves."

In a business situation, Sterling would know what to do to take care of himself. But this was different. He felt a spurt of pain in his temples. "I'm so damn tired. I keep picturing Louis—"

"Don't," his wife said. "It won't get you anywhere. I know, I've been doing the same thing."

She eased in front of him, then lowered herself to

his lap, sinking against his chest. He could feel her exhaustion. "We'll get through this, my love," she whispered, but it seemed almost as if she was addressing someone else. "I'll make sure we do."

He leaned back with her, rocking gently, but he was aware that he had no physical response to her. Not that many years ago, he'd have cleared his desk and made love to her then and there. A tense, difficult situation wouldn't have stopped him. He'd have welcomed the distraction, the release. So would she.

But Jodie was different these days, or he was different, and certainly he'd never dealt with a murder before, the deliberate taking of a human life. A man he knew, a man he'd hired. It changed everything, and he was afraid, terrified to his very core, that his nonreaction to his wife was only the beginning, and ultimately the least of his worries.

Ten

The Mount Chester School for Boys occupied three hundred acres on the outskirts of the village of Cold Ridge, its picturesque campus dotted with huge oak trees still hanging onto their burgundy-and-burnt-orange leaves under the darkening November sky. Carine was almost relieved when Ty said he needed to stop at the school to check on Eric Carrera, Manny's son. It gave her a chance to get her bearings now that she was back in her hometown for the first time in months.

She'd said little during the three-hour trip north. There was no taking back what she'd initiated at her apartment. She'd wanted it to happen. Emotionally, she was over Tyler North. Physically—physically, she thought, he was a hard man to resist.

"Did you notice my abs?" she'd asked him during the drive.

He'd almost driven off the road. "What?"

"My abdominal muscles. I've been running and

swimming, doing all sorts of calisthenics.'' She didn't mention she was trying to pass the PJ preliminary fitness test. ''Chin-ups. Flutter kicks.''

''Sure, Carine. That's what I was thinking. *Gee, she's been doing flutter kicks.*''

''Flutter kicks are the worst, don't you think?''

He hadn't said a word. Now, apparently as tense as she was, he used more force than was necessary to engage the emergency brake. ''I'll be right back.''

She watched him head up the stone walk to the late-nineteenth-century brick administration building, whose design was classic New England prep school, with its tall, black-shuttered windows and ivy vines, that died back in the autumn cold. If she'd lived, Carine thought, her mother could still be here, teaching biology to another generation of boys. Mount Chester was a solid private high school with a good reputation, but it didn't have the prestige of an Andover or Choate. Carine, her sister and her brother—and Ty— had all attended the local public school.

She knew sending Eric to Mount Chester had to be a financial stretch for the Carreras, but they believed it would be good for him to be on his own, although Carine suspected there was more to it than that.

She climbed out of the truck, immediately noticing that the air was colder, a nasty bite in the wind, but she could smell the leaves and the damp ground, not yet frozen for the winter. Fallen leaves covered most of the lawn, most already dry and brown, some still soft, in shades of yellow, orange, maroon, even red— although the reds tended to drop first.

"Eric'll meet us out here," Ty said, returning to the small parking lot.

Carine nodded, sticking her hands into her pockets, trying to acclimatize herself to being back in New Hampshire.

Eric Carrera shambled down the blacktop walk from the main campus and waved, grinning as he picked up his pace. He was dark-haired and dark-eyed like his parents, and small for his age, but the way he walked reminded Carine of his father, although he didn't possess Manny's economy of movement.

"Hey, Uncle Ty, Miss Winter," Eric said cheerfully, "what's up?"

"Your dad asked me to put eyes on you," Ty said.

"Because of what happened? Mom told me. She called a little while ago. She said she wasn't sure if Dad would have a chance to call. You know, because of the police and everything. She wanted me to know what was going on in case I heard it on the news."

"You okay?"

"Yes, sir."

He wore a hooded Dartmouth zip-up sweatshirt and cargo pants, but he looked cold and too thin. He'd joined Manny and Val Carrera at Antonia and Hank's wedding a month ago. Antonia had told Carine that Eric was doing well, managing his asthma and allergies with medication and experience, knowing what triggered attacks, taking action once he felt one coming on—calming himself, using his inhaler. He wore a Medic Alert bracelet and, in addition to his rescue inhaler, carried an EpiPen—a dose of epinephrine—

everywhere he went. He could treat himself in an emergency, save his own life. At least now he knew what his deadly allergy triggers were: bee stings, shellfish, peanuts. His allergies to tree pollen and dust mites, although troublesome, were less likely to produce an anaphylactic reaction that could kill him.

But it had been a long road to this point, and it had taken its toll, not only on Eric, but on his parents. Carine had seen that at Hank and Antonia's wedding.

"How's school?" Ty asked.

"It's okay." Eric shrugged with a fourteen-year-old's nonchalance. "I'm playing soccer. I'm not on the varsity team or anything, I just play for fun."

"That's great. This thing with your dad—it'll get figured out."

The boy nodded. "I know. He called you?"

"No. I was in Boston today and talked to him."

"Oh. Well, I have to go. I have a French test tomorrow."

"Sure." Ty cuffed him gently on the shoulder. "You'll call me if you need anything, right? Anytime. I'm in town for a few days at least."

Eric cheered up, looking more energetic. "Yes, sir. Thanks. I heard about the seniors yesterday. What dopes. They don't think they did anything wrong."

"They did a million things wrong, but they were very, very lucky."

"The school warns us. They have a film. It talks about some of the people who died on the ridge. One of them used to teach biology here—"

"That was my mother," Carine said. "She and my

father both died on the ridge when I was three. They weren't lucky.''

Eric gave her a solemn look. "I'm sorry."

"It was a long time ago, but the ridge is just as dangerous now as it was then. Weather reports are more accurate, and good equipment is readily available, but still.''

"You have to be take proper precautions," Eric said. "I'd like to climb the ridge sometime."

Ty seemed to like that idea. "Your dad and I can take you up there."

Eric shook his head. "Dad doesn't think I can do anything.''

"You think so? Then you'll have to educate him."

"And Mom—Mom worries about me all the time.'' He sighed heavily, as if he had the weight of the world on his shoulders, most of it in the form of his parents. "She keeps encouraging me to do things, but I know it scares her when I do."

"Does it scare you?" Ty asked.

The boy shrugged. "A little. Sometimes. I do it, anyway. The seniors, those guys you rescued—one of them picks on me. He says I'm skinny, and he calls me Wheezer Weasel. Not to my face, behind my back. I think that's worse. His friends laugh. They don't think I hear them, but I do."

"I guess there'll always be a certain percentage of seniors who pick on underclassmen. They see it as their job." Ty winked at the high school freshman. "Wait'll they get the bill for their rescue."

Eric's face lit up. "No kidding, they'll be so pissed! I can't wait!"

He coughed in his excitement, but there was a spring to his step when he headed back to his dorm. Ty watched him, his jaw tightening in disgust. "Wheezer Weasel. Assholes. I wish I'd known before I rescued them. I could have hung them off a ledge by their heels."

Except he wouldn't have, Carine knew. "The Carreras haven't had an easy time of it this past year. I hope the police come to their senses soon and realize Manny's not their murderer."

"He should call his kid."

Ty tore open his truck door and climbed in. Carine followed, shivering, the temperature falling with the approach of dusk. Once he got the engine started, she turned on the heat, but her shivering had as much to do with fraught nerves as it did with being cold.

"Manny told me he had a motive to kill Louis," she said. "Or at least what could be considered a motive. Do you know what he meant?"

"He's not giving anyone the whole story."

Which didn't answer her question, but Carine didn't push it. If Manny had told Ty more than he'd told her, there wasn't a thing she could do about it except respect their bond of friendship—because she wasn't getting it out of Master Sergeant North.

"I figure he meant that people could perceive that he had a motive to kill him," she said, "not that he actually had one."

Ty made no comment, his hands clenched tightly on the wheel.

Yep, she thought. Manny had told him. She leaned back against the cracked, comfortable seat. How many times had they driven along this road? Countless, even before she'd fallen in love with him. She'd known him all her life, but their romance had been a total whirlwind, catching them both by surprise. She'd tried to chalk it up to the adrenaline of her experience in the woods with the smugglers, the shooters, but that wasn't it. If he hadn't called off their wedding, she'd have married him.

"Just drop me off at my cabin," she said quietly. "Then you can go back to Boston and figure out what's going on with Manny. You know it's driving you crazy."

"We're going to Gus's, not your cabin. He said he'd have a pot of beef stew waiting." Ty shifted gears and made the turn into the village. It was just a few streets tucked into a bowl-shaped valley surrounded by the White Mountains, its Main Street dominated by a white-clapboard, early-nineteenth-century church and a smattering of storefronts, although it wasn't a big tourist town. "It was the only way I was going to get out of town. I had to promise to bring you by."

"For what, inspection?"

"Pretty much."

Carine groaned, although this development was not unexpected. She and her sister and brother might all be in their thirties, but their uncle, just fifty himself, liked to see them after a crisis, make sure they were intact. They indulged him, not just because they loved him and life was easier if they complied, but because they understood—he'd survived combat in Vietnam only to come home and lose his only brother and sister-in-law on Cold Ridge. If he sometimes was overprotective, he was allowed. But he'd never let his anxiety spill over into irrationally stopping his nieces and nephew from pursuing their interests, taking risks.

"All right," Carine said. "I'm not going to argue. Drop me off at Gus's. Then you can head back to Boston."

"Not tonight. I need some sleep. Rescuing three kids off a mountain, driving hither and yon, sleeping in my truck—" He glanced at her. "Making love to you. I'm beat."

"You don't get tired, North, and I wouldn't call what we did making love. We—" She grimaced, remembering. "Well, you know what we did."

"Sure do."

"North, I swear—"

"Relax. Gus'll never be able to tell."

Gus lived in the 1919 village house in which his brother and sister-in-law had planned to raise their three children. It was cream stucco with white trim and had a front porch, a small, screened back porch, dormers, bay windows, leaded glass, hardwood floors and a fireplace. Carine used to think he'd sell it once she and her siblings were off on their own, but he didn't. He hung on to it, redoing the kitchen and bathroom, updating the wiring. At the moment, he was wallpapering the downstairs half bath.

But he had the worst taste, and when Carine scooted into the half bath, she wasn't that surprised to be greeted by a tropical oasis of parrots, frogs and palm trees. The design was garish and out of place, but neither would bother Gus—or Stump, his big part-black Lab, part-everything-else dog, who'd tried to follow her in.

When she returned to the kitchen, her uncle was stirring a bubbling pot of stew on the stove. He grinned over his shoulder at her. ''Bathroom makes you think you're in the rain forest, doesn't it? I thought it'd be good during March and April, when you're sure you'll slit your throat if you see another snowflake.''

''I wouldn't mind being in the rain forest right now,'' Carine said, smiling as she hugged him. ''I've missed you, Uncle Gus.''

He'd driven down to Boston a few times to visit her and Antonia, but it wasn't his favorite trip, especially if it didn't involve Celtics, Bruins or Red Sox tickets. Antonia barely knew which team played what sport. Now she was married to a senator—Hank Callahan was Manny's friend, too, a tidbit the media hadn't sunk their teeth into since Louis's murder but no doubt would. Carine expected it was only a matter of time.

Ty had retreated to add wood to the fire, obviously giving uncle and niece a chance to reconnect. Gus nodded in the direction of the front room. "How're you doing with him?"

"Okay. I thought about shoving him into traffic and being done with him, but—Gus, yesterday was so awful—"

"I know, honey. I'm sorry you had to go through that." He set his wooden spoon on the counter. "Being back up here'll help you get your bearings, even with North around."

"I hope you're right." She leaned over his bubbling pot. "Gus, what's that in the stew? The green stuff?"

"Christ, you sound like you did when you were six, always sticking your nose in my cooking." He picked up his spoon again, stirring gently. "It's okra. You know, that stuff they eat down south. I thought I'd toss some in, see if I liked it."

"I'm not sure okra's supposed to be in beef stew."

"It is now. Set the table, okay?"

They ate in the kitchen. The okra wasn't a big hit with Ty, who left it on the side of his plate and said it looked like something out of a swamp. They'd pulled through a fast-food place on their way to New Hampshire, but Carine hadn't eaten much. She ate two plates of Gus's stew, and after dinner, she brought a stack of Oreos out by the fire. She sat on the floor, her knees up, and when Gus and Ty joined her, she told them everything that had happened to her over the past day and a half, start to finish. About her lunch and how she hadn't thought about photographing wild turkeys, about Louis Sanborn asking her if she wanted a ride and the toddler chasing the pigeons on the Commonwealth Avenue mall—and finding Louis dead, what she saw and heard, how she'd run out of the house and straight into Manny Carrera.

She left nothing out, except for launching into bed with Tyler North. He knew, she knew and Gus didn't need to know.

When she finished, her uncle got up and put another log on the fire. "I want you to hear me out on one thing, Carine." He stared into the fire, not at her, and its flames reflected on his lined, lean face. "Don't try to pretend you didn't see a man you know dead in a pool of his own blood."

"Gus, please—"

"Don't fight it. Don't hide from it." He shifted his gaze, glancing down at her. "Give it time. You'll learn to live with the memory."

"I don't have any other choice."

"That's just it. You do have a choice."

He brought in more wood while she and Ty did the dishes. Carine washed, dipping her hands into the hot, sudsy water, trying to stay focused on the simple chore, the routines that reminded her of normalcy. She and her sister and brother used to take turns doing the dishes. In his various home improvements, Gus had never seen the need to buy a dishwasher.

She rinsed a handful of silverware under hot water and set it in the dish strainer. "You've seen dead men," she said. "Men you knew."

"Yes," Ty said.

"What do you do?"

He lifted out the silverware into a threadbare towel. "Focus on the job I'm there to do."

"That must be when all the years of training pay off. Do you think Manny misses the work?"

Ty opened a drawer and sorted the dry silverware into their appropriate slots. "I think Manny's eaten up inside."

After they finished the dishes, Carine put on her barn coat, noticing her reflection in the window. She didn't look as raw-nerved and traumatized as she had earlier, but she was exhausted. "It'll be good to sleep in my own bed tonight."

"Sorry, toots." Ty shook his head, shrugging on his brown leather jacket. "You don't have a guest room, and I'm not sleeping on your couch. Been there, done that. I don't fit, even without you."

"Ty—you can't be serious." Once she got to Cold Ridge, she thought she'd be on her own, at most with only Gus's hovering to deal with. "I'm home. I'm safe. It's okay—"

He wasn't listening. "I have three guest rooms, and there's a pullout sofa in the den. You can have your pick."

"I'm not in any danger!"

"Someone broke into your apartment today."

"We don't know that."

"You were first on the scene after a murder yesterday. We do know that. And we know the police haven't made an arrest and are, in fact, barking up the wrong tree for their man. So—" he zipped up his jacket "—it's my house or here with the parrots and the okra."

"Let's not make this Gus's problem."

"Suits me."

She was left to choose between bad and worse—staying with Gus and Stump was clearly worse. At least at North's place, if it came to actually staying there, which she hoped it wouldn't, she'd be within short walking distance of her cabin, and there wouldn't be dog hair on her blankets. "All right. Have it your way."

"I know you're not giving in, Carine," he said cockily. "You're buying time. You think you can talk me out of it before we get to my place. Put yourself in my position. What would you do?"

"Give me a nine-millimeter to put under my pillow."

"You might be good at flutter kicks, but a gun's a different story."

"Gus gave us basic firearms instruction when we were kids. I can shoot." But she didn't want a nine-millimeter—she wanted her life back, and she thought North knew it. "You're in your Three Musketeers mood, Ty. I'm not going to fight you."

"Because you don't know what happened yesterday."

"No, because I *do* know what happened." Her barn coat, she realized, wasn't warm enough for the dropping nighttime mountain temperatures. "I hope the police don't focus on Manny for too long. Whoever killed Louis—" She swallowed, feeling a fresh wave of uneasiness, even fear. "I don't want anyone else to end up dead. That's all I care about. Just catch whoever killed Louis, and make sure no one else gets hurt."

Ty nodded. "Fair enough."

Gus appeared in the kitchen doorway. "You two leaving? Carine, I'm here if you need me. Got that?"

"I know, Gus. Thanks. I love you."

"Love you, too, kid." His tone hardened. "North? You'll be wanting Carine looking better tomorrow morning, not worse."

A neat trick that'd be, Carine thought, but said nothing as she followed her ex-fiancé outside, the night clear, cold and very dark. But without the ambient light of the city, she could see the stars.

By the time they reached his house, Ty noticed that Carine was ashen, sunken-eyed, drained and distant. He'd watched the energy ooze out of her during their ride out from the village, along the dark, winding road to his place, the ridge outlined against the starlit sky, a full moon creating eerie shadows in the open meadow that surrounded the old brick house her ancestor had built.

He suddenly felt out of his element. What the hell was he doing? Even with the dangers and uncertainties of a combat mission, he would know exactly what was expected of him, exactly what he was supposed to do. Right now, nothing made sense.

Carine was used to his house—she'd been coming there since they were kids. His mother had given her painting lessons, helped to train her artistic eye and encouraged her to pursue her dream of becoming a photographer. As much as odd-duck Saskia North had been a mother to anyone, Ty supposed she'd been one to orphaned Carine Winter.

Carine insisted on carrying her tapestry bag to the end room upstairs and said she could make up the bed herself, but North followed her up, anyway. Her room was next to his mother's old weaving room, which he'd cleared out a couple of years after her death. The different-size looms, the bags and shelves of yarns, the spinning wheel—he had no use for any of it and donated the whole lot to a women's shelter. His mother would sit up there for hours at a time. Her room had a view of the back meadow and the mountains, but she seldom looked out the window. She had a kind of tunnel vision when it came to her work, a concentration so deep, Ty could sneak off as a kid and she wouldn't notice for hours.

He didn't know why the hell he hadn't died up on the ridge. Luck, he supposed. But he'd started to wonder when his luck would run out—how much luck did a person have a right to?

"It's so quiet," Carine said as she set her bag down on the braided rug. "I never really noticed before I moved to the city. One of those things you take for granted, I guess."

"It's supposed to be good weather tomorrow. On the cool side, but maybe we can take a hike."

"That'd be good."

Ty got sheets out of the closet, white ones that had

been around forever, and they made the bed together, but Carine looked like she wouldn't last another ten seconds. "Sit," he told her. "Now, before you pass out."

"I've never passed out."

"Don't make tonight the first time."

"You've got your own medical kit downstairs. What do you call it?" She smiled weakly. "Operating room in a rucksack."

"Yeah, sure. If you start pitching your cookies, I can run an IV."

"Is that a medical term? 'Pitching your cookies'?"

"Universally understood."

"I'm fine."

But she sank onto a chair and started shivering, and he tossed her a wool blanket, then threw another one over the bed. He added a down comforter, thinking, for no reason he could fathom, of her and her ab muscles. Flutter kicks. Hell.

"Tomorrow will be better," he told her.

She gazed out the window at the moonlit sky. "I didn't win any battles today."

"No one was fighting with you, Carine."

"It felt that way. Or maybe I'm just fighting my-self—or I just wish I had someone to fight with, as a distraction. I don't know. It's weird to be this unfo-cused. Last fall, at least we had the police out comb-ing the woods for clues. I heard the bullets. Manny saw the guys, even if he couldn't get a description. This thing—it's like chasing a ghost." She paused, tightening the blanket around her. "What about you? Are you okay? Manny's your friend."

"Manny can take care of himself."

"You PJs. Hard-asses. Trained to handle yourselves in any situation, any environment."

"Carine—"

She didn't let him argue with her. "I know, just average guys doing their job. Thanks for coming after me." She got to her feet and looked for a moment as if she might keel over, but she steadied herself, grabbing the bedpost. "I think I'll just brush my teeth and fall into bed."

He wanted to stay with her, but he'd done enough damage for one day. "You know where to find me if you need anything."

He went back downstairs, hearing her shut the door softly behind her. They'd planned to fix up the place after they were married, turn her cabin into a studio. She was so excited about the possibilities of the house, he'd teased her about falling for him because of it.

Never. It could burn down tonight and I'd still love you.

Ty poured himself a glass of Scotch and sat in front of the fireplace, the wind stirring up the acidic smell of the cold ashes. He felt the isolation of the place. Three hours to the south, a man was dead. Murdered. Shot. The police thought Manny had pulled the trigger.

And he was on Carine duty. Manny was the one in

Boston under police surveillance. Whatever he was dealing with, he was doing it on his own. His choice.

When he finally headed upstairs, Ty walked down the hall and stood in front of Carine's door, listening in case she was throwing up or crying or cursing him to the rafters, although he didn't know what he'd do if it was crying. The other two he could handle. He'd never been able to take her tears, as rare as they were, as much as he told himself she was stronger because she could cry. He remembered coming upon her in the meadow, sobbing for his mother soon after her death, and even then, when he never thought he'd let himself really fall in love with auburn-haired, sweet-souled Carine Winter, it had undone him.

But he didn't hear anything coming from her room, not even the wind, and he went back down the hall to his own bed.

Eleven

Val collapsed into bed early, but she didn't sleep for more than an hour at a time. She finally got so frustrated at her racing thoughts, she threw off her blankets and turned on a light, her gaze landing on her wedding picture. Manny was in uniform, so handsome and full of himself. Clean-cut in his maroon beret. Lately, he didn't even shave every day.

She grabbed the picture and hurled it across the room.

He hadn't called. *Bastard, bastard, bastard.*

But she was so worried about him, it was making her sick. At least Eric was okay. She'd talked to him, and he sounded saner than she did. And her breakfast with Hank and Antonia had gone well—they'd formally offered her the job. An assistant in the Washington, D.C., offices of a United States senator. It sounded exciting.

"Okay, so you won't stick your head in the oven tonight," she said. "You'll get through this."

Manny. Damn him. Why wouldn't he talk to her?

Because he wanted to protect her. Because she couldn't be trusted not to go off the deep end when faced with the truth, even an artful lie.

Except neither was true. He hadn't called her because he was in trouble, and he was a proud man, independent to a fault. Even if she hadn't turned into a nutcase, he wouldn't have called. He was Manny Carrera being Manny Carrera.

Her shrink had suggested she stop referring to herself as a nutcase and playing fast and loose with phrases like "sticking her head in the oven."

She'd promised she would.

She stepped on a book she'd tossed on the floor after three pages. Tolkien. Bookworm that she was, she'd never gotten hobbits. But Eric had read the *Lord of the Rings* trilogy twice, and she'd promised she'd try again.

So many promises.

Her laundry was still stacked on the bureau. She'd meant to put it away after she got back from her meeting with the Callahans, but she hadn't gotten around to it. No energy. No focus. She'd heated up leftover Thai food and checked the Internet for Boston newspapers and television stations, trying to get an update on Manny's situation. Not much new. No arrests yet—that was something. At least it meant he wasn't in jail.

She wandered into the living room and opened the blinds. Damn. Still. Dark. She glanced at the clock— 4:18. Too early to make coffee.

With a husband in the military, she was accustomed to being on her own—she didn't get spooked. She lay down on the couch and pulled a throw over her, but knew she was too fidgety to sleep. She turned on the television and watched CNN. Nothing much going on in the world. That was probably good. She flipped over to the Weather Channel and got the weather for Europe. She wanted to go to Spain one day. Paris and London didn't interest her as much. Rome might be fun.

At six o'clock, with a mug of hot coffee in her and a sketchy plan of action in mind, she flipped through Manny's address book on the computer and found Nate Winter's number in New York.

He answered on the first ring. She almost hung up, but he was a U.S. marshal and probably the naturally suspicious type. "Nate? It's Valerie Carrera, Manny Carrera's wife. We met at your sister's wedding. Actually, we've met a couple of times—"

"Of course, Val, I remember you." He was polite, almost formal, no doubt because he knew he was talking to the wife of a possible murder suspect. Or maybe because she'd never called him before. "What can I do for you?"

God, she was an idiot. A card-carrying idiot. "Nothing," she whispered. "Nothing. I'm sorry to bother you."

She hung up.

She couldn't ask a U.S. marshal to do a background

check on Louis Sanborn on the sly. That just wasn't the way to go. Manny would have her head. Her ass'd be out the door for sure.

She'd have to do it herself.

Twelve

Carine woke up in the wrong bed. Wrong bed, wrong house.

But she knew where she was. She wasn't disoriented for even half a second as she sat up in the snug, four-poster bed and tried to guess what time it was. Seven? Sunlight angled in through the windowpanes. At least seven.

She imagined her life pre-Tyler North, pre-Boston, pre-Louis Sanborn's murder, when she'd get up in her cabin across the meadow on just such a sun-filled, pleasant morning and make herself a pot of tea and build a fire in her woodstove to take any lingering chill out of the air before she got to work. She loved every aspect of what she did. Assignments from various magazines and journals were her mainstay, but she was selling more and more prints, earning a name for herself at shows, and she had her own Web site and taught nature photography workshops. Before moving to Boston, she'd been putting together plans for a set of New England guidebooks, new specialty cards and her annual nature calendar for a local mountain club.

She viewed her life in the city as a kind of sabbatical, not a permanent move. But she'd felt that way about her log cabin, too, when she moved in five years ago. She hadn't meant to spend the rest of her life there.

After his mother died and Ty decided not to sell the house, he'd asked Carine to check on it when he was away, make sure the yard guys were mowing the lawn, let the cleaning people in, pick up packages. He'd offered to pay her, but she considered herself just being a good neighbor. She had no idea how he could afford to keep up the place—a big house with a shed, a long driveway, fifty acres. The property taxes alone had to be astronomical. Even after they became engaged, she hadn't asked for specifics, which, in a way, summed up their relationship. She hadn't taken care of business. But, she hadn't exactly been thinking straight.

Like yesterday in her apartment, she reminded herself with a groan.

She debated going for a run, then remembered collapsing against the lamppost yesterday morning. Ty would have been on her trail then and must have seen her. She didn't like it that he'd caught her at her most vulnerable, in shock, shattered by what she'd seen. But she didn't have to be professional, distance herself. It wasn't her job to catch the killer.

But a run could wait until she was more secure on her feet.

When she got out of bed, she felt steadier, less stripped raw by her experience. She headed down the hall to the shower, taking her time, washing her hair twice, scrubbing her skin with lavender-scented bath salts left over from her last stay there. She took the time to blow-dry her hair and dressed in her most comfortable pair of jeans and her softest shirt, determined to go easy on herself today in every way she could.

She brought her digital camera downstairs with her and set it on the table then she poured herself a cup of grayish coffee. Jodie Rancourt liked the instant gratification of the digital camera, but Carine had explained her preference for film. It'd be a while before she replaced her 35 mm Nikon and 300 mm zoom lens with a digital camera. But she wasn't resistant to change—she would do whatever worked, whatever got her the right picture.

The coffee was undrinkable. Ty must have made it hours ago. Carine spotted him outside at the woodpile, splitting maul in hand as he whacked a thick chunk of wood into two pieces. He looked relaxed, at home. He deserved this time off, she thought, dumping her coffee in the sink. She knew his military career had been intense during the past nine months— he didn't need to spend his leave making sure she didn't meddle in a murder investigation.

She returned to the table and decided she'd take pictures today. That would reassure everyone she was

back in her right mind. She popped out the memory
disk she'd used at the Rancourt house and popped in
another disk with less memory. Whoever broke in to
her apartment yesterday had ignored her less sexy Nikon, but her digital camera might have been too great
a temptation if she hadn't brought it into Boston with
her that morning.

She slipped the Rancourt disk into an inner coat
pocket and headed outside with the camera. The
morning was brisk and clear, the frost just beginning
to melt on the grass. "You need a dog," she said,
joining Ty at the woodpile. "Maybe Stump could father puppies."

He paused, eyeing her as he caught his breath, his
eyes greener somehow in the morning light. "I'm
never here long enough for a dog, and if I were, I
wouldn't get one with any blood relation to Stump.
He digs."

"All dogs dig."

"All dogs *don't* dig. All *Gus's* dogs dig."

She smiled. "Gus has never been much of a dis-
ciplinarian."

Ty lifted another log into place. He was wearing
heavy work gloves, with wood chips and sawdust on
his jeans and canvas shirt. She noticed the play of
muscles in his forearms. "Your brother called," he
said.

"Nate? What did he want?"

"He said Val Carrera called him at the crack of
dawn and hung up." He glanced up at her, everything

about him intense, single-minded. "What do you suppose that was all about?"

"I have no idea. Did Nate?"

"Nope. He and Antonia talked last night—apparently they decided you were in good hands. Or at least you could be in worse hands. He says Hank and Antonia are hiring Val as an assistant."

"With all her bookstore experience, I think she'd be great at just about anything." Carine didn't know Val Carrera all that well but liked her. "It must be weird for her with Eric away at school. She was so devoted to him when he was sick."

"Still is. She knew she had to pull back." Ty swung the heavy maul idly in one hand. "Nate told me to tell you hi."

"He's not happy about this situation, is he?"

"Hates it. But we all do."

Ty raised the maul, then heaved it down onto the log, splitting it in two, both pieces managing to fly in her direction. She jumped aside, and he grinned at her, shrugged without apology. If she didn't know how to get out of the way when someone was splitting wood by now, she deserved her fate. She felt an urge to grab a maul and have at a chunk of wood herself.

"Nate thinks Louis's murder had something to do with Hank, doesn't he? Newly elected senator, and the Rancourts supported him in the campaign—"

"A lot of people supported him."

"But I'm right?"

"Hank didn't know Louis Sanborn. I told Nate that."

"There, you see? That's my brother, ever one for a conspiracy theory." She moved a few steps out of the sun, which was higher in the sky than she'd expected. She hadn't looked at a clock yet, but it was more like nine, not seven. "I'd like to walk over to my cabin. Gus has supposedly been checking on it, but I think he's been preoccupied with his tropical paradise half bath. Do you want to come with me?"

"Want has nothing to do with it. I'm coming." He leaned the splitter against the shed, a mix of weathered wood and black tarpaper that, like the rest of the place, needed work. "I'll scramble you up some eggs first. Gus brought them by the other night. Apparently there's some new egg lady in town. I think he's sweet on her."

"Gus?"

Ty laughed. "Don't look so shocked."

She jumped up on the counter and watched him while he brewed fresh coffee and made eggs and toast, but he finally said she was in the way and shooed her over to the table. He brought her a steaming plate, then sat down with a mug of black coffee. "Gus has already called this morning, too. The Rancourts rolled in last night. They stopped by his shop this morning to congratulate him on the rescue of the boys from Mount Chester. He thinks they were fishing for what he knew about what happened in Boston."

The Rancourts' twenty-acre property was a rare chunk of private land in that part of the surrounding White Mountain National Forest, up an isolated hill with incredible views and just yards from a seldom-used trail, a spoke off the main Cold Ridge trail.

"Did Gary Turner come with them?" Carine asked. "He's their chief of security—"

"The one with the skin and the missing fingers?"

She nodded. "You were paying attention yesterday."

"Always. Gus didn't mention him."

Carine hid her relief. She didn't want to have to deal with the Rancourts, much less Gary Turner. "Turner encouraged me to come up here. So did Sterling. He and Jodie must have decided they liked the idea themselves. Well, I suppose it's their house. They can come and go as they please."

"You don't much care for them, do you? Why'd you take the job if you don't like them?"

She shrugged. "I don't *dislike* them. I'm neutral."

Ty laughed, getting to his feet. "Yeah, right. Define *neutral*. I'm ready to go whenever you are." He dumped out the rest of his coffee in the sink, then stared out the window a moment. "Carine—I never meant to run you out of town."

She took her dishes to the sink. "You didn't."

He shifted, eyeing her. "You know that's not true."

"It's true enough." She rinsed off her plate and put it in the dishwasher, drank the last of her coffee, aware of his gaze still on her, as if even the small things she did might betray her. "I've always lived in Cold Ridge. It's been good to expand my horizons."

"You've traveled all over the Northeast, taken assignments in the Caribbean, Mexico, Costa Rica—don't give me 'I needed to expand my horizons.'"

"I didn't say I needed to. I said it's been good—"

"Hairsplitting. You should have been a lawyer."

She smiled. "This has always been home. I've never lived anywhere else."

"It still is your home."

She sighed at him, slipping her coat back on. "Do you want to listen to me or argue with me?"

He leaned back against the counter, his arms crossed on his chest as he studied her. "Then no bullshit."

"You cut-to-the-chase military types. Think creatively—"

"Carine."

"All right, all right." But she didn't have the emotional resources to dig deep and could only try to explain in a superficial way what the past nine months had been like for her. "After you dumped me—"

"Jesus," he breathed.

"Well? You're the one who doesn't want any BS. Call a spade a spade. After you dumped me, I started to look at my life here in a new way and realized I had taken everything I have for granted."

"You've never taken anything for granted."

He'd always argued with her, pushed her, prodded her. For most of her life, it'd been irritating. But last winter, she'd loved him for it. She'd thought she could talk to him about anything and hoped he could do the same with her. Only that wasn't the way it was. He'd never opened up his soul to her the way she had hers. Maybe that was why it'd been easy—at least possible—for him to walk away.

But she pushed back such thoughts. He wasn't asking about him and their relationship, but about her. "I was too rooted," she said. "I didn't want this to be the only place I'd ever lived, ever *could* live."

"What about men?" He tilted his head back, but if he was trying to be lighthearted, he was failing. There wasn't a hint of amusement in his expression. "Expanding your horizons where men are concerned?"

Carine groaned as she buttoned up her coat. "I give up. I lived a good life before you, and I've been living a good life since you. So don't feel sorry for me because of what you did. Let's just leave it at that. Whatever else that might or might not be going on with me is none of your business. Not anymore."

"Fair enough." He pulled away from the sink and grabbed his leather jacket off the counter, shrugging it on. "People wouldn't blame you if you'd set my house on fire before leaving town."

"I think they're breathing a sigh of relief that we didn't get married, after all. Imagine the kids we'd have had." Her voice caught, but he didn't seem to notice. She quickly headed for the back door. "I'm not still in love with you, if that's what you're worried about. 'Lust' might still be an issue, but, trust me, I can resist."

"Like you did yesterday afternoon?"

"Like I am right now," she said lightly, pushing

open the door, smiling back at him. "There's something about a sweaty man covered in wood chips."

"If that's all it takes—"

But she was out the door, walking quickly down the driveway before she could do anything stupid. So far she'd had a good start to her day. She didn't want to blow it by ending up upstairs with him, or, even worse, having him decide her easy manner with him was an act and she wasn't over him, after all.

Keep practicing, she thought, and maybe the act would become reality.

Thirteen

Her cabin was cold and empty and had an odd nasty smell that she noticed the minute she walked through the back door. Ty located the cause before she did—a recently dead bat in her woodstove.

Lovely, Carine thought, and tried not to view it as an omen.

Ty carried the bat carcass out on a cast-iron poker, and she turned on the heat and stood in her kitchen as if she were a stranger. She touched the scarred, inexpensive countertop, ran her fingers over the small table, which barely fit in front of a window that looked out on the back meadow. The kitchen, bathroom and the small room that served as her studio were all on the back of the cabin. The great room stretched across the front, with its woodstove and hooked rugs, its comfortable furnishings. A ladder led up to a loft under one half of the slanted ceiling. Her bedroom. At night, she could peer through the balcony railing and watch the dying embers of the fire through the tempered-glass door of her woodstove.

It was, at most, a two-person house, all wood and dark greens, rusts, warm browns, intimate and cozy. Carine had done a lot of the work on it herself. Gus would help, Antonia and Nate—and Ty—when they were in Cold Ridge, even Manny Carrera a couple of times.

No one in town had believed Saskia North would sell Carine the one-acre lot. Saskia likes her isolation, they'd said. Her privacy. She's strange, weird. Indeed, she had been a solitary, intensely creative woman, in her late seventies when she surprised her doubters and sold Carine the lot. Even as a neighbor, Saskia was unreliable in many ways, not showing up when she said she would, making and breaking countless promises as if they were nothing. It was as if her brain was so cluttered up with ideas and whims, sparks of imagination, that little else could get in, never mind stick. Anything she thought of would be worth pursuing, at least for a while.

But only her best ideas grabbed her and held on, and when they did, she pursued them with a vengeance—a painting, a tapestry, a collage, whatever it was. That was something to see. Her folk art was sought by collectors, and had become even more popular since her death, although Ty seemed only vaguely aware of either the financial or the artistic value of what his mother did.

After she died, Gus had often said he didn't know

which he liked less, having Carine out there alone, or having her out there alone with Tyler North.

Ty came in through the back door. "Bat's where it won't stink up the joint."

"Did you bury it?"

"No, Carine, I did not bury it or hold a memorial service for it. I threw it in the woods." He zipped up his jacket. "I'll leave you here and go back and finish up the wood. Take you to lunch in town?"

His words caught her off guard. Leave her on her own? Suddenly she didn't want him to leave, or perhaps she just didn't want to be here alone, raking up memories, trying to feel at home. But she didn't want him to notice her ambivalence. "That'd be good."

He winked. "It'll be okay. See you soon."

The door shut softly behind him, and Carine felt the heat come on, clanging in the cold pipes. She checked the refrigerator. Empty, no scum to clean out. She ran the water in the kitchen sink and walked down the short hall to her studio, her desktop computer, her easel, her worktable, her shelves tidy but dusty, as if she'd died and no one had gotten around to cleaning out her house.

"Damn," she breathed, darting outside into the cold air.

Nothing was the same. Nothing would ever be the same again.

She went into her one-car garage, her much-diminished woodpile just as she'd left it months ago. She loaded cordwood into her arms, one chunk of ash, birch and oak after another, until she was leaning backward against the weight of it. Gus had brought her two cords last fall, before the shooting, and dumped it in her driveway, figuring that'd spur her to get it stacked before winter. What was left was super-dry and would burn easily. But she'd need another two cords at least if she planned to spend any part of the winter here.

She dumped her sixteen-inch logs into the wood-box she'd made herself from old barnboards, then went back for another load.

A midnight-blue car with Massachusetts plates pulled into her dirt driveway, and Gary Turner waved from behind the wheel, smiling, as if he thought she might be on edge and wanted to reassure her. He climbed out, wearing a black pea coat with no hat, the slight breeze catching the ends of his white hair. "I was going to call, but I don't have your cell phone number—"

"That's okay. I don't have it on, anyway, and coverage out here is iffy at best." She brushed sawdust off her barn coat. "I heard the Rancourts were in town. I wasn't sure if you'd come up with them."

"I drove up this morning. I was going to drive up with Mrs. Rancourt last night, but Mr. Rancourt decided to join her, so they came on their own." He squinted at her, his eyes washed out, virtually colorless in the sunlight. "You look better, Carine. Being back here must agree with you."

She smiled. "I suppose it does."

"To be honest, I don't know why you left, man problems or not."

"It's complicated."

He laughed, surprising her. "Probably not as complicated as you think. You've just got a knack for complicating things, and that's not an insult. It's why you can do what you do with a picture of a bird. To most people—you know, it's a bird. With you, it's part of a bigger deal." He looked at her a moment, shaking his head. "You can see why I ended up in security work, not in the arts. How're you doing?"

"All right. I was just stacking wood."

He glanced around, sizing up the place. "I've driven past here a number of times. It's nice. Cute. Kind of like Little Red Riding Hood living out here all by yourself, though, isn't it?"

"It was her grandmother who lived in the woods."

"Yeah, she's the one who got eaten by the wolf. I read my fairy tales as a kid. My favorite was Rapunzel. What a little bastard that guy was, stomping his foot when he didn't get his way—" He grinned at Carine, pointing at her with a victorious laugh. "There! I knew I'd get you. A real smile."

"It feels good." She returned to the garage and squatted down, lifting a chunk of wood, its bark mostly peeled off. "But you didn't come out here to talk fairy tales and make me laugh," she said as she rose, grabbing another log on her way up. "Is there something I can do for you?"

"You're right. I have news." He sighed from the open garage doorway, his manner changing, suggesting there was nothing casual about this visit. "I thought you'd want to know. It's being reported in the media, and I have it confirmed by a source, that Manny Carrera was in Boston to recommend that Mr. Rancourt fire Louis Sanborn.''

"Fire Louis? Why?"

"I don't have those details. Mr. Carrera arrived Tuesday night, and he went to see Louis on Wednesday around noontime—"

"Had Manny talked to Sterling already?"

"No. Mr. Rancourt knew Mr. Carrera was in Boston and expected to meet with him later Wednesday afternoon. The Rancourts had an appointment after lunch, that, obviously was canceled due to Louis's death. Mr. Carrera—"

Carine smiled at him. "You can't just use their first names?"

He seemed slightly self-conscious. "It's not my habit. I don't know for certain why he—Manny—went over to the house, but apparently it was to see if he could find Louis and talk to him ahead of his meeting with Mr. Rancourt. It's possible he wanted to give Louis a chance to explain whatever it was Manny had on him."

"I'm sure Manny's cooperating with the police." Carine picked up another log, another bald one, but she couldn't get a good grip on it and dropped it, narrowly missing her toes. She was grateful when Turner didn't jump to help her. "Do you have any idea why he thought Louis should be fired? He must have found out something."

"I don't know. I'm sorry."

"And the police and the media—this story's out there? It's solid?"

"Just that Mr. Carrera was in Boston to recommend Louis be fired. The facts are what they are, Carine. None of us can help that."

She squatted partway down and retrieved her dropped log. "Sterling—what's his role? I still don't understand why he hired Manny in the first place."

"Mr. Rancourt didn't ask Manny to investigate or make recommendations regarding personnel. He was to provide analysis and training. I admit," Turned added coolly, his eyes never leaving Carine as she loaded up her wood, "that I don't know anything about fast-roping out of a helicopter or treating combat injuries. Those aren't typically the skills one needs to do my job."

She peered at him over her armload of logs. "You think Sterling was wasting his time hiring Manny."

"His money, my time. But it wasn't my call. He and Mrs. Rancourt felt they owed Manny for saving their lives last November and wanted to help him get a start." Turner stepped forward, apparently just now noticing she was weighed down. "Can I help you?"

"I've got it, thanks." The load of wood was up to her chin, and she had to maneuver carefully out of the garage to avoid tripping and having it all go flying. "It feels good to get back to my old routines, actually. Did the Rancourts ask you to tell me about Manny and Louis? Is that why you stopped by?"

"It's one reason. They want to keep you up to date. So do I," he added, his voice lowering uncertainly as he followed her out of the garage. "Something's going on here, Carine, beneath the radar, so to speak. I think you should be extra cautious until the police make an arrest."

She paused, glancing back at him. "What do you mean?"

"I wish I could be more specific. Just be alert, more aware of what you say and do than you might normally be—and who you choose to be around." He hesitated, then said quietly, "It's easy for any of us to miss things when it involves our friends."

"Do you mean Manny? Or Ty North, too? You know he's in Cold Ridge, don't you? Gary—I don't get it. You're creeping me out."

He laughed. "Carine—you amaze me. For an artistic type, you're very direct, aren't you? Then again, I mustn't forget you're from New Hampshire."

"Louis called me a granite-head."

"He was a charmer, wasn't he?"

"I liked him. Look, Gary—" She dumped her logs on her small back deck, caught one before it rolled off into the grass. "If you're holding back because you have no choice, I can understand, but if it's to spare me, then please don't."

"I'm not holding back," he said. "I've told you as much as I know. The rest—instinct, experience, speculation. Nothing more. It's easy for me to see the people around you in a different light than you do, because I don't know them as well."

"That can work the other way around, too."

"Of course. Just be vigilant."

"I will. Thanks for the advice."

She thought he'd leave, but he didn't. She sat on her deck, reluctant to invite him in. The air was cool, with a periodic breeze stirring, and she could feel the mountains all around her, Cold Ridge rising up from the wide, flat meadow. A friend of hers from the Midwest, another photographer, had found the mountains oppressive, the valley beautiful but claustrophobic. Not enough flat space. Not enough sky. At least, not until she was atop a high peak gasping at the stunning, panoramic views. Hikers on Mount Washington on a crystal-clear day could see the ocean to the east and as far as Mount Marcy in the Adirondacks, a hundred and thirty miles to the west.

Before she'd moved to Boston, Carine wouldn't have even noticed the ridge on a day like today.

"I didn't come here to upset you." Gary placed one foot on the deck next to her. He wore good hiking boots, but she saw they weren't new. "But I'm not just here about Manny Carrera wanting to recommend Louis be fired. Carine—you took pictures the other morning."

His words caught her off guard, but she was immediately aware of the disk in her inner pocket. She'd almost forgotten about it. "A few, yes. Why?"

He glanced down at her. "Mr. Rancourt would like them."

"I haven't uploaded them—"

"You can give me the disk."

"Actually, I can't. I don't have it with me." She didn't know why she lied, but she had no intention of giving him the disk. "Anyway, now that I think about it, shouldn't I give it to the police?"

"I don't see why. You took the pictures hours before you found Louis."

"Ninety minutes." She could feel herself digging in. "I took the last one ninety minutes before I found him."

"I can't imagine they'd have any significance to the investigation." Turner's manner was calm, almost as if he himself didn't understand why he'd been sent on this errand. He straightened, putting his foot back on the ground. "If you're uncomfortable turning the disk over to me, you can take it up with Mr. Rancourt. I certainly didn't come here to argue with you or force you to do anything that makes you uncomfortable."

Carine stretched out her legs, the grass damp and soft, the icy morning frost long melted. She felt chastised, as if she was being petty and stubborn. "I can provide them with prints and a separate disk of just their pictures, as I have right along."

Turner considered her words, then nodded. "I'll tell them."

Ty's truck pulled into the driveway and bounced over a rut before it came to a stop alongside Turner's car. Ty climbed out, his manner casual, easy-going—deceptively so, Carine thought. "I brought you a load of wood," he told her. "Enough for a few days."

She got to her feet, feeling a self-conscious rush. He'd think Turner showing up proved Manny's point that she needed to have Ty stick to her, keep an eye on her. If she didn't ask for trouble, it'd find her.

The two men introduced themselves and shook hands briefly. "I thought you and I'd get the chance to meet each other before now," Gary said. "I guess we've just missed each other."

"Guess so." Ty walked back to his truck and opened up the tailgate, playing the good neighbor, but Carine could feel his intensity. "Don't let me keep you two."

"I was just leaving," Gary said.

"Glad I didn't block you in."

But, of course, he deliberately *hadn't* parked behind Turner—he meant to run him off, if not to be rude about it. He wasn't even being that subtle. Carine didn't know if she should be relieved, because he wasn't a bad guy to have on her side and Turner had just been ratcheting up the pressure over the pictures, or annoyed, because she'd had the situation under control and Turner was, in fact, taking no for an answer.

Turner shifted back to her, his pale eyes almost transparent in the late morning light. "Now that I've mentioned the memory disk, I know you won't be able to resist looking at it. I warned Mr. Rancourt this could happen if I asked you for it, but it's the risk he decided to take." He smiled faintly. "He knew I wasn't going to wrestle you for it."

"Gary, I honestly don't know what you're talking about—"

"I know you don't. Think back to this conversation when you view the pictures." He seemed more tired, even ill at ease, than irritated. "Remember that I tried to be discreet."

He nodded politely at North, who'd obviously taken in every word as he dumped wood out of the back of his truck. Then, without another word, Turner got into his car, started the engine and backed out.

Carine exhaled, almost choking on tension. "Damn. Ty, listen, I don't know what the hell's going on, but I need—I need to go back to your house and get my camera."

He tossed another couple of hunks of cordwood onto her driveway. He wasn't wearing his work gloves, and she noticed he'd scraped a knuckle, not badly. "Uh-huh. You want to give me a hint what this is all about?"

"First you tell me if you knew Manny planned to recommend Sterling Rancourt fire Louis Sanborn."

"It came up. Why, is it out there?"

"Apparently."

"Pissed I didn't mention it?"

"Does it matter?"

He shrugged, unapologetic. "It doesn't explain anything."

"Then why not tell me? You don't need a security clearance, Ty. Keeping your mouth shut comes naturally to you."

"That's what my third-grade teacher told the security guys when they came up here and checked me out."

"You're making that up."

He jumped out of his truck, landing lightly on the

dirt driveway. "Is Gary Turner going to break into my house and steal your camera if we don't get over there?"

"He might, but I think he credits himself with playing by the rules."

North examined his skinned knuckle, then shrugged it off. "Depends on whose rules we're talking about, doesn't it?"

"Anyway, it won't do him any good if he does steal the camera," Carine said. "I have the disk he's after in my coat pocket."

"Well, well, aren't you lucky he didn't frisk you?"

"I thought about taking pictures today—I didn't want to use the same memory disk. I had my camera with me yesterday when my apartment was searched. If it *was* searched."

"Rancourt and Turner both saw you yesterday with the camera." Ty frowned at her, thinking. "I take it you didn't have it with you during lunch on Wednesday?"

She shook her head. "I left it in the hall of the Rancourt house." She swallowed, not relishing what she had to do. "I hope Gary's wrong and there's nothing on the disk but pictures of the drawing room mantel."

Ty stood very close to her, smelling of wood, reminding her of their intimacy yesterday in her apartment. She'd known he wouldn't refuse her. Somehow, she'd known that.

Had someone slipped into her apartment to find her digital camera?

What was on the damn disk?

Ty smiled at her. "You look like someone's asked you to eat a dead bug."

"That's one way to put it."

"I've done it, babe. It's not so bad."

Her shoulders sagged, and she almost managed a laugh. "Ty, damn it—"

"Come on. Hop in my truck." He slung an arm over her shoulders, still playing the good neighbor, the buddy who'd been at her side for as long as she could remember, even if it was sometimes so he could push her out of a tree. "Let's go see if someone borrowed your camera at lunch and took incriminating pictures before, during or after poor Louis Sanborn got shot with a .38 in the library."

Carine angled a look at him. "You don't know it was a .38."

"It's an educated guess."

"Whose? Yours or Manny's?"

"Colonel Mustard's. Come on, Carine. Give me a break."

"What else did Manny tell you that you haven't told me?"

"That you'd be a meddling pain in the ass if I didn't keep you occupied." He dropped his arm, opening the truck door. "He fed some line about you having a strong moral compass."

She climbed into the passenger seat, fighting an urge to let him take the disk and see what was on it while she stayed here and stacked wood. "I have a feeling if my strong moral compass was working, I'd have given Gary Turner the disk."

* * *

Carine could have popped the memory disk back into her camera and looked at the pictures on its tiny LCD screen, but she waited to boot up the computer in Ty's den, attaching a USB cable to the corresponding port on her camera. A screen came up on the monitor, with a contactlike sheet of all the photos on the disk. It was a fresh disk. The only photos on it, at least as far as she knew, were those she'd taken Wednesday morning on Commonwealth Avenue, before lunch, before she found Louis.

She was supposed to click on what she wanted to do with the pictures—copy them to the hard drive, view a slide show, print them—but she was so stunned, all she could do was gape at the monitor.

The few pictures she'd taken were there, idle shots of the drawing room mantel and chandelier—she hadn't expected to keep any of them. But it was the four pictures she *didn't* take that had her attention.

All four depicted a mostly naked Jodie Rancourt up against the library wall, her legs wrapped around the waist of an apparently fully clothed Louis Sanborn. His back was to the camera, but there was no question of his identity—or what he and Jodie were up to.

Ty whistled, peering over Carine's shoulder. "I wonder who took these last four shots."

Carine shook her head, stunned. "It wasn't me. Someone must have used my camera while I was at lunch. The pictures—the angle—" She paused, making herself breathe, and tried again. "Whoever took the pictures must have stood in the doorway to the hall. My camera was right there on the radiator."

"Talk about nature photography."

She elbowed him. "That's lame, North."

"Just trying to ease the tension in the room. Damn. You didn't have any idea—"

"No. None. Jodie Rancourt and Louis Sanborn? He'd only worked for the Rancourts for *two weeks*."

"Doesn't looked forced on her part, does it?"

"No," Carine said. "No, it doesn't."

Ty squinted, eyeing the pictures more closely, then gave another low whistle. "Agreed. I guess you never know what goes on between two people."

But Carine's throat was tight, her heart racing. "My blood pressure must be a thousand over a thousand. Ty, I swear, I never had an inkling they were having an affair."

"Maybe it was a moment," he said, "not an affair."

"Well, it was a 'moment' not long before one of the two people involved in it was killed. Louis asked me if I wanted a ride while I was on my way back from lunch—he and Jodie must have—" Carine hesitated, trying to steady her breathing, calm herself. "They must have had their liaison before he went out."

"Liaison?"

"Ty, *please*."

"Babe, they were screwing each other blind. Facts are facts. How long were you gone? About ninety minutes?"

She nodded, transfixed by the pictures on the screen, embarrassed for the participants. But if they'd wanted privacy, they could have skipped the library and gone somewhere else. Had there been any clues, any hints she'd missed? Did Sterling know? Turner? "I wasn't in a hurry. There wasn't much going on at the house…that I knew about, anyway."

"Ninety minutes is plenty of time for a quickie in the library." Ty shook his head tightly, obviously as uncomfortable with what they were seeing as she was. "Jesus. What a nasty business. They took a hell of a risk if they didn't want to be caught. Anyone could have walked in on them—"

"Obviously someone did and took pictures."

Carine sank back in the chair, an ergonomic design that she'd helped choose when Ty purchased his computer. The den was tucked in the southwest corner of the house, a sun-filled room with original 1817 twelve-over-twelve paned windows that looked onto the front yard. It was prosaically furnished with a pullout couch, a beat-up leather club chair, a rolltop desk and the computer table. One of Saskia's collages hung on the back wall, depicting images of the White Mountains.

"Do you think Manny knew?" Carine asked quietly.

Ty shook his head. "I don't know."

"What if—" She cleared her throat, her hands shaking as she turned back to the computer screen. "What if he walked in on Jodie and Louis?"

"Manny didn't take those pictures."

"No, but maybe he came in after someone else had. I wonder if he said something to the police, if

Turner found out—Gary obviously knew, or at least guessed, these pictures existed. He said he was asking me for the disk on Sterling's behalf, but I'm not sure now.''

''Maybe Turner took the pictures.''

Carine sighed. ''Lots of questions, no answers.''

''It's not our job to come up with answers,'' Ty said.

She stared at the screen. ''I didn't take these pictures.''

''I didn't ask.''

''Someone will. I don't think there's a way I can prove it, but—I didn't take them. Why would anyone do such a thing?''

''Blackmail. Titillation. To humiliate and embarrass one or both of the two lovers, or the jilted husband.''

''The possibilities are endless, aren't they?'' Carine quickly completed the process of uploading the pictures to Ty's hard drive, as a backup to the disk in case something happened before she could get it to the police. ''We should notify the detectives on the case. If Jodie Rancourt told the police she was out shopping, and instead she was with Louis—''

''She could have told the police the truth,'' Ty said. ''They might just have kept it to themselves. For all we know, this is old news to them.''

''I hope so. I hate the idea of being the rat.'' Carine popped out the memory disk and disconnected the USB cable. ''Gary Turner said to remember he tried to be discreet.''

"Right," Ty said skeptically. "Maybe that's why he took the trouble of using a key instead of a crowbar when he broke into your apartment yesterday."

She tucked the disk into her coat pocket. "We don't know that was him."

"A lot happened on your lunch hour, that's for damn sure."

"And I didn't have a clue."

Ty straightened. "We can call the Boston cops on the way to lunch and ask them what they want us to do with the disk."

"Us? Ty, there's no reason for you to get involved."

"Too late. The minute you found Louis Sanborn, I was involved." He headed for the door, glancing back at her, his eyes a soft green, a real green, but as unreadable as if they'd been green rocks. "But you knew that, didn't you?"

"Maybe I did," she said, and slipped past him into the hall.

Fourteen

His lungs were bursting from sucking in the cold air, rushing up the path too fast. His legs ached. But Sterling pushed himself harder, determined to make it up the last thirty-foot, near-vertical stretch of the path. He'd started from his house, thinking he'd only go for a short walk to blow off some steam, and now he was almost onto the main ridge trail, the same one Abraham Winter had carved almost two hundred years ago.

How had his life gotten so miserably, abominably out of control?

What the hell had happened?

He groaned, lunging upward, crab-walking on the rocks and exposed tree roots. The path was still below the treeline, winding through lichen-covered rocks and fir trees. He had no business being out here alone, but he didn't care.

"Fuck," he muttered, "I don't care about anything."

With a final spurt of energy, he made it to the top of the hill, onto a rounded rock with a blue-splashed cairn marker that indicated he had come, at last, to the Cold Ridge Trail. If he kept going, soon he would be above the treeline, walking along the narrowest section of the ridge, then up to a summit and back down to the cliffs and the famous, awe-inspiring view of valley and ravines, a mountain lake, a river. He'd never gotten that far. Last year, he and Jodie had barely made it above the treeline before they got into trouble.

He paused, sweating, gazing out at the cascade of mountains, some of the highest ones snowcapped, others bald rock against a cloudless sky—which wouldn't last. November was a gray month in northern New England, and the weather forecasters promised that new clouds would move in before sunset.

The days were shorter, the sun lower in the sky. With no city lights, the nights were long and dark, and he could feel the claustrophobia eating at him, just knowing there were only a few more hours of sunlight left. He didn't know how people lived up here all winter.

He wondered if God had intended for him and Jodie to die on the ridge last November and that was why, ever since, their lives had come apart bit by bit, piece by piece.

Exhausted and frightened, shivering uncontrollably, Sterling remembered, with a wince of regret, how he'd grabbed hold of Manny Carrera after their rescue and sobbed. "I was so scared, so damn scared. I thought I could survive up here on my own."

"Nobody survives on their own, pal," Manny had said in his matter-of-fact, unwavering way. "We all need a helping hand."

"You don't—you survive on your own."

"No, I don't. I'm part of a team, they're part of a squadron, and on up the ladder it goes—get it? We each have a job to do. We look out for one another. Right now, I'm looking out for you. So, just rest easy, okay?"

"But if you were stuck behind enemy lines, or attacked or captured, you'd know how to handle yourself. You'd know what to do."

"Yes, sir, but I'd also know I had people who'd never rest until I got back to safety. They'd come for me, the way I am here for you right now. You want to keep talking about this shit, or do you want to get off this goddamn mountain?"

Manny Carrera…*ah, Manny.*

Had Manny taken those pictures of Jodie and Louis Sanborn? Had he known about their affair and that was why he wanted Sanborn fired? Had he tried to take advantage of the situation?

Sterling liked to believe if he'd signed up to become a PJ as a young man, he'd have made it through the rough training. The washout rate was high— often more than eighty-percent. But over celebratory drinks at his house in the mountains, after they'd all warmed up last year after the rescue, Manny had told him he hated the word *washout,* because it implied guys didn't cut it, that they were lesser, somehow, failures. "They just weren't where they were supposed to be. Not everyone figures that out the easy way."

Manny had stared into his beer as if he had bigger worries. It was only later that Sterling learned that Eric Carrera had almost died of an asthma attack.

It was inconceivable Manny Carrera would take pictures like the ones the local police now had in their custody, awaiting two Boston detectives who would arrive later that evening.

Sterling had no doubt that Gary Turner had done his best to get his hands on the disk. He'd been caught between a rock and a hard place. Jodie had told Turner about the pictures and pressed him to get them before anyone found out—including Sterling. Gary had hinted that he needed Carine's pictures from Wednesday morning to prevent a scandal, but he hadn't gone into detail, instead asking Sterling to trust his sense of discretion. When he'd returned empty-handed, Jodie had been forced to come clean about her lunch-hour rendezvous in the library.

Lies and deception—Sterling had no idea what to believe anymore. She said it was her first and only time with Sanborn, and she didn't have a clue anyone had taken the pictures, never mind who. It was a chance encounter, she said. No one could have predicted it. Had Sanborn planned to seduce her, arranged for a cohort to take the pictures? Had someone merely stumbled onto the illicit goings-on and taken advantage of the situation?

Had Manny Carrera seized the moment and snapped four quick shots himself?

But why leave the damn camera behind?

A strong gust of wind blew up the side of the ridge and went right through Sterling's thin jacket. It wasn't a long hike back down the trail, but he knew he needed to get moving soon, before the temperature started dropping with the waning sun. He could feel darkness closing in on him, as if it could suffocate him. His head ached. He hadn't paced himself well.

Although he hadn't seen the pictures himself, he kept imagining them over and over and over. His wife and Louis Sanborn in the library. Dear God.

Jodie herself could have arranged to have the pictures taken.

It would be retaliation. Revenge. Evening the score. Payback. *My turn, Sterling. See? Here's the proof.*

He'd had a short-lived affair with a woman in the office, after their rescue last November. It had lasted six weeks. She was gone now—Jodie had made him fire her. He said he'd drifted because of their near-death experience, and it was nothing as ordinary as a midlife crisis, nothing as tawdry as sex on the side. She claimed to believe him, to have forgiven him. More lies? More deception?

He spotted her down on the trail, circling toward him, moving fast, not hurrying but determined. She was hatless, and the wind caught the ends of her hair. He wondered what she would do if he jumped. He could time it just right and smash onto the rocks at her feet, let her screams of horror be what he heard last as he died.

She could cry buckets at his funeral and get herself a boy toy, play the rich widow, spend all her poor dead husband's money. But she had plenty of her own—she came from a well-heeled family, far better off than his own had been. He'd been so proud when he married her.

He wondered if he'd ever come close to understanding her.

She joined him on his rounded section of rock. "May I?"

"There you go, Jodie. You do what you want, then ask if it's all right."

"I'm sorry," she whispered, although her tone and expression didn't change. She had it all under control, he thought. She stood next to him, squinting out at the mountains, panting slightly from exertion. "Gorgeous, isn't it?"

"I can't focus on the scenery. I keep seeing you—"

"Don't. Don't do it to yourself, Sterling. That's what I did when it was you and your bimbo, and it does no good."

He wondered if he could get away with pushing her. Probably not. Learn your wife screwed a man minutes before he was murdered, that there are pictures—then, oops, she dies in an accident on Cold Ridge. Nobody'd believe it.

"It was like it was happening to someone else." She spoke quietly, staring out at the mountains. She had on her parka and carried water in a hip pack, marginally better prepared than he was for the conditions. "I felt as if I was floating on the ceiling, looking down at myself, at this woman I knew but didn't know. I was horrified, a little fascinated. And frightened because I knew what a risk she —what a risk I was taking."

"Jodie, I don't want to hear about it."

She angled her head up at him. "Was it that way for you when you had your affair?"

"I try not to think about it. I've put it behind me."

"Of course," she added, as if he hadn't spoken, "I was with Louis only that one time."

Sterling turned away from the view, taking the first, precipitous steps back down the steep section of the path. He'd just wanted to make it onto the ridge trail. That was all. He glanced back at his wife. "I suppose I deserved that."

"Neither of us deserves what we're doing to each other. I felt—I feel tainted. Dirty. Then, to have Louis killed."

"Did you do it?"

"What!" She almost fell backward, and automatically—he couldn't help himself—Sterling reached out for her, but she was too far away and had to regain her balance on her own. The near-fall upset her, all that elegant reserve gone now. "No, goddamn it, *no*. I didn't kill him. Where the hell would I have gotten a gun? Why would I—"

"It was a stupid thing to say."

"An affair is one thing, Sterling, if that's even what

it was—but murder—'' She choked back her outrage.
''I'd hoped you wouldn't find out. I had no idea about
the pictures. I never saw, never heard—''

''You were too busy with other things.''

''Goddamn it! I'm trying here, Sterling. I'm trying
to make up for lost ground and be honest with you.
I realized, even before—I realized then and there,
while I was in the library, that I didn't want to hurt
you. All my desire for revenge fell away, and that
was what was left. That I loved you.''

He breathed through his clenched teeth, not knowing what the hell he felt. Anger? Pity? Humiliation?
Not love, not at that moment. ''I should have had
Gary take the damn disk from Carine, steal it if he
had to.''

''I tried to steal it yesterday. I went to her apartment—I have a key—''

''Jodie, for God's sake!''

She blinked through her tears. ''I had no choice. I
told the police I was with Louis, but I never mentioned what we were doing. I didn't lie to them. I just
didn't tell them everything.''

''You lied to me.''

She nodded. ''I know, and I'm sorry.''

But Sterling frowned, her words sinking in, the
holes they presented. ''Jodie, if you didn't hear anyone while you were with Louis, how did you know
there were pictures?''

She didn't speak for a moment. ''I had a call.''

''*What?*'' This time he really did almost lose his
footing.

"It just said, 'There are pictures.'" She licked her lips, not meeting his eye. "That was all. Like it was a friendly warning, and I should take action."

"Christ." Sterling raked a hand over his head, whipped around on the path, stones flying up under his hiking boots. *"Christ Almighty!"*

"I told Gary this morning. I didn't know what else to do. He decided you had to know about the disk, but I begged him not to tell you how I knew, to let me tell you first—"

"For God's sake, Jodie. For *God's sake!* How could you not have told me?"

She ignored his question. "I think it was Manny who called." Her voice was hoarse from the dry wind, the tension. "I think he took the pictures. He must have planned to use them as further leverage against Louis, maybe to get him to quit so he didn't have to tell you what he knew. He probably didn't take the camera because Louis was about to catch him—or he figured he could get it from Carine since they're friends."

Sterling's head was spinning. "The police will look at the pictures as more evidence against him."

"We can't help that," Jodie said quietly.

He bit off a sigh, but his rage had subsided. He was tired and cold, past the point of feeling anything. He took another step down the path, hardly paying attention to the tricky footing. "I'm heading back to the house. You can do what you want to do."

"Can I walk with you?"

He nodded without enthusiasm. "Suit yourself."

"Sterling—we'll get through this together."

"I'll get through it," he said stiffly. "I don't care if you do or not."

Fifteen

Val Carrera waited until midafternoon for Manny to call her. When he didn't, she started calling him and leaving him messages on his voice mail. One every fifteen minutes. After the tenth, he called her back. "Damn it, Val, can't you take a hint? I don't want to talk to you."

"Tough. Where are you? Not in jail, I presume, or you wouldn't have your cell phone."

"My hotel. A different one. I'm on my own dime now. I'm climbing the fucking walls. There, you happy?"

"Police watching you?"

"Yes."

Her heart jumped. It was real. Her husband was under suspicion for murder. "Jesus, Manny. How the hell did this happen? Is there anything I can do?"

"I don't know how the hell this happened. There's nothing you can do. Well, there is." He paused, and she could feel his smile—she swore she could. "You could get a job. You drive people crazy when you're not working.''

"Ass. I've got a job. Hank and Antonia hired me this morning. Manny—'' She choked back a sob, hating herself for displaying any weakness. "Do you want me to come to Boston?''

"No.''

"Have you talked to Eric?''

"No. You?''

"Yesterday. I'll call him again tonight. He's—well, you know how tight-lipped he is. Gee, I wonder where he gets it. But I can tell he's worried about you. I am, too. Sorry, bub, but you can't control how we feel.''

"Val, listen to me. Worry all you want. Tear your hair out, curse me to the rafters. I don't care. Just stay out of this mess. Understood?''

"Manny, you're my husband. What happens to you—''

"What happens to me doesn't happen to you. When I jump out of a helo, I don't see you strapped on my back.''

He clicked off.

She hated him. She really did.

She hit Redial on her phone, since his number was the only one she'd called all day. She got his voice mail again. He'd probably shut off his cell phone, knowing she'd call back.

Her apartment reeked of cheap pizza, half of it still in the open box on the coffee table. She'd had it delivered, and next time, she thought, she was going to make them wait until she got it out and give them the damn box back, let them get rid of it.

"Someone ought to come up with a self-destructing pizza box," she grumbled, carrying it into the kitchen.

She stuck the leftover pizza in the refrigerator, no plate, no aluminum foil—she just laid the two cold slices on the rack by themselves. If she was still here, she'd heat it up for supper. If not, it could rot. The pizza box she dropped onto the floor and jumped on, flattening it, then used her feet to fold it as small as she could, but even that didn't fit into her trash can.

When he was home, Manny did the trash. He never complained about it. They shared the cooking, but she didn't think he'd ever touched a toilet brush in his life. Maybe in PJ indoc somebody made him swab out a toilet. If so, it was the last damn time.

She scooped a stray piece of pepperoni off the floor, dumped it in the trash and wiped up the spot with the toe of her running shoe. Okay, so she wasn't a great housekeeper. She liked books. She could read one a day. She *loved* talking books with her customers back when she was a store manager. She'd read any-thing—mystery, romance, thrillers, the women's book club books, biographies. She'd gotten into self-help for a while, but it always made her feel inadequate, sitting there answering the questions about dreams and goals, writing her own eulogy. That was pretty sick. *Here lies Val Carrera, who read a lot of books and tried to do right by her family, even if she screwed it up most of the time.*

She hoped there were readers on Hank's staff. If they were all policy wonks and just wanted to talk about reforming the health-care system, she'd slit her own throat.

She grabbed her lukewarm Diet Coke off the coffee table and took it with her to the computer, set up in a corner of the living room. Pepperoni pizza and a Diet Coke. Made a lot of sense. But she was wired as it was, and sugar in addition to the caffeine would put her over the top. Then she would get in her car and drive up to Boston. Manny was acting as if he was on a combat mission and she was out of line for wanting to show up. No wives on search-and-rescue missions. Except he wasn't in the air force anymore.

Two years in uniform had done it for her. She had no interest in being career military. She knew women who could be generals and wanted the job a whole lot more than she ever did.

She'd wanted what she'd had. A sexy, irreverent husband who rescued people. A smart, healthy son. A job she loved.

But she didn't have any of those things anymore.

''Negative thinking, negative thinking.''

The monitor had gone into sleep mode. She got it up and running again, but she was having the same problem she'd had since she got back yesterday from breakfast with Hank and Antonia—she couldn't access Manny's files without his password. Why did the bastard need a password? Had he decided she was nuts and couldn't be trusted with access to his files?

She'd tried every possible password combination

she could think of. Eric's middle name, his birthday, the name they'd picked out if he'd been a girl. *Her* middle name. Her maiden name. Their wedding date. Manny was a sentimentalist at heart, and he wasn't particularly creative or intricate in his thinking. It *had* to be something obvious.

Irritated, she typed *bullheaded,* but that didn't work, either.

Tyler North? Nope, not in any combination she tried.

If she called Manny and asked him for his password, he wouldn't tell her. He'd just say "butt out" and hang up. Or not bother to call her back at all.

Stubborn.

Irritating.

Nothing was working. She flopped back against her chair and sipped her Diet Coke. She had to stay busy. If she didn't, she'd think. She'd relive the scary, early days of Eric's illness. She'd relive charging off to the emergency room while Manny was out of the country, facing dangers of his own—he couldn't talk about most of his missions, but she was well aware of what he did.

She didn't think, not then, that she could lose them both, her husband to combat, her son to illness. Only afterward, only when they were safe. It was sick, but there it was.

She suddenly realized she was shaking, crying. Her gaze settled on the number of her therapist, which she'd written on an orange Post-it note and stuck to the side of the computer. She grabbed it and reached

YOUR READER'S SURVEY
THANK YOU FREE GIFTS INCLUDE:

▶ 2 "The Best of the Best™" books

▶ A lovely surprise gift

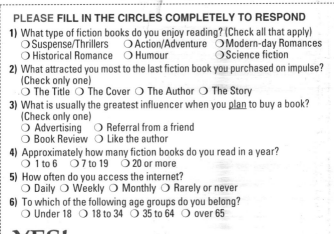

PLEASE FILL IN THE CIRCLES COMPLETELY TO RESPOND

1) What type of fiction books do you enjoy reading? (Check all that apply)
- ○ Suspense/Thrillers   ○ Action/Adventure   ○ Modern-day Romances
- ○ Historical Romance   ○ Humour   ○ Science fiction

2) What attracted you most to the last fiction book you purchased on impulse? (Check only one)
- ○ The Title   ○ The Cover   ○ The Author   ○ The Story

3) What is usually the greatest influencer when you <u>plan</u> to buy a book? (Check only one)
- ○ Advertising   ○ Referral from a friend
- ○ Book Review   ○ Like the author

4) Approximately how many fiction books do you read in a year?
- ○ 1 to 6   ○ 7 to 19   ○ 20 or more

5) How often do you access the internet?
- ○ Daily   ○ Weekly   ○ Monthly   ○ Rarely or never

6) To which of the following age groups do you belong?
- ○ Under 18   ○ 18 to 34   ○ 35 to 64   ○ over 65

YES!
I have completed the Reader's Survey. Please send me the 2 FREE books and gift for which I qualify. I understand that I am under no obligation to purchase any books, as explained on the back and on the opposite page.

385 MDL DRSV   185 MDL DRSR

FIRST NAME	LAST NAME

ADDRESS

APT.#	CITY

STATE/PROV.	ZIP/POSTAL CODE

Offer limited to one per household and not valid to current subscribers of MIRA or "The Best of the Best." All orders subject to approval. Books received may vary.

The Best of the Best™ — Here's How it Works:

Accepting your 2 free books and gift places you under no obligation to buy anything. You may keep the books and gift and return the shipping statement marked "cancel." If you do not cancel, about a month later we'll send you 4 additional books and bill you just $4.74 each in the U.S., or $5.24 each in Canada, plus 25¢ shipping & handling per book and applicable taxes if any.* That's the complete price and — compared to cover prices starting from $5.99 each in the U.S. and $6.99 each in Canada — it's quite a bargain! You may cancel at any time, but if you choose to continue, every month we'll send you 4 more books, which you may either purchase at the discount price or return to us and cancel your subscription.

*Terms and prices subject to change without notice. Sales tax applicable in N.Y. Canadian residents will be charged applicable provincial taxes and GST. Credit or Debit balances in a customer's account(s) may be offset by any other outstanding balance owed by or to the customer.

If offer card is missing write to: The Best of the Best, 3010 Walden Ave., P.O. Box 1867, Buffalo, NY 14240-1867

BUSINESS REPLY MAIL
FIRST-CLASS MAIL   PERMIT NO. 717-003   BUFFALO, NY

POSTAGE WILL BE PAID BY ADDRESSEE

THE BEST OF THE BEST
3010 WALDEN AVE
PO BOX 1867
BUFFALO NY 14240-9952

NO POSTAGE
NECESSARY
IF MAILED
IN THE
UNITED STATES

for the phone, but she didn't dial, instead doing her relaxation and visualization exercises until she felt the incipient panic pass.

It'd be okay. She was getting better.

For grins, she typed *crazywoman*, but nothing happened.

"Maybe I should just shoot the damn thing."

If she couldn't get into Manny's files and he didn't want to talk to her, what *could* she do?

She dug her date book out of her handbag and looked up Tyler North's number in New Hampshire. If he wasn't on duty, he'd be there. She used to be critical of his weird, crazy mother. Not anymore. For the most part, she'd done the best she could. She made mistakes. But she'd been lucky.

If Manny had confided in anyone, it'd be his best friend and fellow PJ. Obviously, Val thought, it wasn't his wife.

Sixteen

Ty tried to concentrate on the scenery as he drove Carine up the notch road, a pass in the mountains with a small lake, a waterfall, a rock-strewn brook, ledges, cliffs and breathtaking views. But it wasn't easy to focus on anything but the tense and distracted woman beside him. She wanted to see the Rancourts. He told her he didn't think it was a good idea. She said, fine, she'd rent a car. She'd take a bus back to Boston and get her own damn car. She'd hike up the ridge to the connecting trail that led down to the Rancourt house.

She wouldn't get Gus to take her, that was for damn sure. Gus didn't like the idea of her going up to the Rancourts, either. She and Ty had dropped off the embarrassing pictures of Jodie Rancourt with the Cold Ridge police and met Gus for lunch at a village café. Gus didn't get it. Why would Carine want to see the Rancourts? Why would they want to see her?

But Gus couldn't talk her out of it, and Ty sure as hell couldn't. They tried all through lunch. The café was owned by a couple of ex-hippies who scrawled their daily menu on a chalkboard. Carine had turned over her digital camera and camera bag as well as the memory disk. The police had warned her to expect a visit from the Boston detectives now on their way to New Hampshire to pick up the evidence—they'd want to talk to her, as well as the Rancourts.

Carine had hardly touched her sweet potato chowder. Gus had a bowl, too, but Ty didn't go near it—he had a bacon-lettuce-and-tomato sandwich. He didn't like Carine's lack of appetite. "Flutter kicks'll really kill you if you don't keep up your strength," he told her.

"They kill me, anyway."

"Why are you doing flutter kicks? Why not just take an exercise class in Cambridge? Pilates. Kickboxing. Something like that."

She'd given him a smile that he couldn't quite read. "Maybe I'm training for a triathlon."

"Okay. You've always been fit. You need to do flutter kicks to train for a triathalon?"

"Can't hurt." She seemed evasive. "I have endurance. I don't have a lot of power and speed. I'm working on it, though. You can swim twenty-five meters under water on one breath, right?"

He suspected she was trying to distract herself—or distract him. "It's not something I do every day—"

"How did you do it at all?"

"Willpower."

"I have willpower."

"When it comes to a picture you want. You'll wait

around for the wind to blow the right way a lot longer than I ever would. But swimming underwater—nothing's at stake for you if you pop up for another breath. For me, it was a requirement. I had to do it.''

"You're saying if you want to be a PJ bad enough, you'll stay under.''

"It helps.''

"That's a crock. I think it has more to do with lung capacity and efficient strokes.''

He grinned. "There's that, too.''

But she hadn't smiled back, and he knew the illicit pictures bothered her. She'd liked and trusted Jodie Rancourt and Louis Sanborn, but they'd committed adultery in such a way that she'd become involved. She felt used, tainted.

Gus had shaken his head over his soup. "I thought you'd be out of the fray up here, but now they're all up here with you. The Rancourts, this Gary Turner. Next it'll be Manny Carrera.''

Gus was all for outfitting his niece for a three-day hike in the mountains. He even said Ty could go with her, seeing how he was more like a brother to her these days. That was designed, Ty had no doubt, to draw a response from Carine, and it did, just not the one Gus expected. He'd wanted, clearly, a hint about what was going on with the two of them. Instead, she shoved her bowl across the table at him and stormed out of the café.

"I guess 'brother' was a bad choice of word,'' Gus said, not particularly remorseful. "North?''

"I'm doing the best I can, Gus.''

"No, you're not. You're just as scared as she is."

"Doesn't matter. I'll do what I have to do."

"To keep her safe—or to keep Manny Carrera safe? Whose side are you on? His or Carine's?"

Ty had attempted a joke. "I'm on the side of truth and justice," he'd said, but Gus didn't laugh, instead sticking him with the bill.

The access road to the Rancourt property snaked up a fifteen-hundred-foot rise of pitted pavement with one bona fide hairpin turn. It wasn't the sort of location people who lived in the region full-time generally chose for their homes, even if they could afford it. Ty glanced at Carine as he negotiated a relatively straight incline, the hill falling away on her side, the bare-limbed trees offering vistas that seemed almost endless. "We still have time to give this up and take Gus's advice and disappear in the mountains for a few days."

She smiled briefly. "Do you still have a taste for beef jerky? I remember as a kid you'd grab a piece of beef jerky and head up the ridge. You weren't even eight years old. I don't know how you lived."

"I don't know, either but I've got MREs these days. Good stuff."

"Purloined 'meals ready to eat.' Well, I understand they're better than they used to be. The prepackaged camping foods certainly are." She looked out her window, the road twisting again now, evergreens hanging over rock outcroppings. "Once I pass the PJ Physical Abilities and Stamina Test, I'm going to take one of the Appalachian Mountain Club winter camping courses. I think that'd be a challenge.''

"Once you pass the what?"

She glanced over at him, a welcome spark in her blue eyes. "The test aspiring PJs take to be accepted into the program."

"Ah. I forgot that's what it's called. Ominous. I just remember running my ass off, nearly drowning a few times, and sweating a lot. Indoc was more of the same, just worse. This explains all the running, swimming and flutter kicks?"

"I'm having fun. I've read up on what you do. All these years with you in and out of my life, and I never really knew much about what a PJ does. Is it true that instructors strap you into a helicopter, blindfold you and throw you in the water to see if you can get out?"

"It's a simulated helicopter."

"Real water."

"I remember," he said.

"You got out?"

He smiled. "I'm a PJ, right? I got out."

She sighed, staring back out her window, the distraction of PJ talk not lasting. "I shouldn't have gotten mad at Gus. He's just trying to help. He doesn't want to see me making the same mistakes all over again with you."

"Maybe, but he was also trying to make you mad. Get your blood up. Put some color in your cheeks."

"Well, it worked."

"You're lucky Gus hasn't locked you in your room by now."

Her vivid eyes stood out against her pale skin. "You taught me how to go out a window on a bedsheet."

"As if you needed teaching."

"It's the age difference. It was more telling when we were six and ten. Now—" She turned back to her window as they passed a steep, eroded embankment. "Never mind."

Ty could see she was preoccupied, dreading her visit with the Rancourts. "I can turn back."

She shook her head. "I need to do this."

He downshifted, taking the last section of hill before the road dead-ended at the Rancourt driveway and the start of the trail that merged with the main Cold Ridge trail. A wild turkey wandered into the road in front of them, and he stopped while it stood sentry for a dozen other turkeys that meandered out from the woods. Carine sat forward with a gasp of excitement, as if she'd never seen a wild turkey before. "Look at them! I wish I had my camera." She bit down on her lower lip, then added, reality intruding, "My Nikon."

Ty couldn't stand another second of seeing her so shattered by her experience in Boston, finding Louis Sanborn dead, running into Manny and now finding the four pictures that had appeared on her camera disk. "Ah, hell." He gripped the wheel, damn near stalling out. "Carine, I'm sorry. I don't know what else to say. If I'd just married you—"

"Don't, Ty." Her voice was surprisingly gentle, more so than he deserved. "It doesn't help. Something worse might have happened if we'd gone through with the wedding. We don't know. We could have been robbed and killed on our honeymoon.''

"We postponed a honeymoon. I only had a few days. I had to get back to Hurlburt—''

"You know what I mean.''

Actually, he did. It was a rationalization, a way to make herself feel better about what he'd put her through. But he said nothing.

"Anyway, you *didn't* marry me,'' she went on. "And I didn't accept Louis's offer of a ride, and I didn't call the police from inside the Rancourt house and not run into Manny.''

"That's not the same.''

"You're not responsible for what's happened to me this week. Or last week. Or ever. I'm responsible for my own actions. Don't you think I understood the risks when I let myself fall for you? Ty—I've known you all my life.''

He let the truck idle a moment. "When did you first want to sleep with me?''

She groaned. "You can be such a jackass, you know.''

"Your sister says the jackass fairy must have visited me every night when I was a kid. You two work that one out together?''

"No, but I like it.'' This time her smile reached her eyes. "I wonder what a jackass fairy looks like.''

"I'm really a nice guy. Everyone says so.''

She went very still, her hands on her thighs. "You're the best, Ty. I've known that for a long, long time. But you're not—'' She sighed, grinning suddenly, unexpectedly. ''You're not normal.''

''Normal?''

She nodded.

''Right. Like you are, she who can outstare an owl.''

''Did you see my barred owl in the woods last fall? I think he knew I was going to be shot at. He flew away. I sometimes think if he hadn't, I might have been killed.''

Ty shook his head. ''Not to burst your bubble, babe, but it wasn't the owl that saved you. Those guys were using a scoped rifle. They missed you on purpose.''

''You're probably right.''

Carine settled back in her seat, and he continued up the road and turned onto the Rancourt driveway. Its blacktop was in better shape than the road, the sprawling house visible farther up on the hill.

''I think my digital camera's cursed,'' she said quietly. ''When the police return it, I'm getting rid of it.''

Ty stopped the truck at the bottom of the driveway and pulled on the emergency brake. When he reached over and touched her cheek, she didn't tell him to go to hell. ''Your camera's not cursed. You're not cursed. And I loved you last winter. I loved you as much as I've ever loved anyone.''

''I know.''

He kissed her cheek, then her mouth, her lips parting. He threaded his fingers into her hair as their kiss deepened, memories flooding over him, regrets, long-ings—for her, for himself—but nothing that he could put to words.

She was the one who pulled away, brushing her fingertips across his jaw before she sat back in her seat. "You're a complicated man, Sergeant North."

"Not that damn complicated. I could pull over somewhere more private—"

"I think you've made your point."

Not very well, he thought. He knew Carine, and she'd be thinking he was just interested in sex and that was why he'd kissed her. And he was—he was very interested in sex. Hell, so was she. But his feel-ings toward her were more involved than that, only he didn't know how to get at them, crystallize them in a few words that made any sense. That was how he'd ended up waiting until the last minute to pull out of their wedding, just trying to think of how to say what he had to say, so that she'd understand and not blame herself. He got the blaming part right—she blamed him instead. But he'd mucked up getting her to understand.

He continued up the Rancourt driveway, which swept them into a parking area in front of an attached three-car garage. They were at a fairly high elevation, the expansive views of the surrounding mountains im-pressive, majestic more than intimate. The landscap-ing was natural and minimalist, designed to blend in with the environment, with a sloping lawn, stone walls and plantings limited to those that occurred in the area—flowers only in pots, no ornamental trees and shrubs. The glass-and-wood house was built into the hillside, two levels in front, one in back, with a screened porch and several decks. A separate dirt track curved up from the parking area to a rustic-looking outbuilding that Ty remembered served as a garden shed in summer and a kind of a warming hut in winter. It had its own potbellied woodstove and a ground-level porch where the Rancourts and their guests could leave their skates and skis.

If they wanted to, Ty thought, Sterling and Jodie Rancourt could convert their place into a bed-and-breakfast or a ski club. It was big enough and had all the right amenities.

"I should go in there alone," Carine said, unbuckling her seat belt.

"I don't think so."

She let the seat belt snap back into place and looked over at him as if he hadn't kissed her at all, never mind that she regretted it. "Back off, okay? I'm not in any danger from the Rancourts."

Ty had no intention of backing off. "What if Louis Sanborn's murder is the result of a garden-variety domestic dispute? Sterling comes in, finds his wife and their new employee in the library and renders his own personal justice."

"And takes pictures before he starts shooting?"

"To keep the wife in line in the future."

"But he leaves the camera."

"Because Manny shows up."

Carine still was skeptical. "Sterling has an alibi."

"So did Jodie Rancourt. Hers didn't hold up, did

it?'' Ty unfastened his own seat belt—she wasn't going in there alone. "I'm playing devil's advocate, babe. All I'm saying is that anything's possible. And I'm with you all the way. That's not so bad, is it?''

She pushed open her door, one leg hanging out as she turned back to him and gave him a quick once-over. "You're not armed. If Sterling or Jodie or whoever decides to shoot me, they'll shoot you, too."

"Consider me a deterrent to violence." He gave her his best cocky smile. "And who says I need to be armed?"

That drew a small laugh. She looked steady enough when she got out of the truck. Ty followed her up a short walkway to a flat stone landing at the front door. He leaned into Carine and whispered, "Don't you feel like you've just climbed the beanstalk to the ogre's castle?"

She bit back a smile, but she had her hands twisted together, obviously trying to keep them from shaking. It wasn't a pleasant errand she was conducting, but Ty knew she wouldn't give up now. That was Carine—in for a penny, in for a pound. Maybe it was her "strong moral compass" at work, but Ty suspected it was also plain stubbornness.

"We can still go camping," Ty said. "I'd keep you warm—"

"So would a good sleeping bag. Will you stop?"

But when Sterling Rancourt pulled open the door a moment later, Carine somehow managed to look less tentative and guilty. It wasn't her fault the police had the pictures of Jodie Rancourt and Louis Sanborn, but that only just now seemed to sink in. Sterling looked like a wealthy country gentleman in his wide-wale corduroys and Patagonia sweater, but it was clear he was prepared for this encounter with his photographer. He must have seen them coming up the driveway, Ty thought.

"Carine, Sergeant North," Rancourt said coolly. "What can I do for you?"

Ty checked out the guy's stiff manner. No tea by the fire today. But Carine, stuffing her hands in her pockets, not intimidated, plunged ahead. "I'm sorry about the disk, and I'm sorry things have turned out the way they have." She paused, but Rancourt didn't say a word, and she went on. "I didn't feel I could give the disk to Gary Turner. I had no idea what was on it—Sterling, I hope you believe me when I say that I had nothing to do with those pictures."

He shifted in the doorway, not meeting her eye. "I'm sure you did what you felt was right. It's not a pleasant situation for any of us, but I haven't seen the pictures. I'm not in a position to discuss them."

"I understand. Given what's happened, I think it's best I quit my job. Jodie has all the pictures I've taken so far. I really appreciate the opportunity you and Jodie gave me—"

"As you wish, Carine. Anything else?"

She took a breath. "No."

Rancourt tipped his head back slightly, studying her, but Ty wasn't fooled by his outward calm or superior manner. The other shoe about to drop—the guy was debating how big a jerk he was going to be to her. Payback. Carine had gone off the reservation. She hadn't turned over the disk to him when asked or consulted him about what to do once she realized what was on it. He'd had no control over what she did. He'd been powerless over her and the entire situation, and he didn't like it. To Ty, it was real simple.

"A bit of friendly advice before you leave." Rancourt's tone was anything but friendly. "If you want to make it in the real world in a big way and not limit yourself to taking pretty pictures of birds and flowers, you'll need to learn to get along with people. You're too independent."

Carine didn't go after him, but Ty saw her hands tighten into fists and knew she wanted to. *He* wanted to. But it was her show, so he kept still and let her handle the bastard. "You're upset," she said calmly, "and you've had a shock, so I'm not going to argue with you."

"I'm not trying to be harsh, but we live in a harsh world." Rancourt wasn't going to back off. "You've been lucky, Carine. You've lived up here in Cold Ridge most of your life. Sheltered, protected."

Right, Ty thought. That was how she'd ended up an orphan at three. Every fiber of his body focused on not interfering, not pounding this prick into the dirt for taking his humiliation and anger out on Carine. But she didn't say a word, just went pale again, as if she'd taken a body blow.

It didn't stop Rancourt. "If you want to achieve the kind of success I think you do. You'll have to change your ways."

She stiffened, but took the hit. She'd always been something of a hothead when it came to him, Ty thought, but she wasn't letting this guy get to her. Maybe she was cutting Rancourt some slack because she'd just given police pictures of his wife with another man. Maybe she didn't have the strength to fight him at the moment. Ty did—he could cheerfully knock Sterling Rancourt on his rich pompous ass.

"Ty," Carine said quietly, "we should leave."

But Rancourt wasn't ready to give up. "I'll take it on faith that you didn't take those pictures on Wednesday, Carine, but there's no proof, either way."

Ignoring him, she started back down the stone walk to the truck.

"It's never easy when you know what someone needs to do." Rancourt had shifted to Ty and spoke in a patronizing man-to-man tone. "I can see the mistakes she's making, not because I'm more brilliant or talented, but because of my circumstances, my experience—"

"You don't know anything about her work or her life."

"Perhaps you're right. But I'm in a position to help her, if she chooses to break from the course she's on—well, that's her call. Not everyone wants to play in the big leagues."

Carine reached the truck and sank against the driver-side door, facing the house. "Ty—whenever you're ready."

Rancourt smiled nastily, his attention still on Ty.

"It's not easy to tell her what she needs to hear, is it? You've been there."

Ty felt every muscle in his body coil, but Rancourt suddenly slumped against the doorjamb and put up his hand, as if to ward off a blow he knew he deserved. "I'm sorry. I—Christ, I'm so sorry. It's been a terrible day. I don't know what I'm saying."

"Yeah. Okay." Ty didn't know what the hell to do. "Carine's right, we should leave."

Jodie Rancourt eased beside her husband. She looked tired and drawn, self-conscious, but also, Ty thought, curiously elegant, as if she was trying to maintain some level of dignity. "Please accept my apology, too. You and Carine. It's been a very difficult few days for all of us. I'm sorry I put you all in such an untenable position."

"Mrs. Rancourt—"

She smiled politely. "Jodie, please. I knew I was taking a risk, just as I knew we were taking a risk last November when we tried to hike Cold Ridge. As then, the consequences have been far worse than I ever imagined." She averted her eyes, her voice lowering, almost as if she were talking to herself. "That's something I'll have to learn to live with."

Her husband positioned himself in such a way that she had to step back into the entry or take an elbow in the cheek. She withdrew, and Rancourt shut the heavy door without another word.

Ty gave a low whistle as he walked back to his truck. "Yep. That went well."

Carine took her hands out of her pockets and

breathed out in a long, cathartic sigh, then managed a halfhearted smile. "Some deterrent you were."

"Think of how much worse it would have been if I hadn't been there. He might have slugged you."

"I don't know, a black eye might have been easier to take."

Ty stood close to her, aware of her hurt, her lingering anger. It was cold on the exposed hill, the wind blowing up from the valley in gusts, penetrating his flannel shirt. He thought about zipping up his jacket, but Carine still had her barn coat unbuttoned. He had to keep up his image of strength. But his attempt at private humor didn't catch hold, and he knew all he wanted to do was get her out of there. "A few days in the mountains," he said. "It's still an option."

"Maybe I'll go take pictures of stupid birds and flowers."

"You're not going to let him get to you, are you?"

Her mouth twitched, her eyes sparking with sudden irreverence. "If I did, would you fly through the door and kick his teeth in?"

Ty shrugged. "Sure."

"Probably get in trouble with some general, wouldn't you?"

"Nah. I'd get a medal."

She sighed, releasing some of her tension. "He was rude and obnoxious, but he's hurting."

"He's not hurting, Carine, at least not in the way you mean. He's pissed that someone else played with his toy without his permission."

"Shoot-the-messenger time."

"Yep. And he doesn't like not being able to control you."

She gazed out at the beautiful view, the seemingly endless cascade of mountains—blue, white and gray against the November clouds. "Maybe it was selfish of me to come. I didn't make anything better."

"Not your job."

One of the garage doors hummed open, and Gary Turner walked out onto the parking area. "I failed in my mission, so now I'm on clean-the-SUV duty," he said with a self-deprecating smile, gesturing back to an expensive white SUV parked in the garage. But his smile didn't last, and he shook his head regretfully. "I overheard you all. Obviously I should have handled this situation differently."

"It's okay," Carine said. "At this point, what's done is done."

Ty opened his truck door, hoping Carine would take the hint and realize it was time to go, but she didn't. "Did Jodie Rancourt use my key yesterday and search my apartment for the disk?" she asked casually, as if it was only of passing interest to her. "The locks are tricky. She must have gotten frustrated or nervous, because she left the door open."

Turner gave an almost imperceptible nod. "She didn't take anything? No one took advantage of the situation?"

Carine shook her head.

"Then I hope we can leave what she did as an act of poor judgment on her part, nothing more. Since you did give her a key—"

"How did she know there were pictures?"

"I can't say. I'm sorry. There's nothing more I can tell you. The police asked us not to discuss our statements with anyone else."

"I understand."

She probably did, Ty thought, but it wouldn't stop her from listening if anyone wanted to talk. But he kept his mouth shut and climbed in behind the wheel. Turner led Carine around to the other side of the truck and opened the door for her. Ty noticed the missing fingers, mentally ticked off various possibilities of how people lose fingers. But mostly he noticed Turner's attentiveness toward Carine. He knew it shouldn't make a damn bit of difference to him, but it did.

"Coming up here was a mistake," Turner said, still very focused on Carine, edging in close to her as she climbed in the truck. "I'll encourage the Rancourts to head back to Boston as soon as possible. We all need to be patient and let the police conclude their investigation. Then we'll know what went on the other day."

"The Rancourts have as much right to be here as I do," Carine said.

"You could use the peace and quiet. I'll see you sometime. Take care of yourself."

"You, too. Thanks."

He shut her door, and Ty started back down the mountain way too fast. He almost two-wheeled it on a curve and slowed down, aware of Carine getting quieter and paler beside him. "You're not going to be sick, are you?"

"I'm fine."

"Good, because I just cleaned my truck."

She lifted her eyes to him, but it was obviously an effort to pull herself out of her thoughts. "You did not. It's filthy."

"It's not filthy. I got out all the wrappers and crud—"

"Look at the dashboard. Dust, grime. And you didn't vacuum."

"Vacuum? Babe, if I vacuumed, I might suck out something this thing needs to keep running. There's a certain balance of nature at work here. It's my New Hampshire truck. My truck on base is spotless."

She let a small smile escape. "Isn't there some general who can call and send you somewhere?"

He grinned. "Am I getting under your skin?"

"Underfoot," she said, "not under my skin. Maybe I miss Boston."

"The cockroaches or the kitty litter in the front hall?"

"There are no roaches in my building."

"I saw one the size of an alligator."

"Watch it, North. Once I've mastered the PAST, I'm going to become a marksman. Try my hand at tactical maneuvers."

"Soon the generals'll be calling you."

She shook her head. "You didn't hear me say I was planning to take up parachuting, did you? That's an unnatural act, jumping out of a perfectly good aircraft.'' She settled back in her seat, watching the passing scenery—rocks, evergreens, birches. No wild turkeys. Wherever they went on late November afternoons, presumably they were there. ''At least I don't mind helicopters. Antonia hates them.''

''And here she is married to a helicopter pilot.''

''Life can be funny that way, can't it? She still says she's never going to be the doctor in the helicopter with the patient, not if she can help it. She'll be the doctor waiting at the hospital for the patient.''

''Have you been on a helicopter?''

''A number of times, on various photography assignments.'' She sighed, adding dryly, ''But I guess that wasn't in the 'real world.'''

''You don't have anything to prove,'' Ty said, slowing down for a series of ruts and potholes, ''you or your sister.''

She glanced over at him. ''Neither do you.''

Seventeen

In the village of Cold Ridge, November was a time between seasons. The leaf-peepers had gone, and the winter sports crowd hadn't yet arrived, leaving the shops and restaurants more or less to the locals for a few short weeks. When Ty parked his beat-up truck in front of Gus's outfitting shop, Carine jumped out first, although by now she knew she wouldn't go far without him. He was definitely in Musketeer mode, her own personal d'Artagnan shadowing her wherever she went—because she'd found a dead man, because his friend had asked him to.

But it didn't seem fair. He was on leave after months leading his pararescue team in combat and training missions that were the subject of speculation and rumor around town but seldom got fleshed out with specifics. Special operations, unconventional warfare. It was all something that happened far away, removed from their northern New England village.

Except Tyler North was one of their own—even if,

Carine thought, he didn't see himself that way, but as the outsider, the boy with the weird mother.

Regardless, he should be hiking and fishing, sitting by the fire with a book, puttering in his rambling house, not traipsing around after her.

But they'd had that discussion on the way into town. "Relax, babe," he'd said. "I haven't fared too badly hanging out with you."

Meaning the sex and the kisses.

That'd teach her to open her damn mouth.

The alternative to having him on her tail—running around on her own—had its appeal, but Carine thought if she could just make the leap to Tyler North as a Musketeer, she wouldn't feel so hemmed in. But it wasn't just his presence, it was that every time she looked at him, a part of her remembered that he was the man she'd loved so much last winter and almost married.

She eyed him as he joined her on the sidewalk and wondered what they'd think of each other if they were meeting for the first time now. He was thirty-seven, she was thirty-three. They weren't kids. She tried to look at him objectively, pretend she hadn't known him forever—hadn't gone to bed with him just yesterday. She took note of his superfit physique, his military-cropped tawny hair, his green eyes and bad-road face. The jeans, the battered brown leather jacket.

She'd be attracted to him, no doubt about it.

Just as well she knew better, experience ever the hard teacher.

He seemed to guess what she was thinking and grinned at her. "Just think. Manny could have asked Gus to keep you out of trouble instead of me."

"Do you see now why I've always hated you?"

"If I'd known what you meant by 'hate,' I could have started sleeping with you when you were sixteen."

"Gus would have killed you."

"Hang on. He might yet."

It was in the fifties in the valley, warm by Gus's standards. He had the wooden front door of his store propped open with a statue of a river otter, the afternoon breeze blowing in through the screen door. Carine went in first, the old, oiled floorboards soft under her feet. Her uncle had started the business, now one of the most respected outfitters in the valley, when she was in the second grade, and he called it Gus & Smitty's. There was no Smitty and never had been, but he insisted that just Gus's was too prosaic. It was located in a former Main Street hardware store. Customers liked the old-fashioned atmosphere, but they came for the state-of-the-art equipment and unparalleled services.

Carine wove through the racks of winter hiking and camping gear to the back wall, where Gus, in a wool shirt and heavyweight chinos, had a map of the Pemigewasset Wilderness opened on the scarred oak counter. They'd hiked in the Pemigewasset countless times. It was a sprawling federally designated wilderness area resurrected from shortsighted logging-and-burning operations that had nearly destroyed it between the mid-nineteenth and the mid-twentieth century. Now it was protected by an act of Congress, and human activity there was strictly regulated.

"Planning a hike?" Carine asked.

He peeled off his bifocals and looked up from his map. "Nah. Just dreaming."

Stump wagged his tail but didn't stir from his bed at Gus's feet.

Ty whistled at a price tag on an expensive ski jacket.

"Only the best," Gus said.

"At that price it should come with its own search-and-rescue team." Ty emerged from the racks, joining them at the counter. "Just add water."

"You come in here to make fun of the merchandise?"

"No, sir. We're here to invite ourselves to dinner."

Gus folded up his map and tucked it back in a drawer. He sold a wide selection of maps, guidebooks, how-to books and outdoor magazines. "I'm cooking a chicken in the clay pot. You two can go over to the house and put it in the oven if you want. I'll close up here in a bit."

"I never can remember what to do with a clay pot," Carine said. "What part you soak in cold water, for how long, if you're supposed to preheat the oven—"

"Instruction book's right in the pot. How'd it go at the Rancourts?"

Ty leaned over a glass cabinet of sunglasses, sports

watches and jackknives. "Sterling was frosty, Jodie was hangdog and Gary Turner drooled over Carine."

She groaned. "Gus, that's *not* how it went."

"It's the short version." North pointed to a pair of Oakleys. "Let me see those."

Gus shook his head. "I'm not wasting my time. You've never paid more than twenty dollars for sunglasses in your life."

"Twenty bucks? When have I ever paid that much for sunglasses?"

"Go to hell."

Ty put a hand to his heart in mock despair. "Is that how you treat a paying customer?"

"The key word is *paying*." Gus dismissed him and turned to Carine, his tone softening. "You don't ever have to see the Rancourts again, you know. You quit, right?"

She nodded. "If I'd just taken my camera with me during lunch—"

"If Jodie Rancourt and Louis Sanborn had just behaved themselves."

"I promised Sterling we'd be discreet."

"Too bad his wife wasn't."

"It's water over the dam at this point," Carine said. "I hope the Boston police will be here soon. I just want to get it over with."

"Go put the chicken on. Cooking'll help keep things in perspective."

The screen door creaked open, and Eric Carrera wandered unexpectedly into the store, making his way back to the counter. Flushed and out of breath, he spoke first to Gus. "My friend and I are in town collecting leaves for earth science class," he said. "How's it going, Mr. Winter?"

"Not bad, Mr. Carrera," Gus replied.

Ty, eyes narrowed as he took in the boy's appearance, stood up from the glass cabinet. "No trees on campus?"

Eric shifted, deliberately avoiding contact with his father's friend. "Yes, sir, there are, but not any ginkgoes and larch trees. There's a ginkgo in front of the Cold Ridge library...." But the boy's voice trailed off, and he sniffled, coughing as he adjusted his backpack and pretended to look at a rack of lip balms. He had on his habitual cargo pants, today's too-big hooded sweatshirt from Amherst College. "I saw your truck out front, and I—I was wondering if you'd heard anything from my dad."

"Not today." He stepped toward Eric, forcing the boy to face him. "You have your meds with you?"

Eric nodded. "I'm okay. I'm just—" He coughed, a sloppy sound in his chest, but he waved off any help, although Ty hadn't made a move in his direction. "My dad...the dead guy...that's not his real name. Louis Sanborn. You know about that, right? It was on the news."

Ty slung an arm over the boy's thin shoulders and maneuvered him to a wall of cross-country skis, sitting down with him on a wooden bench. Carine edged behind a rack of socks to eavesdrop, ignoring Gus's disapproving frown, but she suspected he was as shocked by Eric's news as she was—and wanted the details.

"We haven't heard anything," Ty said gently. "You want to fill me in? Relax, buddy, okay? Take your time."

Eric, who seemed to be making an effort to stay calm, coughed again, but with more control. "The police said the dead guy's identity doesn't check out. They don't know who he is. My dad told the police he doesn't know, either."

"That's what they said on the news?"

"Yeah. Yes, sir."

"Eric, is your dad under arrest?"

He shook his head, sniffling. "The reporter said the police are still not calling him a suspect. I don't know what that means. He's innocent, right, Uncle Ty? He didn't kill anyone?"

"Your dad's not a murderer, Eric."

Carine noticed Ty's careful choice of words and felt her abdominal muscles clamp down, a wave of nausea coming out of nowhere as the news sunk in. Louis Sanborn used a phony name? *Why?* Then who the hell was he? But she didn't move, didn't say anything.

"My mom called," Eric said. "She tried not to sound upset, but I can tell. She said if I need her, just say so and she'll come up here. I told her no."

"You haven't talked to your dad?"

He shook his head. "Not yet."

Ty glanced around the dark, quiet shop. Canoes and kayaks hung from the ceiling, but Gus & Smitty's was in winter mode. "Where's your friend who's collecting leaves with you?" But he'd obviously seen through the boy's lie immediately, and when Eric squirmed, Ty cuffed him on the shoulder and got to his feet. "Come on. I'll give you a ride back to school. If you want to come stay with me, we can work something out with the powers-that-be. Okay?"

"I still have to collect some stupid leaves."

"We can grab some on our way." He glanced back at Carine, pointing at her as if he'd known all along she was there. "Pick me out a pair of socks while you're at it." There was just the slightest hint of sarcasm in his tone. "I'll meet you at Gus's."

"North's good with the kid, I'll give him that," Gus said after they'd left. "I like Eric. He's got a lot of guts, coming up here to school. But, Christ, what next? It doesn't look good for Carrera."

"Something must not add up for the police not to have arrested him yet." Carine grabbed a pair of hiking socks, uneasy, restless. "I should have gone for my run this morning. Ty found a dead bat in my woodstove. I wonder what that means."

"It means you have bats."

"Can I take these socks?"

"Take?"

"I'm unemployed."

"You're self-employed. There's a difference."

She dug in her coat pockets, looking for money. "The police must be putting the thumbscrews to Manny. It's got to be killing Ty not to know what's going on. He doesn't say anything—"

"He won't. It's not his style. And it'd take more than thumbscrews to get Carrera to talk if he doesn't want to."

"Why wouldn't he want to?"

"I didn't say he doesn't. Just don't you worry about it. He can take care of himself. I know, I know—so can you." He rubbed his booted toe over Stump's hind end, the dog wagging his tail in appreciation. "Something like this happens, it's like you're a little kid again. I can't help it."

Carine pulled a few quarters out of one pocket. "It's comforting to know there's someone in my life who cares as much as you do."

"Honey—"

"Don't go there, Gus. Ty's been a perfect gentleman. It's okay."

"Gentleman? Sure. I believe that."

"I'm handling being around him." She set the quarters on the counter. "I don't have my wallet with me."

"You can owe me."

"Do I at least get a discount?"

He offered ten percent. She argued for thirty and settled for twenty. When she tried to throw in new cross-country skis and socks for Ty, he shooed her out the door.

It was dusk, the sun dipping behind the mountains in a pink glow as Carine made the familiar three-quarter mile walk up the hill to her uncle's house. She smelled smoke from a fireplace in the neighborhood. She kicked through dry, fallen leaves on the sidewalk, and when she got to the house, she sat on the top step of the front porch. She could see herself and Ty as kids up in the maple tree in the side yard, still sweating and panting from raking up the huge pile of leaves under their thick branch. He threatened to push her if she didn't jump on her own.

Saskia North had never come up to Gus's house. Not once, not even to pick up her son. Ty had been on his own for a long time. It was what he knew, and Carine wondered if she'd been crazy to think he'd ever really let anyone in.

North dropped Manny's son off at school with his bag of leaves and a full head of worries. But there wasn't much Ty or anyone could do to ease the mind of a fourteen-year-old boy who knew his father was in a mess—who knew his father hadn't called to reassure him and probably wouldn't.

For which Ty could cheerfully strangle his friend. But on one level, he understood. Manny, in his own particular, annoying way, was doing his best to protect his son. He'd put everyone on a need-to-know basis. They could worry, they could get mad, but if he didn't think they needed to know something, he wasn't going to tell them.

Carine could try her burning bamboo shoots on Manny Carrera, too, but they wouldn't work.

Carine. Hell, she'd had no idea Louis Sanborn wasn't Louis Sanborn. It'd been obvious from her reaction. The guy she'd found dead—the guy she'd *liked*—wasn't who he said he was. If Manny had found out, it would explain why he'd headed to Boston to recommend Sterling Rancourt fire him. Rancourt couldn't employ someone who'd lied to him—especially for security.

"Not to mention screwing the poor bastard's wife," Ty muttered to himself.

But had Manny known *that?*

North turned onto Gus's village street, and although it wasn't even six o'clock, Cold Ridge was already engulfed in darkness. Gus's house was all lit up because Carine was there—otherwise, her uncle would have just the kitchen light on. Ty pulled into the short driveway, his cell phone ringing, and he just barely made out Val Carrera's voice through the static. "You must have some kind of mother radar, Val. I just saw Eric. He's worried about Manny, but he's okay."

"Is he eating?"

"Not much from the looks of him, but he had his meds with him. He was coughing, but lungs sounded pretty clear. The house parents at his dorm were waiting for him when we got back—"

"Got back from where?"

"Town. We were leaf-collecting."

"I should—never mind."

"I know it's hard, Val, but he'll make it through this thing. We all will."

"What other choice is there?" She was grumbling, worried and out of sorts, but she didn't sound as fragile as she'd been six months ago. "Manny's not talking to you, either, is he?"

Instinctively, despite his own frustration with his friend, North found himself offering a defense. "Manny doesn't have a lot of room to maneuver."

But Val wasn't one to cut anyone, herself included, much slack. "How much maneuvering does it take to dial a goddamn phone? Okay, never mind. That's not why I called. Look—I'm driving myself crazy here with the computer. You don't happen to know his password?"

"Why would I know his password?"

"I don't know. He tells you things he doesn't tell me. I thought if he knew he might be in deep trouble, he'd maybe clue you in on how you could help him if he really got in over his head."

"I don't know how to help him, Val. I wish I did."

"He's hamstrung. He can't do a damn thing except smile at the cops."

If I can't function…I've got computer files…you'll remember.

Hell, North thought. Only Manny. "Try *I love Val.*"

"What?"

"For the password. Manny said something to me yesterday at the hotel. It didn't make sense at the time—"

"What, that he loves me?" she asked in that wry Val tone.

"No, that he felt the need to mention it. Christ, Val, you can be irritating."

He heard her tapping her keyboard. "It didn't work, so there. Wait, let me try—" She gulped in a breath. "Bingo! I'll be damned, North, that's it! I used a *u* for love and one *v*. I'm in. *I-l-u-v-a-l.*"

"Val—"

"I knew you'd know. I wish I'd thought of you ten million failed passwords ago. I'm surprised this thing didn't self-destruct like in *Mission Impossible,* just start smoking."

"Val, what's on the screen—"

But it was as if her mind was inside the computer. "I'll call you back if I find anything interesting. Watch, it'll just be a spreadsheet of how much he's won in the football pool. He loves those damn spreadsheets."

She clicked off, and Ty could have thrown his phone out the window. He adored Val—everyone did, just like everyone adored Manny. They were straightforward, high energy, fighters. But both of them could drive Ty straight up the wall if he let them.

I love Val.

Why hadn't the big oaf just said it was his goddamn password?

The cop with the PalmPilot, probably. Manny wouldn't want to tip her off. But if he had anything on Louis Sanborn, anything that could help his situation, he needed to be spilling it to the damn police, not making cryptic remarks to a PJ buddy.

Maybe whatever was in the files *didn't* help his situation.

Or maybe there was nothing in his files, North thought, and he and Val were just grasping at straws, trying to help a friend and husband who may have lost it two days ago and blown a man away. It'd been a rough year for Manny. He shouldn't have retired. He needed a couple more years to get Eric out of school, Val back on her feet and in a new job. Starting his own business—it was a different world for Manny Carrera, unfamiliar territory.

But he hadn't lost it. He hadn't blown Louis Sanborn—or whoever he was—away in Boston on Wednesday.

Ty rousted Stump out of a hole he was digging in the backyard and joined the Winters in the kitchen, the uncle and the auburn-haired, blue-eyed niece arguing over butternut squash. Bake or boil. Nutmeg or cinnamon. Real butter or the soft stuff made with olive oil. Boiling won out, because there wasn't enough room in the oven with the clay pot.

Carine retreated with Stump to the front room to sit by the fire, and Ty wondered if he looked as agitated and frustrated as he was, as ready to get into his truck and charge down to Boston.

"You were afraid you'd die on her this year." Gus's quiet words caught him off guard. "You knew what kind of missions you had coming up. She'd just had that business with those assholes shooting at her. What happened to her parents up on the ridge is a part of her—you see that. You let it spook you."

Ty sat at the table; the small kitchen was steamed up, smelling of chicken and baking onions. "Gus, you're off base. I can't do my job if I'm worried about dying. But I'm not going there with you."

"You're not getting my point. You can't do your

job if you know she's back home worried about you dying.'' Gus glanced up from his cutting board. ''That's the devil, isn't it?''

Ty watched him dump the deep orange squash into a pan of water on the stove. The man had done combat in the Central Highlands of Vietnam. An infantryman. A kid plucked out of the mountains of northern New England and sent off to fight a war he didn't understand. He'd probably thought about his family back home worrying about him.

But it didn't matter—Ty's relationship with Carine was for them to sort out. ''You know you could make soup out of that squash?''

Gus returned to his cutting board for another chunk of squash. ''Butternut squash soup is a favorite at the local inns. They put a little apple in it, sometimes a little curry.''

''I'd rather have apple than curry, wouldn't you?''

''North…I was out of line.'' Gus sighed, his paring knife in his hand as he brushed his wrist across his brittle gray hair. ''You and Carine—what's between you two is your business.''

Ty grinned. ''What have I been saying, huh?''

Gus pointed his knife at him. ''You're going to live to be an old man, North, just to torment the rest of us.''

''And you're going to kill yourself with your own cooking.'' Ty was on his feet, frowning at the stove. ''What the hell's that in the frying pan?''

''Braised Brussels sprouts with olive oil and a little parmesan.''

"Jesus. I think I've got an extra MRE out in the truck."

Gus threw him out of the kitchen, and Ty joined Carine in front of the fire. He sat on the couch, and she sat on the floor with her back against his knees, comfortable with him, he thought—and for a moment, it was almost as if he'd never knocked on her cabin door and canceled their wedding.

Eighteen

Carine climbed onto her favorite rock on the lower ridge trail and looked out at the valley and mountains, the view that had captivated her since she was a little girl. It was midmorning, the trees, even the evergreens, almost navy blue against the bleak gray sky. If only she could stand here and let her worries and questions float out on a breeze, dissipate into the wilderness.

She remembered Gus taking her and her brother and sister onto the ridge after their parents died. She'd dreamed about that day for years. She spotted an eagle and swore she saw her mum and dad flying with it in the clear summer sky. The image had been so vivid, so absolutely real to her.

But, so had her dreams, her images, of her life with Ty. So vivid, so real.

She half walked, half slid down the curving granite, rejoining him on the narrow, difficult trail. They'd gone far enough. Neither had the attention span for a long hike. They'd loaded up a day pack after breakfast and set out, crossing the meadow, climbing over a stone wall, then walking up a well-worn path to the trailhead. The dirt access road was quiet, the parking lot empty, not atypical of November. It was Saturday, but still early.

There was a threat of light snow and high winds above the treeline. They weren't going that far, but Carine had gone back to her cabin and dug out her lighter winter layers for the hike. Thermal shirt, windproof fleece jacket, windproof pants, hat, gloves. Her hat and gloves were still in the day pack. She wore her new hiking socks. No cotton—she'd even banned it from her summer hikes.

Ty had approved of her wilderness medical kit, but he'd raised his eyebrows when she tucked the manual into the pack. "Look at it this way," she told him. "If I fall and hit my head, you won't need the manual. If you fall and hit your head, I'll need the manual."

"Only if I'm unconscious."

"Of course, because if you can talk, you'll just tell me what to do."

"If I'm conscious," he said, leaning toward her in that sexy way he had, "I'll treat myself."

She told him she had treating blisters down pat. She knew CPR and basic first aid. She'd have done her best if Louis Sanborn had still been alive when she found him. But Antonia was the doctor in the family—Carine didn't like blood and broken bones, people in pain. Not that Antonia, or Ty, did, but they had a calling when it came to medicine that she simply didn't have.

Of course, Ty's calling also involved guns, diving, fast-roping and the insanity of HALO—High Altitude Low Opening jumping, where he would depart a plane at very high altitudes, with oxygen, a reserve chute, a medical kit and an M16, the bare necessities to survive the jump and get to a crew downed in hostile conditions.

Not that *he* thought HALO was insane. Just another tool in his PJ tool bag of skills, he'd say.

Carine respected his skills and abilities, his nonchalance about them, but she wasn't intimidated, perhaps because they seemed so natural to him, integral to who he was.

She'd spent an hour last night in his kitchen answering questions from the two Boston Police Department detectives, who had been sent to take possession of the memory disk, camera and camera bag. It hadn't occurred to her to have an attorney present. After they left, her brother called on Ty's hard line, which meant Ty could listen in on the extension as Nate told her in no uncertain terms to go mountain climbing today. He wouldn't go into detail about anything he'd found out, but Nate wasn't one to overreact. Although he never said so directly, Carine received the strong implication that her brother had talked to his law enforcement sources and had good reason to make sure his friend and his sister stayed out of what was apparently not a simple case of murder.

After she hung up with Nate, Ty tried to call Manny, got his voice mail and almost threw his phone into the fire. He tried Val Carrera, also without success.

Carine had her Nikon with her on the hike and took several pictures, anything that struck her eye. Ty had said little all morning. Inaction, she thought, was getting to him. She knew he wanted to be in Boston, pulling information out of Manny Carrera, a syllable at a time if he had to.

She slipped the camera into an outer pocket of the day pack, strapped to his back. "Hiking can be a substitute for my run," she said.

"Nope. You hike, then you go back and do your run."

"Says who?"

He grinned over his shoulder at her. "That's something we hear a lot in the military. 'Says who?'"

He was teasing her, a good sign his mood had improved. "Fortunately, I'm not in the military. I'm just a simple photographer who wants to run a mile and a half in ten minutes and thirty seconds or less."

"You can do it. How close are you?"

"Twelve minutes. Well, once, anyway. I'll get there. I told you, it's the swimming that kills me. I always get water up my nose." She zipped up the compartment and patted him on the hip. "Tell you what, Sergeant, if you run with me, I'll do my mile and a half after we get back."

"Think I can't?"

"I think you need to burn off more excess energy

than this little hike of ours will accomplish. You're not sleeping, Ty. You were up at dawn again this morning.''

''Dawn's not that early in November.''

''You're preoccupied, worried about Manny—and Val—''

''Having you down the hall isn't the greatest sleep-inducer, either.''

She sighed. ''Ty, it's not always about sex.''

''It's not?''

''I am trying—''

He winked at her. ''I know you are, babe. Don't worry about me. I'm doing just fine.'' He started down the trail, moving easily over the roots and jutting rocks. ''One thing, though. You're not a simple anything, but you're sure as hell not a simple photographer. You're a brilliant photographer.''

''You don't have to say that.''

''Yes, I do.'' He held out his arm for her to grab as she jumped off a two-foot rock in the middle of the trail. ''You have the talent, the skills, the drive. I look at your pictures—I can't explain it. There's something going on there. I know it's nothing I or most people could do with one of those little throw-away things.''

She was taken aback. ''I appreciate that. Really. Thank you.''

He continued down the trail, not taking any time to enjoy the scenery. ''When we get back, I'll try Val again. Then I'm heading down to Boston to see Manny. You can hang out with Gus and Stump. It's the slow season. You two can wax skis. Argue about squash recipes.''

"I'd rather go to Boston with you."

"I know you would."

"I could get my car, water my plants—"

He glanced back at her. "You don't have any plants."

She kept up with his killing pace, no more pauses to check out the view or pick up the perfect fallen leaf. The steep pitch of the trail eased into a long, gentle downward slope, the trail widening as it took them over a stream and back out to the parking area. When they reached the meadow, the wind gusted and howled down the mountains from the north, blowing an icy snow in their faces.

But the snow ended abrupty as they crossed into Ty's backyard and didn't even cover the ground. The sun beamed white through a thin cloud. Dark, lumpy clouds shifted over the valley, and the long, looming ridge with its high summits. Carine, more aware of the sky than she'd ever been in the city, tried to remember various cloud formations—stratocumulus, lenticular, cirrostratus. Each was associated with its own particular weather, but she was rusty on which was which.

Ty left the back door open for her, and she didn't linger outside. The wind blew into the kitchen, where the fire was almost out. He set the day pack on the table. When the phone rang, Carine, who was closer, picked it up. She didn't even get a chance to say hello. "Tyler? It's Val Carrera. The police are at my damn door with a search warrant."

"Val, it's Carine. Ty—"

Val didn't seem to hear her. "I'm sorry I didn't call back last night. At first I was too stunned, and then I fell asleep at the computer. I tried this morning but didn't get through—Jesus, Ty, he's got all kinds of garbage in these files. PJ stuff. Football scores. I *told* you I'd find football scores. At least I didn't find any porn."

"Slow down, okay? Let me get—"

She was talking rapidly, breathless. Ty made a move for the phone, but Carine was afraid they'd miss something important if she tried to transfer it to him with Val so oblivious to who was on the other end.

"He's got your e-mail address here. I'm sending you the file I think we're interested in. Jesus, will they break down the door if I don't answer?" She yelled, away from the phone, "I'm coming! Hang on a sec!" Then she returned, adding in a lower voice, "They'll haul off his hard drive. You know damn well they will."

In spite of her tough language, Val sounded panicked and fragile. Carine held up a hand, stopping Ty from ripping the phone from her. "I'll tell Ty—"

"It looks like Manny suspected Louis Sanborn was using an alias and having an affair with Jodie Rancourt, maybe extorting money from her. Something. I haven't gone through it all. I hope it doesn't get Manny into hotter water with the police."

Carine went still. "Manny suspected Louis and Jo-die were having an affair *before* he got to Boston?"

"Yeah. I think so. Carine? Is that you?"

Ty snatched the phone. "Val, what the hell's going on?" He listened a moment, then said, "Open the damn door for the police. Do what they tell you. For Christ's sake, don't argue with them. Do you have a gun in the house? Val—" He glared at the phone then sighed at Carine. "She's gone."

"Did you get anything more out of her?"

"I need to check my e-mail. Jesus, those two." He looked ready to kick something. "We don't know what Manny's told the police. Goddamn it, we don't know anything."

Carine knelt down to see if she could revive the coals in the fireplace. She blew on them, and a few glowed red. She lifted a skinny log out of the wood-box and laid it on the coals, trying not to suffocate them, the familiar work only a partial counter to her tension.

She'd found Louis dead, but the Carreras were Ty's friends more than they were hers. He and Manny had been in combat together.

"Go on," she said. "Check your e-mail for what Val sent. I'll join you in a minute."

But Ty came behind her and hooked an arm around her waist, lifting her to her feet and kissing her softly, unexpectedly. He threaded his fingers gently through her hair. "This'll all work out. You know that, don't you?"

She wondered if he was trying to convince her or

himself, but she nodded. "Manny's a rock. Val, too, in her own way."

He headed to the den, and Carine returned to the fire, the log catching with no additional effort on her part. Nate could have called last night and encouraged her to go mountain climbing because he'd found out Louis's murder involved blackmail, extortion, an adulterous affair—people with connections to her and Cold Ridge.

She set another log on her reborn fire, then made her way down the hall to the den. With the gray sky, it seemed more like late afternoon than midday. Ty didn't look up from the monitor. "I downloaded Val's file. It looks like some kind of personal log Manny kept."

Carine resisted the temptation to read over his shoulder. "I'll leave you to it."

She returned to the kitchen and put another larger log on the fire, then stood in front of it, her fingers splayed out over the flames. She remembered those crazy few days last November with the shooting and the Rancourts' rescue, Ty grinning at her and calling her babe, telling her she had pretty eyes, as if he'd never noticed her in all the years they'd known each other. He and Manny Carrera sneaking around after the shooters and pulling Jodie and Sterling Rancourt off the ridge like it was no big deal—and Hank Callahan, the retired air force officer, the senate candidate. They'd all gathered in front of the fire here in Ty's kitchen and eaten chili and drunk beer, talking late into the night—she remembered Ty insisting on walking her back to her cabin as if it wasn't something she'd done on her own a thousand times when his mother was alive. It was cold and so still they could hear their footsteps on the dirt driveway, and when they got to her door, he kissed her good-night.

That was when she should have fled to Boston, not six months later after the damage was done.

He walked into the kitchen and pulled out a chair, turning it so that he could face the fire. He sat down, sighing heavily, collecting his thoughts. "Manny figured going into business for himself would be good for Val and Eric, that it'd give him more freedom to make his own schedule. But he hates it. He doesn't like the work, he doesn't like the people he has to work with. He'd have given it up if the Rancourts hadn't hired him."

"Funny how these things work out sometimes," Carine said, still on her feet.

"He was in Cold Ridge in September to visit Eric. I wasn't here. Neither were you. Gus was on a hiking trip. While Eric was in class one morning, Manny drove up to the Rancourt house to see if anyone might be up there, get the lay of the land so he could make recommendations. It was just something to do, really." He paused, glanced up at Carine. "Guess who was there?"

"Jodie? She's come up here on her own a number of times."

Ty nodded. "Yep. She was here. With Louis Sanborn."

"In *September?* But the Rancourts only hired him

two weeks ago. I didn't realize they already knew each other. Louis acted as if they didn't—''

''Sterling Rancourt didn't know Louis. Only Jodie.''

''Oh.'' Carine sank onto a chair, wincing at the implications. ''Ouch.''

''Somehow or another, the rescue last fall made Sterling feel vulnerable, so he started paying more attention to his personal and corporate security. He hired Gary Turner, then Louis Sanborn. He got Manny in to consult.''

''If Jodie and Louis were already having an affair, you'd think she would have tried to stop her husband from hiring Manny.''

''For all we know, she tried. Manny met with Sterling Rancourt, Gary Turner and Louis Sanborn in Boston a few days after Sanborn was hired. He realized right off the bat that Sanborn was the same guy he met in September.''

''Did Sanborn say anything?''

Ty shook his head. ''And Manny was pretty sure Jodie Rancourt introduced Sanborn under a different name. Tony something. Italian.''

''Jesus—so she knew he was using an alias? Then why hire Manny? If he'd already met Louis under a different name why take the chance? Unless there's an innocent explanation for the alias and no one was worried about it.''

''Manny couldn't swear to what Jodie told him in September, at least according to the log.'' Ty sighed, leaning back in his chair. ''You should see this thing.

He's not a talker on a good day, but there are places he's downright cryptic. A lot of it's in military lingo. No wonder Val couldn't make much sense of it."

"He must have told the police all this."

"I'm not making any assumptions at this point. He decided something wasn't on the level and started digging into Sanborn's background. Nothing added up. He already knew the guy sure as hell wasn't southern—"

"That was an act?"

"According to Manny. He's a Texan. He thinks he can smell a Yankee at a thousand yards."

Carine smiled. "Why isn't the reverse true?"

"Because we Yankees don't give a rat's ass." But Ty's humor was strained, and he leaned over and, without getting up, grabbed a log and pitched it one-handed onto the fire. It landed hard, the sparks just missing Carine's toes. He went on, settling back in his chair. "Manny thought Sanborn might have a Cold Ridge connection."

She shook her head. "I'd have recognized him if he did, wouldn't you think? The way he acted, I'd be surprised if it had occurred to him I might recognize him—I'm sure it didn't. He played the southern guy who thinks fifty degrees is cold. How far did Manny get in his background research before he went up to Boston?"

"Not far enough."

Ty was silent, and the fire hissed, one of Carine's logs breaking up into red-hot chunks. She watched it, trying to piece together different conversations she'd had with the Rancourts in the weeks since she'd started working for them, with Louis—or whoever he was—before he was killed. But there was nothing. She'd had no idea anything was going on beneath the surface until she walked into the library on Wednesday afternoon and found Louis dead. And even then...

But she realized Ty had drifted into silence. "What else?" she asked quietly, knowing there was more.

"Speculation."

"What kind of speculation?"

"Carine—it could all be nonsense. We don't know."

"Okay, with that caveat, what kind of speculation?"

"If Manny's right..." Ty sank back in his chair and rubbed a hand over his head, then sighed, plunging on. "He made a note in his log about the weapons the Rancourts have up here. Expensive rifles. Bolt action and semiautomatic. Scoped. Jodie Rancourt had them out, showing them to Louis the day Manny met them up here. Sterling told him about the guns when he discussed what training he wanted Manny to do."

"A lot of people up here have guns, but I had no idea the Rancourts did."

Ty rose, his back to the fire as he started unloading the day pack. "Manny intended to get to the bottom of whatever was going on with these people. Nothing was going to stop him."

"It makes sense if it was his job—"

"Not because of his job. He has a kid up here. And there's you."

She took her wilderness medical kit off the table where Ty had laid it and slipped it into her coat pocket. "Because I worked for the Rancourts?"

But she knew that wasn't the whole answer, even before Ty spoke. "And because you're from Cold Ridge, and because of last November."

The shooting. The burned-down shack, the missing smugglers. "Manny can't think the Rancourts had anything to do with that smuggling operation. Louis? Could he have been—" She stopped herself, not wanting to phrase the question. Could Louis have been involved? Was that why he came up with an alias? "The police don't have any suspects."

"Not that we know of."

"Nate—he'd know."

Ty shook his head. "He won't tell you even if he does know. Neither would you in his place." He lifted a water bottle out of the pack and set it on the table. "I won't be going to Boston. I see now why Manny put me on Carine Winter duty. You're not on the sidelines, babe. Whatever's going on, you're right in the thick of it."

North split wood until he'd worked up a blister on one hand. He thought about letting Carine treat it. But he was sweating, irritable, ready to jump out of his damn skin. He'd decided to give Val ninety minutes before calling her back. It seemed like enough time for the cops to execute their search warrant and clear out of the Carreras' apartment.

He'd debated heading back up the notch road to ask the Rancourts to explain their relationship with Louis Sanborn, *aka* whoever, but he'd had a good dose of the Rancourts yesterday. And there was Carine.

There was always Carine.

She sat on the back steps, bundled up in a moth-eaten wool blanket she'd dug out of a hall closet, so old it might have been left behind by one of her ancestors.

"Doesn't the wool scratch?" he asked her.

"Not that much. It reminds me of being a kid."

"I think that's the same blanket Nate and I used when we rolled you and Antonia up and sent you down the hill over by the road."

"I remember that. We almost got run over."

He sat next to her, smelling the damn blanket. Mothballs, dust, that musty wool smell. "You didn't almost get run over. Gus just said that when he yelled at us, and it stuck in your mind. You were, what, six or seven? You didn't know enough not to believe everything your uncle said."

Even then, there'd been an unspoken rule in his life. *Never get involved with the little sister.* Nate was his friend. The Winters, in many ways, were his family. Ty had violated the bond between them by falling for Carine—never mind that she hadn't exactly been dragged kicking and screaming into bed with him.

He'd still made the first move. It was his doing more than hers.

And there was no undoing it. He'd learned that in the last few days. Even now, it wouldn't take much for him to carry her and her moth-eaten blanket upstairs for the rest of the afternoon.

Maybe Gus was right, and he needed to sell the house. If not for the damn trust fund, he would have had to by now, anyway.

He could sell the house, quit the air force, buy a boat and sail away.

Or go find other mountains to live in.

Carine had placed his cell phone on the steps. He grabbed it and clicked onto his phone book, found Val's number and hit the button for an automatic dial. She answered almost before it rang, static making her hard to understand. "Ty? They're gone. They took the computer, a bunch of folders he had—he doesn't have an office yet, so he's been working out of here."

"You okay?"

"I just wolfed down cold pepperoni pizza, right out of the refrigerator. You'd have thought I was starving. It was disgusting. All that coagulated grease."

Ty smiled. "Val, you're a trip and a half. Anything out of Manny?"

"Are you kidding? He's lucky I don't drive up to Boston and shoot him myself."

She was handy with a gun. Ty wouldn't put it past her, except he'd never seen a couple more committed to each other than Manny and Val Carrera. "He must be cooperating with the police. He has nothing to hide. If it turns out Louis Sanborn traces back to the shooting here last year, we'll know it. Law enforcement will put the pieces together.''

She sighed, deflating. ''This past year—it hasn't been easy. He did good work as a PJ, you know? He loved it. Then Eric got sick, and I went kerplooey on him—''

''Kerplooey?''

''Yeah.'' He could almost feel her smile. ''It sums up what happened to me rather nicely, a very nasty mix of clinical depression, burn-out, stupidity and guilt.''

''Manny says you just need a job.''

''He does better with other kinds of head injuries than the kind I had. He got sucked into this Rancourt mess, Ty. He's not going to let go until he's got it sorted it. That's the way he is.''

North nodded. ''I know.''

''This business thing wasn't a great idea. I saw that crap in the file about doing it for me. Bullshit. I think—'' She swallowed, no hint of any good humor coming through from her end now. ''I'm not sure he likes the idea of being alone with me for the rest of his days. With Eric away at school—''

''Val, don't do this to yourself, okay? You two are going to the home together. You know that.''

''I keep thinking—'' Her voice quavered. ''I don't know, if I could just do something to bring order back to the universe.''

Ty tried to smile. ''It's not your job to bring order

to the universe, Val. Jesus. Some days it's enough just to get in three meals and eight hours of sleep.''

But she didn't relent. ''Haven't there been times in your life when you've felt as if you're under siege and nothing's ever going to go right again?''

''You bet, Val,'' Ty said gently. ''We've all had those times.''

When he hung up, Carine eyed him, obviously curious about what Val had said, but he put her off and dialed Hank's cell phone, remembering the Pave Hawk pilot he'd flown combat missions with just a few years ago was a senator now. But his voice-mail message was unchanged—''*Hi, it's Hank. Leave a message…*''

''Check on Val Carrera if you can,'' Ty said. ''She's had a bad day. The cops searched—ah, hell, Hank. You're a senator. You can't get mixed up in this mess. Forget it. Val will be fine. So will Manny.'' He clicked off and tossed the phone onto the steps. ''Gus and I agree on one thing. Cell phones should be banned.''

Carine slipped her hand out of her blanket and placed it on his thigh. ''Val knows she has to hang in there. She will.''

He covered her hand with his, noticed that even without the blanket, his was warmer. ''You do realize your brother-in-law is a senator?''

''It's sinking in. I'm not registered to vote in Massachusetts—isn't that awful? I didn't even vote for him.'' She lifted Ty's hand and examined his blister. ''I've still got my first-aid kit. I can treat it.''

"It hardly even counts as a blister. Share a corner of your blanket with me?"

She tossed a section of it over his shoulder, and he scooted in closer to her. But the thing didn't make him feel nostalgic at all. It stunk, and it scratched. He put a finger through one of the holes. She smiled. "Waste not, want not. Saskia got that part of living up here. I tried to explain to Louis that we Yankees are frugal, not cheap. There's a difference." She took a breath, her voice cracking almost imperceptibly. "Except he wasn't southern after all."

"We don't know that for a fact. We just have Manny's notes."

She shook her head. "Ty, I never would have guessed he wasn't on the level. Never. He was funny, irreverent, *nice*. Jodie—she lied, too. I never would have guessed they were having an affair. I must not be a very good judge of character."

"Louis could have been funny, irreverent and nice and still not be on the level."

"Not nice. That's what Manny said to me on Wednesday before the police got there. *Louis Sanborn wasn't a nice man.* I guess he was trying to warn me."

Ty said nothing, just leaned back against the step, taking Carine with him in the blanket. She laid her head against his shoulder, the smell and the roughness of the old blanket apparently not fazing her. He kissed her hair, which was soft and smelled of some citrusy shampoo, not mothballs, and if he smelled like sweat and sawdust, she didn't seem to mind.

Nineteen

❧◈❧

Carine tried to go for her run on her own, but Ty put on running shorts and a ragged shirt and joined her, saying he could provide motivation for her to get her speed up.

Just what she needed.

At some point, he'd mapped out the same mile-and-a-half route she had. He also had the same three-mile, five-mile and ten-mile routes. Ten miles was as far as she'd ever run. Any farther, she was in hiking boots and packing food and a tent.

But her morning hike and the tension of the past few days affected the muscles in her legs, her stamina, her breathing. She couldn't get a rhythm going in her stride. She had on close-fitting leggings, a moisture-repelling running shirt, special running socks and her expensive running shoes, but they weren't doing her any good.

"I'm dying here," she said after they'd made the

turn and were on their way back. "I feel like I'm sprinting."

Ty trotted alongside her with little apparent effort. "Push harder. You can make it."

"You should see me do five miles. It's this damn speed—"

"Carine, you're not running that fast."

"Easy for you to say." They turned into her driveway, and she glowered at him when she saw that he wasn't even breathing hard. "North—I hate you. I've always hated you."

"The refrain." He grinned at her, the run obviously not fazing him. "No, you have not always hated me. That's what kills you."

Her knees were wobbling, and she was sweating and gasping for air, her chest aching, when just a week ago she'd have been fine—not breaking any records, but not ready to drop, either. Ty looked as if he'd just done a warm-up. Plus, he'd chopped wood. *And* he'd gone on the hike with her.

"Couldn't you at least cough and spit?" she asked him. "Get a stitch in your side?"

"Can't stand the heat, get out of the kitchen."

She scowled at him. "My body must have been possessed by aliens when we were engaged."

"Well, maybe your mind was. I know your body wasn't." He swatted her on the rear end. "Now, come on. Hoof it the last few yards. Sprint. Go all out."

She tried to kick him, but he was ready for her and bobbed out of her reach. The hell with it. She dove for his midsection. Headfirst, the way she always had. But he grabbed her by the hips, flipped her over, and before she knew what was happening, she was upside down, looking at the ground. "Hey!" she yelled. "You're going to step on my hair."

Her running shirt dropped down to her chin, and she felt the cool air on her overheated skin—and his hands. "Christ, you have been doing your ab work."

She did her level best to kick him in the jaw.

He laughed and swooped her back over and onto her feet. The blood that had rushed to her face while she was upside down rushed back out again, and she felt herself get dizzy and almost tripped. He caught her by both shoulders, steadying her. "You okay?"

She blinked at him. "I should have thrown up on your shoes."

"Yeah, probably."

"The idea was for me to think twice before I attack you again?"

"No, the idea was for me to feel your abs."

"You felt my abs the other day."

"I wasn't paying attention. I was more interested in other parts of your body."

"Ty." She put her hands on her hips, breathing hard. "Damn, you're not cutting me any slack, are you?"

He shrugged. "Who just plowed into who?"

"I'm standing here having this wonderful fantasy of hanging *you* upside down by your toes. But it'll probably never happen, will it?"

"Not literally. Figuratively—" Something changed

in his eyes. "One way or another, babe, you've got me hanging by my toes every damn day."

His comment, his delivery, unsettled her enough to give her the spurt of energy she needed to sprint the rest of the way to her back deck.

"I'll have to remember that," he said, walking to the deck. "Nice way to get you moving. You showering here?"

"Damn straight," she muttered, scooting inside before he could get to her even more.

She skipped her post-run stretches and climbed up the ladder to her loft, and when she opened a dresser drawer, she heard a distinctive squeaking inside the slanted ceiling. Damn. More bats. And mice droppings in her underwear drawer.

She had visions of scurrying rodents and bats swooping up in the rafters while she slept. Her loft—her bedroom—was in the rafters.

Not a good development.

Ty wandered into the great room below her, and she leaned over the rail. "I'm going to have to sleep up here with a baseball bat."

"Hey—"

"Not because of you. I've got bats and mice. Your house has been empty even longer than mine. Why don't you have rodents?"

"I pay people to take care of the place. You've got Gus." He smiled up at her. "I also have ultrasonic pest-chasers. I think I have a few extra if you'd like me to fetch them."

"Sure. Run there and back so you can work up a

sweat. By the way,'' she said, rising up off the rail, ''your abs aren't so bad, either. I could feel them when you had me upside down.''

''Watch it, toots. If you think I can run fast, you should see how fast I can climb a ladder.''

It felt good to laugh, but after she got out fresh clothes and slipped back down the ladder to shower and change, she found herself making a detour into her studio. She wiped her palm over her dusty filing cabinet and opened the bottom drawer, squatting down to flip through the files, until she came to one labeled simply Hunting Shack, because she needed no further prompting to remember what was inside.

She laid the photos one by one on the floor, on the rug Saskia North had designed and hooked for her one winter.

The police had the memory disk. She'd printed out copies of the photos before it had occurred to anyone to ask her for it. She hadn't touched them in a year. In hindsight now, as she looked at the pictures, she realized the photo of the shack never would have worked as a Christmas card or anything else. The lighting was off, the building itself more an eyesore than a quaint relic of rural New England. There were no vehicles, no people, no snow or footprints—yet minutes after taking the pictures, someone shot at her. Then blew up the shack and let it burn to the ground before the police could get there.

One of the best shots was of the front porch. She'd had to get down low for it. A pair of antique cross-country skis was tacked above the door, and she'd captured about a dozen old-fashioned signs mounted on the outside wall. She took the photograph to her worktable and turned her lamp on it, then got out her magnifying glass for a closer look.

Was someone in the window?

No. And surely the police would have noticed if there were.

She smiled at the moose-crossing sign. There were also cow-crossing signs, but most of the signs were of stores and dairies long out of business—including the Sanborn Dairy. It had gone out of business in the early 1960s. Its old glass bottles were a collectors' item. Carine thought she had a couple in the cellar. They had black lettering, with a line drawing of the heads of two happy-looking cows. The last of the Sanborns had sold off their acreage to the local paper mill that owned the land on which the shack was located. But they owned hundreds of acres, and Sanborn wasn't an uncommon name.

When Ty returned with the pest-chasers, Carine brought him back to her studio and showed him what she'd been up to. "Kind of an odd coincidence, huh?" She handed him her magnifying glass, noticing he'd showered and changed into jeans and a sweater, the ends of his hair still damp. "You've heard of the Sanborn Dairy."

"They delivered pint bottles of milk to school when Gus was a kid."

"Suppose that's where Louis got his alias? He could have grown up in the valley and picked Sanborn because it was convenient, or maybe he's a distant Sanborn cousin or something.''

''That doesn't make him one of the smugglers.''

She shrugged. ''It doesn't *not* make him one of the smugglers.''

Ty peered through the magnifying glass. ''Did you ever steal a deer-crossing sign?''

''That's not a deer, that's a cow and a moose—''

He glanced at her. ''I know it's a cow and a moose. Jesus.''

''*You* stole a deer-crossing sign? Ty, that's low.''

''Nate helped.''

''How come I never knew?''

''You and Antonia would've ratted us out.''

''We were not tattletales!''

He rolled his eyes and handed her back her magnifying glass. ''I think I used a Sanborn Dairy bottle for target practice once. How's that for a coincidence?''

''All right, so it's a weak theory, but it's something, anyway. A nibble. Maybe Louis was one of the smugglers and saw the sign, and when it came to pick an alias, he chose Sanborn, not realizing where he got it. Manny was looking for a connection between the smugglers and Louis.''

''Good. You can tell him it's a defunct dairy.''

''If Louis and Jodie met up here—'' She sighed, knowing she wasn't going to get anywhere with him. ''Oh, never mind. We're just chasing our tails. The police are probably way ahead of us.''

''We? Us?''

She smiled. "Go install your pest-chasers. How many did you scare up?"

"Three. They should help."

Carine quickly put the pictures away and headed for the shower, not wasting any time rinsing off, toweling herself dry and jumping into fresh clothes. Ty had her on edge, no question about it. Val Carrera's call and Manny's computer log didn't help, but they weren't the main cause. The teasing, the sexy comments and looks, the easy manner he had with her all reminded her of their first days together last fall, before they'd tried to commit to something deeper. Marriage. A life together.

Don't think.

Yes. Much better that way. She'd learned her lesson. She wasn't going to get ahead of herself with him again.

She combed her damp hair, not bothering to pull it back, and returned to the kitchen. Gus had called before her run to say he was bringing dinner. She slipped out onto the back deck, shivering, the air chilly against her shower-warmed skin. She noticed Gary Turner's midnight blue car in her driveway. He waved to her over its roof and joined her on the deck, his all-black attire and the fading light emphasizing the whiteness of his hair, the blandness of his eyes and skin.

"Sorry to bother you," he said.

"You're not bothering me. I'm just getting a breath of air."

"Your hair's wet—don't catch cold." He cocked

his head, smiling at her. "Have I ever seen you with your hair down?" But he didn't wait for an answer, straightening, his manner becoming more formal. "I assume you've heard the latest."

"That Louis Sanborn is an alias?" Carine nodded. "I heard yesterday. After my last visit with the Rancourts, I didn't think it appropriate to go up there and chat with them about it."

"Understandable. They're furious with me now, too."

"Because you didn't know?"

He shrugged, not really answering.

She was aware she hadn't invited him inside and wondered where Ty was with his pest-chasers. "Did you hire him?" she asked.

Turner narrowed his colorless eyes on her. "He came well recommended—"

"By Jodie Rancourt?"

He sighed. "Then you know."

"I don't know anything, but they were having an affair."

"She told her husband it was just that one time in the library. It's none of my business. I've tried not to interfere in their relationship. Of course, if anyone believed her affair with Louis had anything to do with his murder, I'd speak up."

"Have you told the police—no, never mind. That's not fair of me to ask. You must be in an incredibly difficult situation."

He paused a moment, his expression unreadable. "Regardless of the circumstances of how Louis came to me, I should have gone deeper into his background. I liked him, and I figured I'd keep an eye on him, see how he worked out.''

She decided not to tell him about Manny's log, how sure he was that it was Louis he'd run into with Jodie Rancourt in Cold Ridge in September—under a different name. Maybe Turner knew, maybe he didn't. It wasn't for her to discuss the contents of a computer file that the police, after all, also had.

''I think we were all taken in,'' she said. ''Gary— do you know who took the pictures in the library? It couldn't have been Jodie or Louis, but I suppose one or the other could have persuaded someone—''

''The pictures are irrelevant. I'm history with the Rancourts. I guess I don't blame them.'' He seemed genuinely unconcerned. ''After this week, they're skittish about the whole idea of hiring their own security experts. They'll probably contract out with an established firm.''

''What will you do?''

''I have options.'' He tilted his head back, the fading light darkening his eyes just a notch. ''What about you? Does the big city still beckon?''

''I like my apartment. No one else seems to.''

He smiled gently. ''That's because they've seen this place.''

''I have great neighbors in the city. I don't have any neighbors here—''

''Tyler North.''

She swallowed. ''He's active-duty military. He's not around much. It just so happens that he's here this week.'' Up in her loft, as a matter of fact, she thought, installing pest-chasers. ''I had a lot of projects in the works before the Rancourts lured me with easy money and a kind of sexy job, taking pictures of a historic mansion.''

''But you don't have that anymore.''

''There's a shop on Newbury Street that's after me to do a brochure for them. I did some work for another shop a couple of months ago—haven't done much commercial work, but it could be fun.''

He seemed amused, but not in a patronizing way. ''Keeping your overhead low preserves your options, so you can pick and choose what jobs you take.''

''It hasn't been easy keeping this place here and renting an apartment in the city, but I've managed. Louis—whoever he was—teased me about being a tight-fisted Yankee.''

Turner laughed, but his heart obviously wasn't in it, the stress of the past few days taking their toll on him, too. ''I wonder if the southern act was real. I wonder if anything we knew about him was real.''

''He's dead. There's no question of that.''

''No, there isn't, and murdering him—that was a terrible thing, no matter who he was. I imagine the police will sort out whatever history exists between Louis and Manny Carrera. I've been ordered not to get involved. 'Let the police handle it' is the mantra.''

''I suppose it makes sense.''

''Carine—'' Turner shifted, intense but quiet, even self-conscious, making no excess movements.

"Please be careful until this situation gets resolved. I told you—something's happening under the radar."

She wondered what he might know that Manny didn't—that she and Ty didn't. "Gary, if there's anything I should know—"

"I'm operating more on instinct and experience than on fact. I'm sorry you found Louis on Wednesday." He paused, taking a breath, and she thought she noticed his hands shaking. "I've enjoyed getting to know you, although I don't claim to know you well. If I can swing it and you plan to stay on there yourself, I'd like to get another job in Boston. I'd appreciate seeing you from time to time. Maybe—" He took another breath, swallowing visibly. "Maybe we could have dinner."

She crossed her arms on her chest, not wanting to hurt his feelings or to encourage him. "Gus is bringing over a lasagna out of the freezer." Her hair felt like ice in the cold breeze, and she smiled, the friend, the woman who liked him but wasn't attracted to him. "We can have dinner right now."

"I meant in Boston, with you." He glanced around, the bare trees clicking in a strong gust of wind, then sighed, calmer, his hands no longer shaking. "I doubt you'll be going back to Boston, at least not for any length of time. You belong here, Carine. But you do know that, don't you?"

"I love it here. I don't know about belonging—I like to think I belong with the people I care about. But I don't know anymore." She dropped her arms, the wind penetrating her lightweight sweater. "It hasn't been an easy year."

"No, I suppose not. Well, I'll see you around. The Rancourts won't give me the boot until they're assured they don't need me to keep them safe. Don't let Mrs. Rancourt's affair with Louis fool you, Carine. She and her husband are two of a kind. Whatever works, I suppose."

"Not me. I value fidelity."

He smiled, a rare warmth coming into his eyes. "And that's a surprise? You're good, Carine, and you expect other people to be good."

"I'm not that good."

He kissed her on the cheek. "Take care of yourself."

"Gary—"

"It's all right."

"I hope things turn out well for you."

He blew her a kiss as he jumped down from the deck. "They will."

When she returned to the kitchen, North was there, chair pushed back, his boots on her small table. She noticed his thick thighs, his flat stomach, the soft color of his eyes as he watched her pull out a chair. "Turner's had a hell of a week, too," he said. "Don't feel bad for him because he took a liking to you."

"I'm not. I just—what just happened isn't a typical experience for me."

"What, guys wanting to take you to dinner? That's because you don't see that many guys. You're always hanging off a cliff somewhere. You might not run fast, babe, but I'd hate to have to chase you up a mountain."

"I haven't hung off a cliff, as you put it, in months. It was good getting out in the woods today. Ty—"

But he caught her by the wrist, throwing her off balance just enough that she landed on his lap, and his arms came around her. "I'm sorry," he whispered. "I should never... Carine, I've loved you for a long time. I love you now. I can't help it, but the thought of another man—"

"Ty, don't."

"I didn't pull out of the wedding because I didn't love you."

"I know. That just makes it worse."

But he didn't let her go, didn't stop. "I hoped you didn't love me as much as I loved you and I'd hurt more than you did, or at least that I'd spare you more pain in the end."

She felt tears coming and turned away so he wouldn't see, then slipped her arms around him and lay her head on his shoulder. "It's easy to love you, Ty. It's the rest that isn't so easy. There's too much going on right now for either of us to think straight." She sat up, and he touched a thumb to a tear that had escaped, but she slid to her feet, then nodded toward the back window and managed a smile. "Gus is here with the lasagna."

He pounded on the back door and walked in, grunting at them knowingly. "Thought I might catch you two up to monkey business."

Carine groaned. "Gus, don't you think we're old enough—"

"Old enough, just not smart enough. Age's got nothing to do with it. People do crazy things in their eighties when it comes to romance. Turns you stupid." He set the foil-covered lasagna pan on the stove. "I'm telling you two right now, I'm not going through again what you did back in February. Get your heads screwed on straight before you drag your family and friends through another drama like that."

"You *two?*" Carine gaped at him. "I didn't do anything!"

"You did plenty."

Ty rolled to his feet. "Relax, Carine, he's just irritable because he's sweet on the local egg lady, and he knows it's stupid."

"Stupid—hell, it's insane. She's got hanging beads for doors." He sighed, switching on the oven to Preheat. "Do you know how many different kinds of chickens there are? Ask her. She'll tell you."

Carine went over to him, slipped her arm around his lean waist and hugged him. "I love you, Uncle Gus."

"Yeah, kid, I know. It won't stop me from chopping your head off if you and North here—"

She changed the subject. "Bats and mice moved in while I was out of town. Ty's been installing pest-chasers."

"They're not working. He's still here."

Ty rolled his eyes without comment.

Gus put the lasagna in the oven, then went to the

back door and yelled for Stump. "Come on, boy. Come inside."

"Gus!" Carine charged to the door, hoping to head off Stump before he got into her kitchen. "There's not enough room in here for Stump—"

But the big dog burst into the kitchen, excited from his romp outside, and he slid on the wood floor all the way into the great room, then crashed into the unlit woodstove. Once he regained his balance, he jumped on the couch and panted.

"I'll get a bottle of wine," Ty said into Carine's ear. "You negotiate house rules with Gus and Stump."

"Stump hasn't been here in a while. He's forgotten," Gus said, then snapped his fingers. "Stump! Off the couch, boy!"

Stump ignored him, and he ignored Carine when she ordered him off the furniture. She finally had to get him by the collar and drag him down to the floor. Abruptly calmer, he slunk under the kitchen table and collapsed.

"He likes to push the limits," Gus said as he returned to the kitchen. "Antonia and Nate both called. Antonia said to tell you Hank would check on Val Carrera tonight. Nate was making sure I knew he'd told you to go mountain-climbing today. He's flying up here tomorrow. I think he knows something."

Carine sank against the counter. "Gus, how did we end up with a doctor and a U.S. marshal in the family? Why not three nature photographers?"

He smiled. "Because you all three were pains in

the ass and each had to be the best at something. Come on. Relax. You look like the weight of the world's on your shoulders. It'll be good to have your brother up for a visit. It's been a while. Hey, here's North with the wine.''

"I grabbed a merlot." Ty gave a mock shudder. "I won't tell you what I found down in the cellar, but bats and mice—they're nothing.''

Twenty

Sterling picked up the phone several times to call Carine Winter and Tyler North and try to make up for his abysmal behavior yesterday. He was embarrassed. Whatever had possessed him? But he didn't make the call, and now Jodie was crying nonstop, ripping his heart out because he could, again, after all, feel sympathy for her. He was shocked by how quickly he'd switched from blaming himself for her infidelity to blaming her. Now he didn't know who—what—to blame.

She staggered into the living room, trembling, visibly weak and overwrought. Her face was red and raw from tears, her eyes puffy, her nose running. She joined him in front of the bank of windows that looked out to the mountains. They could see for miles, but it was dark now, the glass reflecting their own images back at them.

Sterling hit the remote control that shut the shades,

their hum the only sound in the sprawling, empty house.

Jodie sank onto the sectional couch. She looked ugly to him, pitiful. He turned away, wondering what in God's name had happened to them. How had he come to this state of affairs? A murdered employee— a man who'd tricked them, lied to them, betrayed them. Sterling wondered, now that he was calmer, if Louis Sanborn or whoever he was had played on Jodie's weaknesses, used her in one of the worst ways possible.

And Turner. That stupid bastard. Asleep at the switch at best.

Manny Carrera wasn't technically an employee, but there was no doubt the police suspected him of murder. Sterling had read that in the faces of the Boston detectives last night when they interviewed him and Jodie about the pictures. Separately, of course.

Pictures of his wife with another man were now in the hands of the police. They'd promised to be discreet, but he and Jodie were a wealthy, prominent couple—the media would eat up the pictures.

"Dear God," he whispered.

Carine and Tyler…two people he admired. They had to hate him now. Hank, Antonia. They'd have nothing to do with him after his behavior, after this horrible scandal.

Once again, Sterling thought miserably, he'd failed to rise to the occasion.

"Manny Carrera did it." Jodie spoke quietly, stoically, as if she didn't have the strength for any more emotion; but her voice was hoarse from crying. "He killed Louis. All these people—Tyler North, Hank Callahan, Carine Winter. They'll ruin our lives in an attempt to prove Carrera's innocence."

Sterling stared at the blind-covered windows. "They want the truth to come out, Jodie. That's all."

She shook her head, adamant. "No, no, Sterling, you're being naive as usual. The truth, maybe, but how much of it? How much of our privacy will be sacrificed in their effort to deny the reality that their friend killed a man in cold blood?"

"Jodie—Jodie, please don't do this. I'm too tired."

"They'll rip our lives open, just because they can't deal with the fact that Manny Carrera murdered a man."

"That's why we have an attorney."

"It won't matter." She cleared her throat, but her voice remained hoarse. "Manny's a pararescueman. A war hero. He doesn't commit murder. If he kills, it's justified."

Sterling shifted to look at her and wondered if it would be cathartic to cry and scream, fall down on the floor and thrash as she had. Then maybe he could come to this place of calm and certainty. "For all we know at this point, it *was* justified. We don't have enough information."

"Don't we?"

She tucked her feet under her, her robe falling open and revealing the swell of her breasts. Were the police, even now, examining his wife's naked breasts under a magnifying glass? How much of her could they see in the pictures?

"Sterling?"

With an effort that was almost physical, he shook off the image of gloating, drooling detectives. Of Louis Sanborn banging his wife. It was a beautiful, old house with a long history. Were they the first to have illicit sex in the library? Louis was the first murder to occur there. That much Sterling knew for certain. It was a blot—a permanent stain that he knew he and Jodie would never overcome even before he'd learned about her affair.

"Sterling!"

With her voice as hoarse as it was, she hadn't managed much more than an annoyed croak. He sighed. "I'm sorry. What were you saying?"

"I'm saying that Manny was at the house on Wednesday. He was in Boston to get you to fire Louis. What if that wasn't good enough? What if he saw—" She hesitated, placing her hand on a polished toe peeking out from her robe, staring at it as if it had her total attention. She took in a breath, then went on. "He could have decided to capitalize on the situation and grabbed Carine's camera, took those pictures, called me—"

"How could he have called you? He was under police surveillance."

Her brow furrowed, but she didn't let go of her theory. "He'd make it look like an innocent call. The guy's not stupid, Sterling. He'd figure out a way."

He sat on a chair at a diagonal from her. "You're jumping way ahead of yourself."

"No, I'm not. What more do the police need? Why don't they arrest him?" She fought back a fresh, sudden wave of tears, sobbing hoarsely at the ceiling. "I can't stand it! I can't!"

"Jodie…dear God…" What if she were losing it, having a nervous breakdown? Sterling couldn't make himself move toward her. "Jodie—please. Pull yourself together. You're not doing either of us any good."

"Louis used me, and now Manny Carrera and his friends are using both of us." Her voice was angry, bitter, belying the tears that spilled down her cheeks. "We're fair game because we have money. Nobody cares what happens to us. We don't mean anything to them."

"Don't say things like that," he said softly.

"Why not? It's true. You know it is. They resent us." She dropped her feet to the floor and jumped up, fire in her eyes as she sniffled and brushed the sleeve of her robe across her tears. "That idiot Turner—how could he not know about Louis? He'll try to shift the blame. Don't let him."

"Jodie, listen to me. It'll take time. It'll take patience and perseverance." He got to his feet and held her by the elbows, feeling how bony she was under her silky robe. "But I promise you, I'll get to the bottom of what's happened. Who failed us. Why. All of it."

All the heat and anger went out of her. She looked

scared, he thought. Old and scared. "Sterling? What are you saying?"

"I think you're right, Jodie. I think we've been used. By everyone."

He saw her in thirty years, a whining old woman, and couldn't stand it anymore. He had to get away from her. He ran downstairs, out through the front door, not bothering with a coat or hat. The night air was cold, clouds blocking the stars, and even in the darkness, he could see fog swirling in valley pockets.

He'd loved this place. If someone had asked him a month ago if he had to give up one, this house or the one on Commonwealth Avenue, which would it be, he wouldn't have hesitated. The Boston house. No question.

But now he wished he'd never stepped foot in Cold Ridge.

He'd never felt so damn inadequate in his life as the night he and Jodie were rescued by Tyler North, Manny Carrera and Hank Callahan, something he'd never acknowledge to anyone. It wasn't their fault. He admired them.

He was fascinated by their training, their incredible range of skills, everything from emergency trauma medicine to combat maneuvers, scuba diving, parachuting, high-altitude mountain climbing—and he couldn't even do a challenging but popular ridge trail in the White Mountains without getting into trouble.

The cold air drove him back inside.

He and Jodie would pack up and leave Cold Ridge in the morning. Once the police made an arrest for

Louis Sanborn's murder, he'd put this place on the market. Then, after a decent interval that gave people time to forget the horror and scandal of what happened in the library, he'd sell the house on Commonwealth Avenue. He and Jodie might even leave Boston altogether. People moved all the time. So did companies.

In the meantime, he'd soak in the Jacuzzi for twenty minutes and go to bed early. Without Jodie. Until he decided otherwise, she was sleeping in the guest room.

Twenty-One

When the phone rang, Val pounced, hoping it was Manny, or Tyler, someone—anyone—with news. It'd been a long damn day, and she could feel herself creeping past the point of rationality, past her capability to resist her impulses to get off her butt and do something. Act. Waiting. Damn, she'd never been good at it.

"Do you want to help your husband?"

She sat up straight on the couch. The voice on the other end was toneless, dispassionate, not one she recognized. "Of course I do. Who is this?"

"The police are about to arrest your husband."

The voice didn't change—there was no emotion, no way, even, of telling for sure whether it was male or female. Male, Val thought. "How do you know?"

"I know. Trust me. The evidence against him is stacking up. The police can't continue to ignore it. He'll be convicted of murder—"

"No, he won't, because he's innocent."

There was a wry laugh. "Ah. True love. I know he is innocent, Mrs. Carrera—Val. But I also know what will happen if you don't act. I can help him."

"How?"

"I can't do it without your help. You must do exactly as I say. Remember, I know more than you do, and I'm on your side. It won't be easy, but you must follow my instructions."

"This is nuts."

"Don't hang up." The intonation didn't change. "I understand your skepticism. You've seen it all, haven't you, Mrs. Carrera? The wife of a career military man, the mother of a sick son—"

"What do you know about my son? You leave him out of it!"

Again, there was no obvious change in the voice of the other end of the phone. "Listen to me. I'm a friend. I can help."

"The police were here today with a search warrant. Maybe they bugged my phone while they were at it. I hope they're out on the street in some van, listening to you, tracing this stupid-ass call—"

"Quit the tough-girl act, Val. Or is it always Valerie?" This time, she thought she sensed a smile, a touch of kindness. "Here is what you need to do. It's simple, but it's not easy. I need you to bring Hank Callahan to Cold Ridge. Tonight."

"What? Are you out of your goddamn mind? He's a senator. I can't just—"

"You can. You have to. Senator Callahan is the key to proving your husband's innocence. He likes you, Val. He believes in your husband. He'll want to help you. Talk him into driving to Cold Ridge with you tonight.''

"Then what?"

"Everything will be fine. Trust me."

She licked her lips, squeezing her eyes shut as if that might help her figure out what to do. "I don't even know where he is. I can't—"

"You have one chance to help your family. Don't squander it. It's time to trust someone. Trust me, Val."

"But who are you?"

"I told you. A friend."

She shook her head. "No way. I know all of Manny's friends."

"No, you don't."

She took a breath, unable to speak. Was it possible this call was legitimate? At this point, was *anything* possible?

"Hank and your husband performed dangerous combat search-and-rescue missions when they were in the military together. Play on Senator Callahan's sympathies, his sense of loyalty."

"Nothing will happen to him? You won't hurt him?"

"Val, I'm a friend. I'm not going to hurt anyone. I just have to be very careful. The forces against your husband are—let's just say the deck is stacked in their favor."

"The Rancourts, you mean?"

Silence.

"The *police?* Do they have the police in their pockets?"

"I'll call back when you're on the road and give you further instructions. You can do it."

"If I don't?"

"Then I can't help you."

Click.

Shaking, sobbing, Val dialed 911, then slammed down the phone. What if the caller wasn't screwing around? What if powerful people wanted Manny to take the fall for murder?

And how could she just call 911? She needed to call the FBI or something.

She tried Manny's cell phone, but didn't let it connect. Then Nate Winter's number and Tyler North's number, neither time letting the call connect.

She dialed Eric on his cell phone. He answered on the third ring, sounding sleepy. "Eric—it's Mom. Did I wake you?"

"Yes."

"Everything all right?"

He coughed. "Yes, ma'am."

"You're sure?"

"I'm sure."

It was a conversation they'd had dozens of times. She'd tiptoe onto his room at night and stand over his bed, check to see that he was breathing. Sometimes he'd wake up, and she'd scare the hell out of him, standing there like some ghoul.

To him, this was probably the same. Reassure his crazy mom, then go back to sleep.

"I'll call you in the morning when you're more awake, okay?"

"Yes, ma'am. Good night."

She hung up and burst into tears, because there was no way—no way—Eric could bear to lose his father.

Fifteen minutes later, a car pulled up in front of her apartment, and Hank Callahan, the junior senator-elect from Massachusetts, got out and walked up to the front of her building.

"Jesus," Val breathed, as if Hank's presence was a gift from God.

Twenty-Two

***

Carine wrapped herself up in a quilt she'd made one summer and sat on the floor in front of her woodstove. By unspoken agreement, she and Ty had decided to spend the night at her cabin. Gus had left, after a long discussion about defunct dairy farms and how, between farming and logging, much of New Hampshire had been denuded of its forests in the nineteenth and early twentieth century, before so much of it turned into national forest. He'd searched his memory for Sanborns he'd known over the years. But Carine could tell he wasn't that taken with her discovery.

In any case, what did it prove? The man who'd called himself Louis Sanborn was dead. Whether or not he was one of the shooters from last fall, it didn't say who his murderer was.

Ty checked the cabin for various critters—bats, mice, chipmunks, squirrels, God knew what else— and emerged from the cellar, picking cobwebs off his shirt. She had a feeling he'd found a snakeskin down there, but he wouldn't tell her.

"Don't protect me," she said. "Just give it to me straight."

"It was a grizzly bear with cubs."

She laughed, but only for a moment. The fire popped behind the screen, startling her, reminding her of how on edge she still was. "When I think back to Wednesday, finding Louis, it's like my senses were heightened," she said. "I can see myself standing in the hall when I realized something was wrong. I can see the blood oozing toward me—his hand was in it. I can hear myself yelling for help, feel the sun on my neck when I ran outside and Manny was there. I can see the pigeons on the mall. Every detail is etched in my mind in a way it wouldn't have been if I'd just gone back and taken pictures, and it was a normal afternoon."

Ty sat on the floor next to her, not taking any of her quilt. He put one knee up, his other leg stretched out, his toes almost against the stove. He'd pulled off his boots, and she noticed he had on the kind of expensive socks Gus sold. "That can happen when you're under a high level of stress."

"Is it that way for you when you're on a mission?"

"I focus on the job I'm there to do."

"But afterward—"

"Afterward there's another job."

"I didn't have a job to do in the library. I wasn't sent in to rescue Louis or treat him, investigate his murder—I'm a photographer. I'm not a doctor like

Antonia, a U.S. marshal like Nate, a military guy like
you. I didn't have any protocol or orders to follow. I
had no professional responsibility.''

"If any of us came unexpectedly upon the murder
of someone we knew, I doubt we'd react all that differently than you did.''

"Me? I screamed my head off and got the hell out
of there.''

He smiled. "You see?''

"I remember the shooting last fall in excruciating
detail, too. I never thought of my job as having inherent dangers, especially compared to what you do
for a living. Dangling out of a helicopter—''

"I don't dangle. I'd be in a shitload of trouble if I
dangled.''

She looked over at him, picturing him decked out
in a flight suit and all his gear, fast-roping out of a
helicopter. "The idea would be for you to get people
out of trouble, not get in any yourself.''

"That would be the idea, yes. But things can go
wrong.''

"Well, I thought I'd be safe in the woods taking a
picture of an owl. And you and Manny and Hank—
you weren't on a mission. You were just there to steal
my food.''

"Share, not steal.''

"My point is that anything can happen, anytime. I
can't live my life worried about it. I do my job, I take
sensible precautions.''

He gave her a skeptical look. "You were out in
the woods alone.''

"I can't take someone with me every time I go out—that's part of *my* job. I suppose that's one of its inherent risks." She frowned at him and lifted a corner of her quilt. "You cold?"

"No, but I like the idea of being under a blanket with you."

She shook her head. "Only if you tell me what's in the cellar. Snake?"

"Dragon."

She let him under her quilt with her, anyway, and scooted next to him, her leg pressed up against his. "Do you suppose Louis Sanborn really was one of the shooters? He was always so nice to me in Boston." She didn't wait for Ty to answer. "I don't get what's going on. Maybe we're off base totally and Manny was on a secret military mission."

Ty kissed the top of her head. "Maybe you're so tired you're getting screwy."

"I can make us tea—"

But she stopped abruptly, seeing his expression. He didn't want tea.

"Suppose instead of tea," he said, "I carry you up to bed."

"You can't. There's just a ladder."

"Bet?"

She had no time even to scramble to her feet before she was over his shoulder, sack-of-grain style. She didn't ask him to put her down. She didn't kick or thrash. Without even the hint of a misstep, he had her up the ladder and into her loft, then flopped her onto her back on her bed.

She laughed and whacked him on the shoulder. "You're insane!"

He wasn't particularly out of breath. "Tell me this isn't better than tea."

She smiled, rising up off the bed to hook her hands around his neck and kiss him, bringing him back down with her. "Much better," she said against his mouth. "What if you'd tripped?"

"I didn't trip."

He settled on top of her, the weight of him firing her senses, burning up her ability to talk. She let her hands drift down his back to his hips, pulling him against her, knowing they wanted the same thing. They'd been dancing around it for two days, trying to be sensible and not repeat their body-clawing, mind-numbing madness at her apartment.

But he resisted her attempt to get on with it before she could think too much. He eased back, slipping one knee between her legs. "Not so fast."

There'd be no crazed lovemaking that she could attribute to stress and the moment in the morning— it would be slow and deliberate, and she might as well give herself up to it.

It was, and she did. At least for a time.

"We should have been making love like this for months now." His voice was a whisper as he lifted her sweater over her head, tugging it off, casting it onto the floor. "Maybe years."

He touched her breasts through her bra, a kind of erotic torture, then unclasped it, not fumbling even the slightest. Because his movements were unhurried, she had time to think, react, even feel a spurt of self-consciousness when she was exposed to him. In so many ways, they weren't the same people they'd been last winter, before he'd knocked on her door. He'd gone back to fight. She'd fled to Boston. The falling in love, the cutting and running, the pain and anger and embarrassment—they'd all had their effect, not just on her. On him, too. She could feel it in his tenderness, in his determination to give her the chance to make sure this was really what she wanted.

She could have dumped him back down the ladder, but she didn't, and she knew he didn't want her to.

It was warm in the loft, the heat of the woodstove rising, and it was dark in the loft, the only light from the fire's glow through the rail. She could see him outlined above her, feel him as his mouth lowered to her, taking first one nipple, then the other. She moaned, but he didn't pick up his pace. Her jeans came next, an even slower torture of hands, tongue and teeth, as if he was oblivious to her mounting urgency. She fought back, tearing at his clothes, and finally got her chance.

But he was ready for whatever tortures she had in mind.

When at last she straddled him and he lifted her hips, lowering her onto him, his hands smoothing up over her stomach and breasts, she gasped as if it was the first time.

Everything changed. She couldn't hold back and saw that he couldn't, either, not any longer. She wanted speed and heat and ferocity, and he responded in kind, his strokes hard, fast, relentless. She ended up on her back, taking all of him she could get, and when she was filled up, spilling over, he came at her all the harder, again and again. Her release washed over her, endless, and her cries seemed to echo across the isolated meadow. She knew she was spinning out of control and didn't care.

But he didn't stop. He was slick with sweat, his heart beating rapidly against her, and when he came, she thought she would die.

Her vision blurred, and a treacherous mix of love and raw need ripped through her.

She'd promised herself never again. And here she was.

Later, Ty slipped down the ladder and tossed another log on the fire. He debated sleeping on the couch, but Carine would take it the wrong way. Or so went his rationalization as he climbed back up the ladder and into bed with her. She had a mountain of quilts and blankets. He thought he'd suffocate. He peeled one off and threw it on the floor with their clothes.

"Gus says we never returned the snowshoes he gave us for a wedding present," she said sleepily.

"Only Gus would give someone snowshoes for a wedding present, and we did return them. He tried to send them back to the manufacturer. He said they were tainted."

She rolled onto her side, pulling the covers up over her breasts. "I don't have to marry you, Ty, but I can't—I can't just be there whenever you decide you want me there.''

''I know.''

''And you—it's not right for you to be there whenever I want you.''

''Right.''

''Ty?''

He smothered her urge to talk with a kiss. It seemed like the right thing to do, and in a minute, she was the one kicking off blankets.

Twenty-Three

Val talked Hank into going out for coffee. They took her car, but she asked him to drive, because she was too damn nervous and barely knew her way around Washington, D.C., on a good day. For all she knew, her caller was around the corner with night-vision goggles, watching her every move. Maybe he was a law enforcement officer. The CIA. Military intelligence. Maybe she was out of her mind.

Plus, she had an unloaded Glock in her glove compartment, and she couldn't reach it if she was the one driving. And she'd seen in the movies—when you kidnap someone, you make them drive.

Except she wasn't kidnapping Hank. Really, she thought, sitting next to him. She was just going to ask him to drive her to Cold Ridge. Or not? Should she pretend she'd never gotten that bizarre call?

He had on a sweater and a lightweight suede coat. It'd be colder in New Hampshire, but he'd be fine. She'd resisted the impulse to drag out her winter coat and instead pulled on a denim jacket. Jeans, turtleneck, sneakers, denim jacket—she looked perfectly normal, even if she felt as if she should be locked up somewhere.

"Where to?" Hank asked, mercifully oblivious to her wild thoughts.

She chewed on her lower lip. Should she tell him about the call? Or just make up some story about why she wanted him to drive her to Cold Ridge?

"Val? What's wrong?"

He was frowning at her, absolutely one of the best-looking men she'd ever met. And kind. So kind. It was dark on her street, not busy. A beautiful Saturday night in Washington. She and Manny should be at the movies. Eric—even if her life was normal, Eric would be in Cold Ridge. *But that's what he wanted.*

Hank pulled out into the street and headed to the main intersection and onto a four-lane highway of strip malls and chain restaurants. He seemed to sense something was up. He was so quiet, just glancing at her occasionally out of the corner of his eye. Val almost started crying. She couldn't believe what she was about to do. "Hank, I can't stand it," she said. "I—I need to see Eric. He didn't sound that great the last time I talked to him. If I leave now, I can be there by morning. But I can't—I'm too out of it to drive."

"Do you want to take the shuttle? I can drive you to the airport."

"No." She shook her head, not knowing what the hell she was doing. Why not just tell Hank everything and let him help her figure it out? He was a retired air force major. He'd performed combat missions. He was a damn *senator*. A Massachusetts Callahan. He knew everyone. He had connections. "Never mind. There's a place where we can have coffee down the street."

"Val, I know this has been hard on you—"

Her cell phone rang, and she jumped, gasping in an exaggerated startled reaction. She answered it, her hands shaking violently. She could feel Hank's narrowed eyes on her.

"You have him?"

Again it was that toneless voice. Her heart thumped painfully in her chest. "What am I supposed to do now?"

"Do you have him?" the caller repeated calmly.

Hank slowed to a crawl on the busy Arlington street. "Val, who are you talking to?"

"I hear him." But there was no note of satisfaction in the caller's tone. "Good work. Bring him to Cold Ridge. It's your only chance, Val. Do you understand me? Your only chance. *Manny's* only chance. Do what you have to do. Just get Senator Callahan to Cold Ridge."

Her hands were like ice, her fingers gripping the phone as if it might suddenly fly itself out the window. She moaned in despair and frustration. "Don't you get it? I can't drive all the way to New England with a senator!"

Hank slammed on the brake and snatched the phone out of her hand. "Who the hell is this?" He listened a moment, then handed the phone back to her. "Get rid of him. Understood?"

She nodded, although she was past understanding anything.

"Cute trick," the caller said. "I told him I'd only talk to you. Val, be strong. I'm trying to help. The only way I can help is if you bring Hank Callahan to Cold Ridge tonight."

"But—"

"I know it sounds scary and strange." This time, she thought she sensed an undercurrent of friendliness, caring, in the otherwise unchanged voice. "But once I can reveal what I know, once you have the whole picture—both you and the senator will thank me. In the meantime, you *must* follow my instructions to the letter."

"If I don't?"

"Then you'll bear the responsibility for whatever happens. Good or bad. I'm being honest with you. I have the means to help your husband, but only if you're willing to do your part." A pause, calculated, she thought, to further unnerve her. "Mrs. Carrera, please don't mistake me. Some very bad people are after your husband."

"It's something like ten hours to Cold Ridge." She avoided looking at Hank next to her, felt her stomach muscles twist, aching, acid rising up in her throat. "We can take the shuttle and be there in a couple of hours."

But the caller didn't even hesitate. "You know that won't work. Too many air marshals. Drive all night.

It'll be okay. Just do as I say. I'll call back when you're farther north and tell you where to bring the senator.''

"What if I call the police the second I hang up? What if Hank does?''

"If either of you contacts the police—if you tell anyone—all bets are off, and you'll have to live with the consequences.''

He hung up, and Val gulped for air, not thinking as she yanked open the glove compartment and fumbled for her Glock. She pulled it out and pointed it at Hank, who just stared at her, his jaw set, his teeth clenched. He wouldn't know it was unloaded. "Val, for Christ's sake.''

"Please." She didn't know what the hell she was doing. "We can't call the police. Something bad'll happen, and I couldn't live with myself—just drive to Cold Ridge. It's a long way. I'll—I'll figure out something in the meantime.''

Hank was steely-eyed, outwardly calm. "Your hand's shaking. Mind not pointing that thing at me?''

She didn't lower the gun. She'd meant to check out Washington D.C. gun laws but hadn't gotten around to it. She was fairly certain that handguns, concealed or otherwise, were illegal in the nation's capital. But, kidnapping a U.S. senator was illegal everywhere.

"Hank—please, just do as I ask and let me *think*. I need you to drive us to New Hampshire tonight. You and me.''

"I can't do that, Val. I have a wife. I have a job to do.''

She pretended not to hear him. "Take I-95. It's an awful road, but it'll be the fastest."

"Why should I do as you say? What was that call all about? Val—"

"Goddamn it, Hank, my head's spinning. Give me a minute, okay? And get back on the road. Don't fuck with me right now. You know I can shoot."

"You won't shoot me."

"Not dead, but I can make you bleed."

He glanced at her. "And I can feed you that damn gun."

"You won't." She managed a faltering smile, even as she fought back tears. "You know I'm desperate. I'm—I'm trying to buy us some time. I don't know if this guy's on the level. If he is, great, at least he's on our side. If he's not—well, then we're screwed, anyway."

"Val, trust me. Talk to me." His voice was earnest, serious, and she remembered Manny telling her Hank Callahan was one of the coolest pilots under fire he'd ever seen. "Tell me what's going on. I can help."

"Just drive."

"Let me call the police."

"No. I can't risk it." Her head was throbbing, as if she had cobwebs growing in her skull, multiplying, squeezing her brain, so that she couldn't think. "Manny's incommunicado. Tyler's already in Cold Ridge. Eric—I talked to him a little while ago. He's in his dorm, asleep. I'm out of the loop. If I do something wrong—I couldn't live with myself."

"You're doing something wrong now."

"He—at least I think it's a he. Maybe not. Anyway, I'll get another call with more instructions when we're closer to Cold Ridge. Jesus, that's a long time."

"You're goddamn right it is."

"But you'll do it, won't you?"

Hank nodded tightly, turning onto the interstate. Traffic was heavy, endless rows of headlights and brake lights, the whoosh of passing cars and trucks, all of it adding to her confusion and anxiety. He had a thousand options, but Val suspected he wanted to buy himself some time to think, too. And he'd want to find out what was going on in Cold Ridge as much as she did.

He sighed at her with his first hint of real irritation. "Just put the fucking Glock away, will you?"

"The f-word, Hank?" She smiled faintly, not letting go of her gun. "If your constituents could hear you now."

Twenty-Four

Ty reached for the phone when it rang and answered it before he thought about where he was—in Carine's loft bed. But it was Antonia, as collected as ever despite the obvious note of concern in her voice. "Did I wake you?" she asked. "I called your place first. I thought you and Carine were staying there—never mind. Hank got your message and went over to Val's over two hours ago."

"What time is it now?"

"Almost midnight. He's not back, and I haven't heard from him."

Carine stirred, and Ty sat up. He had the inside of the bed, next to the slanted ceiling. "Did you call over there?"

"No answer. I'm trying not to overreact. Hank's cell isn't on, and I don't have Val's number." She sighed, her calm faltering. "Tyler, what the hell's going on? I know Val must be scared to death about Manny's situation. Have you talked to her?"

"Not tonight. Earlier today. The police were at her door—"

"We heard about that. They had a search warrant. Well, that's enough to frighten anyone. I've got the media here—they showed up not long after Hank left for Val's. They've made the connection between him and Manny. I think they're gone now."

Carine touched Ty's arm, and he gave her a reassuring nod, although he felt a twinge of uneasiness. Val Carrera was volatile on a good day—funny as hell when she wasn't depressed, but impulsive. And no one who knew her wanted to piss her off. "Antonia, is there anything I can do?"

"I don't know. I don't give a damn about the media, but—Hank—" She gulped in a breath, revealing some of the stress she was accustomed to keeping so carefully hidden. "He's sympathetic to Val's situation."

"We're all sympathetic, but it's late."

"I could go down to her apartment."

"Not alone."

Carine, impatient, motioned for the phone, and North handed it to her. "Antonia? What's up?" She listened a moment, then shook her head. "No, you listen to me for a change. Give Hank thirty minutes. If he doesn't get in touch with you, you don't go down to Val's. You sound the damn alarm."

Antonia called back twenty minutes later. Carine was in the kitchen making tea, debating whether or not to call Gus and get him up. Ty talked her out of it. He simply had to suggest she put on more water for tea—it put the same image in her head that he had, Gus and Stump in her cabin at one o'clock in the morning.

He could hear the relief in Antonia's voice. "Hank called. He and Val are on their way to Cold Ridge."

"They're driving up here tonight?"

"Val wants to see Eric. Hank says she's very stressed out and hanging by threads, and you know how he is. He's loyal, and he's a good guy. He also said Val's worried about Eric—you know that's all it'd take. Hank's got a soft spot where children are concerned."

Ty knew. Ten years ago, Hank had lost his first wife and three-year-old daughter in a car accident while he was serving overseas. He'd dedicated himself to his work and public service, but it had taken Antonia Winter to get him to let himself take the risk of falling in love again.

"How'd he sound?" Ty asked.

"I don't know—he's very good at concealing what he's really feeling. It's such a stressful situation." She sighed, breaking off. "I'm coming up there. I'll take the first plane I can out of here in the morning."

The kettle whistled, and Carine, frowning at him, grabbed a pot holder and filled her chipped teapot with the hot water. But she didn't snatch the phone out of his hand, and he said, "Nate's coming tomorrow, too. Maybe you two can meet up at the airport."

"That'd be good. I don't want to be a worrywart, but it's just—" Antonia faltered, a rarity for her.

"Never mind. You have enough on your plate without fretting about me. Carine? You're keeping your promise?"

He smiled. "I don't know about that."

"Liar. You know damned well what you've been up to. So do I. I *am* a doctor—and I know you two."

"Goodbye, Antonia. Safe flight tomorrow."

He hung up. Carine unwrapped tea bags and dropped them in the hot water, their tags hanging over the sides of the teapot. Normal tea bags. But Ty could see the tension in the way she held herself. They'd pulled on their clothes, but there was no pretending what happened in the loft hadn't happened. She knew it had, and she wasn't sure she approved.

Well, who would?

But he pushed the thought out of his mind and dialed Manny's cell phone, and when he got his friend's voice mail—again—he left a pointed message. "You have Val's cell phone number? Call her. She's up to something."

Twenty-Five

━━━━∞∞∞━━━━

With as much adrenaline as she had pumping through her, Val didn't get sleepy on the long drive north. Hank wasn't dropping off, either. He sat rigidly as he drove, as if he were on some secret military mission. She'd let him call Antonia and reassure her, although it didn't sound like she was thrilled when he told her he was on his way to Cold Ridge.

After he'd hung up with his new wife, he glared at her. "Get this straight, Val. I'm not driving you to Cold Ridge because you've got your goddamn gun. I'm driving you because I know you're frightened and feel you're out of options. So, let's just get there."

The hours ticked by. It was a dark, cloudy night, but there was no rain. Traffic eased, and when they crossed the border into New Hampshire and the sun came up, she wondered if she'd imagined the calls. Wouldn't that be nice? She'd rather be delusional than have to face the caller again.

The yellow and orange leaves had vanished, in

their place, bare limbs and patches of oaks with brown-and-burgundy leaves. The air was colder. She could feel it even with the heat on in the car. The sun and the blue sky were deceptive. She looked up at the looming mountains, stark against the clear sky, and saw that some of the highest peaks had snow.

They were off the interstate now, almost to Cold Ridge.

She sighed at Hank, trying to distract herself. "Do you ever wish you'd stayed in for thirty instead of retiring?"

He glanced over at her. "Right now I do."

She ignored his tight undertone. "Manny had no business getting out. Don't you think he'd make a great PJ instructor? He's like this old warhorse. He's done all these different kinds of missions. He's seen it all. I don't want him back in combat, but he could be an instructor."

"Val," Hank interrupted softly, "let me help you."

She stared down at the Glock in her lap. "I don't know what to do."

"Talk to me."

Her fatigue was eating away at her reserves. They'd had no food, no water since hitting the road. They'd had to stop for gas, but Val had done the pumping, her unloaded Glock tucked in the waistband of her jeans. They'd managed a bathroom run, and that was really when she'd realized Hank wasn't going to try to escape—he was playing along with her, because he was her friend, he knew her, he knew she was scared and desperate and stupid.

He was so damned caring. Nobody could ever fault Hank Callahan for not caring.

She sank her forehead into her hands and started to sob.

"Val…what would Manny want you to do?" Hank's voice was gentle, breaking through her fog of desperation, her sobs. "He loves you. I've never seen a man love a woman as much as he does you. Twenty years from now, if Antonia and I have what you two have—"

"Don't—Hank, please don't."

"He'd want you to trust me."

She lifted her head, sniffling. "He'd want me to jump out of this car so you could run me over."

She could feel Hank's smile. "Well, that, too."

"Oh, shit." She threw back her head and swore at the top of her lungs, then looked over at him. "I could have been an astronaut, you know."

"Val…"

She told him everything. What was in Manny's computer files, about the police search warrant—and about her caller. Hank listened without interruption. That was another of his virtues. He listened to people. Not Manny, she thought. Mostly, Manny liked to be listened to.

"I'm sorry," she said. "I'm so sorry."

Hank stayed focused on the narrow, winding road. "We're in Cold Ridge now. It's where we both need to be, don't you think?"

She nodded. "When you say it, it sounds sensible."

He reached over and wiped a tear off the end of her nose. "Wait'll Manny sees you. What a mess."

"He didn't kill that guy."

"I know."

Her phone rang, and she managed to answer it without dropping the gun. "Yes?"

"Where are you?" the toneless voice asked.

"I'm not saying until you tell me who you are."

The caller paused, then gave a sad, long-suffering sigh. "You've told Senator Callahan, haven't you? He's calling the shots. I thought it might come to this. Well, allow me to persuade you in another way."

"Look, if you really are a friend—"

"You called your son last night."

"What?" She couldn't grasp what he was saying, couldn't make the leap. "What about my son? How did you know I called him?"

"I was with him. You called him on his cell phone. You assumed he was in his dorm room—"

"No!"

"I made him take the phone with him, Mrs. Carrera. I have your son."

Hank didn't say a word or try to take the phone from her; he just pulled over to the side of the road and waited.

A numbness crept up her neck and into her cheeks. "What—what do you want me to do?"

"Mom?" It was Eric, coughing, scared. "Mom, he made me pretend I was asleep—"

"Where are you?"

But the caller had grabbed the phone away. "Feisty little kid, for an asthmatic." There was no friendliness in the toneless voice now. "He has his rescue inhaler and his EpiPen, but it's November in the mountains. Open the window. Feel the air. He won't last long."

"Don't hurt my son. *Please.*"

"If you cooperate, he'll have a chance. If anything happens to me, I promise you, Mrs. Carrera—Val— no one will find your son in time."

She gulped in a breath. "We're on the main road into the village. What do you want me to do?"

"Turn onto the notch road. Hank knows it. There are two scenic pullovers. The first one is at a lake. Don't take that one. The second one—the one you want—is at a picnic area. A couple of picnic tables, a lot of rocks. Pull in and wait for me. I'll find you."

"Eric—"

"Any cops, any curveball at all, your kid is dead. It's cold, he's sick. But I don't want him. Do you understand?"

"No, I—"

"I want the senator in exchange for your son."

That was all. He was gone. The phone was dead in her hand.

She kept gulping in air, not exhaling.

"Val." It was Hank, his voice gentle, trying to penetrate her shock. "Val, breathe out, sweetheart."

"He's got Eric." She clawed at Hank's arm. "Oh, my God!"

"What does he want?"

She didn't want to tell him. Kids were Hank's weakness. Everyone knew it. If he could exchange himself for Eric, even die in his place, Hank Callahan, senator-elect from Massachusetts, would do it without hesitation.

"Val?"

She clenched his arm, and she could see it in his eyes. He knew.

Twenty-Six

Carine had dozed on the couch in front of the fire, but she doubted Ty had slept at all. They kept expecting Hank or Val to call or roll in the driveway. It'd been hours since they'd set off—they had to be getting close to Cold Ridge. But their cell phones and phone lines remained quiet.

And not a word from Manny Carrera.

They walked back to his house, where Ty made coffee and they tried to eat a couple of pieces of toast. But Carine could see the waiting was getting to him as much as it was to her. She stared out the window at the bleak morning, fog and mist settling on everything. "If Val wants to see Eric, she'll probably go straight to the school—"

"Grab your coat."

The campus of the Mount Chester School for Boys was quiet so early on a Sunday morning, just a couple of intrepid boys out on the track. Ty parked in front of Eric's dorm, another ivy-covered brick building.

He and Carine were greeted at the front door by the young couple who served as house parents. Brendan and Penny O'Neill—Carine had met them before.

Brendan, a bearded man in his late twenties, led them down a carpeted hall to Eric's first-floor room, his door covered in posters. "We saw him last night," Brendan said. "He seemed preoccupied but otherwise all right. Is there any news about his father?"

Ty shook his head and rapped on Eric's door, but he spotted a note folded and tacked to a *Lord of the Rings* poster. He pulled it off, opening it as Carine and Brendan O'Neill read over his shoulder.

> To whom it may concern:
> I have gone on a hike in the mountains. Don't worry about me. I have everything I need. My dad taught me to climb. I have to do this on my own.
>
> Sincerely,
> Eric Carrera

Brendan swore under his breath, but Ty was tight-lipped, rigid in his control. The note oozed all the angst of an unappreciated fourteen-year-old boy with too much on his mind, but it was short on specifics, which, given Eric's reaction to the seniors who'd had to be rescued the other day, surprised Carine. He'd printed the note, obviously hastily, but had signed his name in cursive.

Using his pass key, Brendan unlocked Eric's door and pushed it open. It was a typical dorm room, with a neatly made bed, a chest of drawers, a desk, a chair and a closet—and more posters, the emphasis on *Lord of the Rings*. The room wasn't tidy, but it wasn't a pigsty, either.

"We didn't see him leave," Brendan said, his distress evident. "I can't even imagine where he's gone, what he did for transportation. Damn it! At least it's good weather today, but it's windy up high, and the temperature must be below freezing. If he's not prepared…" He didn't finish.

Ty quickly checked Eric's desk, stacked with binders and textbooks. "Does he keep his meds here?" he asked.

O'Neill shook his head. "The infirmary dispenses all medications. Eric only carries his EpiPen and rescue inhaler. He *must* have those with him—he wouldn't go anywhere without them. He knows that."

"Where's the infirmary?" Ty asked. "Eric takes four different medications on a daily basis. We need to know when he had his last doses."

"It's down the hall, but I can call." Brendan went back out into the hall and grabbed a wall phone, dialing numbers, his hand visibly shaking. He spoke to someone on the other end—obviously a nurse—then hung up. "He was in after dinner yesterday for his second dose of Serevent, a long-acting inhaler, and his dose of Singulair—it's an anti-inflammatory. He's supposed to take an allergy medication and a nasal steroid spray in the morning, but he hasn't been in. I don't—honestly I don't know what he could be thinking."

Ty opened Eric's closet, squatting down. "His hiking boots are here. I don't know if he had a second pair, but I doubt it." He looked up as he stood up straight. "We need to find this boy."

"I'm calling the headmaster," Brendan said shakily, dialing more numbers.

Carine touched Ty's arm as he joined her out in the hall. "We should call Gus and get the ball rolling on a rescue, start checking trails, get the word out—notify the park ranger, the shelters. If Eric shows up in the meantime, great."

"You see what it's like out there. It'll take all his strength to manage the climb in this cold and wind. If he gets above three thousand feet without hiking boots, good clothing, food, he could be in real trouble, fast. Cold and anxiety aren't a good mix for anyone, never mind an asthmatic kid hiking solo."

"Maybe he went with a friend. He must be more upset about his father than any one of us realized." Carine sighed. "Let's hope the wind and cold are to his advantage and they at least deter him from hiking alone."

Penny O'Neill drifted down the hall, obviously sensing there was a problem, but she maintained her composure while Carine quickly explained what was going on. Penny shook her head, firm in her conviction. "I can't believe—it's just not like Eric to go off on his own this way."

"Call the police," Ty said, handing the stricken couple the boy's note. "I don't think Eric did go off on his own."

* * *

They found Gus in his backyard hollering for Stump. "I heard," he said. "The school's not wasting any time. The New Hampshire Department of Fish and Game and the National Park Service are coordinating with the police on an organized search. I'll check the local trails."

But as he opened the passenger door on his truck and Stump roared in, Carine noticed something different in her uncle's manner. "Gus? What is it?"

"I shouldn't tell you—" He slammed the door shut and raked a hand through his brittle hair. He had on his hiking clothes, thoroughly ratty but with years of wear left in them. "I was going to wait and tell Nate when he gets here. It's just a crazy theory. Like you and the Sanborn Dairy."

Ty settled back against the hood of his own truck, but nothing in his manner was easy or calm. "Spit it out, Gus."

"You know that old bastard, Bobby Poulet?"

"Yeah." Ty nodded. "Bobby Chicken, we used to call him."

"Christ, no wonder he's a crank. He's a survivalist these days. He has a place up past the woods where Carine got shot at last fall. I warned her to stay away from him when she went up there."

"I remember," she said. "The police interviewed him."

"Within a day or two after the shooting, right. He's got guns out the yin-yang, but he's harmless. He heard the shots—he said he figured it was some guy exercising his God-given right to bear arms." Gus spoke without inflection, just saying what he had to say. "He didn't see anything. That was the end of it, as far as the police were concerned. But this past spring, he showed up at the shop on his annual trip to town. Gave me shit about the merchandise."

Ty shifted, restless. "Gus, come on—"

"I'm getting to the point. While he was bitching and moaning, Bobby told me about a guy he'd helped out back in late January, early February. He was lost in the woods. He was frostbitten, and he had this skin infection, like it was rotting off. Bobby gave him first aid supplies and something hot to drink and offered to take him to a doctor, which tells you how bad a shape this guy was in. Bobby doesn't offer anybody anything. The guy's lucky he wasn't run off with a shotgun."

Carine grabbed her uncle's arm in shock. "Did Bobby think this man was going to lose a couple of fingers?"

"He was sure of it. He said they practically fell off in his soup bowl."

"Jesus Christ," Ty breathed.

"I tried to get him to talk to the police," Gus went on, "but he didn't want to. He doesn't trust the police. He's pretty much a paranoid old fart."

"Did you tell the police yourself?" Carine asked.

He nodded. "By then, there wasn't much to be done. The guy was long gone. I hadn't thought about the story in ages, until I saw that guy at your cabin last night. I didn't get a good look at him—" He shook off whatever he planned to say next. "Oh, screw it. A lot of people have missing fingers."

Carine turned up the collar of her coat, the cold wind penetrating her light layers of clothing. "You never mentioned Bobby's story to me."

His eyes held hers for a moment. "It was March. You'd just had your heart broken. I didn't want to remind you of the shooting. That's when you went haywire and fell for North." Gus looked tired all of a sudden, as if he'd missed something important and now everyone was paying the consequences. "I talked to the police this morning and reminded them about Bobby's guy, told them about Turner. They went up to the Rancourts. I guess they're leaving for Boston—they're probably gone by now. Turner'd already left. The cop I talked to figured they'd get in touch with the Boston police. I don't know. It could all be bullshit."

Ty ripped open his truck door. "I'm going back to the house. I'll check the ridge trail for any signs of Eric and try Manny again. Carine—maybe you should go with Gus."

"Sure," she said quietly. "But, Gus, if I'm going with you, the dog stays. There's just not enough room."

"All right, all right." He seemed relieved to be back in action, not talking about a crazy survivalist with a tale of a freezing man with rotting fingers. He opened up his truck door. "Come on, Stump. Back inside."

Carine stood next to Ty, could almost feel his concentration. She realized she was an unnecessary distraction for him, and that was why he was sending her off with her uncle. "We can check the trail up by the Rancourt house," she told him. "The Rancourts used it when they got into trouble last year and you and Manny rescued them—Eric'll know that."

"And Hank." Ty said, climbing in the behind wheel. "He was here that weekend. Now he's missing in action, too. So's Val Carrera."

"Everyone in the whole goddamn state'll be on it before too long," Gus said, taking Stump back up the walk to the house. But he sighed, giving North an encouraging look. "We'll find them."

Carine glanced up at the blue, cloudless sky and could almost feel the high winds and cold of past hikes. "We don't have a lot of time."

Twenty-Seven

~~~

Sterling stood in the doorway of the warming hut and let his eyes adjust to the poor light inside, in case he was wrong. The tension and stress of the past few days could have affected his vision—or his mind, making him see what wasn't there. A fire in the pot-bellied stove. A boy tied up in the far corner by the back door. Gary Turner standing in the middle of the hut, his white hair stark against the dark wood walls.

"The local police were just here," Sterling said, his voice sounding almost disembodied. "I told them you'd left."

Turner shrugged, matter-of-fact. "I parked my car out of sight."

Sterling squinted at the back of the hut. The boy wasn't gagged, but he was pale, his breathing labored—the Carrera boy? *Dear God.* "What's going on here? Turner? Who are you?"

"Have you ever wanted something so much you'd do anything?" He withdrew his nine-millimeter pistol from his belt holster, without any obvious change in his calm manner. "Kidnap an innocent boy? Kill your best friend? Risk everything?"

The bite of fear Sterling felt was unlike anything he'd ever experienced. It made him cold. It made him pretend he couldn't see the boy suffering, terrified, in the corner. "Jodie and I are leaving as soon as we get the car packed. I told the police we were on our way. They—" He hesitated, but didn't stop himself from finishing his thought. "They have no reason to come back up here."

But Turner didn't seem to hear him. He fingered the tip of his gun, but his attention was squarely on Sterling. "You were born with a silver spoon in your mouth. What would you know? You've had money and good health all your life. A beautiful wife, even if she does fuck around."

"I should get back to the house—"

"You've never wanted or needed anything, except to prove yourself to a few air force guys who don't think twice about you."

Sterling backed up a step. "I'm sorry things didn't work out."

Turner lifted his colorless eyes. "You pretend it's your wife who doesn't connect with other people, but it's you, Rancourt. It's all about you. Always. What if someone killed her? What would you do?" He continued to speak in that rational, detached manner. "Would you hunt whoever did it to the ends of the earth? Would you make them pay?"

"Revenge—" Sterling coughed, his throat was so

tight that his voice sounded strangled. "Revenge is a complicated thing."

"No, it's not. It's simple. You put it all on the table. You go against the odds. You accept that you'll probably have to die. You accept that you might even have to sacrifice your own moral code."

"I'm not—Gary, I'm not a part of this."

Turner jumped forward, his nine-millimeter pistol at Sterling's throat before he could draw his next breath. "One word and the kid dies for sure. Do you understand? One fucking word to anyone."

"Yes. Yes, I understand."

"Right now it's not my intention to hurt him. He's just a kid. But I will if you talk. Just so you'll have to live with what you caused."

"Nothing. Not a word. Promise."

"Go back to the house. Get your slut wife. It wasn't just the one time in the library with Louis. Ask her. Ask her on the way out of here who he really was." He tucked the gun back into his holster and smiled cockily. "She knows."

Sterling wasn't breathing. Through the dim light, he could see the boy, obviously weak and in pain, staggering to his feet. He was stooped over, but he managed to run for the back door. If he could just incapacitate Turner, Sterling thought—but how? The man had a pistol.

He did nothing, and Turner swooped across the small hut and grabbed the boy around the middle, dumping him onto the blanket on the floor. "You little fuck. I told you to stay put."

The boy erupted into a spasm of coughing, a wet, sloppy sound that turned Sterling's stomach. He'd watched the scene unfold in horror. But there was nothing he could do to help the boy—he had to keep his mouth shut and get himself and Jodie out of there.

Sterling ran down the dirt track to the house, the wind swooping up the hills and blowing hard. Jodie had the back of the SUV open, loading in one of her endless bags. Sterling pushed her aside and shut the tailgate. "Whatever you have packed will have to do. We're leaving. Now."

"What's going on? Who were you talking to up—"

"Don't speak to me. Not now."

He grabbed her by one shoulder and opened the passenger door, pushing her. She stumbled, then quickly got the message and climbed up into the seat. Her lower lip trembled in fear.

Sterling got into the driver's seat, surprising himself that he wasn't shaking. "Be glad I'm even taking you with me," he said. "Just keep your lying mouth shut and come with me."

A car—not Turner's car but an old Audi they kept in New Hampshire—lurched down from the hut. Sterling didn't look to see if the boy was in there with him. How would he know, anyway? Turner could have him stuffed in the trunk.

It was so clear and perfect, it was as if they were in the middle of a postcard, the mountains cascading all around them, a darker blue against the sky.

The Audi quickly disappeared.

"Gary," Jodie said hoarsely. "He's a part of it, isn't he?"

Sterling glared at her. "A part of *what,* Jodie? Hmm? What?"

"Nothing." She was ashen, her voice small. "I don't know what I'm saying. You're right—let's get out of here."

Twenty-Eight

It wasn't much of a picnic area. Val edged forward in her seat, peering out at the rocks, the birch trees and evergreens, the two unpainted picnic tables in a small clearing. A sign said there were no facilities, meaning, she assumed, no rest rooms. No trash cans, either. She didn't know why she noticed such details, except it gave her something to do, something to focus on. She didn't want to think.

The mountains, every inch of them visible on such a clear day, rose up on both sides of the road—a notch, Hank had told her, was basically a pass in the mountains. Yet even with the perfect visibility, she felt claustrophobic, enveloped by the mountains, hemmed in. Probably, she thought, she wouldn't have made a good astronaut, after all.

She was done. Spent. *I'm in over my head...Eric...*

She handed Hank the phone. "Call the police." Even to herself, she sounded exhausted, past the point of coherency, never mind logic. "I'm just playing into this bastard's hands."

He glanced at the readout. "There's no service here. I remember last fall we had trouble getting through—Carine and Ty stopped at a lake down the road."

"That's why the bastard picked this spot. In case I changed my mind, I wouldn't be able to call for help." She shoved the Glock at him. "Here, take it. You make the decisions. It's not loaded, but I think there's a clip in the glove compartment."

He shook his head. "You hang on to it." He pushed her hand back with the gun, then thrust the phone at her. "I'll wait here. You get to a house or a place where you can call."

"No! Hank, he wants *you*."

"Exactly. Val—"

"You can't, Hank. This guy's not going to keep his word."

But Hank was determined—and very clear about his intentions. "I have to try to make the exchange. If there's a chance he'll let Eric go and take me in his place, I have to at least give it a shot. If nothing else, perhaps I can buy the authorities more time."

Val noticed how quiet it was around her. "I wish he wanted me. I can't—Hank, I can't let you do this."

"If you'd go, then let me go."

"He's not your son."

"Does it matter? He's an innocent fourteen-year-old boy who's caught up in something not of his own making.'' He brushed her cheek gently with the back of his hand. ''Trust me, Val.''

It was as if she was on a treetop, looking down at herself, a small, dark-eyed, stupid-assed woman who'd made too many mistakes in the past twenty-four hours. The past year.

She pushed open her door and climbed out, composed, as if she'd disassociated herself from her fear. ''I'll call the police as soon as I can,'' she said. ''Just stall for time, okay? Oh, listen to me, like I'm the combat veteran.''

But something had diverted Hank's attention, and he leaned forward, looking out the windshield, then lunged across the seat at her. ''Val—behind you! Get down!''

She dove onto the front seat, but she felt a burning pain in her left side even as she heard the shot. Hank reached for the Glock, but a white-haired man had his door open, a gun to Hank's head. ''On your feet, Senator. My car's parked on the other side of the rocks. If you want the boy to live, you will do as I say.''

Val could hear Hank's voice. ''Understood.''

''I won't have to kill him. Time and the elements will. He's a very sick kid.''

''Eric...'' Val tried to yell but nothing came out. She tried again. ''Don't hurt—''

But she didn't know if she'd made a sound. She held her side, remembering that Manny had told her to apply pressure to a wound—and it hurt. God, it hurt. She could feel her own blood warm on her hands. She was collapsed face first on the car seat, could hear Hank getting out of the car. She couldn't think, couldn't really see.

"Val—"

Hank's voice. She held her side, unable to move but knowing she couldn't just pass out and die out here in the cold. Not yet.

The man with the white hair snorted. "Val Carrera is dead."

Twenty-Nine

A fourteen-year-old boy hiking alone would draw the attention of any alert hiker, North knew, but when he checked the main trailhead above the meadow, he didn't see signs of *any* hikers, never mind Eric Carrera. It was the off season, and conditions weren't great on the ridge. There weren't going to be many hikers out today.

North, however, had his doubts about Eric's note and didn't believe the boy was on an illicit hike to prove himself, to his father or anyone else.

He headed back to his place. First on tap was to try to reach Manny again, then call Antonia for any word from Hank and Val. And the police. Ty wanted to touch base with the local police *and* the Boston police.

But pulling into the driveway ahead of him was Carine's ancient Subaru sedan, which he'd last seen parked on her street in Cambridge. Ty rolled to a stop behind it and got out.

Manny Carrera unfolded himself from within the small car's confines and climbed out. "What a rattle-trap. Doesn't she know cars don't run forever?" He rolled his big shoulders, stretching, but his eyes were serious when he focused on North. "I got your message about Val and slipped out of town. I'm not under arrest. I can go where I want."

"Manny, this isn't a good idea."

"If it was your wife, what would you do? I talked to Antonia about an hour ago. She said Val and Hank are on their way up here. I figured we could head them off at the pass, so to speak. I tried reaching you but didn't get through up here in the boonies."

"I was at the school."

Manny frowned. "The school?"

Ty's head pounded. "You don't—shit, you don't know. Manny, Eric's missing."

His friend had no visible reaction as he absorbed the news. "Talk to me, North."

"He left a note on his door. It sounds like bullshit to me—he says he's gone hiking. But he didn't stop at the school infirmary to take his morning meds. He could have forgotten—"

"He didn't forget."

"Or not bothered. He's upset. It's possible he just wants to prove himself."

"He's got nothing to prove."

"I know that. The police and forest rangers are on it. Conditions are tough up on the ridge—if his note's legit, he could have changed his mind about a hike and stopped at a coffee shop and had breakfast. Or maybe he went with Val, and she made him write the note for reasons we don't understand.''

Manny thought a moment. He had on a black wool jacket, a lightweight wool sweater, jeans and cowboy boots. ''Where are the Rancourts?''

''On their way to Boston. And Gary Turner's left, too. Supposedly. I don't know what's relevant anymore, but Gus—ah, hell, this sounds screwy.'' Ty looked up toward the ridge, which looked innocuous from his elevation. But he knew the winds would be bad above fifteen hundred feet, and fierce above the treeline. ''Remember the survivalist from last fall? The police questioned him.''

One corner of Manny's mouth twitched. ''The chicken guy.''

''Bobby Poulet. A few months after Carine got shot at, a man surfaced at Bobby's place with frostbite and a skin infection—Bobby said it looked like he was going to lose a couple fingers. Gary Turner's missing a couple of fingers.''

''Christ. You people up here.'' Manny motioned for North, obviously ready to take action. ''Come on. In the car. Let's go see what the story is at the Rancourts'. Shit's hitting the fan at the school because they lost my kid?''

''Major league.''

''Good. He's got his EpiPen, his rescue inhaler?''

Ty nodded. ''Looks like it.''

''One bright spot. All right. If the Rancourts are there, I torture them for information. They've been holding back. If they're not there, I break in and see what's what.''

''Manny. The police—''

''You can stay here.''

North didn't hesitate. ''We'll take my truck.''

''Now you're talking.'' He gave Carine's rusting car a disparaging look. ''I feel like Fred Flinstone driving this goddamn thing.''

Manny's wry humor in a tight situation was legendary, but Ty knew not to underestimate his friend's focus. At this moment, his sole mission was getting to his wife and son. Nothing else mattered—and that, North thought, was where he came in. He couldn't let Manny cross the line. It'd never happened before, but the stakes had never been this personal.

''Did you slip out from under police surveillance?''

''They know I'm not their man.''

Which didn't really answer Ty's question. He got in behind the wheel. Manny didn't argue. ''You know the terrain.'' He gave a mock shiver. ''Hell, it's cold up here. I always forget.''

''Winds above the treeline—''

''Yeah. I know. Close to hurricane force. I listened to the weather station on my way up.''

Ty pulled out onto the main road. ''Your turn, Carrera. Talk to me.''

It seemed to give Manny something to do while they drove. ''Louis Sanborn's real name is Tony Louis Apolonario. Apparently his great-grandfather—''

''Was named Sanborn and owned a local dairy?''

"You figured it out?"

"Carine."

Manny smiled slightly. "She's got bird-dog potential, don't you think? I didn't find out until it was too late. The police have everything I do, by the way. Looks like Louis/Tony was involved in that smuggling ring we ran into last fall. The Canadian authorities were on to them, and the feds were closing in—then came the incident with us and Carine. They burned down the shack, their base of operations, and disappeared. Not nice guys. They were into smuggling guns, people, drugs. Whatever paid."

"You think Gary Turner's one of them? Makes sense. He started work for the Rancourts months ago, but after the shooting. Louis only started a couple of weeks ago—something there, you think?" But Manny didn't answer right away, and North sighed. "This wasn't in your log."

"My computer log? Val was on it?"

"Apparently she tried every password possibility she could think of before she called me. *I-l-u-v-a-l.* Christ, Manny."

He grinned in spite of his obvious tension. "I knew it'd stump her, keep her nose out of my business. I figured if things went south, you'd at least have enough to go on. I pumped a source for information."

"Nate Winter?"

Manny scoffed. "Are you kidding? A Winter as a snitch? I've never seen a more tight-lipped, close-mouthed, stubborn bunch. No, another guy I know in Boston. It started really coming together Tuesday night, Wednesday morning. Then Louis calls me to meet him at the Rancourt house—fool that I am, I went. By the time I got there, he was tits up. Dead as a doornail.''

''You didn't see Jodie Rancourt or whoever took those pictures?''

''Not a thing. I went outside to call the police on my cell. I should have seen Carine going inside and stopped her—''

''She's handling it.''

''Then the cops were all over us. I knew I wasn't the killer. I was pretty sure Louis Sanborn tied back to the shooters last fall. I didn't know about Gary Turner—I thought he could be legit. I was more interested in the Rancourts.''

''Because they'd hired Louis?''

''And me. That didn't make any sense, either.''

''Did you know Louis and Jodie Rancourt were having an affair?''

''Suspected.'' He stared out the side window as Ty turned onto the notch road. ''I thought the police'd sort it out. I cooperated with them. I put you on Carine. I shut Val out. I figured Eric was safe at school.'' He was silent a moment. ''I guess my plan didn't work out that well.''

But North's focus was up the road, where an elderly man had jumped out in front of them, waving them down, a Ford Taurus with Maine plates was parked crookedly in back of him. There was a second car—it had veered off into a dry ditch, its front end smashed against a granite ledge.

Ty pulled over, but Manny was already kicking open his door. "That's Val's car."

He was out of the truck before they'd come to a full stop and charged down into the ditch. When Ty climbed out, the old man, decked out in a winter parka, hat and gloves, was on him. "She was coming from the other direction and crossed right in front of me—I knew something was wrong. I think she must have had a heart attack or something. I didn't know whether to leave her and go call an ambulance."

Manny ripped open the driver's side door. Val fell out into his arms. Ty shoved his cell phone at the old guy. "Call 911. When you connect, give the phone back to me." He grabbed his medical kit out of the back of his truck and ran down to Manny and Val. He could see the blood on her front, mostly on her left side. He opened up his med kit, setting it on the ground. "What's her condition?"

"She's been fucking shot."

"Manny—"

"Airway, breathing, circulation are okay." The ABCs, the basics. "Skin's clammy, she's shivering—she could go into shock."

Ty grabbed gauze and moistened it with IV fluid, then thrust it at Manny, who immediately applied pressure to the wound. It was his wife—he didn't bother with protective gloves. "Abs?" Ty asked.

"Guarding."

They both knew that was a positive sign. Manny checked for bowel sounds in all four quadrants, then nodded, satisfied. They needed to get Val to definitive care, the sooner the better. The "golden hour" rule. Every minute care was delayed, the patient's chances of recovery dimmed.

Ty handed Manny an Ace wrap to hold the dressing in place. "You okay?"

He nodded, concentrating on a task he'd performed hundreds of times in simulations and missions. The training took over, and if he was going to panic in a crisis, Manny Carrera wouldn't have lasted as a PJ for twenty years. Ty helped him put in a saline IV and let it run wide open—Val had suffered enough blood loss that she needed fluid or she might not make it to the hospital.

Ty leaped back up from the ditch and got a blanket out of his truck, and he and Manny laid Val on it and wrapped her up as best they could to keep her warm. Then they elevated her feet, to keep blood flowing to her vital organs.

"Val," Manny said, "what happened, sweetheart?"

"White hair, missing fingers." She tried to sit up, clawed at her husband's arm. "He has Eric and Hank."

"How long have you been out here?"

"A few minutes. Not long."

The old man handed the phone down to Ty. "I've got the dispatcher. There's a lot of static."

Ty nodded and spoke to the dispatcher, explaining that he was a paramedic and knew local procedures—they needed to get an ambulance to pick up Val and take her to the soccer field at Mount Chester, and they needed to get a medevac helicopter there to fly her to the regional trauma center.

Val rose up and hit Manny in the chest. "Goddamn it, leave me out here! Go find Eric and Hank! He'll leave Eric to the elements. Manny, he'll die—"

"Val—Jesus, how can I leave you?"

Ty got to his feet. "Carine and Gus headed up to check the east ridge trail near the Rancourt place. I'm going up there. Ambulance will be here in a few minutes. Val, you hang in there. You're going to be okay."

But her eyes were locked on her husband, her teeth chattering as she shivered, even with the blanket over her. "Go, Manny, for God's sake. There's nothing more you can do for me here. I'll be fine."

She sank back, her breathing rapid, her color not good. Manny looked up at the old man. "You'll stay with her? Apply pressure to the wound. She's not going to die on you."

Despite his obvious confusion, he didn't hesitate. "Of course. I'll do my best."

Manny kissed Val on the forehead. "You hang in there, okay? I love you."

She didn't answer, and Ty could see how hard it was for Manny to leave her. He didn't look back as he climbed up the steep wall of the ditch and got into Ty's truck. "This fuck Turner wants us. It's payback for last fall. He and Louis must have been in cahoots. We put an end to their nice little smuggling operation. He doesn't want Eric. He can have me. He used my wife—my boy—"

"Don't go there." North thought about Turner on the back deck with Carine, talking to her about the pictures, asking about having dinner with him sometime in Boston. "Hell, he wants Carine, too."

"She's up by the Rancourts? We need to warn her. That fuck's out here somewhere."

Ty pulled out onto the road. "Knowing Hank, he'll have this all sorted out by the time the police get there."

"Yeah. Damn pilots."

"It's going to work, Manny. I gave the dispatcher the lowdown. The cavalry's on its way. If we find Turner first, we isolate the situation until a tac team can get in there. Right?"

Manny didn't seem to be paying attention. "Don't you have a gun?"

"No."

"Val did." He pulled a bloodied Glock out of his waistband, then shook his head. "It's unloaded. No ammo. That woman."

Ty manufactured a smile. "This is why she works in a bookstore."

Manny looked down at his wife's bloody gun, his wife's blood on his clothes and hands. He glanced out the window when they turned up the access road to the Rancourt house and the east ridge trailhead. "So, what happens if Callahan's elected president—he gets a mountain named for him up here?"

And Ty relaxed slightly. Manny was with him.

Thirty

~~~∽◦≥◦◦≥◦∾~~~

Gus narrowly missed a head-on collision with the Rancourts' SUV as it careered out of their driveway onto the access road. He veered off to the side, almost plowing into a hemlock. "Jesus Christ! What the hell do they think they're doing?"

"Obviously they didn't expect anyone else to be on the road," Carine said, jumping out of the truck.

Sterling rolled down his window and gave her a cool, unfriendly look. "The sun was in my eyes. Is Gus all right? Is his truck hung up on the rocks?"

"He's fine. I thought you'd gone already." She shivered in a stiff gust of wind. "Have you seen Eric Carrera?"

"Up here, you mean? No, why? Is something wrong?"

"He left a note saying he was on a hike, but it doesn't all add up. The police and forest rangers are on the case, but we were hoping to catch up with him before he'd gone too far."

"I'm sorry. We just don't know anything."

Carine knew she'd been dismissed, but she didn't give up. "What about Gary Turner? Is he here?"

"I assume he's left, but I don't keep track of him. Goodbye—"

"How did you end up hiring him? Did he come to you, or did you go to him?"

"Carine, this isn't the time or the place for this discussion. I'm glad we didn't collide. Give your uncle our best—"

Carine straightened. "The Sanborn Dairy was before your time up here."

"I beg your pardon?"

Gus circled around the back of his truck and took her by the arm. "Come on, honey. We'll go back to North's, figure out what's next."

Jodie Rancourt jumped out of the passenger side of the SUV and came around the front, Sterling banging the steering wheel in frustration. Jodie ignored him. "My God, I wish we'd never met those bastards. Gary and Louis, Tony, whatever his name was. Louis was so charming and sexy. They came to me, separately. First Gary, months ago. Then Louis. I manipulated Sterling into hiring them, playing on his anxieties following our ordeal last fall." Her voice was hoarse, but her words were distinct. She shrugged, and said without sympathy or apology, without so much as a glance at her husband. "I was bored."

Sterling banged the steering wheel again with the palm of his hand and made an angry hissing sound.

''Did you know they were the smugglers?'' Carine asked.

''I was aware Louis had a past he wanted to hide. My God, don't we all? I wasn't sure he and Turner knew each other. I suspected it, but I wasn't positive. And I didn't ask. I—frankly, I wasn't interested.''

''The pictures?''

For the first time, she showed a hint of embarrassment. ''I've wanted to believe it was Manny Carrera. It was more convenient to think that whatever they were involved in, Gary and Louis wouldn't hurt anyone—me included. I don't know who took the pictures. I never saw, never heard, never suspected a thing. I left, and Louis said he was leaving. Then—he was killed. And the next day I got the call about the pictures. It had to be Gary.''

''Why would he want Louis dead?''

''I think Gary wants everyone dead. But specifically Louis—I don't know. I wouldn't be surprised if Louis had his own game, if Gary found he couldn't control him.'' She averted her eyes, staring down at the valley. ''I doubt Gary liked the idea of us having a…whatever it was.''

Carine shoved her hands into her pockets. ''Right now, all I want to do is find Eric. Hank Callahan and Val Carrera are on their way up here, too. If you see them—''

''We're leaving,'' Sterling said, his voice strangled, hoarse.

Jodie Rancourt raised her eyes to Carine. ''The boy is in the warming hut. Turner has him tied up. He threatened to kill us if we said anything, but I can't—he's a child.''

"Eric's *here?*" Carine was stunned. "And you haven't called the police?"

Sterling glared at her. "I don't have to explain myself to you."

Gus swore. "I'm going up there—I won't do anything stupid. Carine, take the truck and get where you can make a call."

"Where's Turner now?" she asked the Rancourts.

Sterling ignored her. "Jodie, get back in the car," he said coldly. "We're leaving. We have to save ourselves from this madman. He'll hunt us down, just the way he has Hank Callahan, Manny Carrera—Carine, you and North are next. I don't know why. Some kind of revenge. Frankly, you're risking making the situation worse by interfering."

"What about Val Carrera and Hank?"

"I have no idea where they are." He winced, the color draining out of his face as he looked down the road. "Christ. We're out of time. Jodie!"

She jumped back into her seat. The SUV screeched forward, narrowly missing an old Audi careering up the road, turning onto the driveway.

Gary Turner was driving, Hank Callahan in the seat next to him.

Carine dove into Gus's truck, hitting the floor, hoping Turner hadn't spotted her. She got onto her knees and peered over the dashboard, and she saw Gus pause and look back, the car charging for him.

She kicked the door open, screaming, "Gus!"

He dove, but too late. Turner was gunning for him and caught him on the right front bumper of the Audi. Gus went sprawling, facedown, onto the damp grass along the side of the driveway.

The Audi sped on up the driveway.

Carine ran to Gus and knelt beside him, pushing back a rush of panic. "Gus—Gus, are you okay? Talk to me!"

He was writhing in agony, every few words a swear. "Fuck…I'm okay. Goddamn it! I think I broke a leg—my ribs…"

"Don't move. Come on, Gus, be still. If you've got a back or a neck injury—"

"I don't. *Shit!*"

Swearing seemed to help his pain. Carine took a breath. "Turner—he's got Hank. I didn't see Val. I have to do something. I can sneak behind the house and try to get a view of the hut and see what's going on. Don't worry, I won't do anything nuts. But if Turner starts hurting anyone—I don't know, maybe I can create a diversion."

"You're a sitting duck out here. Take cover, will you?"

She picked up a softball-size rock off the side of the driveway. "I used to be pretty good with a rock."

"Christ, kid."

She blinked back tears. "Eric…he's just fourteen.…"

"Something starts going down, look to Hank for guidance. Understood? He's got combat experience. You don't—well, you didn't used to." Her uncle winced, holding his right side with one arm, in obvious agony. He was pale, pearls of sweat on his upper lip. "I'll see if I can get into my truck and get a call out to the police."

"You shouldn't move—"

"Just fucking stay out of the line of fire, will you?"

She nodded. "I plan to."

Jodie was white-faced as they drove down the hill, but Sterling kept his eyes on the twisting road. His jaw was clenched, and he had to fight with himself to concentrate on his driving. This was no time to two-wheel a sharp curve or lose control and go airborne off the damn mountain.

"We have to call the police," Jodie said quietly, wringing her hands in her lap.

He glanced at her coldly. "You lied to me about everything, didn't you? Your affair with Louis. When you met. What you knew, what you suspected. What else?"

She turned away, staring out at the scenery. "I met Louis up here over the summer. We didn't—" She broke off awkwardly, and he could see her fighting for the right choice of words. Or perhaps just another lie. "I put him off until he moved to Boston."

"Put him off?"

"He'd made it clear he was…interested."

"I see."

"No, I don't think you do." Her voice was surprisingly flat, as if she didn't care anymore. "I didn't want to tell you that we knew each other. I knew you'd be suspicious—''

"Rightly so." Nothing in his tone or demeanor let her off the hook—he didn't want it to. "He asked you to recommend him to Gary Turner?"

"He pressured me to get Gary to hire him. He never said there was a connection between the two of them. Neither did Gary."

"You had nothing to do with their smuggling operation?"

"No! Of course not. I was just—a pawn."

Sterling gave her a cold look, feeling in control again. He'd lost it up on the hill, when he'd almost plowed into Gus Winter's truck, and then Carine had stood there, so damn self-righteous. "You were more than a pawn, Jodie." His hands relaxed slightly on the wheel. "You were a willing participant. Did you tell the police everything?"

She stared down at her hands and gave a small shake of the head. "No. I didn't tell them I knew Louis from up here. Manny Carrera—he saw us together in September. I'd hoped he wouldn't remember."

"For Christ's sake, Jodie, with his training and experience—''

"He's not a law enforcement officer, he's an air force pararescueman. He wouldn't even be involved in our lives if you hadn't called for help when we were on the ridge. We could have made it on our own."

"We'd have died."

"You've been trying to prove yourself and protect yourself ever since. You hate feeling vulnerable, inadequate. It's made you impossible this entire year."

"Don't blame me for your own failings."

"Sterling—" Her voice cracked, all her remoteness and reserve suddenly gone. "Let me at least try to get through to the police. Eric Carrera could be dying on *our* property. If you don't get the human component, at least, for God's sake, think about how it'll look. Carine and Gus know we left that boy up there."

He said nothing. Big chunks of the puzzle were still missing, but he had a fair idea of what had happened. They'd drawn attention to themselves last fall when they were rescued off the ridge, and Turner and Sanborn had seized the opportunity to take advantage of them, exploit them, use them. Louis had preyed on his wife. They'd both preyed on him.

"Jesus..." Jodie's voice was barely more than a croak now. "You hope Turner kills them, don't you? Then they can't report what a goddamn coward you were."

"What? Jodie, for the love of God, *no,* I'm not hoping he kills anyone. But don't you get it? Turner *is* a killer. We're caught in the middle. He won't harm us unless we give him reason to. If he gets away— what do you think he'll do? He got away last fall, but did he slink off and disappear? No. He used us to get access to the people who ruined him. He wants them dead. What do you think he'll do to us if we ruin his revenge?"

"Nothing if he's in prison!"

He shook his head. "I'm not taking that chance."

Her eyes shone with tears. "What happened to us? We used to be better than this."

"I'm being smart, Jodie, not a coward."

"Sterling…"

He bit off a sigh. "All right. We'll call the police the first chance we have. We'll tell the police we were scared and didn't want to cause more problems. Remember your crisis training classes—your first job is to escape a dangerous situation. The police don't need two more hostages on their hands."

"If we'd helped Eric while Turner was out—"

"I didn't know where Turner was, how fast he'd be back. What if he'd caught us and killed all of us? Killed the boy in front of us? Then how holier than thou would you feel?"

She was crying now. "I just…I just don't know what to do."

"Then shut up and let me think."

When he reached the bottom of the hill, he turned left instead of right toward the village of Cold Ridge. He didn't want to run into the police or any search parties already out looking for Eric Carrera. Jodie stared at her cell phone, but Sterling knew there wouldn't be service—or a house where they could call—for at least several more miles. Any delay wasn't his fault. Then he'd let Jodie notify the police, and he'd call their attorney to meet them when they arrived back at their house on the South Shore.

Thirty-One

Ty pulled in behind Gus's truck, parked off the road just before the Rancourt driveway. Manny, his hands wiped off and disinfected, jumped out and checked the truck, but shook his head. Ty joined him, feeling the drop in temperature even at this elevation.

"No sign of anyone," Manny said, squinting up toward the Rancourt house. "Think they spotted Eric and went after him?"

"The trailhead's just up the road. It's possible—"

But he saw a movement up on the left side of the driveway, someone waving to them from behind a low stone wall, then collapsing back out of sight. Manny saw it, too. "That's Gus. Looks like he's down."

Manny was already on his way. North grabbed his medical kit from the back of the truck and ran, forcing back any intrusive thoughts—Carine? Where the hell was she? What had happened to Gus? But he knew not to get ahead of himself.

Manny leaped over the stone wall and squatted down next to Gus, who was conscious but in obvious pain. "Where are you hurt?" Manny asked. "What happened?"

"Turner bounced me off the bumper of his fucking car. I think I broke a leg, maybe a couple ribs—"

"Christ, Gus," Ty said. "You need to stay still, take it easy."

"Relax, I'm fine." His breathing was rapid, his eyes on Manny. "He's got your son and Hank up in the shed."

Manny had no visible reaction. "You saw them?"

Gus shook his head, wincing. "Just Turner and Hank. The Rancourts said he's got Eric up there, too. They knew and did nothing."

"Where's Carine?" North asked.

Gus winced. "Sneaking around back with a rock."

Ty pictured her last year, zigzagging up the hill from her cover behind the boulder. She was a scrapper. She'd do anything, but she wasn't stupid. He shook his head at Gus. "Jesus. I shouldn't have let you and Carine come up here on your own."

Manny fished a cervical collar out of North's med kit. "Too late, North. We're all here now."

Gus tried to sit up on an elbow. "You're not putting that fucking collar on me. Go find Carine. Turner must have hit me five, ten minutes ago at most. You didn't pass the Rancourts on the road? They said they'd call the police."

"Police are on their way," Ty said, but deliberately didn't tell him about Val. Gus had enough on his mind, and his pulse was rapid, his skin getting clammy. He needed an ambulance. "You warm enough?"

"Yeah. Toasty. Will you quit?" He licked a little blood off the corner of his mouth. "Bit my fucking lip. That hurt."

North quit arguing. "Just stay still."

"Carine won't do anything crazy."

Manny crouched behind the low stone wall and looked up the hill at the remaining length of driveway, the dirt track, the warming hut with its surrounding trees and natural landscaping. There was a lot of rock. "Think he's seen us?"

"I don't know," Ty said. "I'm guessing yes."

"North!"

The shout came from the warming hut. Turner.

Manny gave North a quick sideways look. "Well, he's seen you."

"Do you think I care if you bring in helicopters and every cop in the state?" Turner yelled. "Kill me. It doesn't matter. So long as I kill you and your friends on my way out."

"Shit," Manny said, "one of these suicide types. And he's got my kid."

North gave him a warning look. "You with me?"

Manny exhaled, nodded. "I'm going up there."

"Let's talk money." Turner, although he was shouting down the hill, sounded calm, even conversational. "How much for your senator? For your friend's son? For your woman, Sergeant North? How much for her?"

"No way he has Carine," Manny said. "She'd never go quietly. Gus would have heard something."

Her uncle grunted. "This is bullshit. Turner doesn't want money. He had the Rancourts, for Christ's sake. They've got more money than all of us put together."

Ty took a breath. "Let's talk," he called. "Face-to-face. You send out the boy, I'll come up there and talk money with you."

"I tried that trade once. I was almost double-crossed by Mrs. Bitch Carrera."

"I'm killing him," Manny said. "Understood?"

Ty ignored his friend. "Then let's get it right this time. Let the boy go, Turner. You don't want to hurt a kid."

"I've investigated you, Sergeant North." This time, Turner's voice held a note of sarcasm and superiority. "Suppose you give me some of that trust fund you've got tucked away?"

Manny looked at North. "Trust fund?"

"My father left my mother some money," he said. "When she died, she left it to me."

Gus frowned. "I wondered how she managed to live off making collages and painting waterfalls. Christ, you have a father after all, huh? How much money he leave you?"

"I'm comfortable."

"How comfortable?" Manny asked.

North ignored both of them. They were all, he knew, focused on the job at hand. "I don't think Turner saw you," he told Manny. "I'll keep him talking. You want to get up there?"

Manny nodded. "I'll see what Carine's up to. A rock. I hope it's a big one." He glanced at North. "The Rancourts have rifles. I'll see what I can grab. But if things go south up there, I'm going in."

"Valerie Carrera's dead." Turner's voice seemed louder, almost echoing across the valleys and ravines. "Someone should have found her body by now. Did you pass her on your way up here?"

"Tyler! *Mom!*"

Eric Carrera. His voice wasn't as strong as Turner's, but it was distinct. Manny couldn't stand it and jumped up. "Your mom's alive, son."

North grabbed him and jerked him back down behind the stone wall, but Manny was already diving. A shot sounded, hitting a rock two feet to their left, just above their heads, sending a chunk flying. It struck Manny on the right side of his head, tearing out a two-inch strip of flesh above his ear. "Negotiate, my ass. He's fucking out to kill us. Damn boonies, or we'd have a tac team here by now."

"There's only the one road up. They're not going to come in here with guns blazing. They'll plan it out first." North reached for a bandage in his med kit and handed it to Manny. "At least we know where Turner is."

Manny patched his bleeding head. The flying rock probably would have knocked anyone else unconscious. "Yeah. He's up in the fucking shed with my kid, shooting at us."

"At least Eric can talk," Ty said. "That's a positive."

Gus tried to move but moaned in pain, gritting his teeth. "Hank's up there—I'm betting Turner hasn't hurt him yet. He'll want to keep all his bargaining chips as long as he can."

Blood had dripped down the side of Manny's face onto his neck, but he didn't seem to notice. "He wants us dead, but on his terms."

North nodded. "We contain the situation. We keep Hank and Eric alive until we get help up here."

"Easiest way is to kill this fuck," Manny said, crouching down low, then moving quickly, making his way from cover to cover up the hill.

Thirty-Two

The shot had been close enough that Carine had felt its concussion, as if the air around her was compressed, the oxygen sucked out of it by the velocity of the gun burst. It was so unexpected, so startling, she'd almost screamed, and ended up biting the inside corner of her mouth.

Turner didn't have her. In fact, he'd slipped out of the warming hut and was moving around back, near her position in the trees. She was cold—no hat, no gloves, just her barn coat. At least she was basically out of the wind.

"Carine," Turner said softly, dried leaves crunching under him, "I know you're here. I have a soft spot for you. Join me. You didn't know about North's trust fund, did you? We can get away from here. I won't hurt anyone if you come with me."

Maybe North had a trust fund, maybe he didn't, but she didn't believe Turner planned to do anything but shoot her the first chance he got. Either he really was losing his grip on reality or he was just pretending to, toying with her, manipulating her. She sank low behind a low-branching white pine. If she moved, he'd hear her—she couldn't see him, but she knew he was close.

"I'm sick. I have cancer. It's all through me. No one's fault."

If true.

"It gives me perspective." His voice was eerily calm, almost toneless. "I know what I want before I die. Who I want to see die first. But I'd give that up if I could spend my last days with you."

She stiffened to keep herself from shivering with fear, the cold. She didn't dare look around the tree, make even the slightest sound.

"Tony—Louis—and I had a good thing going. I planned to live out my last months in style. I had a wife." His voice cracked. "The smuggling was to help set her and her idiot brother up for the future."

Carine had no choice but to let him talk. If he was talking—hunting her—he wasn't shooting anyone else. But had he seen her, heard her? Was he just playing with her before he pounced?

"Jodie Rancourt took up with Louis a year ago, before you took the pictures of our base of operations. She knew he was up to something, but she liked the sense of danger, the risk. She let us try out her and her husband's expensive guns."

Good God, Carine thought, wishing she had a tape recorder.

"He had them for show," Turner said as he crept

around in the woods to her right, nearer the Rancourt house. "Louis wanted to kill you. I stopped him. I wanted to get the camera, make sure there were no incriminating pictures and make sure you were too scared to talk. Then the PJs and Hank Callahan showed up on the scene. I had to cut my losses."

She spotted him in the trees, up on the hill above her, still to her left, but if she stayed where she was, he'd see her. She picked up her rock and eased around the other side of her pine, making relatively little noise in the bed of red-brown pine needles. She hit grass, then quickly slipped into the back door of the hut.

Maybe it was what he'd planned all along. Corner her. Shoo her into the hut with Eric and Hank.

Eric was in the corner, sobbing and choking for air. Carine knelt down, setting the rock on the floor next to her, and quickly undid the bungee cords around the boy's wrists and ankles. "You heard your dad out there, right?"

The boy nodded. "He—he only tied me up this morning." But talking was clearly difficult for him, and once free, he immediately grabbed his inhaler, then sagged and threw it down. "None left."

"Look—sit tight," Carine said. "I'm going to untie Hank. Turner's outside looking for me. Maybe your dad and Tyler will intercept him."

She quickly ran to the front of the hut, where Hank was bound and gagged next to the small potbellied woodstove. Carine pulled the gag.

"Eric—he's going out the back. If Turner sees

him—'' Hank sat up straighter. ''Go after him, Carine. I'll be okay.''

He was bound with thin rope, the knots pulled tight. She tugged at them, trying to stretch the rope. ''I can't get them without a knife.''

''Go!''

She could hear Turner out front, stepping onto the ground-level porch. ''What the fuck's going on in there?''

''We're out of time,'' Hank hissed.

She ducked down and ran toward the back of the hut, diving outside and down behind a woodbox next to the door. Eric was up by her pine tree, but he didn't stay put. He made a mad dash up the hill, into the woods, thrashing through the dried leaves.

Carine took a breath, pretending she was the one making the noise. ''Gary,'' she said. ''I told everyone you weren't trying to kill me that day last fall. The shack—you set it on fire?''

He was inside, moving toward her position. ''I had to burn down the evidence. Manny Carrera was almost there—''

''He would have waited for the police. He was unarmed.''

''I couldn't take that chance.''

''What happened?''

''My wife was there. She tried to talk me out of burning everything down. She didn't want to give up. She and Tony Louis—they thought we could kill all of you.'' He kicked at something on the floor just inside the door, probably Eric's bungee cords. ''They were right. I should have listened. The explosion and fire killed her. I watched the woman I love burn to death.''

"I'm sorry, but why didn't anyone find her body?"

"I buried her in the woods, before the ground froze. She didn't die right away, but I couldn't take her to the hospital. Louis ran—Jodie Rancourt helped him. I don't know if she guessed who he was then, knew it all along. I hid in the woods for weeks. I got a skin infection. Frostbite. I lost my fingers, a couple of toes.''

"I'm sorry." She held her rock, wondering if he'd come outside and she could bonk him on the head before he shot her. "But hurting people because you're hurting—that's not your way. I can tell.''

"I don't expect you to understand. It'll feel good to see those bastards go before I do. They think they can do anything.''

He was out the back door, two feet from her. She didn't dare breathe.

"Are you armed, Carine?" he asked in a conversational tone. "The boy won't last. There was peanut oil in the energy bar I made him eat a little while ago. He doesn't know. He's deathly allergic to peanuts.

"North! Carrera!" It was Hank, yelling from inside the hut. "Eric's free. Turner's going after Carine. I'm setting this place on fire. I'm his only hostage.''

Turner spun around. "What? Goddamn it—''

The sound of crashing metal—the potbellied stove—came from the hut, Hank still yelling information, instructions. Carine shot out from her wood-box cover and beaned Turner with her rock and ran, darting up the hill into the woods. He swore viciously, and she glanced back, seeing him down on one knee, grabbing his head where she'd hit him. He hadn't dropped his rifle.

She knew she'd only bought herself a few seconds.

But she could smell smoke. Hank had set the hut on fire, presumably creating a diversion—confusion, chaos—for Manny and Ty to act.

Carine zigzagged up the hill from tree to tree, trying to pick up Eric's trail and stay out of Turner's sight. Had he gone back into the hut to grab Hank? He wouldn't want to lose his only hostage.

But if he had, it wasn't for long.

She could hear him down the hill, behind her in the woods.

Thirty-Three

ᘓᘏᘓᘏ

North and Manny had made it to the trees just below the hut when Hank decided to set the goddamn place on fire.

"Carrera, North—go after Turner!"

But the fire would spread rapidly—smoke was already pouring out of the front door. No way would they leave Hank in there to burn to death.

Without discussion, North ran, Manny with him. Automatically, Manny ducked to one side of the front door, Ty covering his mouth as best he could and bursting inside, crouched down as he grabbed Hank and dragged him out. Manny took over, throwing Hank over his shoulder and running a few yards back down the hill, dumping him behind a boulder.

Ty coughed, but he hadn't inhaled that much smoke. He dove behind the boulder and glanced back. Flames were eating up the wall where the woodstove had been. Hank wouldn't have stood a chance.

Manny got a knife from North's med kit and

quickly cut the ropes on Hank's feet and hands. He was coughing up soot, his lips and cheeks swelling.

"Looks like you singed most of the hair off your face," Ty said. "Eyebrows, eyelashes. That's going to look good on TV."

"I'll be okay." Hank winced in pain, pushed North's hand away when he started to dig in his med kit. "Go after Turner. Intercept him before he gets to Carine and Eric."

Ty had already thrust a tube of burn ointment at him. "This hut's going to keep burning. Stay clear of it."

Hank hissed irritably. "Jesus Christ, I know. I hope I bought Carine enough time. He's gone after her. He knew you'd storm the place once the fire started, and he wouldn't have a chance against all three of us."

"Eric?" Manny asked.

"He's not in good shape. He used the last of his inhaler. He tried—"

North checked a lump on Hank's forehead. "What'd you do, jump the woodstove?"

"Turner hit me on the way up here. He wants Carine dead as much as he does us. Maybe more. She took the pictures last fall, she turned him down on his offer of the good life together—and Eric. Turner'll use him if he has to. He wants revenge. We ruined his life. He'll ruin ours."

North got to his feet. "No one knows these mountains better than Carine."

"Cold, fear, an uphill climb—Eric's going to collapse." Manny's head was bleeding through the bandage and had to be pounding, but Ty knew he wasn't going to stop. "Go, North. Pick up his trail. Don't let me slow you down. If I can't keep up, don't count on me."

Hank coughed and spat black soot. "I'll meet the police when they get here and get a rescue team in place. Gus?"

"Banged up pretty good. He's down by the stone wall."

"I'll hook up with him. If you see this guy—he's done playing games. He wants to kill someone. Don't take any chances."

Carine thought she'd gone too far and must have bypassed Eric somewhere down on the trail. She made the last, steep burst onto the main ridge trail, but kept going, not daring to call him.

Although she was still below the treeline, the wind was blowing hard, the temperatures dropping, the cold penetrating her barn coat and freezing her ears. She couldn't imagine Eric in his sweatshirt. What if he'd fallen? What if he'd collapsed? But she couldn't think about that—she had to keep moving, find him, stay ahead of Turner, hide from him.

She ducked on and off the trail, trying to stay within cover of trees or boulders, intensely aware she was unprepared for the conditions. But Eric had spent the night in the cold hut, kidnapped, terrified, conserving his inhaler as best he could. She could keep moving.

The trail meandered along a section of rock, marked with splashes of blue paint and rock cairns.

And then she saw Eric, collapsed in a patch of grass a few feet off the trail. Carine shot over to him. Fear and determination had gotten him moving fast, but now he was prone, barely breathing as he lay on the cold ground. She glanced around her for Turner, then grabbed the boy and half carried, half dragged him to the base of a fifteen-foot ledge, several stunted fir trees concealing them.

Eric was wheezing, raising his shoulders and lifting his head as he struggled to get air. She noticed he was blue around the mouth and knew that had to be a dire sign. Carine stemmed her panic and tried to talk to him, but he just mumbled incoherently, ripping her heart out. She thought she remembered that it was easier for an asthmatic patient to breathe sitting up, but her first aid skills were limited. She didn't know if he was suffering more from asthma or an allergic reaction. It seemed to make common sense, however, and she put her arms around his thin shoulders. "Come on," she said, "let's sit you up.

She searched his pockets and found his EpiPen, which she knew was intended to combat a severe allergic reaction, but she wasn't sure how to use it. She slipped off her barn coat and wrapped it around him, hoping that if she could get him warm, maybe he could tell her what to do. Self-management had been key for him. He couldn't have gone to Mount Chester without knowing how to deal with his illness.

But nothing Carine did seemed to help. Eric was

laboring to breathe, not even mumbling now. She held him close to her in an attempt to transfer some of her body heat to him—at least they were out of the worst of the wind. She could hear it whistling and howling.

She heard Turner—someone—on the trail nearby.

"You're not armed, Carine."

Turner. Calm. Superior.

"You can't hold out against me. You can't hide."

His voice seemed to be coming from the ledge above where she and Eric were tucked amid the stunted firs. She pulled Eric against the rock wall, in its shadow, where they were less likely to be seen from above. The shallow soil was moist under her. She tried to cover Eric as best she could with her own body and protect him from the elements. But she was cold herself, shivering in her cotton shirt.

Eric gave a rattling, frightening wheeze.

"I hear the kid."

Heartless bastard.

If Turner spotted them, they didn't stand a chance, but Carine knew the area where she and Eric were hiding well. The footing was tricky, deceptive on the ledge. Turner undoubtedly would attempt to track Eric's wheezing—maybe it was something she could use to their advantage.

"Be careful, Gary." She tried to match his tone. "There are places you can get hurt up here. And maybe you've gone up, but your still have to go down. The police, Manny, Tyler and Hank will all be waiting for you. And Gus. Don't count him out."

"But you'll be dead. You killed my wife."

"You killed your own wife."

"And Louis—"

"You killed him, too. Why? He had you take the pictures of him and Jodie Rancourt so the two of you could blackmail her? You realized what a loose cannon he was?"

"He wanted money. He didn't understand that I had other priorities to see to first."

"But you want money—you did try to blackmail her."

"I wanted it all, Carine. I still do. Money, justice. You."

She could hear him moving on the ledge, trying to find her. As she'd hoped, he was well off the trail, onto one of the most treacherous sections of the ledge. It was one of her favorite spots for taking pictures, but a deceptive growth of stunted balsam made it look like there was proper footing where there was none— she'd almost fallen there herself.

"What if I cooperate with you?" She kept her voice low in an effort to lure him, but not to give away their position completely. "What if I help you get Manny, North and Hank? Three for one. That's not a bad deal."

"What about the boy?"

"He's not doing well. I wouldn't worry about him."

"Tell me where you are."

She debated her next answer, but knew she had to take the chance. "We're down here. At the base of the ledge." Then she spotted him above her, slightly down from her, his rifle raised, but she hoped he still couldn't see her and Eric concealed within the rock and trees. She took a shallow breath. "I can see you, but you can't see me. Be very careful. The footing's tricky up there. You don't want to fall. Do what I say and you'll be okay."

"Fine." He sounded shaky, dubious. "Where to from here?"

Carine knew he didn't believe her. He was doing to her what he'd done to Louis with the pictures— pretend to cooperate, then he'd pounce. She held Eric more closely, feeling how cold he was. He was shivering uncontrollably. He kept raising his shoulders and his head, fighting for air. The sand had run out of the hourglass. She had to get him out of here.

She concentrated on what she had to do. "See the small evergreens? They're balsam firs. Stay out of them. You'll fall. Instead, go backward a few steps and up to your right."

They were the proper instructions, but, just as she'd hoped, he did the opposite and went for the fir trees, losing his footing almost immediately. He swore dropping his rifle as he grabbed onto weak branches that couldn't support his weight. It was a precipitous twenty-foot drop, and he yelled all the way down.

Manny appeared up on the ledge, and Ty bounded out of nowhere, getting to Turner just as he landed five feet from where Carine was hidden with Eric. She heard his head hit rock, then saw him sprawl forward onto his left wrist, which snapped under the impact of his fall. But he was conscious, moving—going for his nine-millimeter in his belt.

Ty kicked him in the head, then swooped in, snatched the handgun and pointed it at Turner. "Hands where I can see them. Don't move."

Turner sneered at him. "Fuck you." But his voice was weak, his head bleeding from where he'd struck the granite, never mind where Ty had kicked him and Carine had earlier pelted him with her rock.

Manny dropped silently onto the rocks next to Carine and collected Turner's rifle, handing it to Ty, then dropping down next to Eric. Carine, shivering herself now, was still holding the boy. "I tried to keep him warm. I didn't know what else to do. Turner told me there was peanut oil in an energy bar he made him eat. I don't know if it's true."

Manny quickly examined his son and injected the epinephrine, then shook his head. "Christ. This isn't just asthma. His epiglottis is inflamed from the peanut oil. His airway's getting obstructed—North, I've got to do a crike."

Ty tossed over his med kit. "Want me to do it?"

Manny shook his head. "I've got it."

He got out what he needed—a small scalpel, gauze, first aid tape, a breathing tube. Carine moved out of the way, but she could see Manny was in trouble. He blinked blood out of his eyes from his own head wound. "Manny…"

Ty, keeping the nine-millimeter leveled on Turner, eased in next to his friend. "Manny. Come on. Your head's a mess. I'll do it."

Manny gave a curt, reluctant nod, not speaking as

he stood up and took the guns from Ty, letting him get to work on Eric.

Turner was unconscious, not that Manny took any chances—he kept the gun pointed at him, the rifle cradled in one arm. Carine offered to take the rifle, but he shook his head. "You're shivering. You'll end up shooting someone."

"He wanted us all in the hut. He was going to set fire to it and let us burn to death, set right what he did to his wife last fall. She was badly burned when he blew up the shack and ended up dying. It was an accident. He didn't mean to kill her. He didn't listen to her. She wanted him to shoot us all that day and disappear. That's what he planned to do this time. Kill us all and disappear."

"Better late than never, I guess. Bastard. He tell you all this?"

"Most of it. Some—not in as many words."

By unspoken agreement, she knew, they were trying to focus on something besides Eric's condition, but Manny glanced back as Ty made a small incision in the boy's neck—it bled like crazy, but he quickly stanched the blood with gauze.

"What's a crike?" Carine asked, hoping that talking helped.

"Cricothyroidotomy. It's like a tracheotomy, except you use the cricothyroid space. It opens up the airway. It's a—" Manny paused, swallowing, obviously struggling to control his fear for his son. "It's a simple procedure."

"What happened to your head?"

"Flying rock. Mine got me worse than yours got you last fall." He glanced at her, and she thought he might have tried to smile. "Lucky for you."

Ty inserted a breathing tube into the airway, secured it with tape and packed it with more gauze. "He's got mild hypothermia. We need to get him out of here."

Manny peeled off his coat and covered his son with it, cradling his son against his big body. North took over guard duty, handing his cell phone to Carine. She managed to get hold of Gus, but she was shivering uncontrollably. Her head was fuzzy. She managed to get out the basics of their situation.

"They're stuffing me into an ambulance," Gus said. "A rescue team's on its way on foot."

"Eric's in bad shape. There's no time."

Ty looked at her, his concern for his patient evident. "Tell him we need to get a helicopter up here. Winds are tough, but it'll be okay. They can ask Hank. He'll tell them."

Carine repeated his words to Gus, who grunted at her. "You freezing?"

"More or less."

She clicked off, and Ty eased his leather jacket over her shoulders. "I'm sweating from hoofing it up this goddamn mountain," he said. "You did say you liked a sweaty guy—"

"Covered in wood chips. A key ingredient."

"What if Turner had believed you and did what you said?"

"I had another rock picked out."

"That's the spirit."

She nodded at Turner. "What about him?"

"Broken wrist, concussion. When Manny gets done with Eric, he can hold a gun on Turner and I'll treat him. There's not much I can do."

"Is he—"

Ty read her thoughts. "Nah. He'll live."

She could feel the warmth of his jacket, her shivering slowly subsiding. "He would have killed you, me. Hank. Manny. Eric. Gus. All of us. He waited to get us together, at the right moment—it was like he got satisfaction from manipulating us, playing us."

But Ty didn't answer, edging closer to her. He tucked the nine-millimeter into his waistband and held on to the rifle with one arm, slipping the other around her shoulders. "You need to stay warm. Gus'll have a fit when he sees you up here in cotton. He'll recommend to Fish and Game that you pay for your rescue."

"I did the rescuing. Some of it."

North smiled at her. "Damn, babe. You do have the prettiest eyes."

Thirty-Four

Nobody could get Manny into a litter. He carried one end of his son's litter and climbed into the National Guard rescue helicopter with him. They took Gary Turner, too. He'd regained consciousness, but was incoherent.

A Cold Ridge police officer, part of the rescue team that arrived on foot after the helo took off, relieved North of Turner's rifle and handgun. He was freed to argue with Carine about getting her ass in a litter and letting the rescue team carry her off the ridge.

He didn't win that one, either.

She was determined to walk. North went with her. The rescue party provided them with warm clothes and warm fluids, but Carine had had a hell of a few hours—so had he. By the time they got back down to the Rancourt house, Gus and Hank had already been transported by ambulance to the hospital. All hell was breaking loose over a United States senator turning up in a hut on a New Hampshire mountain with a madman.

Except Gary Turner was stone-cold sane. North had no doubt about that.

Antonia Winter Callahan, M.D., met them at the hospital. She was in trauma-doctor mode, checking on her husband, her uncle, her sister, the entire Carrera family. Val was in surgery. Eric was responding rapidly to treatment for a severe allergic reaction, asthma attack and mild hypothermia. He'd helped save himself. There was no question about it. He'd conserved his Albuterol as best he could and consciously tried to lower the level of his anxiety. If he hadn't responded the way he had, he'd have been dead before Carine found him on the ridge.

Manny, no surprise to North, wasn't the most cooperative patient, but he finally, reluctantly, agreed to let someone do a CT-scan of his head—just so they'd all leave him alone. He said his head was fine. He was right. The CT-scan was negative.

Antonia shoved a cardboard cup of gray-looking coffee at North in the ER waiting room. "The doctor orders you to drink. You've had a hell of a day, but I see you're as indestructible as ever."

"That piece of rock could have hit me instead of Manny."

She smiled faintly. "The key here is that it didn't."

He sipped the awful coffee. "I can tell you, you wouldn't have seen me kicking over a damn wood-stove with my hands and feet tied together—what'd Hank plan to do, slither out of there like a snake?"

"No, he planned for you and Manny to rescue him. He says that's what you guys live for."

But her face was pale, and she looked strained and tired. "I'll bet right now Hank knows exactly why he married an ER doc."

"He won't even be admitted. He'll just need to grow new eyebrows." She teetered suddenly, and North grabbed her. "I think—oh, hell, Tyler, I'm going to be sick."

And she was, right there on the waiting room floor, damn near getting his shoes.

"I know you hate barf," she said, embarrassed.

He got her onto a chair, and a nurse came running, but Antonia waved her off. "I'm all right. I'm—" She smiled through her wooziness. "I'm pregnant."

"Antonia!" It was Carine, coming around the corner into the waiting room, eavesdropping as usual. "That's wonderful. Are you okay? Can I get you anything?"

"Have you told Hank?" Ty asked.

Antonia lifted her head. "It took the cocky pilot right out of him."

North figured the voters of Massachusetts would either get used to their new senator's way of doing things or they'd give him the boot in six years. Kids came first with him. Period. He was the kind of guy who'd kick over a woodstove while he was tied up if it meant giving an asthmatic kid an extra few minutes' lead, to escape his captor.

Nate Winter finally wandered in, pissed off and pacing, in full U.S. marshal mode. He was tall and rangy like his uncle, with about as much patience. He glared at the younger of his two sisters and then at North. "I told you two to go mountain climbing."

Carine ignored him. "How bad a bad guy was Gary Turner?"

"Considering he kidnapped a fourteen-year-old boy and a U.S. senator and planned to kill them and you, Manny Carrera and your ex-fiancé here, I guess he was pretty goddamn bad."

"Yeah, but before that?"

His mouth twitched. "Before that he wasn't so hot, either. He likely committed two murders in Canada. Tony—Louis was a trip, too. Extortion, smuggling, forgery. He was very good at forgery. Smuggle people into a country, they need papers."

"The wife?"

"Turner was devoted to her. They had some weird relationship—looks like he went to pieces when he accidentally killed her. The doctors treating him say it's a wonder he made it out of the mountains last winter. It doesn't look as if he ever sought medical help for his fingers and toes."

"He's talking?" Carine asked.

"Some. He wants credit. Hell—" Nate bit off a sigh. "If he goes downhill or shuts up, investigators can just talk to my baby sister and wrap this one up."

Carine didn't wither under her brother's impatient scrutiny. "Will I get a medal?"

"Pain in the ass," he said.

The Rancourts were talking to the police, but only through their lawyer. They'd stopped ten miles up the notch road to call the police and, according to Nate, acted like victims.

She sipped some of Ty's coffee, made a face and dug money out of one of her endless barn coat pockets for the soda machine. "Antonia, I'll share a Coke with you, provided I don't catch what you've got."

Her sister tried to smile, but she was done in. North winked at her. "Long goddamn night and day for a pregnant lady."

"Long night and day for all of us."

They all went up to Gus's room. He bitched about having his leg in a cast and the prospect of missing even a minute of snowshoeing and cross-country skiing season, but he hadn't incurred any permanent damage. He'd be back on the ridge before the winter was out. He had no sympathy for Carine's brush with hypothermia. Apparently he'd offered to stop at her cabin for her to put on more appropriate clothing, and she'd refused.

"The doctor lectured me on wearing cotton," she told him. "It was an *accident.* I never wear cotton hiking, not even in the summer."

North smiled. Winters, even when they were being treated for their injuries, never liked being told something they already knew. They were a loving but contentious lot, and as he looked from green-at-the-gills Antonia to rangy Nate to brittle-haired Gus to Carine, blue-eyed and auburn-haired and not nearly as fragile as everyone thought, North knew he could never leave Cold Ridge. Not forever, anyway.

* * *

Val figured she was dreaming or maybe dead. She didn't care which, just so long as it didn't end. Manny was there beside her hospital bed, holding her hand and telling her he loved her, that Eric was okay, they were all okay.

He was crying. That part she could do without.

She touched his stubble of beard. She had all kinds of tubes and crap in her, but a doctor had told her she'd be fine, she was lucky. She liked that. Lucky.

Manny kissed her fingertips, and she felt his tears warm on her hand.

"I just didn't know what else to do," she said.

"I know. Neither did I."

Thirty-Five

Carine rented her apartment to a special education teacher who "loved" her bright colors, which was a good thing, because her landlord hadn't had citrus green and mango and lavender in mind when he'd agreed to let her paint the place. She moved back to her cabin on the edge of the meadow and cleaned it from top to bottom. Satisfied there were no more bats, mice, snakes or any of their droppings, bones and skins, she let herself relax.

It was a cold, bright winter morning, with six inches of fresh snow on the ground. She had her winter hiking books out, new crampons, her serious backpack, her sub-zero sleeping bag, her Nikon with her longest lens—she'd taken a Gus-approved workshop on winter camping, and it was definitely more complicated business than summer camping.

She was good on her own, she thought, filling up a water bottle at her kitchen sink. She didn't need anyone to complete her and never had. But Tyler

North was her soul mate. There was no way around it.

He'd gone back to Hurlburt. She wasn't sure exactly what the team leader of a special tactics team did, but she figured she'd find out—she had tickets to Florida. She'd never been on an air force base. She'd go and see how far she got before someone threw her out or pointed her in Ty's direction. She suspected that the incident in November had reinforced his notion that he was dangerous—that he was bad luck and could die on her and she deserved someone "safer." She wanted to disabuse him of that notion As far as she was concerned, it was just an excuse. He wasn't used to letting anyone in. His mother had been like that—it wasn't just the way he was raised. It was the way he was. Independent, solitary, good on his own.

Well, so was she. She'd redone her Web site and got back to work on her series of guidebooks, beginning with one on the White Mountains. She'd dug out her pictures, started jotting down descriptions of her favorite trails and listing people she needed to contact and places she needed to go.

She could work on the guidebook from Florida if she ended up staying. Air force guys moved around a lot. Ty might not stay in Florida. It didn't matter. Cold Ridge was her home—she belonged there in a way she never would anywhere else. But Ty was definitely her soul mate, and she wanted him to know what that meant to her. She hadn't really known what it meant last February when he'd canceled their wedding. She'd needed this past year to figure it out. In the past weeks, she'd thought of him—she'd thought of herself—on Cold Ridge in November with Gus run over, Eric Carrera near death, Hank Callahan tied up—all of them at the mercy of a determined murderer. What if she'd been killed chasing up the ridge after Eric? What if Ty had been killed rescuing Hank from the burning hut? Anything could have happened. But they'd done what they'd had to do.

She thought she heard a dog barking. A small dog—it was more a little yelp than a proper bark. At least it wasn't Stump. A stray? She didn't have any neighbors, except for Ty, and he wasn't around.

But he was. He knocked on her back door and pushed it open before she could even adjust to his presence. He wasn't wearing a hat or gloves, just a fleece pullover and jeans, his boots, and he gave a mock shiver. "Damn, it's cold out there. I've been in Florida too long." He gave a loud whistle out the back door. "Come on, now, be a good girl."

Carine took in his broad shoulders, his green eyes—everything about him—but couldn't believe she hadn't conjured him up. "Ty—what—"

He winked at her. "Thrown you right off balance, haven't I? Wait just a sec." He patted his thigh several times and whistled again. "Don't make me come and get you."

And next thing, a black-and-brown ball of fur charged into her kitchen and banged against the stove, then bounced up and skidded into the great room on Carine's newly polished wood floors.

A puppy, all of eight weeks old.

"She's excited," Ty said.

"What are you doing with a puppy?"

"She was free. Nobody'd pay money for Stump's offspring. She's his granddaughter. She was born the day Gus got out of the hospital. You can tell she and Stump are related, because she just. peed in my truck."

Carine got down low and called the puppy, who came running, lapping her hands, jumping all over her. She laughed. "What's her name?"

"I don't know. I thought you could help me think one up." He stood at her table and fingered her snow-shoes, her backpack. "Going somewhere?"

"Winter camping."

"Alone?"

She rose, the puppy flopping on her feet. She had on cross-country ski pants and a winter hiking top she'd picked up at Gus's at full price. "I told you, solitary hiking is one of the hazards of my profession."

His green eyes settled on her. "Does it have to be?"

She shrugged. "I don't need a lot of distractions."

He picked up her crampons and examined them, as if he wasn't sure they met his standards. "I heard you tried to access my trust fund."

"Nate, that big mouth. I thought since he was a U.S. marshal—" She paused, realizing she wasn't the least embarrassed. "I didn't try to 'access' it. I just wanted information. I can't stand watching your house go to ruin. I figured it was my heritage, too, since my family built it and owned it for almost a hundred years—''

"Less than seventy-five. Mine's gaining on you."

"Well, Nate was no help whatsoever. Gus said the trust fund was from your father?''

"He was an old guy on the Mount Chester board of trustees. He was in his seventies when he and my mother had their fling—supposedly he planned to marry her, but he had a heart attack and died first. But he left her a little money."

"She was a wonderful woman, Ty. You're not her, you won't ever be her—but she was something. Gus is digging in his attic and cellar for any old artwork of hers, now that it's worth something."

"How's he been on crutches?"

"Miserable. He's drawing up plans for redesigning his kitchen."

"Uh-oh."

"I only know it involves chickens. It has something to do with the egg lady."

"Back to Nate," Ty said. "He proved trustworthy?''

"He proved close-mouthed and stubborn. I couldn't even get him to check and see how much money you have."

"Less now. You heard Manny's back in?"

She nodded, trying to follow his ping-ponging changes in subject. "He's a PJ instructor at Kirtland. I told him I passed the PAST, except I did it over a whole day instead of three hours seeing how I am over thirty. I think he should overlook that 'guy only' thing and let me in, don't you?''

''He's at the end of the pipeline. You'd have a shitload to get through before you got to him, and there'd probably not be much time to take pictures of birds.''

She resisted a smile. ''Okay, so what's he got to do with your dwindling trust fund?''

''I invested in a bookstore with Val. She's something else—she'll probably double my money in a year, never mind independent bookstores falling on hard times. Eric's handling the Tolkein section. The dry western air agrees with him, but he loves New Mexico.''

''No more Mount Chester?''

''He went through a hell of an ordeal. He needs to be with his family.''

''Val would have made a good assistant for Hawk, but I never saw her and Manny in Washington.''

Ty scooped up the puppy and held her in his arms, letting her lick his face. ''They're happy. It's good to see. Manny says it's just his luck to end up with a couple of bookworms.''

''Ty—you're a big softie at heart, aren't you?''

He smiled. ''What have I been saying?'' He set the puppy back on the floor, and she charged around the small house. ''I told Eric I was getting a puppy. He says we should name her Strider.''

''Strider's a male character—''

''It's got a nice ring to it, though, doesn't it? Here,

let me see if it works.'' He whistled again, snapping his fingers and calling ''Strider!''

She came running, ears back, tongue wagging.

''You could have called her anything like that and it'd work,'' Carine said.

He ignored her. ''Hey, Strider, good girl.''

The puppy licked his hand and charged off into Carine's studio.

Ty surveyed her stack of camping food on the counter. ''Well, we could scramble up something here and sit by the fire and pet our puppy, or we could have freeze-dried stroganoff on the ridge, after we've set up our tent in below-zero temperatures and hurricane-force winds—''

''Not hurricane-force winds. The wind's relatively calm today.''

''I like how you say 'relatively.'''

Carine hesitated, hearing the fire crackle in her woodstove, remembering how quiet it had been in her cabin just a few minutes ago. ''I have tickets to Florida for when I get back from camping.''

''Thought you'd sneak onto base, did you? I wondered how long you'd last without seeing me.''

''I can do my job from anywhere. You can't. I mean, there are no air force bases in Cold Ridge.'' She breathed out. ''Not that I'm getting ahead of myself. But I have options. I'm not sure I saw that a year ago.''

''We both have options. The military's been my life since I was eighteen, but I'm not going to be doing this job forever. I can become a weekend warrior and go into the reserves, keep my hand in that way and figure out something to do around here. I still have to make a living. The trust fund's helped me hang on to the house, but it's not like I'm a Rockefeller or something. I want to train our puppy. Raise our kids. The rest we can figure out together. Carine—'' His eyes were serious now. "I was wrong in February. Scared, stupid. Crazy.

"I knew you had a tough year ahead of you. You didn't want to put yourself through worrying about me—put me through worrying about you.

"I'm used to doing things on my own. But I love you, Carine. I always have.''

She could barely speak. "I know.''

He brushed a hand over her hair and touched a finger to the side of her mouth. "Let me try again.'' His voice was low, sincere. "Let me get it right. I want to marry you more than anything else in the world.''

"I said yes once.''

"I understand. You trusted me with your heart once—''

"No, no!'' She shook her head, smiling. "You don't understand. What I'm saying is that my yes is still good. I just—wait a minute, okay?''

She ran into the great room and pulled out the ash bucket she kept beside the woodstove, digging down with her hands until she found her ring. She held it up, blowing off the soot and ashes. "I let Stump tear up my wedding dress and bury it in the backyard, but the ring—I guess I couldn't get rid of it.''

"No, but you could bury it in the ashes. What if you'd accidentally used those ashes for compost?"

"Accidentally? That was the plan, but I didn't get to do a garden this summer. Look. It'll clean up nicely." She got to her feet and handed him the sooty ring. "Do you want to put it on my finger?"

"You've got soot all over you. There's a black spot on the end of your nose."

She knew he didn't give a damn about the soot. "I love you," she said. "I've always loved you."

He smiled. "I knew that's what you meant when you'd say you hated me."

"It wasn't, but that's another story."

He slipped the ring on her finger, and kissed her softly, soot and all, their puppy pulling at his boot laces. "It's good to be home."

From the bestselling author of
The Soul Catcher and *Split Second*

A Maggie O'Dell Novel

AT THE STROKE OF MADNESS

In the tomblike silence of an abandoned rock quarry someone is trying to hide a dirty little secret....

When FBI Special Agent Maggie O'Dell travels to New Haven County, Connecticut, on a tip, a routine missing person investigation quickly turns into a full-fledged hunt for a serial killer.

With only an old man who suffers from Alzheimer's as a witness to the killer's identity, can Maggie piece together the clues to solve the puzzle before time runs out?

ALEX KAVA

"Kava uses a strong supporting cast to provide Scarpetta-like authenticity and the psychological insights of Alex Delaware.... This one is sure to be spotted all over the beach by summer's end."
—*Publishers Weekly* on *The Soul Catcher*

Available in hardcover the first week of August 2003 wherever books are sold!

A beautiful novel about desire, healing
and the most powerful medicine of all—love

USA TODAY bestselling author

Susan Wiggs

Isabel Fish-Wooten has spent most of her life on the run.
Blue Calhoun runs a thriving medical practice while raising
his son alone after an unthinkable tragedy.

When Blue is forced at gunpoint to save Isabel's life, her rescue
comes with an unexpected price. He is drawn to her fragile
beauty and the mystery that surrounds her. She is touched
by this remarkable man and his son.

From danger-filled back alleys to the glittering ballrooms of
high society, Isabel and Blue confront the violence and
corruption that threatens their newfound passion. Theirs is an
unforgettable quest to discover a rare and special love, and the
precious gift of a second chance at happiness.

A Summer Affair

Available the first week of August 2003 wherever paperbacks are sold!

CARLA NEGGERS

66923	STONEBROOK COTTAGE	___ $6.50 U.S.	___ $7.99 CAN.
66845	THE CABIN	___ $6.50 U.S.	___ $7.99 CAN.
66790	THE CARRIAGE HOUSE	___ $6.50 U.S.	___ $7.99 CAN.
66651	THE HARBOR	___ $6.99 U.S.	___ $8.50 CAN.
66582	THE WATERFALL	___ $6.50 U.S.	___ $7.99 CAN.
66541	ON FIRE	___ $5.99 U.S.	___ $6.99 CAN.
66485	KISS THE MOON	___ $5.99 U.S.	___ $6.99 CAN.
66266	CLAIM THE CROWN	___ $5.50 U.S.	___ $6.50 CAN.

(limited quantities available)

TOTAL AMOUNT	$_____
POSTAGE & HANDLING	$_____
($1.00 for one book; 50¢ for each additional)	
APPLICABLE TAXES*	$_____
TOTAL PAYABLE	$_____

(check or money order—please do not send cash)

To order, complete this form and send it, along with a check or money order for the total above, payable to MIRA Books®, to: **In the U.S.:** 3010 Walden Avenue, P.O. Box 9077, Buffalo, NY 14269-9077; **In Canada:** P.O. Box 636, Fort Erie, Ontario, L2A 5X3.

Name:_____

Address:_____ City:_____

State/Prov.:_____ Zip/Postal Code:_____

Account Number (if applicable):_____
075 CSAS

*New York residents remit applicable sales taxes.
Canadian residents remit applicable GST and provincial taxes.

MIRA®

Visit us at www.mirabooks.com

MCN0803BL

Lady Grace Mabry was up to something.

Lovingdon wasn't certain what, but he'd bet his last farthing that she had some scheme in mind. Very deliberately, very slowly, her eyes never leaving his, she tugged on each fingertip of her glove and leisurely peeled off the kidskin, exposing her wrist, her palm, her fingers. So slender, so pale. It had been years since the sun had kissed her skin. He wondered if any gentlemen had this evening.

She moved her bared hand over to the other glove, and he cursed her actions and his fascination with the gathering of material, the revealing of skin. Bloody Christ. It was only an arm. Her pale blue ball gown with blue piping and embroidered roses left her shoulders and neck enticingly bare, but the upper swells of her breasts were demurely covered, and yet he found the unrevealed more alluring than everything revealed by any courtesan he'd visited of late.

His world tilted off its axis.

LORRAINE HEATH

WHEN THE DUKE WAS WICKED

AVON

An Imprint of HarperCollinsPublishers

This is a work of fiction. Names, characters, places, and incidents are products of the author's imagination or are used fictitiously and are not to be construed as real. Any resemblance to actual events, locales, organizations, or persons, living or dead, is entirely coincidental.

AVON BOOKS
An Imprint of HarperCollins*Publishers*
10 East 53rd Street
New York, New York 10022-5299

Copyright © 2014 by Jan Nowasky
ISBN 978-0-06-227622-3
www.avonromance.com

First Avon Books mass market printing: March 2014

Avon Trademark Reg. U.S. Pat. Off. and in Other Countries, Marca Registrada, Hecho en U.S.A.
HarperCollins® is a registered trademark of HarperCollins Publishers.

Printed in the U.S.A.

10 9 8 7 6 5 4 3 2 1

*In loving memory of our sweet Duchess,
who became a member of our family after
surviving Katrina. She never met a stranger,
never had a harsh bark for anyone, and
taught us that dogs do indeed smile.*

Prologue

From the Journal of the Duke of Lovingdon

On the morning of February 2, 1872, I, Henry Sidney Stanford, the seventh Duke of Lovingdon, Marquess of Ashleigh, and Earl of Wyndmere, died.

Not that my death was apparent to anyone other than myself.

I continued to breathe. I still walked about. On occasion, I spoke. I seldom smiled. I never laughed.

Because on that morning, that dreadful morning, my heart and soul were ripped from me when my wife and precious daughter succumbed to typhus within hours of each other—and with their passing, I died.

But in time I was reborn into someone my mother barely recognized.

All my life I had sought to do the right and proper thing. I did not frequent gaming hells. I did not imbibe until I became a stumbling drunk. I fell in love at nineteen, married at twenty-one. I did the honorable thing: I did not bed my wife until I wed her. On our wedding night she was not the only virgin between our sheets.

I was above reproach. I had done all that I could to be a good and honorable man.

I was brought up to believe that we were rewarded according to our behavior. Yet the Fates had conspired to punish me, to take away that which I treasured above all else, and I could find no cause for their unkind regard.

And so I said to hell with it all. I would sow the wild oats I had not in my youth. I would gamble, I would drink, I would know many women.

Yet I knew, with my blackened heart, that I would never again love. That no one would ever stir me back to giving a damn about anything beyond pleasure.

Chapter 1

London
1874

The Duke of Lovingdon relished nothing more than being nestled between a woman's sweet thighs.

Unless it was gliding his hands over her warm and supple body while she caressed his shoulders, his chest, his back. Or hearing the hitch of her breath, a murmured sigh, a—

Rap.

He paused, she stilled.

"What was that?" she whispered.

He shook his head, gazing into her brown eyes and fingering back from her blushing cheek the

stray strands of her ebony hair. "The residence settling, no doubt. Pay it no mind."

He lowered his mouth to her silky throat, relishing her heated skin—

Rap. Rap.

Dammit all!

He winked. "Excuse me but a moment."

Rolling out of the massive bed that had been
specially built to accommodate his large frame,
he marched across the thick Aubusson carpet,
his temper barely leashed. His butler—all his
servants—knew better than to disturb him when
he was enjoying the offerings of a woman.

He closed his hand around the handle, released
the latch—

"There damned well better be blood or fire involved—"

He swung open the door. "—in whatever—"

He stared into wide, rounded sapphire eyes that
dipped down before quickly jerking up and clash-
ing with his of amber.

"Sweet Christ, Grace, what the devil?"

Before she could respond, he slammed the door
shut, snatched up his trousers from the floor, hastily drew them on, and proceeded to button them.

"Another one of your paramours?" the luscious
vixen in his bed asked.

He grabbed his linen shirt from where it was draped over a chair. "Good God, no. She's but a child." Or at least she'd been the last time he'd seen her. What the deuce was she doing out and about this time of night? Had she no sense whatsoever?

After pulling on his shirt, he dropped into the chair and tugged on his boots. He didn't know why he was concerned with Grace's sensibilities. It was truly a bit late to worry about them, considering the view he'd given her when he opened the door. Trust her to take the sight with unfettered aplomb. She'd always been a bold little she-devil, but she'd taken things too far tonight.

He shoved himself to his feet and crossed over to the bed. Leaning down, he kissed the lovely's forehead. "I won't be but a moment in dispatching her." After giving her a reassuring wink, he strode across the room, opened the door with a bit more calm, and stepped into the hallway, closing the door behind him.

Grace stood where he'd left her, blushing deeply from her neck to the roots of her coppery hair. Had her freckles not faded, they would have been obliterated. "I'm sorry to have awakened you."

Is that all she thought she was doing? But then she was an innocent miss at nineteen, and while the lads she'd grown up with were more scoundrel than gent, they had all done what they could to preserve her innocence. For her, their wicked ways were little more than rumor.

"It's after midnight. You're in a bachelor's residence. What are you thinking?" he asked.

"I'm in trouble, Lovingdon, a situation most dire. I need your help."

He was on the cusp of telling her to seek assistance elsewhere, but she gazed at him with large blue innocent eyes that left him with little choice except to suggest they adjourn to his library. She'd always had that irritating effect on him, ever since she was a young girl and looked at him as though he were some errant knight capable of slaying dragons.

Perhaps in his youth when the dragon was little more than her foul-tempered cat in need of rescue from its perch on the tree limb—

But he had learned through harsh experience that he was not a dragon slayer.

After they reached the musty scented room, he crossed over to a table that housed an assortment of decanters. In silence, he poured a scotch and a brandy. He hoped beyond hope that when he was done pouring, she would be gone. But when he turned, she was still there, studying him as though she were searching for something, and he found himself wishing that he'd taken a bit more time in dressing. Her attire was far more formal: a white ball gown trimmed in pink velvet.

He'd known Grace all his life. She was not generally one to need help. Certainly she was not one to ask for it. She'd once spent an entire afternoon stranded in a tree because she was too stubborn to alert anyone to her predicament. Wanted to get down on her own. Eventually, as darkness fell, he'd climbed the tree and helped her to the ground, even though he'd been twenty to her eleven, and much too old to be scampering up trees. Then he'd had to reclimb the blasted elm to rescue her mean-spirited cat. He bore the scars from the encounter on his left wrist.

For her to come to him now, she had to be in very bad trouble indeed.

As he held the snifter toward her, he could not mistake the gratitude in her expression as she wrapped slender white-gloved hands around his offering. While it was entirely inappropriate for a lady to be alone in a bachelor's residence, theirs was no ordinary relationship. Their families were close, and she had practically grown up within his shadow, as he had spent much of his youth watching out for her. If she were indeed in trouble, her parents—the Duke and Duchess of Greystone—

were more likely to kill him in a most unpleasant manner if he didn't help her than to harm him in any fashion for allowing her to remain in his residence at this ungodly and scandalous hour.

He indicated the seating area near the fireplace where glowing embers were all that remained of an earlier fire.

Her skirts rustling, her fragrance of roses and lavender drifting toward him, she wandered to a burgundy chair and perched herself on the edge of its cushion. She'd always been a complex creature, never content with the ordinary, not easily defined. One scent was not enough for her. And neither was one gentleman, based upon the conversations he barely gave any notice to at the gaming hells.

He took the wingback chair opposite hers, slowly sipped his scotch and studied her for a moment. Although he knew her age to be nineteen, he couldn't help but wonder when the bloody hell she had grown up. He knew her as a spindly legged and freckled-armed girl who preferred climbing trees to visiting ballrooms, who preferred galloping her horse over the gently rolling hills to attending dance lessons.

She was nine years his junior. He'd known, of course, that she was growing up, but his realization had been more of a vague sort of thing, on the periphery of his life, like knowing the seasons were changing but not being fully aware of each falling leaf or budding blossom. She had certainly blossomed. She was slender with only the barest hint of curves. Her gown, while revealing her neck and upper chest, stopped just short of displaying any swells of her breasts. He would not have expected her to be so modest, yet with her modesty she became more mysterious.

It seemed she was also fearless. He'd heard that she had no qualms traveling about at night to the foundling homes that her parents had opened. While she generally had a chaperone in tow, she was rumored to be skilled at escaping her notice.

Tonight's little visit a prime example.

He tapped his glass, striving to get his thoughts back on track, to her problem, her reason for being here. "So what's this trouble you're in?"

"You weren't at the Ainsley ball," she responded, no censure in her voice, but still it was laced with something that very much resembled disappointment. He tried to remember when she'd had her coming out, if he'd even been aware of it. Respectable activities no longer held any allure, and he managed to successfully avoid them.

"Did some gent take advantage? Do I need to fetch my pistols?"

She smiled, a warm, amused tilt to her plump, soft-looking lips. "No, but it warms the cockles of my heart to know you would champion me."

Yes, he'd champion her. When she was a child. He didn't have the desire to champion anyone these days. What he did desire was waiting for him upstairs in his bed.

"You've never been one to stall," he pointed out impatiently. "Explain what brings you here and be quick about it."

She held up her hand. Dangling from her wrist was a card, her dance card. "I danced every dance tonight. If previous balls are any indication, in the morning dozens of bouquets of flowers will be delivered to the residence."

"You are most popular."

"No," she stated succinctly. "As you are no doubt well aware, I come with an immense dowry that includes land and coin. It is my dowry that is popular."

"Don't be ridiculous. You offer a good deal to a man. You're lovely and charming and poised. I'd wager all my estates that you'll be betrothed before the Season is out."

She rose from the chair with the grace to which he'd alluded and stepped over to the fireplace. She was tall. He was well over six feet, and her head could bump against his chin without her rising up on her toes. The long slope of her throat would draw a gentleman's eye. Small understated pearls circled her neck, adorned her ears. She had no reason to be flashy. Her hair sufficed. It was presently piled on her head, a few tendrils deliberately left to toy with the delicate nape of her neck. He suspected the haphazard ones circling her oval face were not planned but had escaped their bounds during the ball, no doubt when she had waltzed.

"But will I be loved, Lovingdon? You know love, you've experienced it. However can I identify it?"

He gulped down scotch that was meant to be savored. He would not travel that path, not with her, not with anyone. "You'll know it because it'll be someone without whom you cannot live."

Turning slightly, she met his gaze. "I do not doubt that I will know if I love him. But how will I know if he loves me? My dear friend, Lady Bertram, was madly in love with her husband. He has since taken a mistress. It's broken her heart. He was infatuated with her dowry, not her. And Lady Sybil Fitzsimmons? Her husband has taken to scolding and berating her. How can he love her if he berates her, in public no less? With so many men vying for my affections, how can I know if their hearts are true? I shall marry only once, and fortune hunters abound. I want to ensure that I choose well."

"Trust your heart."

"Do you not see? It is obvious to me that in the matter of love, a woman cannot trust her heart. It can be most easily influenced with poetry, and chocolates, and flowers. A lady requires an objective person, one who is familiar enough with love to assist her in identifying and weeding out the insincere, separating the wheat from the chaff, so to speak. Someone like you."

"I am no longer an expert in love, and I have no desire to become embroiled in it again, not even from the outskirts."

"Is that why you've turned to this life of debauchery?"

He eyed her over the rim of his glass. "What do you know of debauchery?"

"I've heard rumors." She stroked her fingers along the edge of the mantel as though searching for dust. "And I know you weren't alone this evening when I disturbed you. Is she your mistress?"

"A mistress implies a certain amount of permanence. I have no interest in permanence."

She peered over at him. "A courtesan, then."

"Is that sharpness on your tongue disapproval?"

"I'm not judging you."

"Aren't you?"

She shook her head, a sadness in her eyes that irritated him. "No. You have every right to be angry with fate for what it stole—"

"I won't discuss it, Grace. Not fate, not Juliette, not love. I don't need you or anyone else to justify my actions. I live as I wish to live. I find satisfaction in it, and make no excuses for it. If you want someone who is an expert on love, I suggest you talk with your parents. They seem to have weathered enough storms."

She scoffed. "Do you truly believe I'm going to discuss my interest in gentlemen with my mother or father? They are each likely to inflict bodily harm on any gentleman I am unsure of, simply by virtue of my being unsure of him. Besides, they will tell me to marry whomever will make me happy."

"Sound advice."

"Have you not been listening? Just because he makes me happy before the vows are exchanged does not mean he will make me happy afterward. If you will not bring your knowledge of love to my quest, you can at least bring your recent experiences to bear. Who better to identify a blackguard than another blackguard? I need you, Lovingdon."

I need you. Juliette had needed him and he'd failed her.

"Please, Lovingdon."

He almost believed there was more to her plea

than met the ears. Where was the harm? He held out his hand. She stared at it as though she didn't recognize what it was.

He snapped his fingers. "I'll take a quick look at your list, assist you in eliminating the cads, so you can be on your way."

"How can you discern a man's feelings for me simply by reading his name?"

"I can identify those with whom you do not wish to invest your heart, those of bad habits and vices."

"If that's what I wanted, I'd go to Drake. He knows men's vices better than anyone."

Drake Darling—a former street urchin and thief who'd grown up within the bosom of Grace's family—managed Dodger's Drawing Room, a gaming hell for respectable gentlemen. Yes, he was certainly familiar with various gentlemen's vices, but he was also very good at holding secrets.

"I need more," she said. "I need you to observe them, to then offer your opinion on them." She knelt before him, and while the glowing embers provided little light, it was enough for him to see the desperation in her blue eyes. "Attend Claybourne's ball. It's the next one of any importance. Be a wallflower, stand behind fronds. Then provide a report on what you've noticed, who you believe truly cares for me."

The thought of being at a place filled with such joviality caused him to grow clammy. It would only serve to remind him of happier times, and how quickly and painfully they'd been snatched from him. "Trust your heart, girl. It won't lead you astray. You'll be able to tell if a man cares for you."

Defeat swept over her features. "I can't trust my heart, Lovingdon. It's betrayed me before."

He felt as though he'd taken a hard punch to the gut. He despised the thought of her hurting. Had some man taken advantage? Why else would she not trust her instincts?

Standing, she returned to the fireplace, presenting him with her back. "When I was younger, I once fell deeply, passionately in love—or as passionately as one can at such a tender age. I thought he returned my affections. But eventually he married another."

"Who? No." He held up a hand. "That is not my concern."

With a sad smile, she glanced over her shoulder at him. "Don't worry. I won't reveal his name. You would think me an utter fool if you knew who he was."

"Just because he took another to wife doesn't mean he didn't love you. Men marry for all sorts of reasons."

"As I'm well aware. Which is the reason that I'm here. Do you not see that you are making my arguments for me? How do I determine that they are marrying me for the right reason, for love, and that their affections are not held elsewhere? I fear that if I were to give my heart to another, and discover that he truly had little regard for it—the devastation could very well be my undoing."

"Little Rose, perhaps it's better not to love."

She glided back to the chair and sat. "Do you truly believe that? Is it not better to hold someone for a short span of time rather than not to have held them at all?"

For the briefest of moments he heard laughter—Juliette's laughter. He saw her smile, felt the warmth of her touch, tasted her lips, felt the heat of her body welcoming his. It had been so long, so very long since he had given himself leave to think of her at all. The agony of it nearly doubled him over.

"I want what you had," Grace said softly. "It was perfection, was it not?"

"I shall never love another as I loved her. That is the honest truth."

She studied him for a long thoughtful moment before asking, "What is it like to have such a grand love?"

It was all-encompassing, permeated everything. How could he put into words an emotion that defied them? "You laugh, you smile. You have secrets to which no one else is privy. You can communicate without words. You know what each other is thinking. There is a sense of euphoria. But it all comes with a price, Grace. Losing it can destroy you, turn you into little more than a hollow shell."

"You cannot dissuade me from wanting it, even if it is only for the blink of an eye. To love someone and to know beyond doubt that he loved me would be the most wondrous experience I can imagine. And therein rests my dilemma—it is not enough to love. I must be loved in return, or what is the point? Will you assist me in my quest for true love? I can think of no better way to honor your Juliette than to help someone acquire what the two of you once held."

Once held and lost. He would not wish his sorrow on his worst enemy.

"I can't help you, Grace. It would serve neither of us well for me to even try. You should be off now, before your father discovers where you are and forces me to marry you. That would be the quickest way to ensure that you do not acquire that which you seek."

"My father trusts you. He knows you would not take advantage."

"Be that as it may, if anyone were to see you leave here, you would be ruined."

"I will not marry a man who does not love me, even in the face of ruination." Her words came with such conviction, but he knew from experience that conviction did not always render the words true.

"Be that as it may, I fear you would have no choice."

"We all have choices." Slowly she rose. "The Claybourne ball."

He did not watch her leave, but instead turned his gaze back to the fireplace, where the embers no longer glowed. She asked the impossible of him—just as Juliette had.

Don't let us die.

I won't.

But he had.

Chapter 2

As the carriage rattled along the cobblestones, Lady Grace Mabry's thoughts traveled to where they ought not: Lovingdon opening his bedchamber door and standing there proudly in the altogether. She'd caught a glimpse of the woman in his bed, knew she'd not awakened him, yet it seemed prudent to act the innocent.

But doing so left her with questions that a lady shouldn't entertain, but they were there nonetheless, and she wasn't certain to whom she could turn for the answers.

The Duke of Lovingdon did not resemble any statuary she had ever gazed upon. She'd seen Michelangelo's David, among others. Lovingdon put them all to shame. She could have stood there staring at him forever, but she'd forced herself to lift her gaze to his because it wouldn't do for him to know that she'd wanted to touch.

All of him. His broad shoulders, his flat stomach, his . . . maleness. No, he was not at all like David in that regard. He'd been quite breathtaking. As the memory caused heat to suffuse her, she pressed her cheek to the cool glass.

She'd been fortunate to find his residence not locked up for the night. She supposed that meant the woman wouldn't be staying. She didn't know why relief accompanied the thought. What did it matter one way or the other when the woman was there now?

Grace had been all of seven when she first came to love Lovingdon. Although in retrospect she knew it was little more than a young girl's fancy, but at the time it had seemed so much more to her young heart.

Spring had only just arrived, and her mother had invited the other families—connected by hearts, not blood—to join them at Mabry Manor, her father's ancestral estate. Some of the young boys had taken to teasing her about her red hair, saying she looked like a carrot. She had been curled in a corner of the stable weeping when Lovingdon found her and crouched beside her. He was sixteen, on the cusp of manhood. With his thumbs, he gently wiped away her tears. No boy had ever touched her so tenderly. Her childish heart had done a little somersault. He could have asked anything of her at that moment and she would have granted it. He could have called her anything—Freckles, Coppery, Hideous—and she would have thought it poetry. Instead he had stolen her heart with his words.

"You're only a bud right now," he'd said. "No one appreciates the bud, but before long you will blossom into a beauty as lovely as a red rose that will put all other ladies to shame. Now come on, Little Rose. No more moping about. Someday you shall have your revenge, and it will be incredibly sweet."

Over the years, he had called her Little Rose. Until he married. Then he had no time for her at all, had given her no attention. While her yearning heart had known that was the way it should be, that her feelings were little more than childish affection, it also felt the sharp sting of rejection.

Tonight had been the first time in years since he referred to her using the endearment. And her heart did that silly little somersault thing in her chest, which had irritated her beyond measure. She didn't want it dancing about for him. He had proven to be a disappointment. She loved him as a friend, a brother. Her woman's heart would never love him as more than that.

But he possessed the knowledge she required to achieve happiness. He knew love, and he knew the wicked ways of men. Who better to assist her? Yet he did not care about her enough to take a holiday from all his sinning. She supposed that said it all. His was not a character to be admired.

What a fool she'd been all those years ago to hold him in such high regard. She could not risk misjudging again, for this time she would be attached to a man for the remainder of her life. She wanted a good man, an honest man, a man willing to be her hero even when she wasn't in need of one.

Sitting at the breakfast table the following morning, Grace could not help but be amused that, just as she'd predicted, an abundance of flowers began arriving before she cracked the top of her soft-boiled egg. She supposed she should have been giddy with excitement, but she was quite simply too practical for such nonsense. It was a result of her upbringing, she speculated, or more to the point—her mother's.

It was no secret that Frannie Mabry, Duchess of Greystone, had grown up on the streets under the care of a kidsman who taught her to survive by cunning, thievery, and fraud. Grace had listened to her stories with fascination, and as she moved toward womanhood gained an immense measure

of respect for her mother. She also gained an unbridled belief in love, having witnessed it firsthand.
Against all odds and her sordid beginnings, her
mother had won the heart of a duke.

Grace dearly wanted the sort of love they shared:
one of adoration, respect, support. For many years
her mother continued to manage the books at
Dodger's Drawing Room. She was part owner of
the gentlemen's club, and her husband took great
pride in her accomplishments and independence.
They worked with common purpose to improve
the plight of orphans. They shared goals, triumphs,
and failure. But nothing deterred them from reaching for what they sought to obtain. Grace was
convinced that in all aspects of their life they had
achieved success and happiness because their relationship was built on a foundation of love.

While she might have asked her parents to help
her determine if a gentleman truly loved her, neither of them thought any man worthy of her.

"Another morning filled with flowers, I see," her
father mused as he wandered into the breakfast
dining room and headed for the sideboard where
an assortment of Cook's best fare awaited him.

Grace only recently learned of his failing eyesight, although it had apparently plagued him for
years. He'd hoped to keep it a secret from his chil-

dren for much longer, but as he had taken to leaning more on their mother, his steps became more
cautious and he tended to squint more often, even
though that action did nothing to widen a world
that was slowly going dark.

Grace wanted to marry before he was completely
blind. A silly reason, she knew, but she wanted him
to see that she was gloriously happy.

"Do you suppose I should let it be known that I
much prefer a gent make a donation to a children's
home?" she said in response to his comment about
the flowers. "It doesn't even necessarily have to be
one of ours."

Her parents had built three homes for orphans
and one for unwed mothers. Grace had always
been aware that some people were less fortunate,
and she was brought up to believe that she had
both an obligation and a duty to help where she
could. She wanted a husband who also believed
in good works, not one who would squander her
dowry. She really wasn't asking for much, was she?

Her father joined her at the table, sitting in his
usual place at its head, while she had always taken
a chair to his right. "Those who are in the flower
trade have bills to pay as well."

"I suppose that's true enough. It's only that
flowers wilt; they don't last."

"So we must enjoy them while we can."

Her stomach tightened with the realization that shortly he would be able to only enjoy their fragrance, not their vibrant colors, the shape of their petals.

"Most girls would be delighted to have a man shower them with flowers as a way of giving them attention," her father said.

"But then I am not most girls."

He smiled. "As I'm certain the gentlemen are coming to realize. How was the ball? Did anyone strike your fancy?"

Her parents seldom attended soirees any longer, as her father could no longer tolerate crowds. He had too much pride to be caught knocking into someone he couldn't see.

"A few gentlemen engaged me in interesting conversation. Lord Somerdale is quite fascinated with the pollination capabilities of bees. Tedious process."

"Equally tedious to hear about, I venture."

She laughed. "Immeasurably tedious. Lord Amber's bones creak when the weather grows cold. He lives in the North, which means I would forever be hearing his bones creaking. Not very appealing, really."

"No." Her father creased his brow. "You are talking about the fifth Lord Amber."

"No, unfortunately. The fourth."

"I thought he'd died some years back."

"Not quite." White-haired, he held a horn-shaped instrument up to his ear in order to hear. He didn't dance. He simply tottered about. "He doesn't need an heir. I think he's just lonely."

"Yes, well, you can mark him off your list. The whole point in giving you an ample dowry was so you would have an abundance of choices and wouldn't have to settle."

"I fear it's given me far too many suitors. I'm finding it a bit difficult to weed out the sincere from the insincere."

"Trust your heart."

She began slathering butter on her toast. "Yes, that's what Lovingdon said."

Not that his advice had been any help at all.

Her father stilled, his teacup halfway to his mouth. "When did you see him?"

She lifted a shoulder. "Oh, recently our paths crossed."

"Last night, perhaps?"

Now she was the one who froze, her lungs refusing to draw in air.

Before she could deny it, he said, "Your maid returned to the residence at half past eleven. You didn't seem to be about."

She should have known he'd be alert to her not arriving. She was surprised he hadn't been waiting in the foyer when she did finally get home. But then, her father was accustomed to her spending nights at the foundling homes. "I went to see him, yes, to ask his opinion about some of the gentlemen courting me."

"Grace, a young lady does not go to a bachelor's residence at all hours of the night."

"It wasn't all hours. It was only one: midnight. He was unhelpful and I promptly took my leave."

"You are missing my point."

"You know Lovingdon wouldn't take advantage. He sees me as a sister." She hated the disgust that wove through her voice with the final words.

"And you wish he considered you as more."

It seemed her father saw far more with his limited vision than most did with all their eyesight intact.

"Once, I admit, when I was a young girl I was infatuated with him, but now he just angers me. He no longer moves about in Society, and I've heard the rumors regarding what a wastrel he's become. It's very disappointing, and sets such a bad example. Still, I must confess that I had rather hoped, when he saw me in my evening attire, that he would cease to think of me as a child."

Her father placed his hand over hers. "I don't

think anyone would mistake you for a child. You've grown into a remarkable woman. You deserve a man who will love and appreciate you. As much as I hate to say it, I don't think he can love or appreciate anyone anymore."

"I fear you're right. He's breaking his mother's heart."

"Olivia can take care of herself. And I won't have him breaking yours. Now," he said, returning his attention to his breakfast, "no more of these late night excursions. I don't want to have to lock you in your room."

She gave him an impish grin. "As though you ever would."

"I will do whatever is necessary to see you safe and happy."

"Well today, happy is a new gown." She rose from her chair, bent down and kissed his cheek. "I love you, Papa."

"Someday, when you least expect it, sweetheart, love will arrive and it will not be at all as you imagined."

"Is that how it was for you?"

"It was so much more."

She retook her seat, threaded her fingers through his and squeezed. "But at what point do I reveal the truth about my . . . situation?"

She could see the sadness and sorrow woven in the depths of his blue eyes.

"You leave that to me. I'll take care of it when they ask for your hand."

"While I appreciate your willingness to stand as my champion, I believe most strongly that the news should come from me. Sometimes I think I should take out an advert. 'Beware! Lady Grace Mabry may come with an immense dowry, but she is far from perfect.' "

"I was far from perfect. It didn't stop your mother from loving me."

"But I think it will take a very special man indeed to accept my imperfection."

"Not so special as you might think."

Lovingdon traveled through the London streets with the coach's shades drawn. He had an ache behind his eyes brought on by too much liquor and the smoke of too many cigars. The disadvantage to playing cards in a room without windows was that one was not able to see night giving way to day.

After Grace had left the evening before, he'd sent the woman in his bed on her merry way with a hefty pouch of coins, while he'd gone in search of liquor and gambling. Those he played with on a regular basis were very skilled, and winning against them required focus, which he had hoped would serve as adequate distraction. But Grace continued to intrude on his musings. She deserved love. He could think of no one who deserved it more. But he couldn't quite wrap his mind around her dilemma. She was sharp, clever, spirited. Surely she could tell if a man's affections were true. Something was amiss but he wasn't quite sure what it was.

Besides, a man would be unwise to play her for a fool. It was no secret that her parents' friends and their family members would defend her to the death. But she could have gone to anyone for assistance. Truth be told, anyone would have been a better choice, as he no longer frequented Society, avoided the trappings of polite merry-making like the plague.

His coach rolled to a stop. A footman hastily opened the door. Sunlight scalded Lovingdon's eyes, but he merely squinted against it as he exited. He wanted a bath and then a bed.

He strode up the steps. Another footman opened the large, thick wooden door for him. He marched through and was accosted by the heavy fragrance of flowers. Little wonder as an absurd amount of blossoms filled the entryway. All colors, all varieties, shapes, and sizes. Nauseatingly sweet.

"Welcome home, Your Grace," his butler, Barrow, said, appearing from down a hallway.

"What's the meaning of all this?"

"They arrived an hour ago, with this missive." Barrow held out the folded parchment.

In spite of his resounding headache, Lovingdon took the paper, unfolded it, and narrowed his eyes at the words.

This morning's arrivals. However is a lady to decide?

He scoffed. Grace, not giving up on acquiring his assistance, it appeared. So like the stubborn little minx.

"What shall I do with them, sir?" Barrow asked.

"Send them back to Greystone's with a message that simply says, 'No.'" He started up the stairs, paused. "On second thought, send them 'round to a hospital or someplace where people are in need of cheering." He had already won the battle. No sense in engaging in further combat. He didn't want Grace bloodied. She would get his message quickly enough when she realized he was ignoring hers.

He had traversed three more steps when he abruptly reversed direction and headed back down. Barrow still stood at attention, as though he'd known Lovingdon was not quite yet finished.

"I'll be sending a missive 'round to Mabry House."

Chapter 3

One did not complain about having in abundance that which others wished desperately to obtain.

So Grace did not complain about her aching toes, because they were the result of enjoying far too many gentlemen's attentions. She merely settled herself on the plush ottoman in the ladies' retiring room and lifted a swollen foot, so her lady's maid could replace her worn-out slippers with new ones. It was the second time this evening that she'd had to retire from the ballroom, promising a disappointed gentleman that she would be more than happy to entertain him in her mother's parlor the following afternoon. She did not reveal that he wouldn't be the only one in attendance. She tried to leave a few dances open so she could have a moment's respite, but the gentlemen were simply so frightfully insistent that their night would be incomplete without a turn about the ballroom floor with her in their arms.

So she succumbed to their charms.

And they were charming. Every last one of them. Which was part of her dilemma. How to separate charm from con.

She had spent a good deal of the night searching the shadows for Lovingdon, but as far as she could tell, he had not come. The message that he sent a few days earlier—*He'll know your favorite flower*—had given her hope that he would be on hand at Claybourne's ball to assist her in discerning who was a fortune hunter and who was not. She couldn't assume that just because a man's coffers were empty he was only after her fortune. On her own she had eliminated some of the men who were. They always had greedy little eyes and spoke of all the things they could accomplish with her dowry in hand.

A rather poor courtship technique.

But most of her suitors were not as overt and rarely mentioned her monetary assets. Courtship was an art, and they had perfected it. As she was the lady of the Season with the largest dowry, she drew the most attention—which did not endear her to many of the other ladies. They knew they would be getting the cast-offs.

With a sigh, she stood. "Thank you, Felicity." While most in the aristocracy did not usually thank servants for doing their tasks, Grace had grown up hearing her mother constantly thanking servants. A product of the streets, her mother took nothing for granted and treated everyone as though they mattered because to her they did. She'd passed that attribute on to Grace.

Felicity helped to straighten her hair, to repin what could be contained. Grace's hair was so curly that the strands were often escaping their constraints. With a last look in the mirror, Grace turned and nearly ran into Lady Cornelia. The woman possessed all the curves that Grace didn't.

"Please release Lord Ambrose from your spell," Lady Cornelia whispered.

"Pardon?"

Lady Cornelia glanced around as though she expected demons to be lurking in the corners, but the only other two ladies in the room were busy chattering while their maids repinned their hair.

"Lord Ambrose—if you were to let him know that he had no chance of gaining your favor—he might look elsewhere for the funds he needs in order to continue raising his horses."

"You fancy him?" Grace asked.

"He is not so hard on the eyes. I will admit to

favoring him. And I'm terribly fond of horses. His in particular, as they are the most beautiful thoroughbreds. And he has a lovely estate. I would like very much to be his countess."

Although love was woefully absent from the lady's reasons, Grace studied her card. It wasn't her place to judge what someone else desired for happiness. "Who do you have for the fifteenth dance?"

"No one. I've had all of three dances claimed. My dowry is nowhere near as large as yours, my father is not as powerful. I have atrocious black hair and am as white as my mother's tablecloth. My brother says I look like a ghoul."

Grace smiled. "Brothers are hideous, aren't they?"

"You're lucky yours aren't about this Season."

"I'm very lucky indeed." Striving to strengthen the bond between them, Grace wrapped her fingers around Lady Cornelia's arm. "Just before the fifteenth dance, meet me by the doors leading onto the terrace. I suspect my feet will be aching too badly for me to enjoy the quadrille. Perhaps you would be kind enough to dance with Lord Ambrose in my stead."

Lady Cornelia beamed, and Grace didn't think she looked at all like a ghoul. She thought she more closely resembled an angel. "The other girls are jealous of the attentions you get, you know."

"I know. But we always want what someone else has."

"What do you want?"

Grace gently squeezed her arm. "I want you to have Lord Ambrose."

Before Lady Cornelia could pepper her further, Grace walked from the room. She wasn't about to admit to anyone—other than Lovingdon—that she desired love. She didn't want to be painted as a pathetic creature who doubted her own self-worth, but there were moments when she feared love would be denied her.

She glided down the stairs that led to the first landing. Lord Vexley was standing there, his elbow resting on the first baluster. He was quite possibly one of the most handsome men she'd ever known. His black hair was styled to perfection. Unlike hers, none of the strands ever rebelled. His deep blue eyes sparkled, his smile was broad and welcoming.

"I was afraid I was going to have to go up those stairs and drag you out of that private room where ladies secret away to do and say who knows what," he teased as she neared.

"You're waiting for me?"

"I am. The next dance is mine, and unlike some of the other gents, I'm not willing to give up a waltz with the most beautiful woman here." He extended his arm as she moved off the last step.

She placed her hand in the crook of his elbow. "You flatter me, my lord."

"I believe we would make a remarkable pair."

He escorted her into the ballroom just as the music was drifting into silence. Very well-timed planning. And he was so deuced handsome. She did wish she felt more for him than mild pleasure at being in his company. Unfortunately none of the gentlemen courting her stirred her heart. It beat its same constant, steady rhythm whether she was thinking about them, dancing with them, or conversing. Nothing was terribly wrong with any of them, but neither was anything terribly right.

"Did my tulips arrive after Ainsley's ball?" he asked.

"They did." Not her favorites, but a close second. "As did the chocolates." She had not bothered to send those around to Lovingdon. She was willing to go only so far to convince him she was in need of his assistance, and giving up chocolate was one step too far. Although she wondered if they may have made a difference toward securing his cooperation. In his youth, chocolate had been his favorite treat, but then he was not who he had once been. If he was, he would have put her needs above his and been willing to assist her. On the other hand he had responded to the arrival of the flowers, although not to the extent she would have wished, but better than not at all.

It occurred to her that in order to gain further help from him, she was going to have to take more drastic measures.

Although it was long past midnight Grace walked with confidence along the dimly lit narrow corridor, her skirts rustling over the thick carpeting. She expected that her arrival would be frowned upon by those she would soon be encountering, but then she'd never cared one whit about obtaining their approval. Neither had they cared about gaining hers. They did as they pleased, when they pleased, with whom they pleased. While they might not want to have anything to do with her, she was not going to give them a choice. Not tonight anyway.

They were men, after all, and as she'd recently learned, a practiced smile accompanied by a fluttering of the eyelashes could turn the most intelligent of men into mindless dolts, who could be led wherever a lady wished to lead. Her problem, however, was that she didn't want a man who was so easily controlled, nor did she want one who sought to control her. She wanted a partner in life, one who saw her as an equal, even if the law didn't.

She finally reached the door located within the darkest of corners. Against the thick mahogany, she delivered three sharp knuckle raps, a pause, and two more, the last dispensed more quickly than the first set. At eye level a tiny door, a small opening in the much larger door, creaked open. A man peered out. The shadows effectively hid from her the details of his face. She would not have been surprised to find him wearing a mask.

Much ado was always made about secretive meetings.

"Only those knowing the special word may pass through here," he growled, his voice deep and rumbling, as though he were auditioning for the role of ogre in a child's fairy tale.

Ah, the dramatics. She was allowed to come and play here on her birthday, and so she knew how to gain entry.

"Feagan."

Homage paid to the kidsman who had once managed the den of child thieves that included her mother.

The oaf barring her way grunted. A lock clanked as it was released, then he swung the door open and Grace waltzed past him through the narrow portal. He was a big, hulking brute whom she had never encountered before. She suspected his size alone intimidated quite a few, and his large meaty fists would intimidate anyone else.

"I'll take you to the others—" he began.

"No need."

She moved on, parting heavy velvet draperies that appeared black with the absence of light, though she knew they were a deep, rich burgundy. Sitting areas and tables adorned with decanters were in this section, but no one was making use of the lounging area in which to sulk, which meant that in all likelihood the games had not been going on long enough for anyone to have been separated from too many of his coins. Parting another set of draperies, she glided through—

"No! God, Grace, what are you doing here?" Drake Darling came up out of his chair at a large round table covered in green baize. It appeared he had repeatedly tunneled his fingers through his dark hair, a sign that the evening was not going his way. He managed Dodger's; she suspected a day would come when he would own it.

Her eyes momentarily stung in the smoke-hazed room. Tables with more decanters lined the walls. Servants liveried in red stood at the ready. One tall fellow moved toward her. Drake held up a hand to stay him.

"I've come to play," she stated succinctly.

Viscount Langdon, son to the Earl of Claybourne, groaned while glaring at her. "I'm not in the mood to lose tonight."

"Then give up your chair and be off," she said. Knowing that Langdon would do neither, she signaled to the nearest footman, whom she recognized from earlier visits. Without hesitation he brought her a chair, apparently well aware which side his bread was buttered on.

Amidst grumbling, three of the gents at the table scooted their chairs over to make room for her. The fourth moved nary a muscle, merely focused his amber gaze on her as though he could see clear through to her soul. His perusal caused an uncomfortable knot to form behind her breastbone. His dark blond hair curled where neck met broad shoulder. The darker bristle shadowing his jaw made him appear dangerous. She had the uneasy feeling that he knew exactly why she was there and the game she was about to play. "Lovingdon."

"This particular game is invitation only."

His rough voice washed over her, fairly skittered along her flesh. Why was it that no other gentleman's voice had quite the same impact on her?

"As my mother is part owner of this establishment, I believe the invitation is implied."

Grace settled into the chair, which put them at eye level or nearly so. She was relieved to find him here, though the men within this room were men not so different from him. They played by special rules. Jackets, waistcoats, neck cloths were discarded. Sleeves were rolled up past elbows. She was astonished that they didn't insist upon playing without shirts. They were all skilled cheaters, their upbringing influenced by at least one person who had survived the streets. They had all grown up fascinated by cons, dodges, sleight of hand, and misdirection. Among the aristocracy, they were uncommon, but among themselves— regardless of title, rank, or heritage—they were equal.

Well, almost so. Lovingdon, she'd always felt, was a cut above. She could not help but notice now the firm, solid muscle of his forearms that hinted at firm, solid muscle elsewhere. She suspected he could pick her up with very little effort. Not that she wanted him to. All she wanted was for him to guide her toward love.

"How did you know we were here?" the Duke of Avendale asked.

She turned her attention to the dark-haired,

dark-eyed man sitting beside her. Like Lovingdon, he'd inherited his title at a tender age. His connection to her family came through the man who had married his widowed mother: William Graves, one of London's finest physicians. "None of you were at Claybourne's ball. What else was I to think?" A heartbeat of silence before she continued. "You do realize, do you not, that with your absence you are breaking the heart of many a mother—and daughter, for that matter?"

"There are many lords in need of a wife. I'm certain we're not missed."

"But none come from such powerful and wealthy families as you lot." Her gaze skipped back over to Lovingdon. Focusing his attention on the center of the table, he rolled a silver coin under and over his fingers, creating an undulating wave of light and dark again and again. She wondered if he was remembering when he had attended balls, when he had fallen in love.

The joy of it, the magic of it.

She desperately yearned for that joy, that magic. It had been sorely absent last Season, and this Season so far was little more than a repeat of the last.

"You're not here to play matchmaker, are you?" Langdon asked. He had his father's black hair and silver eyes. Every Earl of Claybourne had looked out at the world through eyes of pewter.

She laughed lightly. "No, I'm here to win your money. I'm in need of funds for one of the foundling homes."

The coin rolling faster over his fingers, Lovingdon grumbled, "I shall gladly make a donation if you'll but leave us in peace."

She gave him a cocky smile. "I'd rather take your money." And with any luck would take a great deal more than that. "It's such fun to beat you all, and I'm in need of entertainment this evening. I found the ball rather dull."

"My mother will be disappointed to hear that," Langdon said.

"It wasn't her fault I assure you." She eyed him. "I'm rather surprised she let you get away with not attending."

"I feigned illness."

"Well, she shan't hear the truth from me, unless of course I find myself ousted from here."

He bowed his head slightly. "You may play as long as I have coin."

Considering that his father was also part owner of Dodger's, she suspected he had a good many coins. She reached into her reticule, withdrew her blunt, housed in a red velvet pouch, and set it before Drake. He had grown up within the bosom of her family, was more brother than friend, but he studied her now as though he didn't quite trust her. She knew she was rather skilled at appearing innocent when she wasn't. It was the reason that the blame for little pranks—which she usually initiated—fell to her two older brothers and not her, the reason they suffered through punishments while she went blithely on her way. She was the one who had inherited their mother's quick mind and nimble fingers. Her brothers had inherited their father's cunning—and they always found a way to get even with her for causing them trouble. But as she was the youngest, they loved her all the same. And she adored them.

As they were presently traveling the Continent, they would not be interfering with her plans. Drake, however, was another matter entirely.

He finally pushed a stack of colorful wooden chips her way. Leaning forward, she scooped her hands around them and—

"You're not serious about allowing her to stay," Lovingdon said.

"She's as fine a gambler as you are," Drake replied, "and her money spends just as easily."

"If I wanted a woman's company I would seek one."

"Pretend I'm simply one of the boys, Lovingdon," Grace put in. "You seemed to have no trouble accomplishing that goal when I was younger."

His gaze took a leisurely sojourn over her, and she cursed the tiny pricks of pleasure that erupted along her bared skin. She wanted to be unaffected by his perusal. Instead she found herself shamelessly wishing to reveal more, to bare everything, to see a look of adoration in his eyes, when she feared that what she might very well see was revulsion. His first wife had been perfection. There had not been a handsomer couple in all of Great Britain.

He reached for his tumbler of amber liquid, his grip so hard that she could see the white of his knuckles. "Fine," he ground out. "But don't expect us to cease our smoking, drinking, or swearing because you're here."

She tilted her chin at a haughty angle. "Have I ever?" She glanced around the table. "So, gentlemen, what are we playing this evening?"

And with that, she began rolling her kidskin glove down from above her elbow to her wrist, where her pulse thrummed.

She was up to something. Lovingdon wasn't certain what, but he'd bet his last farthing that she had some scheme in mind.

Very deliberately, very slowly, her eyes never leaving his, she tugged on each fingertip of her glove and leisurely peeled off the kidskin, exposing her wrist, her palm, her fingers. So slender, so pale. It had been years since the sun had kissed her skin. He wondered if any gentlemen had this evening.

She moved her bared hand over to the other glove, and he cursed her actions and his fascination with the gathering of material, the revealing of skin. Bloody Christ. It was only an arm. Her pale blue ball gown with blue piping and embroidered roses left her shoulders and neck enticingly bare, but the upper swells of her breasts were demurely covered, and yet he found the unrevealed more alluring than everything revealed by any courtesan he'd visited of late.

His world tilted off its axis.

Even when she'd come to see him the week before, he'd still gazed upon her as a young girl, not a woman. But it was a woman whose sultry eyes met his, whose pouting mouth was waiting to be kissed.

With a great deal of effort, he righted his world, setting it back properly on its course, and mentally kicked himself for even being intrigued by that show of flesh. She was a dear friend, no more than that. He shouldn't find anything about her desirable. His younger version would not have noticed. However, he knew he was no longer who he had once been.

But then apparently neither was Grace. She could have taken the time to change into something less enticing before beginning her journey to the club. They would no doubt be here all night, which she would have known. She knew their habits, their sins, as well as they did. But she had chosen instead to make a grand entrance.

For what purpose?

He knew she had an aversion to losing, but was she really here to gain funds for a foundling home? He doubted it immensely. All she had to do was ask and they'd each reach into their pockets to find their last coin. No, something else was afoot, and he suspected it had to do with her midnight visit to his residence last week.

Realizing that he'd been studying her for too long, Lovingdon lowered his eyes to his two cards, one down-turned, one up, that had been dealt as soon as her gloves were secure in her reticule. With this lot, no hiding places were allowed. They were playing stud poker. Grace's brothers had taken a voyage to New Orleans and discovered it while there. When they returned and revealed the intricacies of the game, it became a favorite among their friends and added to the repertoire of entertainments at Dodger's Drawing Room.

Downstairs, however, it wasn't nearly as cutthroat, nor were the stakes as high. He wondered if he should mention to Greystone that he was giving his daughter far too much allowance if she had enough blunt to allow her into their private games.

More cards were dealt, more wagers made, until Grace won the round. Her smile of victory was bright enough to light the room without the gaslights burning. The others groaned, which only caused her lips to widen further in triumph. "You never know when to stop betting, Langdon," she said, her voice laced with teasing that skittered down Lovingdon's spine. When was the last time he'd laughed, or even smiled, for that matter?

"You should play my father," Langdon replied. "I hear he never loses at cards."

"Grace seldom does either," Drake said, beginning to deal the next round. "Even when she played silly card games as a child that required little more than matching two pictures, she always managed to beat me."

"All these years I thought you let me win."

Drake did little more than wink at her. He had begun his life as a street urchin until he was brought into the bosom of Grace's family. He never spoke of his life before, but there were times when Lovingdon could see that it weighed heavily on him. He was devoted to his work here, ensuring that the gaming hell made a tidy profit, his way of repaying those who had given him so much.

"Anything interesting occur at Claybourne's ball?" Avendale asked.

Grace lifted one slender alabaster shoulder. "If you want to know what happens at the balls, you should attend."

"I don't truly care. I was simply trying to make polite conversation."

"Trying to distract me from noticing the cards dealt, more like. Although I did hear that a certain young lady was spotted in the garden with a particular older gentleman."

"Who?"

She gave him a pointed look. "I'm not one to gossip."

"Then why even mention it?"

She smiled, that alluring smile that Lovingdon suspected brought some men to their knees. "To distract you. Now you'll be wondering if perhaps it was a lady who might have made you an excellent duchess."

"I have no interest in marriage. I daresay none of us at this table, with the exception of you, do."

"You all require heirs."

"There's no rush," Lovingdon said laconically. "My father was quite old when he sired me."

"Which left your mother a young widow."

"Marrying young is no guarantee that you won't be left alone." As soon as the words left his mouth, he regretted them. After two years the bite of loss was still sharp. His mother encouraged him to move on. She had done it quickly enough after his father died, but then theirs had not been a love match. No, she had not known love until Jack Dodger, the notorious public owner of Dodger's Drawing Room, had been named Lovingdon's guardian.

Grace blushed, and he suspected if she still possessed her freckles that they would have disappeared within the redness of her face. "Of course not. I'm sorry. I . . . I was thoughtless there."

"Think nothing of it. My words were uncalled for." Tension descended to surround them. No one ever spoke of Juliette. Sometimes it was as though she had existed only in his mind. Of late he found it increasingly difficult to recall her scent, the exact shade of her hair, the precise blue of her eyes. Had they been a sky at dawn or sunset?

Grace turned her attention to her cards, and he found himself watching as her bright blush receded. Her face would be warm to the touch, but then he suspected all of her would be warm. He should leave the cards and find himself a woman, but tonight he had no interest in the women he'd been visiting recently. Yes, they brought surcease to his flesh, but he failed to feel alive when he was with them. He went through the motions, but it seemed for the past two years, in all aspects of his life, he'd merely been going through the motions. Putting one foot in front of the other without thought or purpose. He refocused on his pair of jacks, holding dark thoughts at bay.

It came as no surprise to him that neither he nor Grace won that hand. The game seemed trite and yet it was a relief to concentrate on something that didn't truly matter. He had enough money in his coffers that losing was no hardship. He had been brought up to adhere to his father's belief that debt was the work of the devil. A man paid as he went. He never owed another man anything because debts had a way of bringing a man down when he least expected it.

The night wore on, conversation dwindling to nothing as everyone concentrated on the cards they were dealt. Lovingdon watched as half his chips made their way into Grace's stash. It should have irritated the devil out of him, but he was intrigued by the glow of her cheeks and the sparkle of her blue eyes with each round that she won. That she cared so much about something so trivial when he cared not at all about the most important things . . .

The present hand showed Grace with two queens and a jack, while Lovingdon showed a king, a ten, and a nine. Drake and Langdon had withdrawn from the round earlier. The final cards were now placed facedown in front of the remaining players.

Graced tapped her finger on a card. "I shall bet fifty." She tossed her chips onto the pile in the center of the table as though the amount was of no consequence, but then it wasn't really the money that enticed any of them into playing. It was the thrill of beating the others. The chips simply served as a measurement of success.

"I believe I'm finished for the night," Avendale said, turning all his cards facedown.

Lovingdon peered at his last card, shifted his gaze to Grace. She wore confidence with the ease that most women donned a cloak. He met her fifty and raised her fifty more.

Without hesitation she met his fifty. "I want to increase the pot," she said.

"Then do so."

"I wish to wager something a little different."

He wasn't the only one who came to attention at

that. He could fairly feel the curiosity and interest rolling off the others. He hoped he had managed to keep his own fascination from showing. "Explain."

She licked her lips, the delicate muscles of her throat moving slightly as she swallowed. "We each wager a boon. If your cards beat mine, you may ask anything of me and I shall comply. If my cards beat yours, you will honor my request."

"Don't be ridiculous," Drake said. "That's not the way the game is played. Use your chips or forfeit."

"Hold on," Lovingdon drawled, studying her intently. The glow that alighted in her eyes, the fine blush beneath her skin. "I wager she's been waiting for this moment all night. I say we let her have it."

"Why do I feel as though I've stepped into the middle of some muck here?" Drake asked. "Do you know what's going on?"

Lovingdon rolled his lucky coin over and under his fingers. "I have a fairly good idea."

He had to give her credit: she didn't flinch, but met his gaze head on. So he was right. She planned to win his assistance.

"You're not seriously considering calling her on it," Drake insisted. "You have no idea what she'll ask."

"I doubt she'll ask anything that I would find revolting. The danger is to her, for she knows not what I might ask, and my standards are not as high as hers."

"You can't ask anything that would be unseemly or might put her reputation at risk," Drake insisted.

"Are there rules to this wager?" Lovingdon asked her.

She angled her chin. "None at all."

"I won't allow this," Drake said.

"The lady is willing to suffer the consequences of so rash an action, so you have no choice," Lovingdon reminded him.

"I rule here. It's my gaming house," Drake insisted.

"It's not actually. It's owned by my stepfather, Langdon's father, and Grace's mother. As much as I respect how well you manage it, I must also respect that the lady has the right to wager as she wants. As long as she understands that she will not be at all pleased with my request should I win."

Drake leaned toward her. "Grace, this is an unwise course of action. You have no earthly clue what he might demand of you."

Never removing her gaze from Lovingdon, she smiled, and the slight upturn of her lips nearly undid him. She was daring him to do something wicked. Oh, he thought of the fun he could have teaching her the ways of men with scandalous reputations—

His thoughts slammed to a halt as though he had hit a brick wall. She was Lady Grace Mabry, lover of kittens, thief of biscuit tins, and climber of trees. What the devil was he doing thinking of her wrapped in silk sheets? He should have his back flayed, and he suspected Drake would be more than willing to do just that if his friend realized the journey his wayward thoughts had just taken.

"That you would think he might do something dastardly has piqued my curiosity beyond all measure," Grace said. "Still, I'm willing to wager a boon as long as you, Lovingdon, understand that you will not be happy with what I request, but you will be obligated to fulfill it until I am satisfied with the outcome."

He almost purred that he could most certainly satisfy her. He felt a thrumming of excitement, the first bit that he'd felt in a good long while. It was odd to think of all the drinking, gambling, and bedding he'd done, and the thrill of it paling in comparison to this one moment, the possibility of beating her . . . and the chance he wouldn't and that her request would no doubt set his blood to boiling, because he had a damned good idea what she wanted of him. It was strange to be so alert, so on edge after being in a fog for so long. He nodded with certainty. "By all means. I call your wager."

Bless her, but she looked triumphant and he knew what she held, before she turned up the first card she had received and the queen of hearts winked up at him. "Three queens."

"I can count, my lady." He flipped over both of his downturned cards and watched as her face drained of all color. Three kings sealed her fate.

"I see." She lifted her sapphire gaze to his, narrowed her eyes, licked her lips. "That is quite astonishing."

"I tried to warn you off."

She nodded, her jaw so tight that he thought she might be grinding her teeth down to nubs. "Your request of me?"

He would not feel guilty, because the cards had favored him and not her. He would not. He was well aware of the other gentlemen waiting on bated breath for his pronouncement. While he was known to take advantage of situations, it irked him to realize that they thought he would take advantage of her, a girl he considered a sister in spite of the fact they shared no blood. "You know what I require."

"And what exactly is that?" Drake asked.

"Something quite innocent, I assure you," she said as she stood, as graceful and proud as a queen who had been disappointed by her minions but refused to succumb to tears. With the exception of Lovingdon, all the gentlemen stood as well. "Drake, will you see about arranging a carriage for me? I sent my driver home earlier."

"I've had quite enough of the evening," Lovingdon said, shoving back his chair and coming to his feet. "I'll see you home."

Chapter 4

❧❧❧

The coach rattled through the streets. Inside, the silence was as thick and heavy as the fog settling in. Lovingdon sat opposite Grace. While she stared out the window, she could feel his gaze homed in on her. "You cheated," she said softly.

"So did you."

She didn't bother to deny it. It was one thing to cheat, another to lie.

"Then I should not have to pay the boon," she said.

"Would you have been so gracious if the circumstances were reversed?"

Her sigh was one of impatience, a bit of anger. She had expected him to play as a gentleman, not a scoundrel. She shouldn't be surprised. The rumors she'd heard that he had lost his moral compass were apparently true. And damn him. Even if she had won unfairly, she would have required he pay the boon.

"No, you're quite right. We were evenly matched, regardless of the outcome." Turning her head slightly to peer at him, she rubbed her hands up and down her arms. "Thank you for not telling them what it was I wanted."

He shrugged out of his jacket, leaned across the distance separating them and settled it around her shoulders.

"So warm," she murmured, inhaling the scent of cigar, whiskey, and something deeper, darker, unique to him. "It smells of you."

"You'll not distract me from my purpose here. I want you to get this absurd notion out of your head that I could assist you in any conceivable manner regarding your quest for a grand love. You must know what qualities you seek in a man. Finding love is a personal journey, Grace."

"I know." She sighed, nodded, glanced back out the window. "Lord Bentley, I should think."

"What of him?" His words were terse.

"I believe his attentions are sincere. He has told me that I am beautiful, that he carries me into his dreams every night."

"But then so do I."

Her heart thundering, Grace jerked her head around to stare at Lovingdon's silhouette. She wished she could see his eyes. They were lost in the shadows. He moved. Smoothly. Swiftly. Until his hand was caressing her cheek, a light touch that was almost no touch at all, yet still it almost scorched her flesh.

She inhaled his rugged masculine scent. Hardly a hairbreadth separated them.

"You are so beautiful." His voice was a low rasp that sent tiny shivers of pleasure coursing through her. "I've long thought of confessing my infatuation, but we have been friends for so long that I thought you might laugh—"

"No. Never."

"In my dreams, we're on a hillock, lying upon the cool grass, our bodies so close that they provide heat as warm as the sun bearing down on us."

"Lovingdon—"

"Were Bentley's words as sweet?"

"Not quite, but near enough."

"And you believed such poppycock?"

She stilled, not even daring to breathe. "You think he lied?"

He leaned away. "All men lie, Grace, to obtain what they want."

Lovingdon's sweet words had meant nothing. What a fool she was to have been lured—

She lashed out and punched his shoulder with all the strength she could muster. "You blackguard!"

His laughter was dark, rough, as he moved back to his seat across from her. "You deserved it. In the space of a sennight you've ruined two of my evenings."

"Why? Because I gave you a challenge tonight? No one plays cards as well as I do."

"No one cheats as well as you do."

"Except you." And that knowledge irritated her because like Drake he'd always let her win, but in her case she thought she'd bested him. The blighter. "So tell me, regarding Bentley, how can I determine truth from lie?"

"If the words are too sweet they are insincere."

"Always?"

"Always."

"So if a man tells me I am beautiful, I am to discount him as a suitor?"

"It would probably be wise to do so, although I suppose there are exceptions."

"Do you tell women they are beautiful?"

"All the time."

"And you never mean it?"

His harsh sigh echoed through the confines of the coach. "The words are designed to make a woman feel treasured, to seduce her. To make her believe that she alone holds my interest—and for the moment she does. But she will not hold me for long."

"So you'll break her heart."

"I'm honest, Grace. The women in my life have no false expectations."

"I think you're mistaken about Bentley."

"Ask around. I'm sure you'll find he's used the words on others."

"Oh, yes, by all means, allow me to be seen as a fool." Beneath his jacket, she rubbed her arms. She was suddenly quite chilled again. "What else must I look out for?"

"False flattery is usually poetic, ridiculous, flowery. At least mine is."

"You never flattered Juliette?"

"We will not speak of my courtship of Juliette. Ever."

"I'm sor—"

"Don't apologize for it. Just heed my words."

"As you wish. Back to the matter at hand, then, the lesson you sought to teach. I feel like such a ninny. Here I am with so many men declaring their affections, yet I am unable to discern their hearts. Even though you instruct me to trust mine."

"Bentley is not for you."

"As you refuse to assist me, I'm not sure I can value your opinion on the matter."

"It's not opinion. It's fact."

The horses slowed as the coach turned onto the circular drive. Soon the driver brought the vehicle to a halt. A footman opened the door. Lovingdon stepped out and then handed her down. Offering his arm, he escorted her up the stairs.

"How can you be so sure about Lord Bentley?" she asked.

"I know Lord Bentley."

Turning to face him, without thought she reached up and brushed the thick strands of blond hair from his brow. "Can a man not reform?"

"You deserve better than a man who requires reforming."

Laughing lightly, she gave her hand leave to fall softly onto his shoulder, to feel the firmness there, the sturdiness, the strength. "Now I am suspect of all praise."

"I would never lie to you, Grace."

Her hand slid down a fraction, to his chest, to where his heart pounded so steadily. But he appeared not to notice. "Yet, you did. In the coach."

"That was merely a lesson, one I hope you took to heart."

"You're an abominable teacher. You might as well have taken a switch to my palm."

"It was not my intent to harm you, but to spare you from harm."

With a quick release of breath, she stepped back. "So in the future I shall not take flowery words to heart." She glanced up at the eaves. "Unless, of course, I know him to be a poet."

"Not even then, Grace."

"We shall see what my heart says. One more question."

"There's always one more question with you."

She ignored the irascibility in his voice. "Do you think you might see your way clear to coming to the Midsummer Eve's celebration that my family hosts?"

"Probably not."

She nodded, bit her lower lip, debated—there was always so much left unsaid between them. "I remember watching you dance with Juliette at the Midsummer Eve's ball, the summer before you married." He went so still, she wasn't even certain he was breathing. "Does it hurt when people speak of her?"

"Sometimes. It's equally hard, though, when no one speaks of her."

"I'm always available to listen, Lovingdon."

He glanced down at his shoes. "We were so young, she and I. We met at the very first ball I ever attended. I've never been to one when she wasn't there."

With his admission tears stung her eyes and her chest tightened until it ached. "You think you'll feel an emptiness."

He lifted his gaze to her. "I don't know what I'll feel."

Nodding, she swallowed hard. "I've not experienced the kind of loss that you have. I can't know the depth of your pain. But I have suffered loss, and I have found it is easier to carry on if I focus on what I have to be grateful for."

He turned to face her fully. "What loss, Grace?"

She shook her head. "I don't wish to talk about it."

"Does it have to do with this fellow you loved? The one who married someone else?"

She released a quick bubble of laughter and lied, because it was easier than baring the truth. She wished she'd not traveled this path and wanted to get off it as quickly as possible. "Yes. Silly really. To compare the two. Good night, Lovingdon. May you sleep well."

She was aware of his gaze following her as she entered the residence. She was grateful that he didn't pursue the conversation, although a part of her wished he'd called her back, wrapped his arms around her, and insisted she tell him everything.

Drake Darling made a final notation in the ledger. It was late, he should be abed, but sleep did not come easily to him. He always felt as though he had something to prove, something to make right, something left undone.

Closing the ledger and his eyes, he settled back and let his past have its way with him. He'd been born Peter Sykes, the son of a thief and a murderer, although that he was aware of the last was his secret. No one knew that he'd made his way to the gallows, watched his father swing for murdering his mother. Frannie Darling had thought she'd protected him from the truth. But he was a child of the streets. No matter what he changed, he could not change that.

When Miss Darling married the Duke of Greystone, she no longer had use for her surname, so Peter had taken it to use as his own in an attempt to wash off his father. When he was a lad, he'd sometimes pretend that Greystone was his true father. He'd had a dragon inked onto his back because the duke had one. When the duke pointed out the constellation Draco, Peter had insisted he be called Drake, in honor of the dragon shaped by stars. Although he'd been embraced by the Mabry family, he'd always known he wasn't one of them. At seventeen he'd come to work at Dodger's, determined to earn his own way, to prove—

"Tell me what you know of Bentley."

Drake opened his eyes. A storm in the form of Lovingdon had just blown into his office. The man looked as though he needed to rip something—or someone—apart. They were close in age, had become fast friends as they'd traveled similar yet different paths. "Viscount Bentley?"

Lovingdon gave a brusque nod. "What is his financial situation?"

"I don't know all the particulars. He runs up a debt here, pays it at the end of the month, repeats the cycle. Boring, predictable really."

"Yes, boring, predictable." Lovingdon walked to the window, gazed out. "I don't understand what she sees in him."

"She who?"

"Grace."

"Sees in whom?"

"Bentley," Lovingdon snapped. "Aren't you paying attention?"

"Grace told you she has an interest in him?"

"In the carriage. She mentioned that he was reciting garbage."

"Garbage? And that appealed to her?"

Lovingdon glared at him as though he hadn't the sense to come in out of a rainstorm. "She thought it was poetry, beautiful. But it was garbage—how he dreams of her and such dribble."

Why would Lovingdon care? Why would Grace confide in him? "What was her appearance here earlier truly about?"

"You'll have to ask her, and while you're at it, warn her off of Bentley."

He watched as Lovingdon charged from his office. Something very strange going on here tonight. Perhaps a word with Grace was in order.

"What are you up to, Grace?"

Within the duchess's sitting room, which looked out upon a rain-drenched garden, Grace lifted her gaze from *Little Women* to see Drake leaning against the doorjamb, arms crossed over his chest. "Surely you recognize a book and the act of reading."

It was early afternoon. She'd slept into the late morning hours and was still recovering from her clandestine adventure the night before. It did not bode well that Drake, who usually slept until early evening, was disregarding his own habits.

"Bentley?" Drake's voice dripped with sarcasm.

"What of him?"

Drake uncrossed his arms, strode to the chair across from her and dropped into it. "You would no more consider Bentley a serious suitor than I would consider pursuing a March hare for a wife."

She smiled brightly. "Are you considering marriage? Mother won't be half pleased."

"Dammit, Grace."

"Who have you set your sights on?"

"Be forthcoming with me, will you?"

She settled back against the plush chair. "How do you know about Bentley?"

With dark eyes narrowing, he studied her long and hard. She refused to squirm. "Lovingdon returned to the club last night, asked after Bentley's debt."

She tried not to appear too satisfied with the knowledge that Lovingdon, for all his blustering that he didn't care whom she married, did in fact care.

"What dodge have you got going on?" Drake asked.

Like her mother, Drake had begun his life on the streets, and in spite of the years since he'd fought to survive on them, he still remembered the tricks of his trade. A dodge referred to a swindle. "Don't be silly."

Leaning forward, resting his elbows on his thighs, he scrutinized her as though he could see clear into her soul. "You're scheming something, and it has to do with Lovingdon. I'd wager that you lost that last hand on purpose."

"You'd lose that wager. My intent was to win."

"And the boon?"

Drake was as close to her as either of her brothers, more so. He was the one who had held her hand when they went to the country fairs, hoisted her upon his back when she grew too tired to walk, stolen pastries from the kitchen and given her half. He would not betray her confidence, even without a promise exchanged. "Men are swarming around me like bees to honey. I wanted him to help me determine if a gentleman truly loved me."

"You're too wise to fall for some man's ruse, and I'm too smart to believe that's all there is to your request." Drake's eyes widened. "You want him to be one of the bees?"

"Absolutely not. He's completely inappropriate." Setting aside the book, she rose to her feet and glided over to the window. Raindrops rolled along the glass, nature weeping.

"He won't marry again, Grace. Something inside him broke with the death of Juliette and Margaret. You can't put him back together, sweetheart, not the way he was."

"Were you not listening? I have no interest in him as a suitor, but that doesn't mean I shouldn't try. That we shouldn't. Try to put him back together, I mean. I don't care that he doesn't love me—but I do care that he is wasting his life."

"I've watched him for two years, Grace. Been his companion through the worst of his grief. If he mends at all, he'll still have cracks and jagged edges."

"We all have jagged edges." Hers more hideous than any Lovingdon might possess. Only when Drake came to stand beside her did she notice her own faint reflection in the glass.

"Those on the inside are much worse than those on the outside," he said.

"But those on the inside are not as ugly. They're invisible."

"Which is what makes them all the more dangerous." He sighed. "How long have you loved him?"

She shook her head. "I don't love him. Oh, I was enamored of him when I was younger, but that was little more than childish fantasy. I am not so dense as not to recognize it for what it was. Besides, I won't be a man's second choice, and I fear with him any other woman would always fall short. But he has knowledge that can assist me, and if in the process he becomes part of Society again, more's the better. He won't be vying for my attention, as he certainly has no need of my dowry."

"Neither do I."

Before she could read his expression, he turned about and was heading for the door.

"Tread carefully, Grace. If you place him in a position where he hurts you, I will be forced to kill him."

She should have gone after him. Instead, she

sank down to the footstool. To her, Drake had always been an older brother. They were not connected by blood, but by their hearts.

What she had felt for Lovingdon when she was a child was far different. He stole her breath with a look, warmed her body with an inadvertent touch, caused her heart to sing with a single word spoken. But he no longer had such power over her. He was the means to an end—one that mattered far more than she dared tell him.

She was grateful that he had given her a bit of advice regarding Bentley. But could she trust it? He had promised to never lie to her—

But what if the promise were a lie?

"**W**ords that are too flowery," Grace said as she poured tea at the cast-iron table in the garden.

"Too flowery?" Lady Penelope, her cousin, and daughter to the Countess and Earl of Claybourne, asked. Grace had always envied her black as midnight hair because it made her blue eyes stand out.

"Yes, you know. Lots of adjectives and adverbs and pretty words."

"But I like pretty words," Lady Ophelia, sister to Lord Somerdale said. Her hair was a flaxen blond that reminded Grace of wheat blowing in a field. Her eyes were the most startling green.

"Yes, that's the whole point. That's why they use them, but if they do use them, then they don't truly fancy us."

"Where did you learn this?" Miss Minerva Dodger asked. As she was Lovingdon's half sister, Grace knew she couldn't very well tell her the truth. She would no doubt confront her brother and any hope Grace had of securing his assistance would be dashed. Minerva was not nearly as fair of complexion as Lovingdon. It came from having vastly different fathers, she supposed. Minerva's hair had the fine sheen of mahogany, her eyes were as black as sin.

"A gentleman told me."

"Which gentleman?"

"It's not important who. He's had a great deal of experience on the matter."

"Very well. I'll write it down, but it sounds like poppycock to me."

"You don't have to write it down."

"I thought we were going to publish a book to help ladies determine when a gentleman was merely after their dowry. *A Lady's Guide to Ferreting Out Fortune Hunters*."

"Well, yes, but I don't know that we'll have enough material."

"I think we need to do it," Lady Ophelia said.

"Even if it's only two pages. Look at Lady Sybil. Her husband nearly had her in tears last night at the ball with all his ranting just because she wore a new gown in the same shade as the one his sister wore. Why would he care? If you ask me he should put her ahead of his sister, tell his sister to go change her frock."

"I always thought he was so nice," Minerva said.

"We all did," Grace said with conviction. "Last Season, I was even considering him as a serious suitor, but then I realized that Syb was terribly fond of him. I feared I'd lose her friendship if I encouraged him. Now I feel rather badly that she's with him."

"It's not your fault," Lady Penelope assured her. "I would have stepped aside as well in favor of a friend. Which is why we must help each other identify the worst of the lot, so we might all avoid a similar sorrow-filled fate."

"I've heard something rather disturbing," Lady Ophelia said, "but as it involves my dear friend Lady Chloe, you must not tell a soul."

"We never would," Penelope said. "This round table is like the one at King Arthur's court. We are honor bound to hold the secrets spoken here."

Minerva laughed. "You are always so dramatic. You should go on the stage."

"Don't think I haven't considered it. I don't think Father would mind. He doesn't care much what anyone thinks, but Mother is another matter entirely. She says our behavior reflects not only on our father but on our uncle." She gave Grace a pointed look.

"I doubt Father would mind."

"I'll think about it if I don't find a beau this Season. Meanwhile, Ophelia, tell us about Chloe."

"Well." She glanced around the garden. "She's making merry with Lord Monroe. She has been since last Season, but he hasn't asked for her hand in marriage. She'll be ruined if he doesn't."

"Surely he will," Grace assured her. "If they're . . . well, you know, being cozy and all, surely it's only a matter of time."

"I've thought about confronting him . . ."

"Bad idea, there. Don't want to get into the middle of it."

"Yes, I suppose you're right." Lady Ophelia gazed out over the lawn. "Finding a good husband should not be so difficult."

"Who are you going to choose?" Minerva asked Grace.

"Oh, I haven't a clue. The first one to send me my favorite flower, I suppose."

"Your favorite flower. What has that to do with anything?" Penelope asked.

"Something my elusive gentleman told me. A man who loves me will know my favorite flower."

"I'm going to jot that down as well," Minerva assured them. "Is this gentleman advisor of yours happily married? I'd like to know how he came to be such an expert."

"He's a widower."

She looked up. "He's old, then?"

Grace forced her expression not to give anything away. "Terribly old." To a child of two.

"I'd like to meet this mysterious gentleman of yours," Minerva said.

"I'll see what can be arranged, but I must confess that he is not one for going out."

"Decrepit as well, then. Does he still have his mind? Is he sharp enough to remember how he came to have his wife?"

Grace fought not to reveal any sorrow when she said, "He's sharp enough to remember everything."

Chapter 5

Noon was far too early for a disreputable man to awaken, but when Lovingdon received word that his mother was waiting in the parlor, staying abed no longer seemed wise. She was not averse to barging into his bedchamber, and while his bed was empty of female companionship, she did not need to see him in his present state, when he had not shaved in eons, his eyes were red and puffy, and he reeked of tobacco and strong drink.

So he hastily bathed and shaved, donned proper attire, and went downstairs to pretend that he was glad she had come to see him.

Pouring tea, she sat in a green wingback chair, and it struck him with the force of a battering ram that she had aged considerably since he'd last seen her. He doubted any son loved his mother as much as he did, and if it made him a coddled mother's boy, so be it.

"Mother," he said as he strode across the room, then leaned down and kissed her cheek. "You're looking well."

"Liar. I look dreadful. I'm not sleeping much."

"And which of your children is to blame for that?" he asked, taking the chair near her and stretching out his legs. After she married Jack Dodger, she'd given birth to two sons and a daughter. Her lineage gained them entry into Society, while Jack Dodger's wealth made them acceptable. Lovingdon had no doubt that they would each marry someone who carried some aristocratic blood in their veins.

His mother said nothing, simply sipped her tea, and that was answer enough.

"You needn't worry about me. I'm fine," he assured her.

"It's been two years. You're not back into Society. You can't mourn forever."

He removed his pocket watch from his waistcoat. It had been his father's. Originally, it went to his father's bastard son, but Jack had given it to Lovingdon on the day he turned one and twenty. Inside the cover of the watch, his father had kept a miniature of a young woman, a servant girl whom he claimed was the love of his life. A girl who gave birth to Jack. Now there was a miniature of Juliette inside the watch. "Father loved only once. Perhaps I'm like him."

"He never tried to love again. Guilt held him back."

Lovingdon understood guilt. *Don't let us die.*

They never should have gotten sick. If only he'd stayed away from the slums like Juliette had asked, if only he hadn't felt the need to be a good Samaritan. If only he'd been content to provide the funds for clearing out some of the slums, if only he'd not felt a need to oversee the work. If only he'd sent his family away when he became ill. If only he'd died instead of them.

His mother set aside her teacup. "I'm not saying that you must love again, but I do think it would do you a world of good to immerse yourself back into Society."

"I immerse myself plenty," he said dryly.

"Yes, in women, I'm sure."

His jaw dropped and he almost had to nudge it to get it back into position.

She quirked a brow. "I'm married to a gambling house owner who shares everything with me. I have long since lost my innocence when it comes to wickedness."

He had to make his mind a blank slate so he didn't conjure images of his mother engaging in wicked activities. But then he supposed he shouldn't be surprised. It was Jack who had given him his first taste of liquor and tobacco. Jack who had taught him to curse and introduced him to cards.

She reached across and squeezed his hand. "Henry, I want you to be happy."

He shook his head. "Not yet, Mother. It's obscene to even contemplate it."

"Take a small step. The Countess of Westcliffe is having her annual garden party this afternoon. You should go."

"I can think of nothing more boring than swinging a mallet."

She furrowed her delicate brow. "I think you've forgotten how much you enjoy croquet. If you won't go for yourself, go for me. I shall sleep so much better if I know you're at least engaging with others."

"I engage—"

"Yes, I'm sure you do engage yourself with less reputable women, but that's not what I had in mind. Do something proper for a change."

"I'll think about it . . . for you."

"I suppose I can't ask for more."

"You could."

She smiled. "But I won't." She rose to her feet and he stood. "I need to be off making arrangements for Minerva's birthday party next week. You will come, won't you? It's only a small, intimate gathering. She'll be so disappointed if you're not there again."

He couldn't even recall how many he'd missed: one or two. Guilt pricked his conscience. He wasn't ashamed of his behavior but he had taken great pains not to flaunt his bad habits around his younger siblings. They'd always looked up to him. He recognized now that it was wrong of him to avoid them. He felt as though he'd been wandering through a fog and sunshine was beginning to burn it away. Although he didn't have a clue regarding what had caused the sun to appear.

"I shall try to be there."

She patted his cheek. "Do more than try for goodness' sakes. I don't ask for much."

No, she didn't. He walked with her into the entryway.

"By the by, have you seen Lady Grace this Season?" his mother asked. "I hear she's considering Lord Bentley."

"For what?"

"Why marriage, of course."

The Countess of Westcliffe was known for her garden parties, and Grace didn't think the lady could have asked for a lovelier afternoon. The sun was bright and joyful. It warmed the air and brought forth the fragrance of freshly cut grass. Most of the Marlborough House Set was in attendance. Some guests took refuge in the shade provided by canopies. Others played badminton or croquet. Many sipped champagne and nibbled on delicious pastries.

Grace sat on a stool beneath the wide full-leafed bough of an elm. Circling her, half a dozen gentlemen vied for her attention, and she was most grateful to see that Lord Ambrose was not among them. She was as charming as one could be under the circumstances, but she was not inspired to passion by any of the gents circling her. They all looked remarkably alike, desperate for her attention. She wanted someone who wasn't quite so needy, and yet she understood that the generosity of her dowry called to those in need. She did not hold their unfavorable circumstance against them. God knew she had been brought up to fully understand that not everyone was as well off as her family, but she preferred a man who was at least striving to make a go of it on his own.

Still, she smiled at Lord Winslow, laughed at Lord Canby's atrocious jokes, which held no humor at all, and listened with rapt attention to Lord Carlton's description of a babbling brook and how he had moved the stones around in order to make it sound different. She refrained from commenting that perhaps if he had assisted in moving stones from his land, the fields might have produced more grain and he wouldn't now be dashing off to fetch her more champagne in order to impress her.

It was a curse to have inherited her mother's knack for numbers, along with her penchant toward the sensible.

Lord Renken was a terrible stutterer and he said not a word. Grace didn't mind his affliction. She wasn't looking for perfection. She wanted love. Her mother had not held her father's approaching blindness against him. She could not have loved him more if his eyesight were perfect. But it was difficult to get to know a man if he never spoke.

Although, Lord Vexley was mute as well. He exchanged glances with her from time to time, secretive little looks that seemed to indicate he felt none of these gentlemen were competition for her affections. She couldn't deny that Vexley was handsome, intelligent, and easy to speak with while they danced. He seemed to appreciate *her* more than her fortune, but how was one to know for sure?

She cursed Lovingdon for not taking her problem seriously, but then she supposed it wasn't truly a serious problem. No one would go hungry, be without shelter, or die because of her choice. And if she didn't choose, her parents weren't likely to disown her. She supposed she could live very happily without a husband, but it was the absence of love that was troubling. As far as she knew, no one had ever been madly, deeply, passionately in love with her. She believed that a woman should experience the mad rush of unbridled passion at least once in her lifetime. Was she being greedy to want it permanently?

Lord Canby was beginning to recite another joke when Grace rose and shook out her skirts. He stopped mid-word, the expression on his face nearly making her laugh. Instead, she adjusted her hat to more effectively shade her eyes and said, "Gentlemen, if you'll be so kind as to excuse me—"

"I'll accompany you," Lord Vexley said, hopping to his feet.

She smiled warmly. "Where I need to go, ladies prefer to go alone. I shan't be long."

He bowed his head slightly. "As you wish."

His voice carried an undercurrent she couldn't quite identify. Disappointment? Impatience? She supposed it was much less frustrating being the pursued rather than the pursuer. She wasn't in danger of being rebuffed, while all these gentlemen were striving to impress. Perhaps she would assuage her guilt by trying to lead them toward ladies more likely to embrace their courtship with enthusiasm. It seemed to have worked for Lady Cornelia and Lord Ambrose.

Walking toward the residence, she was well aware of a prickling sensation along her neck, no doubt Lord Vexley's gaze on her back. She was so aware of his presence, his attentions . . . that had to count for something, didn't it?

As she neared the residence, out of the corner of her eye she spied Lord Fitzsimmons speaking to her dear friend Lady Sybil. They were standing at the far edge of the terrace, where several trees and bushes provided thick shade and coverage. She could not hear the words, but she could tell by Sybil's paling features that her husband was once again deriding her for something. It was no doubt some trivial matter that in the grand scheme of things held no consequence. The man was a toad. A prince who had turned into a frog instead of a frog who had turned into a prince. She knew it was none of her concern, that she should march on, but Sybil deserved far better.

Before she knew what she was about, she was striding toward the couple. Lord Fitzsimmons's nose was less than an inch from his wife's. His eyes were narrowed in anger, while she was cringing.

"My lord?" Grace called out. "My lord Fitzsimmons?"

Jerking his head around, he glared at her, the force of it nearly causing her to stumble back. If she were wise, she would walk right past. Unfortunately, a cowardly streak did not run through her veins and she tended to become stubborn when faced with bullies. It had to do with having older brothers and growing up playing with boys more than girls. She could hold her own in a pillow fight or when it came to playing pranks.

"I'm certain you didn't mean to embarrass your wife here," she stated succinctly, striving to edge her way in front of Sybil.

"Grace—" Sybil began.

"Lady Grace, this does not concern you," Fitzsimmons declared.

"I'm afraid it does. Lady Sybil is a dear friend."

He leaned toward her, his face a hard mask, his finger darting toward her nose. "Be on your—"

He yelped, and Grace was suddenly aware of a large hand holding that offending finger in such a way that it was nearly doubled back. Lord Fitzsimmons's eyes bulged. She had only to turn her head slightly to see Lovingdon standing there, his expression a barely contained murderous rage.

"If you ever point your finger in her face again, I shall snap it in two," he ground out.

"Your Grace, she was interfering—"

"Be grateful she did before I got here. I'd have used my fist rather than my words. You make a spectacle of yourself, man, when you treat your wife with such disrespect. I won't have it."

"You don't rule me— Ah!"

Grace realized that Lovingdon had yet to release his hold. It took only a bit of maneuvering for him to have Fitzsimmons bending his knees as though he would fall to the ground in agony.

"You will treat your wife better or you will answer to me. Have I made myself clear?"

"All marriages have discord."

"This isn't you, Fitz."

He jerked up his chin. "You don't know me, Lovingdon. Not anymore. We all change. You're certainly not the lad I knew in school."

"I'm not the one acting a fool here. Now apologize to your wife for not behaving as a gentleman."

Fitzsimmons hesitated, then said, "I'm sorry, m'dear. Won't happen again."

Lovingdon released his hold. "I suggest you take a brisk walk to cool off that temper."

"You don't control me."

Lovingdon arched a brow.

"But I can see the wisdom in your suggestion." With that he strode off.

Sybil looked first at Grace and then at Lovingdon. "Thank you, thank you both. I don't know what comes over him. As you say, Your Grace, it's absolutely unlike him to be so disagreeable."

"When did these bouts of foul temper begin?"

She lifted a delicate shoulder. "I'm not sure. Three or four months ago, I suppose. But no matter. I'm sure all will be well now."

Oh, Sybil, Grace thought, you are too much an optimist.

"If he should ever hurt you," Lovingdon said, "do not hesitate to send word 'round to me."

Apparently, he, too, had doubts regarding Sybil's optimism.

"He's a lamb at home. It's only when we're out in public. I don't understand it, but we'll be fine." Her cheeks flushing, she walked away.

Grace watched her go, wondering if she should go with her, yet reluctant to leave Lovingdon. She turned back to him. "Thank you for coming to my rescue."

"You could have handled him easily enough I suspect."

That didn't mean she didn't appreciate the steps he had taken to spare Lady Sybil any more embarrassment. Others around had noticed, yet no one else had bothered to step in.

"I didn't realize you were here," Grace said.

"Obviously."

"You're angry."

"I came very close to introducing him to my fist."

She smiled. "I was about to introduce him to mine."

She saw the barest hint of a grin before he brought it back into submission. "You're no longer a child. You can't get into tumbles."

She rolled her eyes at the absurdity of that conclusion. "Nothing wrong with a lady who isn't afraid to defend herself. You taught me how to beat up my brothers. It's a lesson I've never forgotten, and one that I see no reason to delegate to childhood."

He shook his head, and she could see the anger dissipating, perhaps in light of happier memories. Thanks to him, she knew how to hold her fist to minimize damage to herself while maximizing it to others. She knew how to hit hard and quick, how to fight dirty in order to win. Perhaps she should give Sybil a lesson or two. She sobered. "Do you think Fitzsimmons will take your threat to heart, that he'll treat her better? I fear she's being overly optimistic."

He glanced in the direction that Fitzsimmons had gone. "I'll have another word with him. Don't worry yourself over it."

"Difficult to accomplish when I love Sybil so." She studied him for a moment. "I would not have expected to see you at this garden party."

He shrugged. "I had nothing pressing this afternoon, so I thought I would stop by. I noticed you holding court."

She groaned at the censure in his voice. "I have little choice when so many come 'round. The alternative is to queue them up so they each have a few moments of my time, and I think that far worse."

His gaze slid past her, and she could see he was deep in thought. His brow furrowed slightly, and it was all she could do not to reach up and flatten the shallow creases with her thumb. She wanted to comb the locks off his forehead with her fingers. Silly things to want.

"None of those who were gathered at your feet will provide what you are seeking." His gaze came back to her, and in the amber depths, she saw the conviction of his words.

"How do you know?"

"A man who would love you would not have been content to keep his distance." He wrapped his hand around hers, and she was immediately aware of the largeness of his. While hers was slender and long, his was broader, stronger, more powerful. Gently, he tugged her nearer until they were both enveloped in the cool shade and his musky male scent won out over the sweet fading fragrance of the distant roses.

"He would want you near enough," he said, his voice low and raspy, "that when he gazed into your eyes he could see the darker blue that circles the sapphires everyone notices, the darker ring known to only a few. He would want to inhale your fragrance of rose and lavender, feel the warmth radiating off your skin. He would not be content to share you."

For the first time, she noticed the black ring that encircled the amber depths of his eyes. The discovery pleased her because everything else about him was so very familiar: the sharp lines, the acute definitions. When he angled his head just so, he appeared haughty, but at that moment he appeared enthralled, as though he had only just noticed every aspect of her, as though he were mesmerized to discover that she had grown to womanhood.

She was aware of their shallow breathing, of each forceful pump of her heart, the way his smoldering gaze roamed over her face until it settled on her mouth, her lips slightly parted, her tongue darting out in invitation—

Invitation for what, she wasn't sure, but she found it difficult to think, to analyze, to decipher all that was happening. The sun was making her far too warm. Or was it him, his nearness, his attention?

"He would stare at me?" she whispered, swaying toward him.

"He would touch you in ways he could not touch you with his hands—not in public. But images would be filling his mind. He would be unable to tear his gaze away." Clearing his throat, he broke the connection that was joining them and looked up into the trees. "He will look at you, Little Rose, as though you are everything, because to him you will be."

He lowered his gaze. The heat had been doused and she wondered if it had ever been there or whether she simply imagined it. Embarrassed, hoping beyond hope that he had not been aware of the extent to which she'd been enthralled, she swallowed hard and turned her attention to the flowers. They paled in comparison to Lovingdon. She would much prefer watching him.

"It takes a while for love that intense to develop, doesn't it?" she asked.

Slowly he shook his head. "I fell in love with Juliette the moment I set eyes on her."

He stepped back as though he needed to distance himself from the memory.

"She wouldn't want you to be alone," she said.

He grinned, the cocky yet sad smile that had become such a part of him. "I'm hardly alone."

"Love, then. She wouldn't want you to go without love."

"Love is rare. There are those who never know it, but having known it"—he shook his head—"I have no desire to know it again. I could never love anyone as I loved her."

"I find that sad, and such a waste. You must have an heir."

"I can have an heir without loving the woman. My father did." His taut expression revealed that he regretted the words as soon as they left his mouth. "I've told you what you need to know to find the man who loves you."

Abruptly, he turned on his heel—

"Wait! One more question," she called after him.

He turned to her, his face without curiosity. He didn't truly care about her troubles or woes. Why had he come? Did it matter?

Biting on her lower lip, she took a step nearer.

"If a gentleman is bedding a lady and has not asked for her hand in marriage, is it likely that he fancies her?"

"No."

He might as well have slapped her with the terse word. Something must have shown on her face, because he said, "Tell me who it is and I'll kill him for taking advantage of you."

She laughed lightly. "No one is bedding me. It's a friend. She thinks he loves her—"

"He might lust after her, but he doesn't love her. It would be prudent for her to end this relationship before she finds herself completely ruined."

"And you know this because you've been with ladies you didn't love."

"Not with a lady who has a reputation to protect. I've told you before, Grace, the women I frequent know the rules of the game I play. It sounds to me as though your friend doesn't—especially if she still expects marriage."

"Gentlemen don't play by the same rules as ladies, do they?"

"I fear not. We can be beasts when we set our mind to it. Warn her off." He retreated farther into the shadows, toward a side gate that would lead him into the street. She dearly wanted to go after him. Did he have memories of his mother not being loved? Was that the reason he was here, offering advice, small as it was? She'd known of course that his father, much older than his mother, had married out of duty. It was a common practice among the aristocracy, although now love was more often beginning to hold sway and duty was less a factor.

Turning, she jerked back and released a tiny squeal at the sight of the man standing there, fairly hovering over her. "Lord Vexley, you took me by surprise."

"My apologies, Lady Grace. I saw an opportunity to have a moment alone with you. I could hardly let it pass." He stepped nearer, his gaze holding hers, his focus intense, almost captivating. "Lovingdon seems to have upset you."

"No, not at all. He was simply in the area, I suppose, and we had a little chat." She shook her head. "He hardly attends social affairs these days. I was hoping this one might do him some good."

"I feel sorry for any lady who might try to claim his heart. It is very difficult to live with a ghost."

"I don't think—"

"My mother was my father's second wife. She never held his heart. It made her a very sad woman. It is much better to be the first to claim a man's heart." He placed his palm flat against his chest and grinned at her. "Mine has yet to be claimed."

It was an invitation that she thought she should be delighted to receive, eager to accept, and yet she couldn't quite bring herself to do it. Instead she tried to make light of it without causing hurt feelings, as she couldn't deny that of all the gents vying for her affections, he was the one she most looked forward to spending time with. "I find it difficult to believe that your heart has not been touched by another when you are so incredibly charming."

"But I am not so easily charmed. You, however, my lady . . ." He looked toward the gardens. "Perhaps you would be kind enough to join me for a stroll about the roses."

"I should be most delighted." She placed her hand on the crook of his elbow. His words were not overly poetic, and he knew enough to take her through the roses. Now if he but knew which shade she favored.

"Red, I should think," he said, as though he'd read her mind. "Red roses are what I should send you tomorrow."

"Better to leave them where they are. They don't die so quickly that way."

"Ah, a lady who doesn't appreciate a courtship accompanied by flowers. What would you prefer, I wonder?"

She opened her mouth, and he quickly touched a gloved finger to her lips. "No, don't tell me. I shall deduce it on my own."

He gave her a warm smile, and she found herself wishing that her heart would do a somersault.

Having sent his carriage on its way, Lovingdon walked. He needed to walk. He needed his muscles tightening and aching, he needed the pounding of his heels on ground. He needed distance, distance from Grace, the dark blue rings that circled her irises, the damn freckle near the corner of her mouth. Why had it remained when all the others had disappeared, why did it taunt him? Why had he noticed?

The sun had kissed her there. Why had he wanted to as well?

He'd come because he simply wanted to observe, to make certain that Bentley wasn't monopolizing Grace's time. Step in if needed. He certainly hadn't expected to step into Fitzsimmons. What a scapegrace. If any man berated Grace in that manner, public or privately—

How the deuce would he know if it was happening privately?

She would tell him, of course. He'd have her word on it.

She would no doubt inform him it was no longer any of his concern, the stubborn little witch. If he wouldn't assist her in finding a man who loved her, he couldn't very well complain if she ended up with one who didn't.

He probably should have hesitated before stepping in to save her from Fitzsimmons. He would like to have seen the man's face when it met up with Grace's fist. Yes, she would have struck him. She was not demure, not like Juliette.

When Grace wanted something, she went after it, even if it meant asking a recent reprobate for assistance. Which he was not so keen on giving. Whatever had possessed him to gaze at her as he had, to draw her into gazing at him?

He never gazed into women's eyes anymore. He never noticed freckles tucked in near to the corner of a mouth. He didn't pay attention to quick breaths or fingers lifting of their own accord to touch him. He wondered if she'd even been aware of her action. If he'd not moved, she would have touched him, as she had the evening before—and it simply wouldn't do to know the warmth of her again.

Her skin, her sighs, her heated glances would all belong to someone else, someone with the where-withal to love her as she deserved.

"You must tell Lady Chloe," Grace told Lady Ophelia. After her walk with Vexley, she'd met up with her closest unmarried friends near the rhododendrons. "He doesn't fancy her. He's never going to ask for her hand in marriage."

"How do you know?" Ophelia asked.

"My gentleman."

"Vexley? Is Vexley your man? I saw you walking with him."

"No, he's someone else."

"Is he here?" Minerva asked.

"No, no. But he was most insistent that if a man takes a woman to bed without asking for her hand in marriage, it's only lust. And it makes sense. After all this time, why would he ask her? He's searching for someone with a larger dowry."

"Blighter," Ophelia grumbled.

"You must do it."

"All right. All right. I'll talk with her." She opened her eyes wide and smiled brightly. "Ah, there's Lord Ambrose. Think I shall flirt with him a bit. Makes Lady Cornelia bonkers."

"Don't ruin things for her," Grace said adamantly. "I worked very hard to get them together."

"Did your gentleman tell you that Ambrose fancied her?"

"We didn't discuss them."

"Maybe you should. Would be interesting to know his opinion regarding all the various couples that are forming as you break one gentleman's heart after another."

"I'm hardly breaking hearts."

"We all break hearts; we all have our hearts broken. It's the way of things."

Chapter 6

Slowly sipping his scotch and rolling a coin over, under, between his fingers, Lovingdon paid little heed to the men with whom he was playing cards—save one.

Fitzsimmons.

The man downed liquor as though he believed drinking enough of it would cure all ills, when in truth it was only adding to his troubles. Cards required that a man keep his wits about him if he hoped to have any chance at all of winning. Fitzsimmons's wits seemed to have deserted him completely.

He growled when Lovingdon had taken a chair at the table. Not that his behavior was particularly unusual. With the exception of Avendale, the other gentlemen had expressed their displeasure at his arrival by clearing throats, shifting in chairs, and signaling for more drink. Lovingdon was not known for his charity when it came to cards. He believed a man should never wager what he was unwilling—or could ill afford—to lose.

It seemed Fitzsimmons was of the opposite opinion. If this hand didn't go his way, he was going to lose all the chips that remained to him. And Lovingdon already knew Fitzsimmons wasn't going to win. He'd known three cards ago, and yet the man continued to raise the amount being wagered as though he thought continually upping the stakes would disguise the fact that the cards showing before him revealed an atrocious hand.

The final card was dealt facedown. Lovingdon set his glass aside, lifted the corner of his card—

Did not display his pleasure at what he'd been dealt. Fitzsimmons, on the other hand, looked as though he might cast up his accounts. Then in a remarkably stupid move, he shoved his remaining chips into the pile in the center of the table.

The gentleman to Fitzsimmons's left cleared his throat and folded. As did the one beside him.

Lovingdon didn't consider for one moment being as charitable. He matched the wager. Fitzsimmons was obviously on the verge of having an apoplectic fit, if the amount of white showing in his eyes was any indication.

To Lovingdon's left, Avendale folded.

Lovingdon held Fitzsimmons's gaze, watched as the man slowly turned over his cards.

"Ace high," Fitzsimmons ground out.

Lovingdon could feel the stares, the held breaths, the anticipation. It wasn't too late to gather up his cards without revealing them, to simply utter, "I daresay that beats me." Instead he flipped over his cards to reveal a pair of jacks.

Fitzsimmons appeared to be a man who had just felt the cold fingers of death circling his neck. "You cheated, damn you."

One man gasped, another scooted his chair back as though he expected Lovingdon to leap across the table and throttle the insolent Fitzsimmons.

"See here," Avendale proclaimed. "We're gentlemen. We do not accuse—"

"I'm not offended," Lovingdon broke in. "I'm amused. Tell me, my lord, how do I cheat when I keep my hands on the table, one constantly rolling a coin and the other occupied with drink?"

"I don't know." Fitzsimmons's voice was unsteady. "I don't bloody well know."

"I'm certain your credit is good here. You can get additional chips at the cage, although I would recommend against it. Lady Luck isn't with you tonight."

"Shows what little you know. She hasn't been with me in a good long while." Fitzsimmons scraped back his chair, stood, and angled up his chin, gathering as much dignity as possible into that small movement. "Gentlemen."

Then he headed toward the lounge, stumbling only twice.

"One should not mix drink and cards," Avendale declared. He shifted his gaze to Lovingdon. "As Lady Luck does seem to be with *you* tonight, and I have no interest in losing more coins, I'm off to Cremorne."

"You'll lose coins there just as easily."

"Yes, but to ladies who show their gratitude in more inventive ways. Care to join me?"

"In a bit, perhaps. I have another matter to which I must attend first." Lovingdon signaled to a young lad, who rushed over. "Those are my winnings." With a sweep of his hand over the table, he indicated all that belonged to him. "Disperse them evenly between yourself and the other lads."

"Thank you, Your Grace."

The lad eagerly set to the task of scooping the chips into a bowl. Lovingdon bid a good evening to the gentlemen who remained, then strode toward the lounge. He'd barely taken his place in a chair opposite Fitzsimmons before a footman placed a tumbler of scotch on the table beside him. Knowing each lord's drink preferences was a thirty-year tradition at Dodger's. Lovingdon lifted his glass and savored the excellent flavor.

"Come to gloat, have you?" Fitzsimmons asked.

"If I were going to gloat, I would have done it out there. Gloating with witnesses is so much more enjoyable." He tapped his finger against his glass. "You couldn't afford to lose tonight."

Averting his gaze, Fitzsimmons gnawed on his lower lip. Finally he murmured, "I've not been able to afford it in some time."

Placing his forearms on his thighs, Lovingdon leaned forward and lowered his voice. "I knew you at Eton. You weren't a bully—and God knows there were bullies. But not you. Why would you bully your wife? Lady Grace Mabry told me that Lady Sybil believed you loved her—"

"I do love her." Heat ignited his eyes, simmered, then was snuffed out. "I've not been myself of late."

"I've paid little attention to marriages the past few years, but I heard she came with a nice dowry."

"She also came with a penchant for spending. And I had not the heart to deny her the pleasure of it. I thought to increase my assets with investments. I chose poorly. I don't know why the bloody hell I'm telling you all this. Although it'll come out soon enough. I have nothing left. I squandered her dowry. I doubt she'll love me once she realizes the dire straits we're in. My ill temper with her—I think I wanted her to leave me so she would never learn the truth."

"She doesn't know?"

"Would you want your wife to view you as a disappointment?"

Lovingdon felt as though he'd taken a blow to the chest. He'd disappointed Juliette in the worst way imaginable.

Fitzsimmons blanched. "Apologies. That was bad form to mention—"

Lovingdon held up a hand to stem further stammering. He didn't want Juliette's name echoing in this place. "Have you any funds left?"

Fitzsimmons slowly shook his head.

"Right, then. I shall provide you with capital and advise you on how to invest it wisely. You will return my investment with interest once you see an acceptable profit."

"Why would you do this? We're hardly the best of friends."

"Lady Sybil's happiness matters to Lady Grace, and Lady Grace's happiness matters to me. But understand that I can just as easily destroy you as assist you. Our goal here is to ensure you no longer feel a need to take out your frustrations on your wife."

"I won't. I do love her."

"Then treat her as such." He stood. "Be at my residence at two tomorrow afternoon and we'll work out the details."

Fitzsimmons shot to his feet. "I could be there at half past eight in the morning."

Such eagerness. He did hope he wasn't misjudging Fitz. He had known him as a good and honorable man, but he also knew what it was to have life's challenges divert one's course. "You won't find me available at that time of the morning. I intend to spend the night carousing. Tomorrow afternoon will be soon enough."

"I hardly know how to thank you, Your Grace."

"Be kind to your wife."

"I will be. You can count on it."

"And stay away from the cards, man."

"I will."

Lovingdon strode from the room. He decided that he'd head to Cremorne, where ladies and drink were in abundance. He was suddenly in want of both.

He'd known exactly where to find Avendale: at their favorite booth where ale flowed freely. Avendale spotted him, smiled broadly and extended a tankard toward Lovingdon. As soon as he took it, Avendale tapped his against Lovingdon's.

"I knew you couldn't stay away."

Not tonight. Tonight he needed . . . he wasn't certain what he needed. He knew only that he'd not found it at Dodger's. He emptied his tankard in one long deep swallow and called for another.

Avendale leaned back against the counter, placing his elbows on it and crossing his feet at the ankles. He looked to be a man entirely too comfortable here, but then his purview was sin. When they'd been younger men, he'd always sought to entice Lovingdon into joining him. It wasn't until after Juliette died that Lovingdon had finally accepted the invitation. It only took one night for him to wonder why he'd been so resistant in his youth.

Proper behavior was no way for a man to live, he reflected as he downed half the second tankard.

"What were you trying to prove with Fitzsimmons?" Avendale asked.

Lovingdon looked out over the crowd. Cremorne Gardens served two purposes. In the early evening it was for the respectable crowd. Until the fireworks. When they were naught but smoke on the night air, they signaled the beginning of the witching hour—when good folk left and the less reputable arrived. Swells were strutting about now, and buxom ladies were doing their best to entice them.

"Yesterday I witnessed him treating his wife rather poorly," Lovingdon explained. "He wasn't behaving as himself."

"As himself? Or as you remembered him from school?"

"As himself. It seems he's in a bit of a financial bind. Poor investments and all that."

"I suspect it's more than poor investments," Avendale said. "It's this damned industrialization, taking tenants from the land to the cities and factories. It'll be the death of the aristocracy. Mark my words."

Lovingdon chuckled. "Don't be such a defeatist. The aristocracy will survive."

Avendale straightened and lifted his tankard. "Survival is no fun. We want to flourish, have more coin than we'll ever need, so we are men of leisure with no troubles to weigh us down."

"I've never known you to be weighed down with troubles."

Something serious, somber, flashed across Avendale's face before he downed what remained in his tankard and set it on the counter. "What say we find a couple of willing ladies, whisk them off to my residence, and sample them until dawn?"

Lovingdon tried to recollect if he'd heard any rumors regarding Avendale's situation, but he couldn't recall anything. Their relationship was more surface than depth. "Is all well with you?"

Avendale laughed. "It will be once I find a willing wench."

His companion was on the hunt before Lovingdon blinked. After having his tankard refilled, he fell into step beside him.

"So I assume we're looking for our usual fare? Brunettes?" Avendale asked.

Lovingdon didn't answer. The question was moot, and well his cousin knew it.

"I understand you not having an interest in blondes," Avendale went on, "but gingers? They can be as fiery as their hair."

"I'll leave them to you." Juliette was the only blonde he would ever want. As for the reds, he wasn't certain why he didn't gravitate toward them. He supposed it had something to do with Grace and how she had despised her hair and freckles.

He was grateful that Avendale was not of a mind to take an interest in Grace. While he had no need of her dowry, Avendale was not one to remain faithful—or at least Lovingdon couldn't imagine him doing so. As far as he knew, the man had never even bothered to set up a mistress. Sameness bored him. He made a good friend, but as a husband, he would no doubt fail miserably.

Avendale drifted away when a woman crooked her finger at him. While Lovingdon intended to find company for the night, he found himself studying the gents who were about. Were any of them worthy of Grace?

She could be stubborn, and yet there was a softness to her, an innocence. She needed a man who wouldn't break her, who wouldn't berate her. A man who understood that sometimes she tended to behave in a way that wasn't quite acceptable. Coming to a man's residence in the middle of the night, drinking liquor, playing cards, cheating at cards, driving him to madness with her—

He staggered to a stop as he caught sight of red hair beneath the hood of a cape before the woman turned away. She was tall, slender . . . she couldn't be Grace.

"Hello, fancy man. What are you up to tonight?" A golden-haired vixen stroked his shoulder. He hadn't even realized she was near. He'd been so focused on the hooded woman, anyone could have fleeced his pockets.

"Pardon me," he uttered before striding away. Where the deuce was the woman in the cape? It would be just like Grace to decide to come to

Cremorne and make her own assessment of the suitability of gentlemen. Ah, there. There she was. He darted around one gentleman, then another. He edged around a large woman, moved aside a smaller one. She was walking toward the trees. Once she disappeared into the darkness, he'd lose her.

He quickened his pace. Grew nearer. Reached out. Clamped his hand on her shoulder, spun her about—

It wasn't Grace at all. Her eyes were the wrong color, her nose the wrong shape. Her chin was square when it should be round. Her cheeks were not high enough. Her hair . . . her hair was not the correct shade. It was a harsher red. It did not call to a man to comb his fingers through it.

Lovingdon looked into her kohl-lined eyes. No spark, no joy, no laughter resided there. He shook his head. "My apologies. I mistook you for someone else."

He backed up a step, and then another. What the devil was he doing thinking of Grace when he was here? She would never be in this part of London at this time of night. His entire evening had been about her, first with Fitz and now this.

He pivoted and went in search of Avendale. Perhaps he would venture away from brunettes tonight. Someone to take his mind off Grace, a place she should not be at all.

He spotted Avendale staggering toward him, a blonde on one arm, a dark-haired beauty on the other. He whispered something to her. She separated herself from him and strolled, her hips swaying enticingly, over to Lovingdon. When she reached him, she ran her hand up his chest, over his shoulder, and circled it around his neck. "His lordship tells me that you can remove my corset with one hand tied behind your back."

Lovingdon grinned broadly. "I can do it with both hands tied behind my back."

"Ah, you're putting me on now."

He leaned toward her. "I have a very talented mouth."

She laughed, a deep, full-throated laugh. "I'd like to see that."

"It will be my pleasure to demonstrate."

So for tonight, a brunette it would be.

"I had to speak with you before tonight's ball," Lady Sybil said, her arm wound around Grace's as they strolled through the Mabry House gardens.

It had been two days since the Westcliffe garden party, and Grace hadn't seen her friend since, although she had to admit that Sybil appeared more relaxed than she'd been then—but of course her husband wasn't with her at that moment, which could account for her ease. "Has Lord Fitzsimmons been unkind?"

"No. That's the thing of it. He's been terribly solicitous."

"Well, then, I'm glad Lovingdon had words with him at Westcliffe's." She had not heard from nor seen him since that afternoon. She'd decided to give up on his helping her. It was so obvious that he didn't want to be involved in Society any longer.

"I daresay, he did more than speak with him at the party." Sybil spun away, wandered to the roses and touched their fragile petals.

Something was amiss. Grace cautiously joined her friend. "Syb, whatever it is, you can tell me."

"Yes, I know, it's just so terribly difficult. I know you won't tell anyone, but . . ." She looked at Grace. "Fitz lost my dowry."

"How does one go about losing a dow— Wait, you mean he spent it all?"

"More like, I spent it. A good deal of it anyway. Then he made some bad investments—" She glanced quickly around before leaning in. "We're poor. At least for a time. Thank goodness I already have all my gowns for the Season, because Lovingdon gave us the most horrid rules for when we can spend money."

Startled, Grace stared at her. "Lovingdon gave you the rules? What has he to do with any of this?"

"I don't quite understand it all, to be honest, but apparently he's gone into some sort of partnership with Fitz, who is quite convinced that he shall recoup his losses and then some. That's the reason he's been so irritable. He's been under a great deal of strain, striving to pay our debts, and I wasn't helping at all."

"That's still not an excuse for how he berated you. I'd have not put up with it, and you shouldn't have either."

Sybil shook her head. "I knew something was amiss. But he wouldn't talk to me. Pride and all that, I suppose." She grabbed Grace's arm and squeezed. "But I wanted you to know that all will be well. You'll see tonight at the ball. He's once again the man I fell in love with."

Grace hugged her, unable to embrace the optimism but hoping her friend was correct. "I'm happy for you, Syb."

When they drew apart, Sybil smiled at her. "Now we simply must find a gent who loves you, so that you can be as happy as I am. It would be so lovely if you were to receive a proposal at the Midsummer Eve's ball."

Every year, for as long as Grace could remember, her family hosted a ball at their ancestral estate to celebrate the summer solstice. Their guests always welcomed a few days away from the city. She'd often slipped out of her bed and secreted herself in a dark corner of the terrace where she could watch the merriment. She thought, then, that the time would never come when she would be old enough to attend. She'd always longed to dance with Lovingdon and never had occasion to do it.

But Fate seemed to have little regard for the yearnings of her tender heart. She'd been too young to attend balls and parties when he was old enough to make the rounds. When she was finally of an age where she could attend the social affairs, Lovingdon had become a widower and withdrawn from Society. Based on their recent encounters, she doubted he would come to her family's estate for the midsummer festivities.

"You seem to be narrowing your choices down," Sybil said.

Grace shook her head. "It's a decision that will affect the remainder of my life. I don't intend to make it in haste."

"Nor should you be overly cautious. You don't want to lose your chance at the perfect man."

"I assure you that I don't want perfect. Rather, I want someone who can appreciate the allure of imperfection."

There was something decidedly sinful in the way Lovingdon was sprawled over the bed. His hair was flattened on one side, sticking up on the other. His jaw was heavily shadowed, his face rugged, even in sleep. The hand curled on his pillow flinched, the one resting near his thigh didn't move. Nor did the rest of him. The sheets were pooled at his waist. He possessed a magnificent chest. While Grace had seen it before, she'd been distracted by other areas and hadn't given it the attention it deserved. A light sprinkling of hair in the center continued down, narrowed over a flat stomach, and disappeared beneath the covers.

She knew she should leave, but she couldn't quite bring herself to do it. Surely he would awaken soon. And no doubt be furious to find her here. His fury would be justified. A man had the right not to be intruded upon while he slept, but she hadn't snuck in here. She'd knocked on the door several times, then marched in not bothering to soften her footfalls, but he'd barely stirred.

She sighed heavily. She would wait in the parlor, she supposed, as she was determined to speak with him. She spun on her heel and headed for the door.

"Grace?"

The word came out raspy and rough. She didn't want to contemplate that it was the voice with which he greeted his paramours in the morning. Glancing back over her shoulder, she saw his eyes squeezed shut, his brow furrowed, and his fingers pressed against his temples. "I thought you might—"

He held up a hand. "Shh. No need to shout."

If he were one of her brothers, she'd shout that she hadn't been shouting. But he'd done her a favor, so she lowered her voice to a soft whisper. "I prepared something for you." She walked back over to the bed. "It's a concoction that Drake puts together on occasion. Tastes ghastly but you'll feel better once you've had it."

He pushed at the air as though it were enough to physically remove her from the room. "Just go away."

"I can't leave you suffering like this."

"I suffer like this every day. Leave me in peace."

But that was the thing of it. He wasn't in peace and well she knew it. She picked up the glass from where she'd left it earlier on the bedside table. "Humor me, Lovingdon. And then I'll go."

With a low growl, he rose up on an elbow and took the offering.

"Down it in one swallow."

"I know how to manage it," he grumbled.

In fascination, she watched his throat muscles working. Why did every physical aspect of him have to be so remarkably pleasing? Perfection, while she required a man of some imperfection. It would be easier to be accepted fully by a man who had not been chiseled by the gods. She wondered if he had any notion how fortunate he was to have been so carefully sculpted by nature's loving hand.

She took the empty glass from him and set it on the bedside table. "Just lie there for a bit. It won't be long before you're up to snuff."

He eased back down to the pillow, brought the sheet up and eased his right leg up, bending it at the knee, hiding from her view a rise in the covers that she'd noticed earlier but had fought extremely hard not to contemplate. He squinted at her. "What is it with you coming to gentlemen's bedchambers at all hours?"

"You're not a gentleman. You're a scoundrel."

"All the more reason you shouldn't be here."

"You won't take advantage."

"Maybe I should, just to teach you a lesson."

"You won't." She clasped her hands in front of

her to stop herself from reaching out and brushing the wayward locks from his brow. "I know what you did for Sybil."

"I don't know what you're talking about. And you need to leave. On your way out, tell the butler to send up some breakfast."

"Breakfast? It's half past two in the afternoon."

"It's my first meal of the day. Call it what you like. But leave."

"I need to speak with you."

"I'm not presentable," he barked.

"Judging by the volume of your voice, your headache is gone."

He rubbed his brow. "It seems so, yes, and as I asked for breakfast, my stomach is settled as well. Thank you for your witch's brew. Now be off."

"It's a warlock's brew, as it's Drake's recipe." She turned for the door. "I'll see to getting your breakfast, but make yourself presentable while I'm gone, as I fully intend to discuss some matters with you."

"Grace."

She spun around, and the sight of him raised up on an elbow, his other arm draped over his raised knee, the sheet gathered at his waist, nearly took her breath. She'd never given any thought to the fact that she might see her husband in this same position, that he would be as comfortable with his body and might expect her to be the same. "Please, Lovingdon, it won't take long."

He sighed heavily. "I'll meet you in the dining room."

"No need. The sitting area in here works fine. And you needn't tidy up completely. Just enough so we're both comfortable."

Before he could respond, she quit the room and went in search of the butler. She encountered a footman first and gave the orders to him. The butler knew she was in the residence, had assisted her by showing her to the kitchen so she could make her brew, but he'd been quite disapproving of her delivering it to the duke herself. She wasn't particularly anxious to have him scowl at her over her present request. The footman could see that food was delivered.

She returned to Lovingdon's bedchamber and knocked.

"Come!"

She opened the door to find him standing, shoulders bent as he grasped the edges of the table holding the washbasin. He wore trousers, a white linen shirt. No boots. Why did his present attire seem more intimate than seeing him in bed with naught but a sheet covering him? She approached cautiously. "Lovingdon?"

He peered over at her with bloodshot eyes. Droplets of water coated his face. His hair was damp. "I don't think I would have made it to the dining room."

"You made quite merry last night, it seems."

He shook his head. "I don't remember half of it."

"I don't understand the appeal in that."

"No, you probably wouldn't." He splashed more water on his face, then reached for a towel and rubbed it roughly over his bristled skin. She wondered what it might be like to shave him, to scrape the razor over the defined lines and strong jaw. Perhaps she'd shave her husband. It was a thought she'd never entertained before. After tossing the towel aside, he combed his wet hair back from his face and sauntered over to a sofa, his movements relaxed, loose-jointed. She had an odd sensation of being in his lair. Perhaps she should have accepted his offer to meet her in the dining room.

A rap sounded. She opened the door. While the maid set the tray of food on the low table in the sitting area, Grace walked over to the windows and drew back the draperies. He had such lovely gardens to look out on, and she suspected that he didn't even appreciate them. After the servant left, she took a chair near the sofa and began pouring tea.

"You don't have to wait on me," he said as he snatched up a piece of bacon with his fingers, then began to eat like a savage, as though there would be no formality in this room, as though it contained its own set of rules.

"Don't be so grumpy," she insisted.

"My house, my bedchamber. I can be as I want. If you don't like it, you can leave."

"I have no intention of leaving, and your foul mood will not send me scurrying away."

Slowly chewing, he studied her. "How did you know the miracle of Drake's concoction?" he finally asked.

With a smile, she set the teacup before him. "Because he prepared it for me once."

He raised a brow. "Lady Grace Mabry, three sheets to the wind? I would have liked to have seen that."

She chuckled softly. "No, I don't think you would have." It had been after a visit to Dr. Graves. She'd not been at all pleased by his diagnosis or his recommendation for treatment. And so that evening she'd indulged in a bit more liquor than was wise.

He nudged a platter of fruit, cheese, and toast toward her. "Eat."

She took a strawberry. "Are you always so pleasant upon first awakening?"

"My morning was disturbed."

"Again, it's afternoon." She finished off her strawberry. "Truly, Lovingdon, I appreciate what you did for Sybil. She came to see me this morning, explained the situation with Fitzsimmons and how you offered your assistance."

He shrugged. "I needed a new investment partner."

"Yes, but you're providing all the investment, from what I understand."

"Only until he gets back on his feet."

She shifted in her chair. "She said he's more like himself, treating her as he did when they first married. Do you think it'll continue?"

He met and held her gaze, and she could see the conviction in his eyes. "He's not a bad man, Grace. I'm not making excuses for his behavior. It was deplorable. But sometimes when a man feels as though he's no longer in control, he can lose sight of himself."

She almost asked him if that was what had happened to him. This life he led now was so very different from the one he'd led before. He was so very different.

"I've known Fitz since my school days," he added. "His comportment in the garden was unlike him. We'll get his financial situation back in hand,

and I'll teach him how to guard it better, and all should be well for Lady Sybil."

"You'd think he'd know how to guard his money."

"Unfortunately, Grace, sometimes when the coffers have been empty for a while and are suddenly filled, one can forget what is needed not to squander the coins. And if the coffers have been bare for a while, one may have never learned."

"Another reason that I prefer a man who isn't dependent upon my dowry."

"Then you need a man whose fortune is not tied to land."

He was lounging back, so very relaxed, like a great big lazy cat at the zoological gardens. Yet she had the sense that he was very much alert, could spring into action with the slightest provocation—or enticement, if the right woman walked into the room. She took another sip of her tea and set down her cup. "May I ask you something else, Lovingdon?"

A corner of his mouth quirked up. "As though my saying no would stop you."

Oh, he knew her well, and she loved when he teased her like that. No barbs were ever hidden within his words, even when he was put out with her.

"The night I came to ask for your assistance and you opened the door . . . you didn't resemble David."

He blinked. "David?"

"Michelangelo's David."

"Ah." He gave a brusque nod. "I should hope not. My hair is not nearly that curly."

She laughed in spite of the fact that he was deliberately making this difficult for her. "I wasn't referring to your locks, but rather lower. Were you aroused?"

He sounded as though he was strangling, and she wasn't certain if he were choking or laughing. He held up a hand. "I'm not having this conversation."

"I don't know who else to ask about these matters. Not my mother, surely. Minerva, I suppose."

"My sister won't know the answers," he said tersely. "Or at least she'd best not."

"So I must depend on you."

He scowled, and she feared his next words would be a command for her to leave. Instead he rubbed his bristled chin while studying her. She'd been glad that he'd not had time to shave while she saw to breakfast. She liked how dark and dangerous he appeared when he wasn't properly decked out. Three buttons on his shirt were undone to reveal a narrow V of chest and he hadn't bothered with his cuffs. Yes, there was no formality here.

"I had a woman in my bed, Grace," he finally said. "Of course I was aroused."

"A man's—" She pointed her finger at his lap, scratched her neck. "—it's quite a fascinating bit of anatomy. Can you control it?"

"A *bit* . . . of anatomy?"

She felt the heat suffuse her face. "Well, somewhat more than a bit, but you know what I mean. Can you control it?"

He rolled his shoulders as though they'd suddenly grown tense. She supposed she shouldn't continue with this line of questioning but she wanted some answers.

He cleared his throat. "Sometimes, sometimes not. Where are we going with this? For God's sake, hasn't your mother spoken to you about it?"

She shook her head. "As I understand it, it's a topic that only comes up the morning that a woman marries."

"Ask Lady Sybil."

"I have, but she's very vague. Here's my concern. If a man isn't aroused, then he can't make love or produce children, can he?"

He shifted his position as though he were exceedingly uncomfortable. "You have the gist of it, yes."

"Is love enough to arouse a man?"

He shifted again, leaning forward, planting his elbows on his thighs, bringing himself nearer to her. "Little Rose, are you worried that a man won't find you attractive? I assure you that you are in danger of having more children than you can count."

"You're only saying that because you're my friend. I'm thin. There are no paintings of thin women."

"What has that to do with anything?"

"Art reflects what one finds beautiful. Women without an abundance of curves do not find their way into art."

"Of course they do."

"Name one artist who portrays thin women."

He looked at his ceiling—

"Nymphs," she said, as though he'd gone blind. "Chubby nymphs frolicking in the gardens."

Scowling, he looked at the fireplace, at the window. Snapped his fingers and looked at her with satisfaction. "Monet."

"But the women are clothed."

His jaw dropped. "I beg your pardon?"

"In every painting, every statue, that I've seen of nude women, the subjects are plump, which leads me to believe that's what men prefer. What if a man doesn't find me enticing?"

She might have died if he'd laughed. She was certain any other gentleman would have, but ever since he'd discovered her weeping in the stables, he seemed to have an understanding of her insecurities, even though he had no knowledge of how they'd grown tenfold of late. He scooted nearer to her.

"Trust me, Grace, that is not something about which you need to worry. You are lovely beyond—"

"I'm not searching for compliments, Lovingdon. I'm quite disappointed in myself for needing reassurances, but there you are. I can be in a man's bedchamber and not entice him in the least."

Based on the way his gaze slowly roamed over her, she feared she might have overstepped the mark with that comment.

"Are you attempting to seduce me?" he asked in a silky voice.

"No, but I've always been able to talk with you as I can talk to few others. I thought if I understood men a little better, I might have more luck at securing that which I seek."

"Men are aroused by all sorts of things, Grace. For a man who loves you, the thought of being with you will be enough."

"Will it?"

"Of course."

She sighed. She didn't believe him. She'd caught sight of the courtesan in his bed. She suspected the woman's toes were even voluptuous. "I shall embrace your optimism."

"As well you should."

"I don't suppose you'll attend tonight's ball."

He slowly shook his head. "I intend to take a long soak in a tub of hot water that shall last the remainder of the afternoon."

An image of naked limbs, long and muscular, flashed through her mind. She really shouldn't have these sorts of thoughts where he was concerned. They only served to cause her stomach to quiver.

"So how will you spend your evening?" she asked.

"I shall join Avendale for an evening of merry-making and a visit to Cremorne Gardens." He narrowed his eyes. "You don't go there, do you?"

"On occasion."

"But not after the fireworks."

Smiling mischievously, she half lowered her eyelids. "Perhaps."

The lounging duke was replaced by one who sat up stiffly and gave her his complete attention. "You've not been to Cremorne during the wicked hours."

She lifted a shoulder slightly. "Once."

"Do you have any notion how dangerous it is for a woman alone—"

"I never said I was alone."

His jaw dropped, although he recovered quickly enough and gave her a blistering glare. "Who was with you?"

"I can't tell you. You wouldn't approve."

He settled back, but he didn't appear nearly as relaxed as he had earlier. "Well whoever it was, you should no doubt marry him, as it's obvious you've wrapped him around your little finger."

"I never said it was a gent." She rose, and he came to his feet. "I must be off to begin preparing for the ball. I only stopped by to thank you for what you did for Sybil. It means a great deal to me. Enjoy your adventures this evening."

She could only hope that she would enjoy hers.

Lovingdon settled for a cold bath rather than a hot one because he was warm enough as it was. He'd had other women in his bedchamber, most with far less clothing than Grace, but he'd never felt so fevered. He was fairly certain she'd not meant to be a seductress, but when she picked up the strawberry, studied it as though it was the most interesting object in the room, and then closed her lips around it—

His body had reacted as though she'd closed her

lips around him. And then when she began speaking about nude women in paintings, he'd envisioned her lounging over a bed, with sheets draped over her enticingly revealing just enough to set a man's blood to boiling.

He dropped his head back against the rim of the copper tub and stared at the nymphs cavorting over the ceiling. Surely they weren't all Rubenesque. When he realized he was searching for a tall, willowy one with long limbs and narrow hips, he cursed soundly, closed his eyes, and immersed himself in the frigid water.

Blast her! The girl had no sense whatsoever. Spending the afternoon in a scoundrel's bedchamber, licking strawberry juice from the corner of her mouth, touching her tongue to that damned little freckle, talking of nudity, conjuring up images of her in repose, flesh bared—

He came up out of the water and shoved himself to his feet. He had to get these thoughts out of his mind and had to keep them out. He needed her to stop showing up at his bedchamber. He needed her to leave him in peace.

Stepping out of the tub, he snatched up a towel. "Bailey!"

His valet rushed into the bathing room. "Yes, Your Grace."

"I need evening attire for tonight's outing."

Bailey looked as though he'd said he intended to dispense with clothing altogether. "Evening attire, sir?"

To be honest, Lovingdon realized he shouldn't have been surprised by the man's reaction. He'd not donned evening attire in more than two years. "Yes, Bailey, surely it's around here somewhere, buried in moth balls."

"I'm afraid, Your Grace, that it might be a bit outdated."

"I'm not striving to be named the most fashionably dressed man in London. Find it. Then have the carriage brought 'round."

"Yes, Your Grace. Are you celebrating something this evening?"

Bailey's ill-conceived attempt to get to the heart of the matter.

"No, Bailey, I'm determined to get a woman out of my life." Before he did something they would both regret.

Chapter 7

Lovingdon wanted to bury himself in a woman, drown himself in drink, and show Lady Luck that no matter how atrocious the cards were, he didn't need her. He could make do very well on his own.

So other than cursing Grace, what the devil was he doing here? He'd expected the first time that he attended a ball after Juliette's passing would very much resemble taking a hard kick between the legs. He couldn't deny that when he first entered the ballroom, he'd glanced around, out of habit, searching for her.

But then his gaze was arrested by coppery hair held in place with pearl combs, and a smile that had threatened to steal his breath—even if it wasn't directed at him. With whom the deuce was she dancing? He didn't recognize the young upstart, but then he was obviously closer to Grace's age than his own. He'd have to ask around, he thought, then decided it was pointless to do so. Grace needed someone more established with a bit more maturity. That he'd fallen in love at nineteen had no bearing on the situation. Besides, he didn't like the way the lad looked, too moony-eyed.

He'd managed to slip in through the back gardens, through the open doors that led onto the terrace. To his immense satisfaction, he succeeded in observing the festivities unbothered. That had not been the case at the first ball he'd attended. There, the moment he'd walked through the door, he was pounced on by every mother with an eligible daughter. But he'd been a different man then. While he still had a respected title and a generous yearly income, his behavior of late made him less than desirable as a suitor. An eligible bachelor he might be, but husband material he was not.

Grace had spotted Lovingdon three dances earlier, while she was waltzing with Lord Edmund Manning, a second son who was looking to better his position in life through marriage. She did not consider him a serious suitor, but based on Lovingdon's scowling, she couldn't help but brighten her smile. He lurked in the shadows like some misbegotten miscreant. She couldn't deny the pleasure that swept through her at the sight of him, halfway hidden behind the fronds. He wasn't the shy sort, so she knew he was imitating a wallflower because he didn't want to deal with desperate mothers who might take delight in his presence. She could almost feel his gaze upon her, following her.

When the present dance ended, her latest partner escorted her from the dance floor.

"Thank you, Lord Ekroth," Grace said once she reached the sitting area where her maid waited for her.

"I hope at the next ball, you will be kind enough to reserve two dances for me." He lifted her hand to his lips, raised his gaze to hers. "And that I might call on you tomorrow."

"I can't promise you two dances, but I would, however, be delighted to have you pay a call."

"Until tomorrow, then."

He walked off and exited up the stairs, no doubt to join the gents in the gaming room. He had made it clear where his interest resided and that she was the only one with whom he would dance. He was tall with dark hair and swarthy skin. His mother came from Italy and had brought with her a small fortune. If rumors were to be believed, however, his father had not tended it well.

"I hope you're not considering him."

She swung her gaze around and smiled at Lovingdon. "Lord Ekroth?"

He nodded. "He doesn't fancy you overmuch."

She released a laugh of incredulity. "I daresay you're quick to judge. I have it on good authority that the opposite is true."

"Well, then, if you have such good authority, you have no need of my observations." He turned to go. She grabbed his arm.

"Wait. I . . ." What could she say to hold him near? "I do value your opinion."

He gave her a dark smile. "As well you should."

She wanted to roll her eyes at his arrogance. Instead, she said with sincerity, "I didn't expect you to show."

"I decided that I can't avoid balls for the rest of my life."

"Actually, I suppose you could, but I'm glad you didn't. Has it been difficult?"

"Not as difficult as I thought. I've been concentrating on who is here rather than who isn't. Who was that child you were dancing with earlier? I daresay he's not taken a razor to his face yet."

Discreetly, she gave his arm a light punch. "Lord Edmund Manning. A second son who was honest enough to tell me that he is determined to better himself through marriage."

"I hope you informed him it would not be through marriage to you."

"I was not that blunt, but I doubt he'll send me flowers in the morning. So upon what do you base your opinion regarding Lord Ekroth?"

"Watching him dance with you."

"He was the perfect gentleman."

"Exactly."

She furrowed her brow. "All your cryptic comments will have to be discussed later. The next dance will be upon us soon and my card is full." A pity, she thought, wishing one spot remained for him.

"Let me see it." He held out his gloved hand.

"I've told you before that looking at the names—"

"I've observed several gentlemen dancing with you." He snapped his fingers. "Your card and your pencil."

He could be so irritating, and yet what she valued in him was his tendency to speak his mind. With a sigh, she handed over the requested items and watched in dawning horror as he struck through one name after another before handing the card back to her. The names of all the gentlemen with whom she'd danced had been obliterated. "All of them?"

"All of them."

She laughed caustically. "And Lord Vexley? You struck through his name, and I haven't even danced with him yet." At least not at this ball, not where Lovingdon could observe him. Out of the corner of her eye she saw him approaching to claim his dance. The music was starting up.

"He vexes me," Lovingdon said.

"He vexes you? He doesn't vex me."

"He should, if you have any sense about you. Besides, you'll be dancing with me."

Her heart tripped over itself. "I didn't think you were interested in marriage, and based upon your reputation of late, you could very well ruin mine. You were only to observe."

He gave her a caustic look, as though she was perhaps *vexing* him. "Observation is not sufficient. You need a lesson. I intend to show you how a gentleman who fancies you would dance with you."

"But I promised Lord Vex—"

"I'll handle it." He took her arm and fairly propelled her toward the dance floor, passing Vexley on the way. "Sorry, old chap, but I'm claiming this dance."

Without a pause in his stride, he had her in the midst of the dancers before she could object further. And while she knew she should protest heartily, should leave him where he stood, she couldn't deny that she wanted to dance with him, wanted this moment. She might never have another opportunity. She placed one hand on his shoulder, while he held the other and pressed his free hand to the small of her back. Even with his glove and her clothing providing a barrier between their flesh, she could feel the warmth from his hand seeping into her.

"That was quite rude," she said.

"Unfortunately, the only way you would ever realize how much in my debt you should be would be if you were to marry the poor sod."

"I don't think he's as bad as all that. We've danced before and I find his conversation quite delightful."

"He talks while you're dancing?"

"Of course."

"Then he's not fond of you."

"Because we converse?"

"While dancing. The purpose of dancing is to provide an excuse for a gentleman to get very close to a woman, and if he has an interest in her, he is going to take advantage of that. The gents I crossed off your list spent their time looking about."

"So that we didn't run into someone."

"I've not taken my eyes from yours since we began waltzing, and yet neither have we stumbled into anyone."

As much as she wanted, she couldn't deny the truth of his words. "Loving—"

"Shh."

She almost blurted for him not to shush her, but the words that followed caused her heart to still.

"Pay attention to what we're doing."

She knew exactly what they were doing. She'd been doing it most of the night. Dancing. Waltzing, at this particular moment. But his hand holding hers tightened around her fingers and his eyes bore into hers. She became aware of his closeness, his bergamot scent. His legs brushed against her skirts.

"We're improperly close," she whispered.

"Exactly."

"We'll create scandal."

"If a man fancies you, truly fancies you, what will he care?"

"If he loves me, he'll want to preserve my reputation, ensure that his actions don't embarrass me."

"If he cares for you, he won't be glancing around, searching out his next dance partner—or striving to catch the eye of the woman with whom he wishes to have a tryst in the garden."

Her eyes widened. "Lord Ekroth . . . a tryst in the garden? With whom?"

"We're conversing far too much."

The change was subtle but there all the same. His fingers pressing more firmly against her back, tightening their hold on her hand, his gaze delving more deeply into hers, his legs in danger of becoming entangled with hers. The lights from the chandeliers reflected over his dark golden hair. He didn't smile, and yet those lips were soft, relaxed, as though waiting patiently for a kiss. Lovingdon captured her, drew her in, until she forgot that anyone else surrounded them. They moved with a harmony that required no thought. Her toes were safe with him, everything was safe with him.

Even as she had the thought, she knew it was a lie. He had no interest in marriage or love or her, for that matter, except as a friend. Which made him very dangerous to her heart, because it was not nearly as practical as her mind.

The final strains of the music lingered on the air. He ceased his movements but did not release her. She had the odd sensation that he was truly seeing her for the first time.

"He certainly wouldn't rush you off the dance floor," he said.

The words burst her bubble of captivity. "Pardon?"

"A gent who fancied you would be in no hurry to turn you over to another man." He tucked her hand within the crook of his elbow and began leading her from the dance area. Slowly, so very slowly, as though he could scarcely fathom the notion of leaving her. "Ekroth was fairly loping to get you to the chairs so he could make his rendezvous."

He had seemed rather anxious, now that she thought about it. She indicated a couple standing near the doors that led onto the terrace. "Lady Beatrix is certain Lord Winthrop is going to ask for her hand at Season's end."

"He's not."

"How can you be so sure?"

"Watch. See how his gaze keeps darting to those three ladies near that potted palm? He fancies Lady Marianne."

"Maybe he fancies one of the other two."

"Observe him through the remainder of the evening. I think you'll eventually agree I'm correct in my assessment."

Finally they reached the area where her maid awaited her, and Lord Canton was impatiently bouncing on the balls of his feet. The next dance was starting up, and Lovingdon had not struck the earl's name from her dance card.

"My lord," she said in greeting.

"Lady Grace." He tipped his head. "Your Grace. Odd seeing you here. I didn't think you were one to attend functions such as this."

"How else is a gentleman to have the honor of dancing with Lady Grace?"

Canton stilled in mid-bounce, which almost put the top of his head level with Lovingdon's shoulder. "You came here specifically for her?"

"Everything I do is specifically for her."

Had he not already demonstrated in the coach the other evening that his words were meant to toy and teach, were not spoken with true intention, she might have experienced a fluttering beneath her ribs. Instead, she unobtrusively slipped her hand free of his arm and extended it toward Canton. "I believe this dance is yours."

Offering his arm, he gave Lovingdon a final glare before escorting Grace back into the throng of dancers.

"You need to be careful of him," Canton said, his voice low, practically seething.

"I have known Lovingdon since childhood. There is little he could do that would take me by surprise."

Although he had surprised her tonight by coming here.

What the devil had he been thinking to dance with her?

Lovingdon stood in the shadowed corner of the terrace, staring out on the gardens, rolling a coin over and under his fingers. Calming, bringing back a sense of balance. Jack had taught him how to use the coin to keep his fingers nimble. He doubted there was a gent in all of London who could get a lady out of her corset with the same swiftness that he could.

But dancing with Grace, he hadn't thought about doing anything with her quickly. Instead, he'd imagined going very slowly, painfully slowly, unwrapping her like a treasured gift, the joy in the unraveling as great as the pleasure of gazing on what was previously hidden.

"Have you an interest in Lady Grace Mabry?" Lord Vexley asked from behind him.

He didn't bother to turn around. "My interests are no concern of yours."

"She deserves better than you."

"The same could be said of you."

"At least I would be faithful to her. Can you claim the same?"

He no longer stayed with a woman long. They bored him after a time. A short time. He enjoyed sampling but not lingering. "I've already warned her away from you."

"If I understand anything at all about Lady Grace, it is that she is a woman who knows her own mind."

"And if I know anything at all about you, it is that you are in desperate need of funds." He did turn around then. Vexley was only a partial silhouette, most of him lost to the shadows. "She deserves better than a man who sees only a fortune when he gazes on her."

Until that moment he hadn't realized the truth of those words. She did deserve the love she so desperately sought. He'd come here tonight in an effort to rid himself of her, but he feared now that one night might not be enough.

"My coffers may be empty, but my heart is not."

Lovingdon nearly cast up his accounts at the atrocious sentiment. He had little doubt that Vexley would seek to woo her with such ridiculously scripted prose.

Before he even knew what he was about, Lovingdon grabbed Vexley's lapels and jerked him forward. The man's eyes grew so wide that the whites were clearly visible, even in the dimly lit gardens. "Seek your wife elsewhere. Grace is not for you."

"That is for the lady to decide. I was merely attempting to discern your interest in her. I like to know my competition."

"You overstate your worth if you think you could compete with me on any level, for anything."

"Ah, have you not heard, Your Grace, that pride goeth before the fall? Now if you'll be kind enough to unhand me . . ."

Lovingdon flung the man back as he released his hold. "Stay clear of her."

Without another word, Vexley walked off. Only then did Lovingdon become aware of the ache in his hand. He didn't know when he'd stopped rolling his coin about, but based on his tightly closed fist, knew that if not for his glove he'd have broken skin. Very slowly he unfurled his fingers.

He couldn't say exactly what it was about Vexley that vexed him. He'd never placed much stock in the rumors that Vexley had mistreated some girls, but when he thought of the man touching Grace—

Dammit all! When he thought of any man touching Grace, his blood fairly began to boil. He didn't want to assist her in her quest for a husband, but how could he live with himself if she ended up unhappily wed?

Later that night the woman sitting on Lovingdon's lap was all curves, not a sharp angle to be found. She was the sort in whom a man could become lost. She was scantily clad, a nymph who would dance through gardens. She'd loosened his cravat, unfastened the buttons on his waistcoat and shirt, and was presently nuzzling his neck with warm lips coated in wine. He should be focused on her, but instead men dancing with Grace paraded through his mind. More specifically, Grace was the center of his focus: her smile, her laughter, the way her eyes sparkled brighter than any chandelier.

He'd come to Avendale's in hopes of purging all thoughts of Grace from his mind, at least for an hour or so. Avendale was the most debauched of any man he knew. When he wasn't at Cremorne, his residence was populated with women of all sorts and sizes. Liquor flowed constantly, food was in abundance, bedchambers were open to one and all. The man believed in living life to the fullest without regret. Lovingdon had embraced his example.

At this moment he should be embracing Aphrodite. He doubted that was her true name. The women here called themselves whatever they thought a man wanted to hear. It was all pretense, nothing real about it.

"Perhaps you should give Persephone a go," Avendale said laconically.

Aphrodite halted her ministrations. Lovingdon lifted his gaze to Avendale, who stood before him holding a silver goblet no doubt filled to the brim.

"You look as though you're striving to solve a complicated mathematical formula," Avendale continued. "Or perhaps a physics problem."

Lovingdon patted Aphrodite's hip. "Sweetheart, fetch us some more wine."

Without a word or care, she scrambled off his lap and went to do his bidding. That was the thing of it. The women he'd had of late were so eager to please, which he supposed he should find appealing. Instead, he found himself thinking of Grace, too innocent one moment, too worldly the next. She had no qualms about castigating him, challenging him, revealing her disappointments in him. It would take a special man to love her as she deserved, to accept her forthrightness, to not strive to dampen her spirit in order to control her.

Avendale dropped into a nearby chair and stretched out his legs. "I hear you attended a ball tonight."

"Who told you that?"

Avendale shrugged. "I hear all sorts of things from all sorts of people. Are you going back on the marriage market?"

"No, God no. Assisting Grace. I told you that."

"I thought you'd decided to decline that responsibility."

"It's not a responsibility. It's . . ." Blast it. It was a responsibility, one he didn't want, but one he was feeling increasingly obligated to take on. He glanced around. "Do you ever get bored with all this?"

Tapping his goblet, Avendale shook his head. "Without all this to serve as a distraction, I'd go mad."

Lovingdon furrowed his brow and studied the cousin he'd only come to know well during the past two years. At least, he thought he'd come to know him. "A distraction from what?"

"Boredom, of course."

"I think you meant something else."

Avendale lifted his mug. "I'm not far enough into my cups to discuss it. I think I shall seek out some female companionship. You're not jolly enough tonight."

"What do you know of Vexley?"

"Hasn't two ha'pennies to rub together, from what I hear. But he's handsome, titled, has three estates. What more could a woman with a dowry want?"

She could want a great deal more. Deserved it, even.

Chapter 8

"There were fewer flowers this morning," Grace said, sitting astride her bay mare as it plodded along Rotten Row, keeping pace with Lovingdon's chestnut gelding.

"That should please you," he said. He'd arrived one hour before the respectable hour for a morning visit and suggested a ride through Hyde Park. As it was not the fashionable hour, few were about. "It's what you wanted, wasn't it? To separate the chaff from the wheat?"

"Yes, but I'm not exactly sure how it came about."

"Those who sent flowers yesterday but not today care more for your reputation than they do you."

"That's the reason you danced with me. You knew that some men would be put off by my being in the company of a rakehell."

"Don't sound surprised. You're the one who pointed out that dancing with me might sully your reputation."

"But one dance? Not beyond repair, surely. Besides, you're a friend of the family. If you're in the midst of reforming, where better to begin than by waltzing with me?"

He laughed darkly. "I'm not reforming, Grace." Straightening, he took his gaze over her in a slow sojourn. "Is that what this little request of yours is about? Trying to put me back on the straight and narrow?"

"Absolutely not." *Well, maybe a little.* Not that she would confess that to him. "I care only about not making a ghastly mistake when it comes to love. Your appearance at the ball did me a great service. If I'm understanding correctly, a man who truly held affections for me wouldn't give a care who danced with me."

"Exactly."

"You're absolutely certain that you're responsible for my diminished number of suitors?"

"Without question."

"Thank God." She released a tight laugh. "I was fearful someone had seen Lord Somerdale kiss me in the garden and that—"

Reaching out, he grabbed the reins and jerked

her horse to a stop. Beneath his hat, his eyes were narrowed slits. "Somerdale kissed you?"

She wasn't certain why she experienced such triumph. He didn't seem to have a problem when his behavior was questionable. Why should she not be afforded the same consideration? "During the eleventh dance. He had claimed it, but suggested we cool off by taking a turn about the garden. Then he"—she felt her cheeks warming with a blush—"drew me into the shadows and kissed me. I'd never been kissed before."

She pulled the reins from his fingers and urged her horse forward. She was irritated by her reaction. He hadn't the courtesy to blush when he'd opened his door without a stitch of clothing. Why were men so much more comfortable with their bodies than women? He quickly caught up.

"Are you mad?" he asked. "If you want to marry for love, the very last thing you need to be doing is going into the garden with a gent alone at night. If you'd been caught in that compromising position, you would have found yourself at the altar with him."

Beneath her riding hat, she peered over at him. "Yes, I don't quite understand that. What in the world did I compromise? A kiss is pleasant enough I suppose, but hardly worth casting aspersions on a lady's reputation."

"Then Somerdale doesn't fancy you as much as you seem to think."

"I beg your pardon?"

"If he fancied you, he would have given you a kiss that would have had you understanding how one could damn well ruin your reputation."

She shifted her gaze to his lips, plump lower, thin upper. They appeared soft. Somerdale's had been chapped, rough, cold. Lovingdon's looked anything but. She swallowed hard. "But you don't love every woman you kiss."

"I've only ever loved one. As for the others . . ." He shrugged.

"So we're talking lust, not love."

A corner of that luscious mouth of his eased up. "What do you know of lust?"

That based upon the way she wanted to squirm in her saddle, she might be experiencing it at that very moment. She wanted to run her fingers through his hair, caress her hands over his shoulders, unfasten his shirt buttons and catch another glimpse of his chest. "I'm not so innocent as you might think. I have two older brothers. I've listened to some of their conversations."

"Unknown to them, I take it."

She despised hearing the censure in his voice. He was the blackguard here, not her. "As though you are without sin."

His smile faded, his face hardened. "We won't talk of my sins."

She would have taken back the words if she could, but more than that she wondered what had caused his reaction. She suspected whatever he was referring to was darker, deeper than his current follies.

"Lady Grace!"

Glancing over, she saw Lord Somerdale sitting astride a bay horse and trotting toward her. This could prove awkward. "Please don't mention the kiss."

"Not to worry. I won't allow rumors to propel you to the altar."

She drew some comfort from knowing he was still her champion, but she wondered why she didn't feel content with the knowledge.

As Somerdale urged his horse around to the other side of Grace, with little more than a curt nod as acknowledgment to him, Lovingdon wondered how the earl would manage without his teeth. He was contemplating knocking every one of them out of his mouth. How dare the man kiss Grace?

When Grace had confessed about her encounter with Somerdale in the garden, the fury that shot through Lovingdon had nearly toppled him from his horse. It was one thing to watch men flirt and dance with her, but to take it further? To woo her into a darkened garden and kiss her—

That she would allow such liberties, that she didn't realize the risk not only to her reputation but to herself should a man take advantage was beyond the pale. Some man would push her farther than he ought. Vexley for example.

He crossed their path shortly after Somerdale's arrival. He didn't acknowledge Lovingdon, but damned if his cold glare when Grace wasn't looking didn't count as a challenge. He, too, had wisely sidled his horse on the other side of Grace, keeping a safe distance from Lovingdon, who wondered how Vexley would manage with a broken jaw. It was unlike him to have a penchant toward violence, and he certainly wasn't jealous of the attention they were giving her. It was quite simply that they were not the proper marriage material for a lady of her caliber. They were wasting their time, hers, and his.

Two other gentlemen came over on horseback, giving him a curt greeting before turning their full attention onto Grace. Their little entourage had come to a stop, and he was anxious to get them going again. It seemed Grace was not of a like mind.

"I'm going to sit beneath the tree for a while. You needn't stay, Lovingdon."

Was she dismissing him?

"I know my parents appreciate your serving as my escort." She glanced around and smiled. "Lest it not be clear, he is not a suitor."

A few nervous chuckles echoed around them while a couple of the gents eyed him warily. He supposed he couldn't blame her for wanting to lay out his position in her life so there would be no doubts, not that he thought anyone would see him as a serious suitor. He'd made it quite plain that he had no intention of marrying again.

"I've nothing else to do," he said. "I'll escort you home before I take my leave."

Without question she was capable of taking care of herself, but she was still somewhat innocent and naive. A man could take advantage. One no doubt would. Some gent was going to grow weary of competing with the others and seek to force her into marriage by compromising her. A man who was desperately in need of funds. Like the four flocking around her now. He knew their worth, not only in terms of money, but in terms of character. None of them was good enough for her.

But who was? There had to be someone with whom he wouldn't find fault, someone who would love her as she deserved to be loved. But for the life of him, he could think of no one.

While Lovingdon remained mounted, Lord Vexley dismounted quickly and fairly loped over to Grace, placing his hands on her waist—

Lovingdon's horse shied away and he realized he was gripping the reins, yanking them. After settling his gelding, he reached into a pocket, removed a coin and began weaving it through his fingers, seeking calm. Using his knees, he urged his horse forward, reached down and grabbed the reins to Grace's horse. He'd relegated himself to groomsman, but he certainly wasn't going to play the part of swain, especially after she'd already announced that he was nothing more than a family friend.

Lord Chesney came galloping over, a puppy nestled in his arms. He quickly dismounted, not at all hindered by the creature. As he handed Grace the squirming bundle of fur, she looked as though she would marry Chesney on the spot. Like his father before him, he bred dogs, had bred Lovingdon's most recent collie. That alone should have at least earned him some favor, but he couldn't see the man marrying Grace.

Grace's laughter wafted toward him. She was sitting on the ground, playing with the puppy in her lap while entertaining the gentlemen around her. He studied each and every one. In his more charitable moments he wished them each to hell. In his less charitable moments, he decided hell would be too good for them.

Grace shuffled into her bedchamber and looked at the bed with longing. It was wearying to be always smiling, to pretend to care about subjects that held no interest, to not want to hurt some gentleman's feelings because she knew with every fiber of her being that he was not the one.

Although she suspected her tiredness had to do with Lovingdon more than it did the other gents. He kept her alert, aware of every nuance of his movements, every tone of his voice. She'd been acutely aware of him watching her while she flirted with each of the lords who had joined her in the park today. She'd wanted to order him to get off his blasted horse and join her but refrained. If he'd barged into the midst of their group, she had little doubt the others would have scattered. But he maintained his distance, just as he had since Juliette's passing. Even when he was with her, it was obvious his mind drifted elsewhere.

Felicity entered and without a word began assisting her in removing her riding habit. She had left the dog with the boot boy. He would see to its needs until it learned not to make puddles in the house. It was such a sweet gesture on Chesney's part, but Lovingdon had grumbled on the way back to the residence, "A man who loves you would know that you prefer cats. Nasty vile creatures that they are."

He'd made her laugh, naturally and honestly, her first true laugh since Somerdale had arrived. It had felt marvelous to be carefree, to be herself. She never had to worry about impressing him. He'd always accepted her as she was. She was grateful that aspect to their relationship had not changed.

"I'm going to lie down for a while," she said, once all the outer garments were gone and only a layering of cotton separated her skin from the air.

"Are you feeling well, m'lady?" Felicity asked.

"Yes, just tired. Return in time to prepare me for dinner."

"Yes, m'lady."

After the maid closed the door, Grace walked to the bed, stopped, considered, then crossed over to the mirror. Very slowly, she unlaced her chemise. With her eyes on the mirror, she gingerly parted the cloth and, as she had a hundred times during the past two years, imagined her husband doing the same, tried to imagine herself through his eyes. Still, after all this time, when she was completely revealed she felt as though she were taking a punch to the gut. The familiar sight should no longer take her off guard, and yet it did.

"The scars aren't so bad," she whispered, but in her mind she heard a man's voice, deep and rich, roughened by passion. Her husband's voice, on their wedding night. Mayhap he wouldn't notice in the dark. She sighed. He'd notice.

Not bothering to lace herself back up, she wandered over to the bed and stretched out on her side. Her cat, Lancelot, leapt upon the counterpane, circled around, and finally nestled against her hip. She slid her fingers through his fur. "Don't worry, the dog won't replace you. I suspect he'll become Father's more than mine. They seem to have hit it off."

And then because Lancelot was the one in whom she had confided regarding her first love, her first heartbreak, she said, "What if the man I determine loves me doesn't love me enough to remain once he learns everything?"

Her scars were such a personal matter. No one outside of the family knew. Her mother insisted that there was no reason for anyone to know. It wasn't that anyone was ashamed. It was quite simply that things of this nature weren't talked about.

But Grace knew she would tell the man who proposed to her, on the day he proposed. She could not in all good conscience accept a proposal with secrets between them. But again she asked Lancelot, "What if he doesn't love me enough?"

She wasn't aware of going to sleep, but she opened her eyes to darkness warded off by a lamp on the bedside table, and a man hovering near the foot of her bed. William Graves, physician extraordinaire. When he wasn't serving the queen, he served the poor and those he considered friends.

Her mother sat in a nearby chair, hands folded in her lap, concern in her blue eyes. "Felicity said you weren't feeling well."

Grace rolled her eyes. "I was tired, that's all."

"Will you let Dr. Graves examine you?" her mother asked. "Please."

Dear God, she wanted to say no. He'd examined her so many times. But she understood her mother's fears. Reluctantly, she nodded. It was a small thing for her mother to ask. Swinging her legs off the bed, she sat up. Dr. Graves knelt before her, his pale locks curling around his head. She wondered if they would ever turn silver.

"You'll tell me if anything hurts," he ordered quietly.

Nothing had hurt before. That was the thing of it. Had Graves not warned her that eventually she would experience excruciating pain and eventual death, she'd have not believed it, but he'd been most adamant about the death part. So, yes, she understood her mother's fears.

Nodding again, she stared at the corner where shadows waltzed. The doctor was gentle, careful, but thorough. It seemed to take hours, but it was only minutes before he moved away.

"Everything appears to be all right."

The relief washing over her mother's face made Grace feel guilty for inadvertently raising an alarm. She'd only been tired. Reaching out, her mother squeezed his hand. "Thank you, Bill."

"Send word if you need me, Frannie. Any time."

With that, he quit the room. Her mother rose, wrapped her arms around Grace's shoulders, brought her in close to her bosom and rocked from side to side. "Thank God, thank God."

"Mother, I wish you wouldn't worry so. I keep a watch just like he taught me. I'd alert him if there was anything amiss."

Her mother kissed her forehead. "I know, but it is a mother's job to worry." Then she returned to the chair, while Grace retied her chemise. "How was your afternoon in the park with Lovingdon?" her mother asked.

"Lovely. Some other gentlemen caught up with us there, so we didn't have much time to converse about anything other than the weather."

"I doubt you discuss the weather with any of these gentlemen." Her mother studied her for a moment. "I was quite surprised he came to call."

"It's been two years. His mourning period has ended."

"Based upon what I heard, it ended some time ago. I'm also aware that he danced with you last night."

"I don't know why you're beating around the bush. I'm sure Father told you. I spoke with Lovingdon. I thought he could provide some perspective on the men who have been courting me."

Her mother flexed fingers that had once been nimble enough to pick pockets. "Grace, I'm very much aware that you were quite infatuated with him when you were younger."

"When I was a child," she said impatiently. "He can be quite charming. Or at least he was. What I feel for him now . . ." She struggled to find the correct word. "I suppose it's confusion more than anything. Sometimes I catch a glimpse of the young man from years ago, but mostly he's not there anymore. The person he is now is a friend, nothing more." She rolled her eyes. "Well, he's also an expert on rakehells. He's managed to give me some advice there."

"Are you certain you're not running a con, striving to snag something that has always been beyond reach?"

"Drake asked me the same thing. I'm not so desperate that I would try to trick a man into loving me. I'm insulted you would both think so poorly of me."

"Perhaps it is just that I fear a bit of the swindler resides in your blood."

"My grandfather, you mean. I do wish I'd met him."

Standing, her mother reached into her pocket and withdrew an envelope. "Lovingdon's man delivered a missive for you while you were sleeping. Take care, my darling. Games seldom end the way we imagined."

"I'm not playing a game, and I won't fall for him."

"Hmm," her mother murmured. "Funny thing is, I told myself I wouldn't fall for your father. The heart will have its way."

Grace waited until her mother left before opening the sealed envelope and removing the single sheet of paper. The message was short and to the point.

Midnight.
The garden.
—Lovingdon

The garden path was lit by gas lamps, and yet the darkness still dominated. Grace walked slowly, cautiously, searching through the shadows for a familiar silhouette. She wondered what Lovingdon wished to discuss with her and why he had chosen this setting rather than the parlor. He was always welcome in their home. He was well aware of that fact, although she did have to admit that the clandestine meeting appealed to her, the thought of doing that which she shouldn't.

And why so late at night? What was so urgent that it couldn't wait until morning? She was not usually lacking in imagination, but she was quite stumped.

"Grace."

She swung around. In the darkest recesses of the rose garden, she thought she could make out the form of a man. Her heart was hammering so strongly that she feared it might crack a rib. "Lovingdon?"

She watched as the shadows separated and he strolled toward her. "I wasn't certain you would come."

"I'd never ignore a summons from you. What's this about? What's—"

His strong arms latched around her as he pulled her from the path, into a corner where light could not seep. Before she could scream or utter a word of protest, he latched his mouth onto hers with such swiftness that she was momentarily disoriented. His large hand was suddenly resting against her throat, tilting up her chin as he angled her head, all the while urging her lips to part. She acquiesced and his tongue swept forcefully through her mouth, as though aspects of it needed to be explored and conquered.

With a sigh and a soft moan, she sank against him. She had thought about kissing him for far too long to resist—and his skill made resistance unappealing. His other arm came around her back, pressed her nearer. As tall as she was, she supposed she shouldn't have been surprised by how well they fit together, thigh to thigh, hips to hips, chest to chest, and yet she was taken off guard by the intimacy, the heat radiating off him.

His roughened thumb stroked the sensitive flesh beneath her chin, near her ear. No gloves, just bare flesh to bare flesh. A slight alteration of position and his fingers were working her buttons. One loosened. Two. Three.

She knew she should pull back now, should insist that he stop, but when his warm, moist mouth trailed along her throat, she did little more than tip her head back to give him easier access.

Another button granted freedom, and his tongue dipped into the hollow at her throat. Fire surged through her, nearly scorched her from the inside out. Desire rolled in ever increasing waves.

He groaned, low and deep, his fingers pressing more insistently into her back as though he wished for her to become part of him, as though he couldn't tolerate even a hairbreadth separating them.

He dragged his lips up her neck, behind her ear. Then he was outlining the shell of her ear with his tongue, only to cease those delicious attentions in order to nibble on her lobe. She was close to sinking to the ground, her knees growing weak, her entire body becoming lethargic.

"Do you understand now," he rasped, "how, when a man desires a woman, his kiss might very well ruin her reputation?"

He desired her. A sensation, rich, sweet, and decadent coursed through her. He desired her. The words echoed through her mind, wove through her heart.

"But he is not likely to stop here," he murmured.

He? Who the devil was he talking about?

"He will leave no button undone, no skin covered. He will remove your clothes, lie you down on the grass, and have his way with you. You will cry out with pleasure only to weep with despair because you're ruined. If you're discovered, you'll be forced to marry him. If not discovered—"

He gave her a tiny shake and she realized his fingers were digging into her shoulders, jerking her out of her lethargy. She opened her eyes, and though they were in darkness, she could still feel the intensity of his gaze.

"You play with fire when you go into gardens with gentlemen."

Abruptly he released her and spun away. Three steps later his silhouette was visible from the faint light of the lamps. She saw him plow one hand through his hair.

"You said you desired me," she whispered.

"I was demonstrating how a man who desired you would kiss you. If Somerdale didn't kiss you until your toes curled, then he doesn't desire you and it is very unlikely that he would ever love you."

"Demonstrating." Forcing her legs to regain their strength, she strode toward him. "How could you kiss me like that if you didn't desire me?"

"I've desired enough women to know the particulars."

Without thought, she swung her hand around and slapped him with all her might. He staggered back. Her palm stung. "How dare you! How dare you lure me out here and kiss me as though it meant something, as though *I* meant something."

"You need to understand the danger you place yourself in when you allow men to take liberties. And you need to understand that you will never be happy with a man who kisses you as Somerdale did."

"You place too much emphasis on his kiss. Perhaps he simply possesses the wherewithal to hold back his passions."

"Not if he loves you."

"You don't love me and yet you kissed me as though your very life depended on it. I should think that a man who cared deeply for me would be able to accomplish the opposite."

He sighed heavily. "Little Rose, I'm trying to impart a lesson—"

"Well I don't bloody well want your lessons." She hadn't gone to him all those nights ago to seek his assistance because she wanted his love, although perhaps her mother and Drake had the right of it. Perhaps she had been striving to rekindle what she had felt as a child. It had made her feel such joy, made her believe there was nothing she could not conquer. But what she had felt then was composed of childish things: simple and without basis.

She didn't love the man standing before her. She longed for the young lad of her youth, and he was nowhere to be found.

She marched past him. He grabbed her arm and she wrenched free of his hold. "Do not touch me when it means nothing to you, when *I* mean nothing to you."

"You mean . . . you mean a great deal to me. I want you to be happy, to have this man you want who will love you."

"Why can't it be you?"

The swirling shadows created an illusion of him jerking back as though she'd struck him again, but she knew her words meant little. He was helping her because she'd been insistent, not because he had any true desire to be of service. He didn't care what happened to her.

"I don't have it within me to love like that again." His voice was somber, reflective, filled with pain and anguish.

Although she knew the words would slice, she couldn't seem to hold her tongue. "Perhaps you never truly did love."

"You know nothing at all about love if you believe that."

Spinning on his heel, he disappeared into the shadows. She'd meant to hurt him, because he'd hurt her, the one person whom she'd thought would never cause her pain. Her father was right. She wasn't going to find love where she was looking for it.

So she'd damned well find it elsewhere.

Whipping around, she headed to the residence.

Why can't it be you?

What had prompted her to ask such an absurd question? He had only himself to blame for tonight's debacle. Meeting her in the garden had been a mistake. A colossal mistake. Five minutes after sending the message, he'd known it, and yet had been unable to not make the rendezvous.

From the moment he learned that Somerdale had kissed her, Lovingdon had thought of nothing except her lips, what it might be like to press his against them.

It had been unlike anything he'd ever experienced before. He was so young when he married Juliette, so untried, so blasted naive. He had been determined never to offend her with a man's lustful cravings. Oh, certainly passion had characterized their lovemaking. He had adored and desired her.

But with Grace it had been something else, something more. She responded with fervor that matched his own. And while his original intent had been to teach her a lesson, he feared he was the one tutored.

She held nothing back. As in all things, she was fearless.

Had she not been a friend, had he not cared about her, he would have done exactly what he'd predicted a man who didn't love her would—he would have taken her to the verdant grass and had his way with her. He would have slowly loosened her buttons, her ties, her bows. He would have bared her body—

His mind came to a screeching halt. *Grace.* These lustful thoughts centered on Grace.

She wanted love. He could give her lust in abundance, but not love. He had closed his heart to the possibility. He would never again experience the devastating pain of loss. He would not love. He would not.

Perhaps you never truly did love.

How he wished that were true, because he was so damned tired of the agony of loss. He never wanted to experience it again. It wasn't just losing the physical presence of Juliette and Margaret. It was losing the memory of them as well that tormented him. Sometimes he couldn't remember the exact shade of their hair or the peal of their laughter. Sometimes he would go days without thinking of them, and when he did, the guilt blasted into him because he was beginning to accept their absence. That hurt worst of all.

But he was thinking of Juliette now, with a vengeance, as he slowly sipped the whiskey while in a darkened corner in the sitting room at Dodger's. He'd considered returning to his residence, but he couldn't stand the thought of facing the many portraits of Juliette that adorned his home. She would look down at him from above the mantel and judge him, no more harshly than he judged himself.

In his mind she began to recede and Grace came to the fore. Grace who had no qualms whatsoever about displaying her ill temper to him. Juliette had certainly never been angry with him. They'd never exchanged harsh words.

Grace frustrated him to no end with her quest for love. Did she think he could pull it out of his pocket and hand it to her?

"Contemplating murdering someone?"

Lovingdon jerked his head up to find Drake studying him intently. Drake was older by three years, and Lovingdon had once trailed after him like a faithful pup. Drake never seemed to mind, but he had taught Lovingdon some skills that he suspected his mother would rather he not know. He could pick a lock, lift a treasured piece without being caught, pilfer a pocket. With a sleight of hand, he could pluck out the cards that would ensure he won.

"Why would you think that?"

Drake lifted a shoulder. "I'm accustomed to your dark expressions, but this one seems to be almost black." He sat in the nearby chair. "Want to talk about it?"

Lovingdon shook his head.

"Doesn't have anything to do with my sister, does it?"

Lovingdon stilled. While Drake and Grace were not joined by blood, they were as close as any siblings who were.

Drake lounged back. "I thought so."

"She's trying to find love, and making poor choices in the process. She's asked for my assistance, but I don't understand why she has doubts about her ability to recognize love when it arrives."

"She has an air of confidence about her that can be misleading." Drake scratched his thumb over the fabric, studying the motion as though it could help him gather his thoughts. "She's not certain that a man can truly love her. *Her, for herself.*"

"That's ridiculous. She has much to offer a man."

"While I agree—unfortunately she is not as confident." With a growl, Drake leaned forward and planted his elbows on his thighs, his head hanging as though the weight of his thoughts was too much. "Take care with her, Lovingdon. She's always admired you the most, thought you the smartest, the cleverest, the kindest. Without meaning to, you could devastate her."

Based on her reaction in the garden, the warning may have come a tad too late. "You could marry her."

Drake shook his head. "I was raised within the bosom of a noble family, but I am not nobility. I know my place in the world."

"It's standing beside the rest of us."

"I appreciate the sentiment, but you can take a boy out of the streets but you can't take the streets out of a boy. And our topic of discussion is Grace, not me. She's more vulnerable than you might think. Help her if you've a mind to. Otherwise walk away. I value your friendship, but I value hers more. I could destroy you within the blink of an eye."

Sitting in a rocking chair, cradling a sleeping infant who had been left on the foundling doorstep a month earlier, Grace relaxed into the rhythmic motion and gave her mind freedom to wander. As it most often did since the kiss in the garden four nights ago, she found herself thinking not only of lips but of every aspect of a man's mouth.

She had not expected a kiss to encompass so much. Somerdale's lips had been chapped and remained sealed as tightly as a lady's corset, not that she had attempted entry into his mouth—the thought had not even occurred to her. But now it was all she could think of.

Three of his teeth overlapped, which gave him an endearing grin. She imagined kissing him as Lovingdon had kissed her. She would notice the little imperfections, just as she'd noticed Lovingdon's perfections. His teeth were as disciplined as he, lined up perfectly.

She had never thought beyond the lips, but now everything seemed important: breath, tongue, size. Chesney's mouth covered the area of a small horse's. It would swallow her up. Lord Branson was fond of onions. She didn't think he would provide as flavorful a kiss as Lovingdon's, which was rich with the lingering taste of brandy.

Could she love a man whose kiss did not tempt her into kissing him again? She'd never wanted to break away from Lovingdon's mouth. She had wanted to stay there until the lark warbled and the nightingale went to sleep. She had wanted—

"Hiding out?"

She looked to the doorway. Lovingdon stood there in his evening attire, so blasted handsome that he fairly took her breath. She felt the unwanted heat sweep through her as she noticed his lips, as straight as a poker, not curling upward or downward, and yet so frightfully kissable.

"What are you doing here?" She was rather pleased that her voice didn't betray the turmoil burning inside her at the sight of him. She wanted to remain aloof, uninterested. She wanted to leap from the chair and throw her arms around him. She'd feared after their encounter in the garden, after her unkind words, that she'd never see him again. She'd written him a dozen lengthy letters of apology but none seemed quite right. In the end, she'd merely sent him a note that read:

I'm sorry.
—G

"Looking for you," he said. "Do you have any notion as to the number of balls I've slipped in and out of, searching for you?"

A spark of joy should not be rekindled by the words, and yet there it was struggling to burst into a full-fledged flame. "How many?"

"It seemed like a thousand."

The joy ignited and she smiled. "I doubt it even came close to that number. How did you know I was here?"

"Spoke with Drake. He said you spend considerable time at the foundling homes and orphanages your mother has built. Naturally you would be at the last one I visited."

"So what did you want?"

He studied his well-shined shoes. "To apologize for the kiss."

"No need. I thoroughly enjoyed it."

His head came up. "You slapped me."

"Because of the reason behind it. I don't fancy your lessons."

"I thought demonstrating would be more efficient than explaining. Why don't you put that little one to bed and I'll escort you home? We can discuss a different strategy on the way."

"What sort of strategy?"

"One that will ensure that you marry a man who loves you."

"I'm beginning to think that can't be assured."

"Only if you focus on the wrong man."

And that would be you, she thought.

He walked across the room and sat on the floor at her feet, but his attention was not on her, but rather the babe she held. Her heart lurched as he skimmed a long, narrow finger along the child's chubby cheek. As thin as the child was elsewhere, her cheeks had remained rosy and fat.

"I can't love again, Grace," he said quietly. "It hurts too damned much."

"I think it sad that you would go the remainder of your life without love. You are not old, Lovingdon, and you have years ahead of you, years to be lonely."

"Just because I don't have love doesn't mean I will be lonely." He lifted his gaze to hers. "I don't want for women."

"And I don't want for men circling about, but it's not enough. It's superficial, it's—"

"Undemanding."

"Juliette never struck me as demanding."

"She demanded that I not let her and Margaret die."

With that admission, her stomach fairly fell to the floor. She realized there was more to his change in character than loss. There was the burden of guilt, horrible guilt. It was a wonder he managed to get out of bed at all with the weight of it. "Oh, Lovingdon, do you not see? You could not have stopped their deaths. You're not God."

"I brought the typhus to them. Juliette asked

me not to go into the poorer sections of London, but I felt I had a duty to help the less fortunate. I'd contributed money for improvements and felt I needed to oversee the work. In addition, I was striving to collect data, to provide reports to Parliament. I wanted to change things, I wanted to do something worthwhile. Instead I fell ill." His voice caught, turned ragged. "I should have been the one to die, but I survived. My darling wife and precious daughter died, because I put others before them."

"No, no." Her need to ease his suffering was a physical ache that threatened to crush her chest. "You don't know that it was being in the slums that caused your illness. Maybe you came too close to someone at the opera or your tailor or a man you strolled past outside your home. Maybe all three of you were at a park together. Someone, not realizing he was ill, stopped by to say good day. People fall ill for all sorts of reasons. Sometimes it's little more than Nature's cruel ways." She was far too familiar with the truth of those words. "You can't blame yourself for something that's not your fault."

"I can. I do." His voice sounded stronger, as though he'd found his way onto a path that he'd traveled far too frequently. "But I have an even greater sin." He gently, so very gently, combed his fingers over the infant's hair, as though the motion could calm his wretched soul. "I lied to Juliette, you see. She asked me to protect our child, not to let Margaret die. I promised her that I would do all in my power to see that our daughter got well." She saw tears welling in the corner of his eye. "I promised her, and in that promise resided my lie, because our daughter was already gone, and I hadn't the courage to tell Juliette, because I knew she would hate me and I didn't want her leaving this world hating me."

"Lovingdon." Grace wasn't certain how she managed it, but she slid from the rocker to the floor without losing her balance, without toppling over, and she carried the babe with her. Cradling her in one arm between herself and Lovingdon, she wound her other arm around him. "Courage had nothing to do with it. It was your love that stopped your words. You let Juliette go in peace, without having to grieve."

While the whole of the grieving was left to him.

She held him, listening to his harsh breathing, willing him to unleash the tears that she was certain he had been holding at bay ever since his wife and daughter died. She understood now the burden he carried, the life he led, the reasons behind his determination not to love again. Within her breast she wept for him, but she knew if he were aware of the secret tears she shed, he would distance himself further. He was too proud to welcome her sympathy. He was lost in guilt, grief, and remorse, and she didn't know how to convince him that he was forgiven.

Leaning back slightly, he cupped her cheek with his hand, his eyes reflecting his sorrow. "You deserve someone who loves you with every bit of his being. But he is not me. Still, if you wish me to assist you, I will do it with more enthusiasm."

She thought more enthusiasm might very well kill her if that enthusiasm included another kiss. She dropped her gaze to his lips. It was all she could do not to lean in, not to taste them one more time.

"Nothing improper between us," he whispered as though he read her thoughts.

The babe began to mewl and squirm, and she realized she was holding the girl much too tightly, that she had wedged her small body between hers and Lovingdon's. She welcomed the reprieve, the distraction.

She eased away, turning her attention to the child, so he wouldn't see the disappointment in her eyes. "Yes, I still welcome your assistance, along with your proper behavior."

He chuckled low. "You forget that I knew you as a child. Proper was not what you relished then."

"But now I'm grown."

She dared to look at him then, keeping all her yearnings buried. He would not love again. She was certain of it now. She did not agree with his reasons, but then it was not her place to agree. Unfortunately, as much as she cared for him, she thought too much of herself to settle for less than she deserved. She deserved a man who loved her wholeheartedly. "I believe my plan to approach you was misguided. I will truly understand if you prefer to return to your debauched life."

"Helping you doesn't mean I have to leave my debauched life behind."

Pushing himself to his feet, he helped her up. "Tomorrow we will begin our earnest quest for your love."

Chapter 9

Glass. It was an exhibit of glass. Glasses. Things out of which people drank. Why would anyone bloody care?

Lovingdon could not help but recognize that of late there were exhibits on everything. Grace had been interested in visiting this one. He would have been more entertained by cow dung.

There was a reason he preferred nightly entertainments. The day ones were numbing, but apparently very popular. He could hardly reconcile all the people who were entranced with drinking vessels.

With her arm nestled in the crook of his elbow, she said, "Of the couples here, which of the gentlemen truly fancy the lady they have accompanied?"

"All of them. A man would have to be truly, madly, deeply in love to force himself through this."

She smiled and that deuced tiny freckle at her mouth winked. "You're bored."

"It's glass, Grace. Now if it had a pour of whiskey or rum in it . . . or God, I'd even be grateful for rye."

She laughed and he made a mental note that he shouldn't cause her to laugh. He loved the way her throat worked so delicately, the way her lips parted in merriment, the absolute joy that lit her eyes . . . over something as mundane as stemware.

"I don't think you're taking this outing seriously. We're a bit early so it's the perfect opportunity for you to provide me with some clues as to what I should look for. But soon the Set will be descending, because everyone knows that Bertie is keen to see the exhibit, and I will no doubt be swept away by numerous suitors. So that couple over there by the blue glassware. Does he fancy her?"

"He's here, isn't he?"

"You're here and you don't fancy me. Perhaps he's a relation. Is there anything that says he can't live without her?"

This was an idiotic exercise. He needed to see her suitors buzzing about her in order to know which ones she should avoid. But as they were here, and she had asked—

"He fancies her."

She jerked her head around to stare at him. "Oh, I think you're wrong, there. He can barely drag his gaze from the glass. Surely if he fancied her, he'd be looking at her."

"He touches her . . . constantly. Small touches. On the shoulder, on the arm, on the small of her back. That's the big one. The small of her back. Solicitous. Every time she speaks, he leans in so he doesn't miss a word. If he didn't fancy her, he wouldn't care what she said. He'd simply grunt or mutter something unintelligible, because women, bless them, don't care whether or not we listen. They simply want to speak. As long as we offer an occasional, 'Yes, dear, you're quite right, couldn't have said it better myself,' women are overjoyed— even when we haven't a clue as to what it was we couldn't have said better ourselves."

"No." She gave him a discreet punch in the side. "We talk because we have something of import to say."

"Something that a man generally has no desire to hear, and will hardly ever classify as important."

She stepped away from him, anger igniting her eyes into a blue that was only seen in the heart of a fire. "Is that how you feel about me?"

No words existed to describe how he felt about her. He wanted to see her happy; he wanted her to have love. He wanted to whisk her away to a tower somewhere so she would never know the pain of loss. It occurred to him at that moment that by helping her acquire what she desired, he was condemning her to unbearable suffering. He could only hope that she would be up in years and too senile to fully experience it. Yes, a love that lasted her entire lifetime was what he wanted for her. What he could not guarantee. *That* realization had him speaking a bit more testily than he might have otherwise. "No, of course not. You have things of interest to say, and I never know what is going to come out of that pretty little mouth of yours."

That pretty little mouth set into a stubborn line, and he knew she was trying to decipher whether he had just said something that was too flowery to be true. Therein resided one of the problems with giving women too much information. While most men wouldn't agree, he knew not to underestimate a woman's intelligence and reasoning abilities. He suspected if the gents of town discovered what he was revealing about their habits, they would hang him from London Bridge. He needed to get her thoughts elsewhere.

"I can also tell you that she is married to someone else, someone who probably doesn't fancy her."

She shifted her gaze over to the couple, her

mulish mouth now a soft O. "They're lovers? How did you discern that?"

"Why else would they be at such a place where they are unlikely to be seen because no cares about glasses?"

The humor was back in her eyes. "They are likely to be seen, as there are several people here, and soon there will be a good deal more. You obviously don't appreciate the setting. Exhibits are designed as a way to expose us to the world. Here, come with me."

He shouldn't indulge her. To make his point, he should stay where he was, but she had piqued his curiosity. He followed her to a glass case that housed decanters in numerous shapes, all in various shades of red.

"Imagine what it took to create these," she said softly. "Heat, such immense heat, melting the glass, then a craftsman carefully gathering it up on a rod like honey."

He couldn't help but think of a woman's heat, a woman's honey. Nor did he seem capable of preventing his gaze from trailing over her, but she didn't notice. She was focused entirely on the goblets and pitcher in the case, and her mesmerized expression was almost as intoxicating as her words.

"Glass blown with care—just the right amount

of breath, of pressure, of force. Heating, cooling, shaping, reheating. The red added. All the work, the artistry, the passion that must go into creating something so beautiful." She looked up at him then. "Can you imagine it?"

He could imagine it. Vividly. Too vividly. Her skin flushed with the fire of passion. Her lips plump from pressure. Her gaze smoldering with blazing desire. He imagined taking her mouth, burning his brand on her soul.

What the devil was wrong with him?

"How can you not appreciate a work of art, even if it is a common item?" she asked.

There was nothing common about it, about her. She shortchanged herself if she believed men were after only her dowry. Even if they didn't love her, they would gain so much by having her—a work of art herself—at their side. Her fortune, her land, paled when compared with her worth.

"I think what I like best," she said softly, "is that even its imperfections don't detract from its beauty."

"You say that as though you have imperfections."

"We all have imperfections." A sorrow and something that went deeper touched her eyes.

"They add character," he told her, mimicking words his mother had once told him.

She laughed lightly. "So my mother says."

He wondered if all mothers relied on the same counsel. He had a strong urge to want to make her believe the truth of them, if there was something about herself with which she found fault. He wondered if it was that small freckle, the one that had been left behind when all the others had deserted her. He remembered how much she had detested them when she was a child.

She turned her attention back to the glass. "Some of these items are hundreds of years old. They've managed to survive the centuries. If only they could talk. They were lovingly created by someone who is no longer here, being enjoyed by people whom the creator never met, would never meet because they were yet to be born."

"Perhaps they weren't lovingly created. Perhaps they were nothing more than a way to pay creditors."

"What a cynic you are. No, whoever made these cared about them a great deal. They would not be so beautiful otherwise. I won't accept any other answer."

"You're a romantic."

She laughed again. "Frightfully so. But then I don't suppose that comes as a surprise, considering the reason behind your presence here."

Before he could respond, a commotion caught his attention. A group of people was barreling down the passageway. Apparently, the Marlborough House Set had arrived.

They swarmed in, bees to a fresh dusting of pollen, and swept her away as easily as driftwood on an outgoing tide. It was rather amazing to watch, as though he weren't even there, as though it were impossible to conceive that they might have been together.

Jolly good for his reputation as a man who no longer had any interest in marriage.

He supposed he could have inserted himself, but she expected him to observe and share those observations later. Instead, his gaze kept drifting down to one of the vases. The red was muted, the shade of her hair, and he imagined the artisan blowing a soft breath into it, gliding his hands lovingly over it. He envisioned her as the inspiration for the piece, that somehow three, six, eight hundred, a thousand years ago another man had pictured her as he'd worked to create a vase that would outlast his lifetime.

Death had come, and yet the vase carried on. Whoever had served as the inspiration was gone as well. And yet, she, too, in an odd manner was still bringing beauty to the world.

The poetic nonsense of his thoughts could only be attributed to how ghastly bored he was looking at glass. Because on the heel of those musings he was struck with the uncanny certainty that they belonged elsewhere, and that he wanted them.

Exhibits were collections. Someone had put this one together. Someone owned these pieces. He wanted them. He intended to have them, regardless of the price.

It had been a long time since he'd wanted something this badly.

That evening, curled on a divan in the front parlor, Grace fought not to be disappointed that in the crush of admirers, she had lost sight of Lovingdon at the exhibit. His driver had alerted her that His Grace had taken his leave but left his carriage for her convenience. She supposed he had gotten rather bored with the glass and decided to go in search of a more interesting activity.

She was presently in search of entertainment as well. Undecided regarding how she would spend her evening, she sorted through various invitations. No grand balls tonight. Instead it was a night for small affairs. A reading at Lady Evelyn Easton's. A concert at Marlborough House. A dinner at Chetwyn's. The gentlemen had tried to tease her into revealing where she'd be tonight, but she hadn't a clue, so it was easy to tell them the truth.

She wondered what plans Lovingdon had for the evening and if he would be in the back room at Dodger's. Her fingers itched for another round of cards, a chance to get even. How the deuce had he cheated anyway? She kept careful watch of his movements. How had he known she'd cheat?

Because she always had. It was unseemly, but the lads had always bested her at so much. Swindling them had been her small victory.

She heard the doorbell. A caller. She wasn't up to it. Besides, Lovingdon would probably tell her that a gentleman who bothered calling wasn't truly interested. It seemed all his examples involved the various ways that demonstrated when a man didn't fancy her. How would she know if he did?

He'll know your favorite flower.

There had to be more to it than that.

She looked up as the butler walked in carrying a large box.

"The Duke of Lovingdon's man just delivered this package for you."

It was a large box, plain as a dirty road, not wrapped in fancy paper or decorated with ribbons. He set it on the small table in front of her.

"Whatever could it be?" she asked.

"I'm certain I don't know, m'lady."

"What have we here?" her mother asked as she glided into the room. "I heard the bell—"

"A gift from Lovingdon."

"Fancy that. Whatever prompted such a gesture?"

She laughed self-consciously, because she wanted the gift to mean something when she knew that it probably was merely another lesson to be learned. How would she explain that to her mother? "I haven't a clue."

"Shall we see what it is?"

"I suppose we should."

She lifted the lid, set it aside. Amidst black velvet rested red glass. Very gingerly she lifted out the pitcher.

"Oh my word. Isn't that's lovely?" her mother asked.

"I saw it at the exhibit today." Overwhelmed, she didn't know what else to say. The goblets were also there but it was the pitcher that had arrested her attention. She held it up toward the gas-lit chandeliers and the color lightened, glimmered. So magnificent.

"Is there a note?"

"What? Oh." Moving the velvet aside, she saw the parchment, pulled it out and read the neat script.

For your future household. I suspect the artisan would rather it be used than collecting dust in an exhibit.

She supposed she would forgive him for not appreciating the exhibit, when he had managed so successfully to touch her heart. Water served from this pitcher would taste incredibly sweet, and she would never be able to sip it without thinking of him.

"He's optimistic at least," her mother said after reading the missive.

"Optimistic that I'll find a man who loves me. He knows I won't marry one who doesn't."

"I suspect it's been a long time since he's been optimistic about anything. Perhaps it's not such a bad thing that he's been coming around."

Not a bad thing at all.

Chapter 10

Lovingdon couldn't recall how he'd come to be on the floor of his library. He thought after he retrieved his last bottle of whiskey that he'd been heading for the chair. But here he was with his back against it and his bottom on the floor. Which worked well, because it gave him a sturdy place to put the bottle when he wasn't drinking from it.

It also gave him a lovely angle from which to gaze at the vase. With the lamp on the desk off to the side, it cast a halo around the glass container, changed the way it looked. Shadow and light. Copper and red.

"I expected to find you at Dodger's."

Grace's sweet voice filled his ears. He lolled his head to the side. Shadow and light. Copper and red. "I really must talk with my butler about his penchant for allowing you to wander through my residence unannounced."

She glided nearer, no provocative sway to her hips, no enticing roll of her shoulders, no flirtatious lowering of her eyelids, yet he considered her more alluring than any woman he'd known of late.

"He understands that I'm practically family."

"I suspect it more likely that he understands your nature to do as you please."

She grinned. "That as well."

"I didn't think you had any plans for the night."

"I didn't, but I wanted to thank you for the lovely glass. I suppose you were demonstrating another rule. If he loves me, he'll know when I covet something."

He couldn't stop himself from smiling. He did hope he didn't look as silly as he felt. "It pleased you?"

"Very much." She was standing over him now. "Would you like me to help you into a chair?"

He shook his head. "No, I'm where I want to be."

"Not very high standards." She turned, came up short. "You bought the vase as well."

"It appeared lonely with all the other red pieces gone."

"Careful there. You're almost sounding poetic."

"Never."

He watched as she strolled over to his decanter table, grabbed a crystal carafe and glass, and walked back over to him. She settled onto the floor facing him, working her back against the chair opposite his, her legs stretched out alongside his.

"What are you doing?" he asked, his tone not nearly as firm as it should be, failing to convey the inappropriateness of her actions. "You shouldn't be here."

"It's bad form to drink alone. Besides, Mother and Father don't know that I'm here. They think I went to bed early with a headache." She poured—what was it she had? Ah, yes, the rum—into her glass. She lifted it a bit. "Cheers."

And proceeded to take a healthy swallow. No coughing or choking. She wasn't a novice to hard liquor, but he hadn't expected her to take so well to the rum.

"I have sherry, if you'd like," he told her.

"I prefer rum. Awful of me not to prefer the more dainty drinks, I know. I mastered rum because my brothers were drinking it. It's not fair that men go off to a private room to smoke and drink, and ladies sip tea. We should be able to end our evening with a hearty drink." She lifted her glass in another salute before sipping the golden brew. "So I came to a get a report."

"A report?"

"Yes, about what you observed today. Anyone who doesn't fancy me."

"Bertie fancies you."

She laughed lightly. "The Prince of Wales?"

"Indeed, but you want to steer clear of married men, especially one who might one day rule an empire."

"No worries there, as I have no interest in married men. Sort of defeats my purpose, since I am in search of a husband."

He studied her, sipped his whiskey. It was loosening his tongue. Probably not a good thing, but—

"Why the urgency, Grace? Why the urgency to marry?"

She ran her finger around the rim of her glass. "You won't understand."

"Whatever the reason, I promise not to judge you."

She sighed. "I probably shouldn't have had spirits tonight. It makes it so easy to talk, to say things that I wouldn't normally say. Why does it do that?"

She hadn't had a great deal yet, so maybe she wasn't as accustomed to it as he thought. "That's the whole point of it, to make you lose your inhibitions, to not give a damn one way or another. You can tell me because I'm so far gone that I probably won't remember in the morning what you said."

She tapped her glass, and he had an insane flash of her tapping that finger against his bare chest, of her running that nail down his breastbone, scoring his flesh. Yes, he should stop drinking now.

"My father," she said.

He blinked, fought not to look surprised. But he was off his game. He suspected he looked like a deer that had suddenly found itself crossing the path of a hunter. "He's forcing you to marry?"

"Of course not, but he's losing his sight. You mustn't tell anyone. He's so proud and he's hid it for years. I want him to see me as a bride, to know I'm happy. I want him to be able to dance with me on the day I marry."

There was little that he could imagine that was worse than going blind, unless it was to lose the one you loved, but he suspected that others could tell him something worse. Everything was perspective. Everything was subjective.

"I'm sorry," he said, words he meant from the depths of his blackened heart.

"I don't know if it's better to have been born blind and to never know what the world looks like or to have seen the world and then be condemned to blackness."

"It's rather like that question you posed the night you asked for my assistance: is it better to have loved and lost than to have never loved at all?"

"I would rather have love for a little while."

Because she'd never had it. Things that one never possessed always shined more brightly than the things that were held.

They sat in silence for several long moments, with the fire crackling, the clock ticking, his collie snoring in the corner. Her dress buttoned up to her chin. The sleeves were long. No need for gloves when she was here in such an informal capacity. She drew up her knees to her chest, wound one arm around her legs. She couldn't have had on more than one petticoat, because her skirt draped over her as though nothing existed between her and her skin. He wanted to touch her ankle, her knee, her hip, her shoulder, her chin. Light touches.

Sometimes they could be the most intimate.

Oh, but he needed to get his thoughts onto something else, so he said, "The couple at the exhibit, looking at the blue glass—I had it wrong. They were married to each other."

She perked up. "How do you know?"

"Because of the way he touched her. Without thought, without artifice. He wanted her to know he was there, enjoying the moment with her, but he was careful not to intrude."

Her brow pleated. "But you said they were lovers."

"They are. One does not exclude the other."

"But you were quite sure that she was married to someone else," she reminded him.

"I'm not perfect, Grace. I do know they have six children, and so they frequent exhibits in order to be alone for a bit."

"How did you acquire that information?"

"Spoke with him for a few moments when she went to the necessary room."

Smiling brightly, she settled back against the chair. "I'm glad they're married. That they're lovers, and in love. So if a gentleman touches me, he loves me."

"If he touches you without thinking, if he touches you simply because you're near."

Silence again. He didn't know if he'd adequately explained the sort of action to which he was referring.

"Why are you here alone tonight?" she asked quietly.

"Sometimes I need to be alone."

She craned her head back to see the portrait above the fireplace, the one of Juliette. "I was so young when you got married—too young for her and I to become dear friends. I wonder why I always saw her as so old, but never was bothered by the years separating you and I."

"Perhaps because I was always in your life, and she came into it later." Now he looked up. He couldn't see Juliette from that angle, which was a good thing. She'd never approved of his drinking, so he only had a glass on special occasions. She'd never even developed a taste for wine. She didn't like card games. Had she played, she certainly never would have cheated at them.

Unlike the woman across from him who was pouring herself more rum. She didn't chastise him for sitting here, three sheets to the wind. She simply grabbed a decanter and joined him.

"What are you smiling at?" Grace asked.

Jolted from his reverie by her question, he jerked his head back. "Am I?"

"I can't see your teeth, but your lips are curled up. I always liked your smile."

"Always liked yours."

"My teeth were too big for a bit there."

"I never noticed."

"Liar."

He thought his smile grew. He always felt comfortable with her, as though there were no judgments, no wrongs, no sins. But at that moment he wanted more with her.

Perhaps it was because he'd had too much to drink.

Perhaps it was because they were alone.

Perhaps it was the shadows promising to hide secrets.

Leaning over, reaching down, he wrapped his hand around her ankle and pulled her toward him.

Startled, she looked up, but she didn't resist, and he quickly had them hip-to-hip. He splayed his fingers along the back of her head, tucked the other hand beneath her chin, tilted her head up and sipped at her mouth. He circled his tongue around the outer edges of her lips before running it along the seam. An opening, a slight parting, an invitation.

He slid his tongue inside and groaned when he discovered hers waiting, ready to parry. No shy miss, his Little Rose.

She tasted dark, rich, and decadent. The rum added a tartness, a sweetness, a uniqueness. He swept his tongue through her mouth as though he'd never explored it before. Where in the garden there had been a hungry need, tonight the need was leashed. He didn't want madness or haste. He wanted to linger, to enjoy, to relish.

He felt her fingers scraping his scalp, combing through his hair. Touching, caressing. Marvelous, so marvelous. He felt like a cat stretching beneath the sun. It was so very long since he'd been stroked with such tenderness. So long since any woman had given to him as she was doing now. No frenzy, no hurry. Only savoring.

In the garden, he had taken her mouth on a rush of passion and the hard edge of something that resembled jealousy, although he'd never been jealous in his life, not even when it came to Juliette. He'd known she was his, that no one would take her from him.

Yet the Fates had.

But with Grace it was different. He couldn't define her or what he felt for her. It wasn't love, yet it was more than the hollowness that accompanied him when rutting. He wanted to kiss her. He'd wanted to kiss her at the exhibit when she rhapsodized on about silly glass. Her passion for the creation of the pieces had sparked a passion in him.

But tonight it was just his whiskey and her rum, and a darkness that said, *Taste, taste me again*.

She sighed and he was acutely aware of her falling into him. It was a good thing they were sitting, as he thought his knees might have buckled with the force of the desire that slammed into him.

He'd had far too much liquor to perform. That

was a good thing. He wouldn't ruin her, but damn, she tasted so tempting, cream on strawberries, chocolate on cake. He didn't ever want to leave the little paradise that was her mouth—

And it was that thought that had him leaving it. She wanted a man capable of great love. She deserved that sort of man. And that wasn't him.

He pressed his forehead to hers, listened as she gathered her breath, enjoyed the sensation as she trailed her fingers across his shoulders, down his arms, leaving only the memory of her touch behind.

His chest tightened into a painful knot. With gentleness and his fingers, he brushed the strands of hair from her face. "Ah, Grace, I've always loved you. Surely you know that. I just can't love you with the depth of caring that you want."

"It's scary to love, isn't it? It doesn't seem that it should be so, but it is."

"Not always."

"You weren't scared when you fell in love with Juliette?"

He shook his head. He'd known no fear. He'd thought it marvelous, all the rioting emotions he felt.

"If you'd known on the day that you met her that you'd only have a few years with her, would you have still fallen in love with her?"

He didn't know the answer to that. Because he hadn't known, he'd gone into it with naive innocence. Innocence he could never regain. Now he knew that forever was a myth, and that "until death do you part" was not a promise of growing old together.

"It's bad form to speak of another lady when a man is kissing you," he told her.

"You're not kissing me at this precise moment."

"Perhaps I should remedy that." And he did, taking her mouth again, unhurriedly swirling his tongue through the dark depths until he'd had his fill of her, for the moment at least. "I've never kissed a woman who tasted of rum," he said quietly.

"What about the naughty women you visit?"

"I don't kiss them."

Jerking her head back, she couldn't have looked more surprised if he'd jumped to his feet and done a jig around the room.

"But you're intimate with them."

"I'm not intimate with them. I'm not making love to them. I'm rutting."

"It sounds so ugly."

He'd not wanted to travel there. He'd wanted to travel back to her mouth. "I ensure they are pleasured. They have a pleasant time. They are unaware that the only thing engaged is my cock."

And with the uttering of that word to a lady, he realized he was probably *six* sheets to the wind. "My apologies. I should not have—"

"No." She touched her finger to his lips. "I came to you, Lovingdon, because I knew you would be honest with me. Your words and sentiments might be crude, but you have never put a veil of protection between us. Your words reaffirm what I've believed all along. I don't want a man rutting over me. I don't want him thinking, 'Let's get on with this, I need an heir.' I want pleasure. I want him to want to come to my bed. I believe love is the key, which is why I want to find a man who loves me. I don't want to make a mistake, with which I would have to live for the remainder of my life."

He skimmed his fingers along the side of her face. "You won't. It would be a rather poor reflection on my knowledge of blackguards if you end up with a man who doesn't love you. Trust me, Little Rose. I can spot a blackguard a mile away."

"I do trust you."

More's the pity. Because at that moment his words were no more sincere than any of the dribble that Bentley had spouted. It was her lips, glistening and swollen, that prompted his wicked behavior. He wanted those lips, he wanted that mouth.

Don't don't don't.

But he was beyond listening to his conscience. Just one more taste, one more little sip. She tilted her face up slightly, the most beautiful invitation he'd ever received. He framed her face between his hands. "Just one more taste."

She nodded, her mistake, his undoing.

He started with the freckle, the one on the corner, the one that went into hiding when she smiled. He wondered if all the other lords had noticed it. He should tell her about it. *If he loves you, he'll notice that you have the tiniest freckle at the corner of your mouth.*

If he loves you, he'll be fully engaged in the kiss. He won't be thinking of other women or exhibits or laws that need to be passed. He won't be thinking of anything beyond the flavor and feel of you.

But he *was* thinking of other things. He was thinking of fire molding glass, he was thinking of flames licking at red, he was thinking of hands fashioning and shaping—

Hands skimming over her from toe to crown. His hands wrapping around her small ankles, traveling over her slender calves.

He carried her down to the carpet. She didn't protest. She simply went, with the trust she had spoken of earlier. He wouldn't ruin her, but there were other lips to taste, other flames to fan.

Don't don't don't.

He didn't love her, he couldn't love her, he wouldn't love her—not in the manner she desired, not in the manner she deserved.

But she wanted lessons in blackguards, and tonight he was just drunk enough to give her one she wouldn't soon forget.

She knew there was danger in coming here so late at night when he'd no doubt be well into his cups, yet she'd not been able to keep away. When she walked into the library, she had felt the energy like a storm just before lightning struck. She should have said, "Thank you for the gift. I'll be on my way now."

But she had seldom been one for doing what she ought.

Life was too short. Life could be snatched away.

She needed his kisses the way she needed air. This kiss was different from the one before, gentler and yet hungrier. It made no sense. The other had seemed to be about possession.

This one was more about ownership. He was beginning to own her heart.

Beware! her mind cried. *Beware, beware, beware.*

She couldn't love him as a woman loved a man,

not when he was unwilling to love in return. She was fairly certain this was another lesson to be learned, that when he was done he would reveal whether a man who worked his mouth over hers with such determination would love her.

Not that she cared at that particular moment. She loved the taste of whiskey on his tongue, loved the way her mouth molded to his.

He trailed his lips over her chin and lower, lower. She held her breath. His hot mouth closed over her right breast, and the heat of it shot straight into her core. It mattered not that she wore a dress and chemise, that she had left her petticoats draped over a chair in her bedchamber. She had chosen comfort over propriety.

It seemed he wasn't of a mood for propriety either.

His hands bracketed her waist and he pushed himself down farther, rose up on an elbow and watched as his hand traveled over her hip, along her thigh. His gaze came to rest on hers, his holding a challenge that went unanswered.

She didn't know how to respond. Her body was thrumming with need, with something she didn't quite understand.

His large hand knotted around a section of her skirt, began gathering it up.

"Lovingdon—"

"Shh. You'll leave here a virgin, I promise you that."

She trusted him, but she wasn't ready for him to know everything. She doubted she ever would be, but neither was she quite ready to leave him, to lose these warm sensations that were purring through her. "Are you mimicking a man in love with me or a blackguard?"

He raised his eyes to hers. "A blackguard. Most definitely a blackguard."

"I should stop these advances," she said.

"Yes, for other blackguards. But don't you want to know what lies at the end of them? You'll spend the rest of your life with a gentleman. Why not know what it is to be with a scoundrel for a time?"

Her throat was tight, her heart fluttering, her chest barely able to take in a breath. She thought she nodded. Perhaps it was only that she didn't shake her head. Whatever, she'd apparently given him permission to go further.

He pooled the hem of her skirt at her waist. "Silk underdrawers," he rasped, his voice tight, controlled.

"I like the way they feel against my skin."

"I think you'll like more what I'm about to place against your skin."

He unlaced her drawers and began easing them down. Her face burned as she was exposed to him, and she thought of flames shaping the glass. She wondered what he was molding her into. A wanton, no doubt. Or a girl on the verge of truly becoming a woman. Would her husband touch her like this or was such behavior only the purview of rogues?

"Ah, Little Rose, red everywhere."

Especially her cheeks, her neck, her chest. The heat was consuming, and only grew hotter when he pressed his lips to the inside of her thigh.

She had heard about the dangers of rum, how it released inhibitions, made one not care. She knew she should clap her legs together, shove him aside. Instead she opened herself more fully to his questing mouth.

She would no doubt have regrets when she was sober, but for now the scrape of his shadowed jaw against her inner thigh was too tantalizing to warrant regrets. He moved up, half inch by agonizing half inch. She felt his breath wafting through her curls.

Lifting his head, he reached for the crystal decanter.

"What are you doing?" she asked.

"Tasting rum on lips, remember?"

Before she could respond, he poured the golden

liquid over her most intimate region. She squealed, kicked ineffectually at him, an instinctual reaction.

He dropped his head back and laughed, a bold, joyous sound that reverberated around the room. Suddenly the sound stopped, but the essence of it continued to vibrate as though it had become a permanent part of the air surrounding them.

With a somberness that didn't seem to fit with what had just happened, he held her gaze. "God, I can't remember the last time I laughed." He laid his head on the pillow of rumpled skirts at her belly. "Damn, but it felt good."

"Laughter is a balm for the soul."

"Especially one as black as mine."

His eyes came to bear on hers again, and there was something different in them, something heated and dangerous. "It was a release, as good as any I've had with women of the night. You're deserving of one as well."

He lowered his head, and she felt his tongue lapping at the rum, lapping at her. Velvet over silk, and so much nicer than undergarments. She wouldn't mind having that sensation over her entire body—but then he would learn the truth, and while she trusted him, some things a woman simply did not share.

She shoved dark thoughts aside and instead focused on the pleasure, the laughter of her senses. Oh, he was wicked, doing things that she was certain no husband would ever do. It was so inappropriate, so naughty. It was not for the refined, for ladies.

It was decadence at its most decadent.

She knotted her fingers in his hair because she couldn't stand the thought of not touching him. Pressing her thighs against his shoulders, she wished she felt the silk of flesh there instead of soft linen. She should have asked him to remove his shirt. Had she known where he had planned to take her, she might have asked him to remove everything.

He kissed, he stroked, he suckled. He created sensations that were beyond description. Pleasure rolled through her in undulating waves that threatened to take her under, to lift her up. If she were glass, she would have melted by now.

Her breaths came in short gasps, her sighs evolved into ever higher pitches.

"Lovingdon—"

"Let it happen, Grace. Let your body succumb to the ultimate joy of pleasure."

Then there were no more words, only his tongue urging her on with its determined actions. Swirls of red spun behind her closed eyes. Faster, faster, a vortex that flung her over a precipice—

She screamed as her body tightened, her back arched, her fingers dug into his scalp. She shuddered and trembled, reached heaven before floating mindlessly back to earth.

There was silence in the coach. It wasn't heavy or awkward. It was simply present, because after that mind-shattering experience, Grace had been without words.

So had Lovingdon apparently.

Quietly, he had reassembled her skewed attire. With his hand on the small of her back, he led her to the coach and climbed in after her. It didn't seem to matter that it was her family's coach, that it would either need to return him home or he would have to walk.

Perhaps he was aware that she wasn't yet ready to be alone.

Otherwise, why would he be holding her now, his arm around her shoulders, her face tucked into the hollow of his neck? He smelled sultry and wicked. Every now and then she thought she caught a fragrance that might be her.

"I'm beginning to see the appeal of marrying a blackguard, whether he loves me or not," she finally said.

He chuckled darkly. "I thought you might."

"I suppose the best thing would be to marry a blackguard who loves me."

"Blackguards don't love."

"Pity that."

Silence again.

"I suspect," he began, "that I shall forever think of you when I drink rum."

Heat and pleasure swarmed through her. She would never again drink rum without thinking of him. "I fear your carpet is ruined."

"Simple enough to have it replaced."

She placed her hand on his chest, felt the steady pounding of his heart. "I'm not certain what I should take away from tonight's lesson."

"Not all men would have stopped where I did. Never allow a man to lift your skirts."

Pressing her lips to his neck, she tasted the salt of his skin. "Tonight I'm ever so glad I did."

She was aware of him stiffening, was certain he would regret his actions on the morrow when whiskey was no longer coursing through his veins. Perhaps she would as well, but she also knew that even a man who loved her might never make passionate love to her. When all was revealed, he might find bedding her a chore.

The coach came to a halt. Lovingdon leapt out, then handed her down.

"Your father is much too lenient, allowing you out at all hours."

"As I told you earlier, he doesn't know." Rising up on her toes, she kissed his cheek. "Thank you for the glass. That's all I intended when I came to see you, to thank you for the glass."

"Intentions—bad or good—have a way of going astray."

"Good night, Lovingdon."

She headed up the walk and heard the coach rattling away. At the top of the steps she turned back and saw Lovingdon walking down the drive, a solitary figure, encased in loneliness. She wanted to rush after him, return to his residence, curl up in his large bed and hold him. Just hold him. Have him hold her.

She waited until he was no longer in sight. Then she turned and pressed her forehead to the door.

Oh dear Lord, now she'd gone and done it.

She'd fallen in love with him all over again.

Chapter 11

"If a man is keen on us, he will look us in the eye when we speak, and if we speak low, he will lean in to hear what we say. If he doesn't lean in, he doesn't fancy us." Grace was standing in a distant corner of Uncle Jack's parlor, speaking with Minerva and Ophelia. A small gathering of family and friends had arrived for dinner to celebrate Minerva's birthday.

She had hoped to see Lovingdon here, but he had yet to show. He'd not attended a family gathering in two years. She was disappointed tonight would be no exception. She knew Minerva was equally disappointed. It was not every day that a girl turned nineteen. Her oldest brother should be on hand.

"You know, my grandmother always insisted that a lady speak extremely softly. I wonder now if this was her reasoning," Ophelia said.

"Oh, I've no doubt," Grace said.

"Did your gentleman tell you this?" Minerva asked.

Grace nodded perfunctorily.

"I suppose it should go on our list, but it seems that there should be more to it."

"How often have you spoken to a man, only to have him murmur 'Yes, yes' when you hadn't even posed a question?"

"Yes, but—"

"I say we test it tonight," Lady Ophelia announced with authority. "We have the perfect opportunity. The gathering is small, intimate. Several gentlemen are in attendance. We should be able to get results very quickly. We shall hold a meeting afterward in the garden."

"Yes, all right," Minerva agreed. "Although Lovingdon would be a perfect test sample. He cares not one whit anymore about love or women."

Grace felt her face heat up as visions of him caring about bringing her pleasure swamped her. She could readily recall every sensation he elicited with seeming ease. "A more accurate statement might be love or marriage. I'm sure he's not being celibate."

"Why would you think that?"

Experience. A recent ill-advised late-night visit that left her lying in bed each night since wondering if she should pay another visit, but she thought it unlikely that she would find him at home, or if he were, alone. That time had been an aberration. He was very much in want of the company of women. "Celibacy does not a scoundrel make, or so I've heard."

From your brother himself.

"You're quite right," Ophelia confirmed. "Wine, women, and gambling, according to my brother."

"Lovingdon!" Minerva's mother called out.

Grace turned to see her embrace her firstborn child in the doorway, two footmen behind him holding a rather large box. More glass?

"He came," Minerva breathed, the delight in her voice palpable as she rushed across the room.

Grace hurried along behind her, not wanting to miss the welcoming. She knew he had distanced himself from his family after Juliette passed. Unfortunate timing, as she thought those who loved him could have helped him the most with his grief, could have ensured that his foundation didn't crumble.

Minerva stopped just shy of him. "I'm so glad you're here."

"It's your birthday, isn't it?" Lovingdon said. "I've brought you something. It's rather heavy. Lads, set it on the floor."

The footmen did as instructed. Minerva, in spite of wearing a dinner gown, knelt down and lifted the lid. "Oh, my word! What is it?"

Lovingdon signaled to the footmen, who worked to release it from the box and set it on the floor with a clunk. It looked to be some sort of machine with four rows containing oval disks, a letter marked on each one—

"It's a typing machine," he said. "You want to be a writer, don't you? You punch the letter you want and it prints it on paper that you put in the machine. I can show you later."

"It's wonderful."

"Well as I can barely decipher your handwriting, I thought it might prove useful. Don't want publishers attributing incorrect words to you."

"You're the best big brother a girl could have." Tears welled in her eyes as she flung her arms around his neck.

"I'm sorry, Minnie," he whispered. "Sorry, I haven't been here . . . for a while."

His gaze caught Grace's, and she saw the regret there, but more than that, she saw the gratitude, and her heart did three little somersaults, when it shouldn't be jumping about at all. Not for him. She couldn't help but believe that slowly, irrevocably, his heart was healing and that he might one day fall in love again. Not with her, of course. She was far too stubborn and bold for his tastes. She remembered Juliette as being extremely genteel and reserved. They could not have been more opposite in that regard.

When Minnie finally released her hold on him, he stepped over and shook Uncle Jack's hand. While Jack Dodger was not related to Grace by blood, he was dear friends with her mother, and to her he had always been Uncle Jack.

Then Lovingdon was standing in front of her, a devilish twinkle in his eyes that caused her heart to skip a beat. How long had it been since he appeared less burdened? "Are they serving rum this evening?"

She gave him an impish smile, doing all in her power not to let her cheeks turn red. "Not to the ladies."

He gave her a secretive grin. "More's the pity."

To get his mind and hers away from things they shouldn't ponder, she nodded toward the typing machine. "Interesting contraption. I've never heard of such a thing."

"They're a relatively recent invention. However, I don't know that they have much of a future. They seem rather clunky and slow-going to me."

"You remembered her dream, though, and that's what matters."

"**S**trangest thing," Avendale said. "All the ladies are speaking so softly I can barely hear them without leaning in."

During dinner Lovingdon had noticed the odd behavior as well. They were presently in the gentlemen's parlor, drinking port and smoking cigars, while the ladies were off sipping tea. He could well imagine Grace fuming over that little ritual. He knew she'd much rather be in here.

He, Avendale, and Langdon had separated themselves from the other gents. He was ridiculously glad that the bachelors on hand were few in number. The men who were here had not given an unusual amount of attention to Grace. He didn't know if it was because of the occasion or that they had given up hope of securing her hand. He hoped for the latter, then wondered at the reasoning behind his hope.

If she were narrowing down her selections, then soon she would make a decision and no longer need his advice. He could avoid exhibits, balls, and other social niceties. So why wasn't he overjoyed at the prospect of his life returning to what it had been before she knocked on his bedchamber door?

"Well, I could do with some cards," Avendale said. "Think I'll head to Dodger's after this. At least there I can hear what's being said." He rubbed the back of his neck. "All that leaning in has given me a cramp in my neck."

They began talking about stopping by Cremorne on the way to Dodger's. But for some reason it didn't appeal to Lovingdon that night, and he wondered why it ever had. "If you gentlemen will excuse me, I'm going out for a bit of fresh air."

He used the side door that led onto the terrace. Gaslights lit the garden path. He had grown up in this house and was familiar with every aspect of it. He could walk the paths in the dark without tripping over anything. He heard the chirping of the insects and the rustling of the foliage brushing over the brick wall. He knew all the normal night sounds. They did not include whisperings.

As quietly as possible he walked off the terrace and around to the side, where he peered around a hedgerow and spotted three ladies. Were they? No, they couldn't be. Yes, they were—passing a cheroot among them.

" . . . a failure," Lady Ophelia said. "Every gentleman leaned in. They can't all fancy us."

"We simply need another sampling," Minerva said. "The gathering was too small and it was comprised of people who love us, so naturally they're going to try to hear what we have to say."

"I suppose, but could it be, Grace, that your gentleman had it wrong?"

Lovingdon was dumbstruck. She was telling *them* what he was telling her? Had she gone mad? He thought he had her trust, that what he revealed would go no further.

"He's extremely knowledgeable about such matters," Grace said, "so I doubt it."

"Ask your gentleman what it means if a man spends dinner sneaking glances at a lady near whom he is not sitting," Minerva ordered. "As I noticed one gentleman in particular seemed quite taken with you."

Was Minnie talking about him? He had been sneaking glances at Grace, but every man would have. She'd been radiant, her smiles in abundance, her laughter becoming.

"Who was sneaking glances?" he heard Grace ask.

Before his half sister could reply, he stepped around the hedge. "Ladies."

Jumping back, they released tiny squeaks, rather like dormice caught by the cat, and at that moment he felt feral in a way he suspected most felines didn't. He wasn't tamed, but was ready to pounce.

"Lovingdon!" Minnie chided. "You shouldn't sneak up on us like that."

"And you shouldn't be sneaking off with your father's cigars."

"Only one. And they're for guests. He prefers a pipe so he never notices how many are about."

He held out his hand to Grace, as she was the one holding the pilfered cheroot. She tilted up her chin and took a long inhalation before passing it off to Lady Ophelia, who at least had the wherewithal to hesitate a moment before inhaling deeply. Minnie then took a turn. As none of them were coughing—

"How long have you ladies been engaging in this vile habit?" he asked.

"Oh, I'd say about five minutes now," Grace mused with a righteousness in her voice that implied she'd not be intimidated. Not that he'd ever had any success in that regard where she was concerned.

"I meant: how old were you when you first started smoking?"

"Last year," Minnie responded as she took another drag, before handing it to him. "It's not fair that men get port and cigars while ladies get needlepoint and tea. And my needlepoint is more atrocious than my handwriting."

"Fair or not, ladies are not to engage in such behavior."

"Why is it vile if we do it and not if you do it?" Grace had the audacity to ask.

While it was a rather good point, he had no intention of addressing it. "You know what you're doing is wrong, or you wouldn't be out here sneaking about," he said, using his big brother voice.

"The wrong of it," Grace said, "is what makes it so enjoyable."

He couldn't argue with her there, but it also made him wonder how many other wrong things she might have done. "The gentlemen are finishing up. You should probably go inside."

"Are you going to tell Papa?" Minnie asked.

"It's your birthday, so no." Although Lovingdon suspected Jack would applaud her actions. He'd never been much of a rule follower, and while Jack had encouraged him to stray from time to time, he'd always walked the straight path until he became a widower. Then he'd seen some merit in Jack's advice. "Just promise that you won't do it again."

"I promise not to pilfer Father's cigars."

That promise came too fast, and he was quite certain the words allowed her to do as she pleased without breaking her word, but he wasn't in the mood to examine her statement too closely. She was a young lady now, and he had something else he wished to examine. "Inside with you."

"You're a wonderful older brother," Minerva said, before she began leading her merry crew toward the back terrace doors.

"Lady Grace," he murmured, "might I have a word?"

All the ladies stopped, and he almost told them to recall their names and the fact that he wasn't talking to them, but Grace shooed them on before coming over to join him.

"Yes, Your Grace?" she asked, her voice more challenge than inquiry.

"You've been sharing my observations with them?"

"They have as much right as anyone to marry a man who loves them."

The thought of Minnie, dear Minnie, marrying a man who didn't love her sent chills through him. He hadn't even attended her coming out. While her father had a reputation that would scare any lord into behaving, it didn't mean the man would love her. He needed to be paying more attention to what was going on in the world, among Society. His world had narrowed down, and for the first time in two years it was beginning to feel too tight.

He dropped the smoldering cheroot onto the ground and smashed it with his boot. He would smash anyone who made Minnie unhappy.

"They don't know who's been giving me the advice," Grace said softly.

And now he knew why all the women were speaking so quietly tonight. God, but he wanted to laugh. But he wanted something else more.

He advanced on her. She backed up until she hit the brick wall.

"Don't be angry," she said.

"I'm not angry, but I just realized that I've never kissed a woman who tastes of tobacco."

"Oh."

Hers was a short, breathless sound that pierced his gut and lower. Dangerous, so dangerous. Yet he seemed unable to walk away. Cradling her face, he layered his mouth over hers. The smoky taste he'd imagined was elusive, but there was Grace, the sweet temptation of Grace.

He must have kissed her a thousand times in his mind since the night she'd come to his library to thank him for the glass stemware. He'd forgone evenings' entertainments to stare at the blasted vase and to think of heat and red and copper. He'd sipped on rum, striving to bring back the flavor of her.

For the past two years women had floated in and out of his life. He couldn't remember the flavor of a single one.

He'll remember your flavor.

He'll remember your scent.

But he refused to put himself into the category of a man who might fall in love with her. He didn't want to love again, but he had learned that a man didn't always get what he wanted.

Just as at this precise moment he wanted more from her, a kiss that went on until dawn, an unbuttoned bodice that revealed her breasts, a hiking of her skirts that exposed the sweet center of her. But the other ladies would be waiting for her, and he knew Minnie's impatience well enough to expect her to intrude at any moment, so he fought down his desires until he thought he would choke on them and pulled back.

"I prefer the rum," he said.

A corner of her mouth hitched up mischievously and her eyes twinkled. "I prefer the whiskey to the port."

"I shall have to see about accommodating you next time."

Turning on his heel, he started to walk away, wondering why he thought there would be a next time, knowing all the while that if he had any say in the matter, there would be.

"Lovingdon?"

He stopped, glanced back.

"What does it mean if a man sneaks glances at a lady during dinner?"

"I suspect it means she's the most beautiful woman there."

Grace *had* been the most beautiful woman there. Lovingdon meant no insult to the others in attendance, especially the ones to whom he was related by blood, but Grace embodied her name with her poise and elegance. While her features were pleasing, her beauty went beyond the physical, to include an inner loveliness that radiated through to the surface.

Now, playing cards in the private room at Dodger's, Lovingdon glanced up when he heard the door open. Waited, waited, not breathing . . . anticipating—

Cursing inwardly when Avendale parted the heavy draperies and stepped into the room. "Sorry I'm late, gents. Hope Lovingdon hasn't relieved you of all your coins yet."

Good-natured laughter and ribbing followed that pronouncement. He didn't know why he'd wanted to see Grace barging in. She would only serve to upset the others, distract them, change the tenor of the game.

He downed his whiskey and waited impatiently

while his glass was refilled by one of the footmen. He'd always enjoyed these games, but tonight he was antsy, and no matter how many times he turned the coin he could not find the calm within the storm.

"Any of you planning to go to Greystone's for the Midsummer's Eve ball?" Avendale asked as he drew up a chair.

"I shall be there," Langdon said. "I'm looking forward to leaving the city for a bit. Seems ghastly hot for some reason."

Lovingdon had noticed the heat, but only when Grace was around. She had a way of raising his temperature, if not his temper. He'd thought the two reactions were related. Perhaps it was the weather. Easier to attribute it to the climate than to her nearness.

"The duchess will be disappointed if I don't make an appearance," Drake murmured as he shuffled the cards. "So I shall be there for the ball although I doubt that I'll stay beyond that. What of you, Lovingdon?"

The annual event at Greystone's estate tended to extend into several days, with balls, plays, concerts, hunting, riding. It was a nice break from the London Season. Lovingdon had always anticipated it, never missed going until Juliette died. "I haven't decided."

"Anyone who is anyone will be there," Drake told him. "It'll be deuced boring here. You might as well join us."

Joining them meant joining Grace. He wondered if she were sneaking into his library at that very moment. He supposed he should have left word with his butler to alert him if he had any visitors, although there was only one for whom he would put aside whatever activity he was engaged in and rush to his residence. Any activity, he suddenly realized. Even if it involved a woman.

It had been a mere three hours since he'd seen her. Why the devil was he thinking about her? Why did he want to know what she'd been doing since his sister's party ended? Any proper woman would have done little more than gone to bed.

And that thought, blast it, had him wondering if she slept on her back, her stomach, her side. She'd watched him sleep. It was hardly fair that he didn't have a clue regarding her sleeping habits.

" . . . in or out."

He knew how to pick a lock, thanks to Drake's tutelage. Perhaps he would head on over to Mabry House—

"Lovingdon, where the deuce are you?" Drake asked.

He snapped to attention and realized that cards

had been dealt, wagers were being made. If he didn't focus, he was in danger of losing badly tonight. The problem was, he didn't care about proving his prowess with cards. He didn't care if he lost a fortune, didn't care if he won. Not the best attitude when the stakes were as high as they were at this table.

"I'm out." He stood. "As a matter of fact, I've decided I'm not in the mood for cards. I'm off to find some other sport."

Lovingdon stood in the doorway of an exclusive drawing room that catered to the needs of the elite. The girls were clean and the clientele wealthy. Business was handled most discretely. Wine flowed into goblets as smoothly as women floated around the dimly lit room. Candles provided a soft glow, the flickering flames causing light to dance with the shadows, swirling them around bodies. Intriguing. Revealing, hiding.

A Titan of a woman approached him. Plenty of her to hold on to. She wasn't his usual fare. She wasn't dark-haired or dark-eyed. Her hair was a fiery red that he suspected was not the result of Nature. But he didn't care.

When she neared, he grabbed her hand. "You'll do nicely." And in the back of his mind he wondered when he had become content with someone who would "do."

Unlike Grace, who wanted sweet words and love, this woman required nothing more than knowing she was the one chosen for the moment. He would make it well worth her time, not only with the pleasure but also with the coins that would follow. Theirs would be a brief but honest relationship.

He escorted her out of the room and up the stairs that led to the bedchambers. At the landing, he continued on down the hallways to the room she indicated.

After opening the door, he stepped back to allow the woman to precede him. Her silky covering outlined her broad hips and floated around her legs as she swayed provocatively with her movements. Everything about her was designed to entice. She knew what she was and was comfortable with it.

Shutting the door, he needed only two strides to have her in his arms, his lips nibbling her throat. She smelled of vanilla, tasted of oranges.

"I know about you, Your Grace," she said in a raspy voice, arching her head back so he had easier access to the long length of her throat. "You don't bother with kissing."

"No."

"I could make you change your mind."

"I doubt it."

Beneath his hands, her skin was soft and warm, but it didn't tremble or quake. She didn't sigh with longing. She skimmed her hands over him, but they didn't dig into him as though if she could she would press him into her until they could no longer tell where one of them began and the other ended.

He inhaled her fragrance again, and it struck him that it was wrong. It wasn't rose and lavender. He could trail his mouth over her but she would not taste of rum, she wouldn't taste of desire.

She would taste of boredom.

Briskly, he moved away from her, marched to the window and gazed out on the night, on a street that would lead to his residence, that would eventually lead to Grace's.

"Did I do something wrong?" she asked.

"No." But neither had she done anything right. She wasn't what he wanted. Not tonight. And what he wanted he could not have.

Grace deserved love, and he didn't love her. He wasn't sure exactly why she plagued him or what he was feeling, but he knew what it was to love. The torment he was experiencing now was nothing more than lust and frustration.

"Shall I send up a different girl?" she asked.

He was struck by how easily interchangeable they all were. Perhaps it was time he took on a mistress, a woman who would know and meet his expectations. He looked back at the woman standing uncertainly near him, knowing he would be sending her an extremely expensive bauble on the morrow to make amends for his disinterest tonight.

He slowly shook his head. "No, I don't want another girl."

"But you don't appear to want me either."

"It's not a question of want. I just shouldn't have come here."

A slow knowing smile crept over her face. "Another is always a poor substitute for the one we truly want."

He was not at all pleased that somehow he had failed at keeping his thoughts to himself. Crossing his arms over his chest, he leaned back against the wall. "And who do you want?"

"Who every woman wants. A man who will appreciate me."

Curled on her side on her bed, Grace stroked Lancelot, but thought of Lovingdon. She felt beautiful with him. She forgot about her scars and imperfections. She became lost in the sensations he elicited with such ease. The moment his lips touched hers, the rest of the world ceased to exist. It was only the two of them, him giving so much, her receiving. She hoped in the receiving that she was giving as well.

She considered slipping out of the residence, going to his, and doing what she might to bring him pleasure, without receiving it herself. But she knew danger rested on that path. She might give her heart to him completely, but he could no longer give his heart at all.

She thought of all his pronouncements.

He'll know your favorite flower.

He'll gaze into your eyes.

He'll care about what you're saying.

Lovingdon did those things, but then he also did the blackguard things—kissing her at every opportunity, bringing her pleasure . . .

Why would only blackguards do those things? It seemed like a man in love would as well.

Was it possible that he cared for her more than she realized, more than he realized?

Chapter 12

As Grace sat on the blanket, sketching the swans on the lake, she decided that she very much enjoyed Vexley's company. He seemed not to have a care in the world. He wasn't brooding or irascible. He didn't seek to teach her lessons, no matter that she had implied she wanted those lessons from Lovingdon.

Vexley had invited her to picnic with him. Sitting beneath a nearby tree, Felicity was serving as chaperone. Not that one was really needed here at the park. A good many people were about. Vexley could not take advantage—

And neither could she.

She pretended to be fascinated by the swans, because she found herself spending far too much time studying his mouth, striving to envision it moving over hers. It was no hardship whatsoever whenever she thought of Lovingdon, but with Vexley she couldn't quite see it. He had thin lips. The upper tended to disappear when he smiled, which he did quite often. Would it disappear when he kissed or would it become plumper?

Her own swelled considerably when Lovingdon gave attention to her mouth. It was just that he was so thorough. Whether he was kissing her slowly and provocatively or with a ravishing hunger, he was never brief. He lingered, he sipped, he came back for more. He had done her a great disservice by demonstrating how a man who loved her would kiss her. How could any man measure up to that?

How could she survive a kiss that was not a demonstration but was instigated by love? It would contain an emotional richness, delve deeper—

"You have the most lovely blush."

Familiar with the sight of her blushes, she suspected it wasn't lovely, but it no doubt encompassed most of her body, reflecting the path her thoughts had wandered onto. She also suspected with his comment that the rosy hue was darkening. She forced herself to smile at him and not let on that she was embarrassed to be caught musing about things she ought not. "I've grown a little warm."

Understatement.

"You're a very good artist," he said. He was

resting up on an elbow, peering over at the sketch-pad on her lap.

"I inherited my father's talent for putting images on paper. Although he prefers oils, I like pencils."

"Most ladies do needlework."

"Is that what you expect your wife to do?"

"I expect her to do anything she likes."

She wondered if he intended to stand by those words or if they were just meant to lure her in. Why could she not take them at face value?

"She will be a most fortunate woman," she said. "Some husbands have keen expectations."

Sybil's had, although Grace had seen her the day before and all continued to remain calm within her household. Lovingdon's influence had made a dif-ference. Would Vexley step up to assist her friends if they were in need of help?

"I want the sort of marriage my father had," Vexley said. "Very amiable, no discord."

Amiable might be pleasant but it could also be quite boring. She thought of how she could speak honestly and openly with Lovingdon. She couldn't imagine posing the same sort of questions to Vexley, nor could she imagine Vexley responding with Lovingdon's candidness. That was what she desired: someone with whom she could be completely herself.

Out of the corner of her eye she caught sight of

Lady Cornelia walking with Lord Ambrose. Arms linked, they were both smiling. Grace took satisfaction in her role as matchmaker for them.

"That's an odd couple," Vexley said, and she glanced over to see that he was looking in the same direction that she'd been.

"They seem to get along famously." As though to prove her point, at that moment Lady Cornelia's laughter floated toward her.

"Her dowry won't allow them to live with any sort of largesse."

During all of his courtship, Vexley had never once mentioned the assets he would gain with marriage to her. She had begun to lure herself into believing that it wasn't important to him—or at least not more important than her.

"And will mine allow you to live more in the manner to which you desire?" she asked.

The change in his features was subtle but she knew he had realized his mistake. "I was only talking about them." Reaching out, he took her hand. While his was warm, his touch was not as powerful as Lovingdon's. As much as she wished she didn't, she felt Lovingdon's touch all through her body, no matter how slight, how unintentional. "Things are very different between you and I. We are well-suited, dowry be damned."

"So would we still be here had I no dowry?"

"Without doubt."

Yet, she doubted. Blast it all.

The mood of their outing changed. He read her poetry, but the poems weren't written by her favorite poet. They wandered among the trees and along the lake, never touching. She wanted the inadvertent placing of a hand on the small of her back. She didn't care how inappropriate it might be. He talked at her, not to her. He never sought her opinion. She would not have cared if he asked her what color she thought the sky was. She was merely seeking some evidence that he cared about what she thought.

When she spoke softly, he didn't lean in. He merely responded with, "Quite right."

Which didn't seem right at all considering her comment had been that she thought she had spotted a whale in the pond. Not that she had, of course. She'd simply been testing his interest, and discovered it lacking.

She'd had such high hopes for the afternoon, but found herself quite relieved when he returned her to the residence with the promise of seeing her at her family's estate later in the week.

When she walked into the foyer, she heard voices coming from the front parlor, one much deeper, one that sent fissures of pleasure spiraling through her. Cursing Lovingdon soundly for affecting her at all, she strolled into the room to find her mother serving tea to the duke.

Very slowly, he shifted his gaze to her, and she felt as though she'd been smashed in the ribs with Drake's cricket bat. In a smooth, feral way, Lovingdon unfolded his body from the chair.

Her mother glanced over. "Oh, you're here. Lovingdon was just telling me about a lecture on the American hummingbird that he's taking his sister to this evening. He thought you might be keen to learn about it."

"I believe you'll find a lecture far more interesting than an exhibit," he drawled laconically, and she couldn't help but believe there was more to his invitation than her mother realized.

"I thought you'd come around regarding the merits of exhibits," Grace said. Had he not purchased the red glass? Had she not found him studying it? Warmth swept through her with the thoughts of how much he had seemed to appreciate it—had appreciated her—that night.

"They have their place, but I prefer the opportunity to listen as knowledge is shared."

She couldn't be sure, but she thought she caught an undercurrent to his words, a warning. Had she

somehow managed to upset him? That seemed unlikely as she'd not seen him since Minerva's party.
But something was amiss. If she were smart, she
would no doubt decline the invitation, but when it
came to Lovingdon, she'd never been terribly brilliant. She suspected she might regret the evening,
but then she decided it was better to regret doing
something than not doing it. She'd once thought
there were a great many things that she'd never
have the opportunity to do. She wasn't going to shy
away from experiences simply because she wasn't
certain how they might end.

"I'd be delighted to go. May I have some time to
dress properly for the occasion?"

"Take all the time you require."

The undercurrent became a raging river of fury.
Or at least that was the sense Grace had as Lovingdon's coach traveled through the city. Glaring out
the window, he sat opposite her, his back straight
and stiff. Had she brought her parasol, she might
have whacked him on the head with it.

She was acutely aware of the direction in which
they traveled—the incorrect one. "Are we not stopping off to retrieve Minerva?" she asked.

"No."

"Are we going to a lecture?"

"I haven't decided."

"So you lied to my mother? For what purpose?"

His gaze landed on her then with the full weight of it taking her by surprise. He was fairly smoldering. "To get you into my carriage alone. Men lie. Often. When they want something."

"And you want something?"

"I want you to stay clear of Vexley. I've already told you that he doesn't love you."

"I like Vexley."

"So you're going to ignore my advice? Why ask me for it if you're going to discount it? My time is valuable—"

"So valuable that you've hardly given me any, in spite of your promise to be more involved. You didn't attend the ball last night. Are you even going to bother with our affair at Mabry Manor?"

He returned his attention to the passing scenery visible through the window. "I haven't decided."

"It seems there is quite a bit you haven't decided." She sighed. "Come to Mabry Manor, stay a few days, make your observations, give me a report. I shan't bother you anymore after that."

"You're not bothering me now."

"I find that difficult to believe considering how disgruntled you sound."

A corner of his mouth quirked up. She longed

to hear him laugh. "Come early. We'll go riding," she said.

"How will that help you find a husband?"

Maybe it would help her find her friend. "Blast it all, Lovingdon, don't be so cantankerous. Come to our estate, and I promise you can do it without making observations or presenting me with a report. Just enjoy yourself. When was the last time you truly enjoyed yourself?"

He was enjoying himself at that very moment, dammit all. He'd never had harsh words with Juliette. They'd never argued. She'd never been short with him or looked as though she were on the verge of reaching across the expanse separating them in order to give him a good hard shake.

It was odd that igniting a fire within Grace was such fun. He was riding through the park when he spotted her with that scapegrace Vexley. He almost interrupted them there and then, probably should have, but he feared he would come across as some sort of jealous lover. He wasn't jealous, not at all. He was simply disappointed she didn't have the cunning to see Vexley for what he was—completely undeserving of her.

The problem was that he had yet to meet a man whom he thought *was* deserving of her. He didn't like imagining her laughing with some other fellow, sharing exhibits with him, growing warm beneath his touch, saying his name on a soft moan as passion burned through her.

"Did he kiss you?" he asked, immediately hating that he posed the question.

She appeared surprised. "Vexley? Of course not. He's a perfect gentleman." She released a great huff of air. "The trouble is that I'm not certain I want a perfect gentleman. None of the gents courting me excite me the way that you do."

An inappropriate fissure of pleasure shot through him with her admission.

"I spend far too much time thinking of red vases and what transpired near one," she said. "I think of your kisses and wonder if all men kiss with as much enthusiasm."

"I assure you that if he loves you, he'll kiss you with more enthusiasm."

"And if I love him—"

He stiffened in surprise as she breached the distance separating them and sat beside him. She grazed her hand along his cheek, his jaw. When had she removed her gloves? "I'll want to kiss him, won't I?"

"Naturally."

"I'll want him to be keen on having me kiss him

again, so I'll want to ensure that I do it in such a way that he'll be unable to resist begging for more. Mayhap I should practice with someone for whom I haven't a care." She leaned in.

"Grace," he cautioned.

"What's the matter, Lovingdon? Afraid you'll be enticed into wanting more?"

He was already enticed. What he feared was that he might not be able to resist taking more than she was offering. "You play with fire, m'lady."

"I'm not afraid of getting burned. Are you?"

It wasn't the burn she should fear but the aftermath, for it could be painful indeed. But before he could even think of a way in which to explain that to her, she had covered his mouth with hers as though she owned every inch of it, inside and out.

Practice, indeed. If he hadn't experienced her enthusiasm the first time he kissed her, he might well believe she had spent considerable time practicing, but passion seemed to be such a natural part of her. What amazed him was how well she managed to hold it in check. When she released it, God help the man she loved. At that moment, however, God help him.

He knew he should show shock at her boldness, but too much honesty resided within their friendship for him to feign surprise or castigate her for doing what he had been contemplating since he first saw her with Vexley. Publicly claiming her mouth, however, would have resulted in her having the one thing she didn't want: a husband incapable of loving her.

He wished he could reach past the shards of his broken heart and find a fragment of love that remained unclaimed that he could offer her, but she deserved so much more than a scrap. She was worthy of the whole of a heart and then some.

She would give to a man all she had to give and she deserved to receive no less in return. A man would be better for having loved her. She would cause him to rise above mediocrity. Of that he had no doubt.

She skimmed her hand along his thigh.

"Grace." It seemed to be the only word he was capable of uttering.

"You've touched me intimately, Lovingdon. Why shouldn't I be able to touch you?"

"Because you're a lady." Thank God, he managed to find more words, not that they were particularly adequate.

She laughed against his mouth, and he breathed in the scent of cinnamon. He wondered if she'd enjoyed a hard sweet while she prepared herself for the lecture.

Then she nipped at the underside of his jaw, and he groaned. Her fingers tugged at his cravat. "This is in the way," she said. "I want to kiss your neck. Everything is in the way." She reached for the buttons of his waistcoat.

"Grace, we're traveling in a coach through the London streets. Your reputation—"

"Who's to see? When did you become such a prude?"

He'd been born one, had lived as one until two years ago. He'd certainly never taken Juliette in a moving conveyance. He wasn't going to take Grace either, but he could damn well enjoy her, and if she wanted to explore him in the sheltered confines so be it. His neck cloth had disappeared, and she was suckling at his flesh, nipping the tender skin along his collarbone. He might bare evidence of her conquest on the morrow. Wicked, wicked girl.

Bracing a foot on the opposite bench, he drew her across his lap. Her hands were in his hair, traveling over his shoulders, touching, touching, touching. Her mouth slipped inside his unbuttoned shirt collar. "So what can you tell me of hummingbirds?" she asked.

Hummingbirds? "Who the bloody hell cares?" he asked, just before reclaiming her mouth. With her, he had no rules about kisses. He kissed her and wanted to kiss her again. He wanted to touch her, be touched by her. Lust, it was only lust, and yet it was a fiery need unlike any he'd ever possessed.

She pushed back slightly, dragging her mouth across his bristled jaw and he wished he'd shaved recently. "My mother will care," she whispered. "She'll ask me what I learned this evening. I can't very well tell her the truth of it."

"They hum," he answered, distracted as she wedged her hand between them and began caressing him through his trousers.

"When they sing?" she asked.

"I suppose. No, that's not right." He couldn't think. "Perhaps it comes from their feet. Is it important?"

"Depends what Mother asks."

"It's a sound they make, when they fly, I think."

"Their wings, then?"

"Yes, all right." He should take her to the lecture but how could he possibly sit contentedly beside her when he knew he could have her sprawled over his lap?

Reaching for the laces on the back of her dress, he began to make short work of the knots and bows. She straightened so quickly that her head nearly sent his jaw out the window, snapping his head back. The suddenness of her movement, with no warning, allowed him only enough time to bite back part of a harsh groan.

"I'm sorry," she said, gently rubbing his chin, massaging his cheeks. "But you can't undo my bodice."

"Grace, I've seen you below the waist."

"Yes, I know. I was there when you did."

Had his passion frightened her? That made no sense as she was the one who instigated what was happening between them now. "You can tear off my clothing, but I can't reciprocate?"

"No. I . . . I apologize. I think I lost sight of myself there." She scrambled off him, returned to her side of the coach, and gazed out the window. "I'm sorry."

"They have a name for women who lead a man on a merry chase and then leave him in agony. It's not very complimentary."

"Are you in agony?"

He was close to dying. He was angry, but more so at himself for not stopping things before they got to this point. Shifting on the seat, he straightened himself. He would most assuredly be taking a frigid bath when he returned to his residence.

"I'll survive," he said harsher than he intended. "But I suggest you not take such liberties with any gentleman courting you. He might not stop when you ask."

"He will if he loves me."

"It's the ones who don't love you who cause the problems."

"You stopped," she pointed out, and he wondered if she was hoping for some declaration of affection. No, she was too smart for that.

"I stopped because it never should have begun," he told her.

"You care for me."

"Of course, I do, but I don't love you as I loved Juliette. And that's what you're seeking, isn't it? A love such as I had?"

"You judge love by her," she stated. No question, and yet he felt obligated to answer.

"I judge everything by her."

She'd known that of course, which made her wanton actions incredibly embarrassing. His desire for her didn't go below the surface, and while the sensations were incredibly lovely, they left her wanting.

"What aren't you telling me?" he asked.

Her heart hammering with trepidation, she snapped her gaze over to his. "Pardon?"

In spite of the shadows, she could feel his gaze homed in on her like a physical presence.

"Sometimes I have the sense you're not being quite honest with me, that there's something more going on here than a quest for love."

She clutched her hands tightly together until they began to ache. She couldn't tell him everything. She didn't want her truth revealed in a coach, especially with a man who loved another and not her. Love was the key to acceptance. She was sure of it. Yet she knew she must tell him something. "If you must know I don't much like this life you lead. I thought that in your helping me, you might also help yourself to again become the man you were."

"He no longer exists."

"So I'm beginning to realize. You're never going to return to Society completely, are you?"

"No."

His certainty was disheartening. Although she should have expected it.

Reaching up, he rapped on the ceiling. The coach slowed, and she was aware of it turning down another street. She had little doubt he was returning her home.

"I should fasten you back up," he said somberly.

"Yes, all right." While she turned slightly to give him easier access to her back, he crossed over to sit beside her.

With a solitary finger, he caressed her nape.

Closing her eyes, she wished she possessed the courage to give him permission to undo all the fastenings.

"I apologize for what I said earlier," he whispered softly. "You're an incredibly beautiful woman, Grace. You entice me, but I am not yet blackguard enough to take complete advantage. I would have stopped short of ruining you."

"But you don't think Vexley will."

"Do you really like him?"

"He seems nice enough. They all seem nice enough. I should be content with that, I suppose."

He began tying her laces. He'd loosened so many so quickly. She fought not to consider where he might have obtained that experience.

"You deserve more than contentment," he said. "You deserve a man who smiles every time he sees you."

"Unlike you, who scowls."

"Precisely. A man who loves you will want an accounting of every moment when you're away from him—not because he's jealous but because he missed you dreadfully and wants to assure himself that your time apart brought you a measure of happiness, because the price he paid was loneliness in your absence. Nearly everything he sees will remind him of you. No matter what he is doing, he will wish you were there to experience it with him. No matter how boring he may find the things that interest *you*, he'll willingly be there to share them with you.

"Within a pocket, he will carry something that reminds him of you. It can be the silliest or seemingly most inconsequential item: a button from a dress, a handkerchief that carries your perfume, a locket of your hair, a petal from your favorite flower, a missive that you penned. Not a particularly endearing missive, but it's from you and so it matters.

"He'll hoard every smile you give him. He'll want to make you laugh. He'll awaken in the middle of the night simply to watch you sleep. "

"How will I know that he's doing all these things?" she asked.

Done with his task, he folded his hands over her shoulders. "You probably won't." He pressed a light kiss to the sensitive spot just below her ear. "Just as he'll never know the myriad ways in which you privately express your devotion to him."

The coach came to a halt, and she couldn't help but believe a good deal remained unsaid, that the task of knowing that a man loved her for herself was an impossible one.

A footman opened the door, and Lovingdon

stepped out, then handed her down. He offered her his arm and escorted her up the steps.

At the door, he faced her. "When he leaves you, he'll count the moments until he'll be with you again. He'll find excuses to delay saying goodbye." He touched her cheek. "Good night."

Abruptly, he turned and jaunted down the steps. No delays, no excuses. He might not have intentionally done it, but he'd provided her with another lesson.

"Will you be coming to Mabry Manor?" she called after him.

"I still haven't decided."

"I wish you would."

"Unfortunately we don't always get what we wish for."

No, she thought, as he leaped into the carriage and she watched it disappear onto the street, we don't always get what we wish for.

But it seldom stopped one from wishing.

Chapter 13

Several days later, as the coach bounced along, Lovingdon couldn't remember the last time he'd gone to the country for merriment. After deciding not to attend the gathering at Mabry Manor, he received a missive from Grace alerting him that his assistance would be required, as she fully intended to narrow the selection down to one.

Which he supposed meant there were some gents she was beginning to love or perhaps was leaning toward loving.

He wanted that for her, to love and be loved.

So why had he nearly thrown his red and coppery vase across his library?

On her wedding day he would send it to her to complete her collection, as he certainly had no plans to attend the ceremony. He needed no reminders of his own wedding, no reminders of what he had held and lost.

Although he was hit with a sudden jolt of guilt, as he had not thought of his loss in . . . days. He recalled when he counted not thinking of it in minutes. A minute had passed without thinking of them, then two. Sometimes with enough liquor and a woman, he could go hours.

But days?

It was the blasted vase. He would go into his library and see it, and images of Grace would start circling through his mind like a damned carousel. Her smiling, laughing, sipping rum. Then his gaze would drop to the wine stain on his carpet, and he would feel the silk of her flesh against his tongue, hear the cries of her being pleasured.

And here he was thinking of her again. Well, that would end quickly enough when she was married.

He rapped on the ceiling, and the coach slowed to a stop. He leaped out before a footman could open the door. "Prepare my horse. I'm going to ride."

He always brought his horse to Greystone's when he came to visit. While they had a fine stable of horses, nothing was better than having one's own horseflesh beneath him, a horse who knew his moods, his movements, and his hands.

When Beau was ready, he mounted him easily and set off in a hard gallop. The coach driver knew the way, so he didn't have to wait. He needed to feel the horse beneath him, the wind in his face. He needed to concentrate on keeping the beast in line. He needed something to keep his mind off Grace.

Ever since their carriage ride, she had been a constant in his thoughts. If she wasn't so desperate for love, if he didn't care for her as much as he did, if he didn't want to see her happy, he might have considered taking her to wife.

Without a doubt their nights would be fulfilling. She was as carnal a creature as he'd ever met. But she wanted what he dared not give.

And therein rested his dilemma. He didn't love her as he'd loved Juliette.

They were such different women. What he felt for Grace was beyond description.

He would not dance with her while at Mabry Manor. He would barely speak with her. He would seriously observe the men who still held her attention, provide what insights he could, and be done with the entire affair. She would be married by year's end and happy for the remainder of her life. It was what he wished for her, what he would strive—

At the sight of a horse and rider loping over the gently rolling green, he drew Beau up short. He'd forgotten how well Grace rode, how she seemed to be one with the beast. She gave her all to everything she did. She'd do the same with marriage.

It was imperative that he secure her a husband who would give equally.

For half a second, he considered staying on his current path, but she was so damned alluring. What would it hurt to spend a little time with her before the festivities began?

Kicking his horse into a harder gallop, he raced after her.

Her hair had come undone and was flying out behind her. He'd never seen it unpinned. It appeared that it went past her waist. He had an absurd thought that brushing out the tangles would be a pleasurable task, a task that some other man would have the opportunity to relish.

She must have heard the hard pounding of his horse's hooves as they ate up the ground, because she glanced back. Any other lady would have drawn her horse to a halt, but then he had forever known that Grace was unlike anyone else.

He was near enough that he saw her triumphant grin before she urged her horse into a faster lope. A gentleman would have half heartedly accepted the challenge and then let her win, but he was far from being a gentleman. He gave Beau the freedom to try to overtake them.

"You won't catch me!" Grace yelled over her shoulder, taunting him.

Impressed with Grace's skill as she maneuvered her horse over the slight hills and around the trees that dotted the land, he considered letting her have the victory. Then decided against it. He was almost upon them.

After glancing back, Grace barreled on. "Three dances if I get to the top of the next rise first!"

Her laughter echoed around them, and the excitement thrummed through him. He wanted this victory. He wanted her. Stretched out on the green grass among the wildflowers. He wanted to run his mouth over her body with the sun beating down on them. Though that was unlikely to last long with the dark clouds gathering in the distance.

They were neck and neck now. She looked over, and he saw the determination in her blue eyes. It ignited his blood. He was tempted to reach out, snag her from the saddle, settle her across his lap, and take her mouth until she begged for mercy.

To escape those thoughts he gave Beau a final kick, and his horse reached the top of the rise a nose ahead of hers.

"Blast you!" Grace yelled, drawing her mare to a halt near his gelding. "I almost had you."

"Almost doesn't count."

"You could have let me win."

"You would have despised me for it."

"True enough." Her hair a wild mess, she breathed almost as heavily as her horse.

Against his better judgment, he took several strands between his fingers. "You have the most gorgeous hair."

"Men seem to prefer blondes or brunettes."

He cocked up a corner of his mouth. "Men are fools."

Smiling brightly, she pressed her teeth to her lower lip. "I didn't think you'd come."

He didn't want to acknowledge the pleasure it brought him to have pleased her so. "One last effort to help you find the right man."

"Someone I've overlooked all Season, you think?"

"Perhaps."

"Such a noncommittal response. Still, I'm glad you're here."

"You won't be so glad when I chastise you for being out here with no escort."

She rolled her eyes. "It's my father's land, Lovingdon. I've ridden out here alone for as long as I can remember. I could walk about blindfolded and not get lost."

"You have gentlemen arriving, and some of those might seek an opportunity to be alone with you."

"Not this afternoon. Drake's keeping them occupied with billiards, cards, and drink until dinner."

"I suppose I should carry on to the residence then."

"I suppose you should." She held his gaze, a question in hers, but more an answer that he recognized.

Slowly he dismounted, removed his gloves, stuffed them in a pocket, and approached her horse. It shied away, but he grabbed the reins and calmed it, before placing his hands on Grace's waist. "You should give your horse a rest after that jaunt."

With a barely perceptible nod of acknowledgment, she curled her hands over his shoulders and he brought her down, deliberately allowing her body to brush against his. He should have released her then, but he was loath to do so. It didn't help his convictions any that she neither moved away nor lowered her hands from his shoulders.

Tucking the hair behind her left ear, he wondered how it could feel so soft when it appeared so untamed, but then it seemed to mirror her: bold, yet with an undercurrent of vulnerability that he would have never suspected had he not witnessed it. "My assisting you in your quest isn't doing either of us any favors. After this affair, I'll be returning to my debauched life."

"Are you saying you left it?"

"I'm saying I haven't been as devoted to it as I once was." The fingers that had curled her hair around the shell of her ear lingered, skimmed over her cheek, and came to rest near the freckle. He touched it with his thumb. "You're not quite so brazen this afternoon as you were in the coach."

Her cheeks flushed. "It's easier in the dark, don't you think?"

"Not always."

Lowering his mouth to hers, he took because he could, because he knew she wouldn't object, and because he was hungry for the taste of her. Kissing her was wrong on so many levels, but he had ceased to care. No one was about to witness their transgressions.

Her fingers scraped his scalp, tugged on his hair, held him in place while her sweet sighs echoed around them. He wound his arm around her back, and brought her in closer, pressing her breasts to his chest, breasts he wanted to see, touch, taste. Why was she so protective regarding what was beneath her bodice and not what was beneath her skirts? In his experience, the opposite was usually true.

But then again, Grace had never been common, ordinary, or like anyone else.

When she pulled back, her lips were swollen and damp. He wanted to swoop in and claim them again.

"I have the impression that you're not teaching me a lesson," she said.

"No, I'm simply being wicked and taking what I have no right to hold."

"Too much power is given over a kiss."

"I've shown you where they can lead."

"As long as it's mutual, I don't understand why it must be forbidden." She slipped out of his hold and began walking, swaying her hips slightly.

Grabbing the reins of both horses, he fell into step beside her. "Because women are supposed to remain pure."

Peering over at him, she scoffed. "But not gentlemen. So unfair. Perhaps I shall stand in the center of the ballroom and invite every gent to kiss me. Surely if he makes my toes curl, he's the correct one."

Do I make your toes curl? hung on the tip of his tongue.

"I mean, I can't possibly wait until my wedding night to discover if he is a marvelous kisser. What if he slobbers or has rancid breath or doesn't like using his tongue?"

Although he knew he had no right he despised

the thought of another man kissing her. Reaching out, he pulled her to him, cupped her face between his hands, and blanketed her mouth with his own. He didn't want to discuss potential suitors for Grace. He didn't want to be here. He didn't want to be elsewhere.

Sometimes he thought he might go mad. But at that particular moment, madness was the farthest thing from his mind. Grace took over his thoughts. The feel of her in his arms, the sweep of her tongue through his mouth. He backed up until he landed against a tree that he could use for support while he nestled her between his thighs.

Sweet Christ. She writhed against him as though she sought the same surcease that he did. But he wouldn't take it, couldn't take it, not with her, not when he couldn't give her a marriage based on love. But that didn't mean that he couldn't make her glad that their paths had crossed.

As smoothly as possible, without breaking from the kiss, he turned them around until she was supported by the tree. Her riding habit was perfect for what he had in mind as it lacked the layers of petticoats that would prove bothersome to his quest. Reaching down, he wrapped his hand around her knee and lifted her long leg, settling it just below his hip. Bless her height and long limbs.

"Lovingdon," she whispered on a breathy sigh, and he gritted his teeth at the thought of her saying another man's name. She opened her eyes, and he saw the heated passion that was burning inside her. Had he ever known a woman who was so quick to ignite? "We shouldn't be doing this."

"No, we shouldn't, but you tend to do things that you shouldn't. Why stop now?"

"Is this a lesson?"

How he wished it was. "No. I just want to feel you shuddering in my arms."

"I want to shudder in your arms."

With a growl, he buried his face in the curve of her neck, inhaling her sweet fragrance along with the earthy scent of her earlier exertions. She dropped her head back, giving him easier access to the silky, sensitive flesh as her fingers dug into his upper arms.

He slipped his hand beneath the hem of her skirt until he could cup the bare skin of her calf. Firm muscle. He skimmed his fingers higher, along the back of her knee.

She gasped, giggled, sighed.

"Ticklish?" he rasped near her ear, wondering when his voice had grown so rough.

"A little, but don't stop."

"I have no intention of stopping." Although

if she asked, he would. He hoped only that she wouldn't ask. He wanted to give her this, even as he recognized that in the giving he was also receiving. Her happiness, her joy, mattered to him. It was the reason that he'd made this journey, that he would suffer through this deplorable event when he'd much rather be in London focusing only on his needs. But somewhere along the way, she'd become a need, a need not to disappoint.

He trailed his fingers along the marvelous length of her silken thigh. If they were in a bed, she could wrap her legs around him three times over. He fought back that thought before he became of a mind to search out a mattress. He couldn't put his finger on when she'd become so damned appealing. He'd always liked her, but what he felt now went beyond that. Still, he had no desire to examine it. He wanted only to become lost in her pleasure.

His fingers found her sweet center. She was already so wet and hot. Releasing a tiny moan, she pressed herself against him and clutched his shoulders as though she would soar into the heavens without anchor. Then one of her hands was traveling down his chest, his stomach, lower still—

"No," he growled.

"Not fair," she said on a thready breath. "I want you to feel what I'm feeling."

"I do feel it." He slipped a finger inside, and she throbbed around him. She was so tight. He didn't want to think about how marvelous it would be to be buried inside her. "Let me just enjoy you."

Grabbing the back of his head, she held him near while her heated mouth worked its way over his neck, stirring him in ways that the most experienced courtesans hadn't. It took so little with her to build a raging fire of need, a need that would go unfulfilled this day. While he stroked and caressed her intimately, he ran his tongue along the shell of her ear, taking satisfaction in her gasps. Latching her mouth onto his, there was a frenzy to her kiss as though she could not have enough of him.

Her hand dug more deeply into his shoulder. Then she flung her head back, her cry echoing around them, as she pulsed against his fingers. Shuddering, going limp, she fell against him. With one arm, he held her upright, absorbing each tiny tremor. Ironically, for a man who wanted no commitments, he knew he would be content to hold her here all day, into the night and morning.

Unfair to tease her with things he was not willing to give her forever. Very slowly, he pulled his hand away, and lowered her leg.

Gently, she pushed away from him, giving her weight back to the tree. Her skin was flushed, her eyes sultry. With a sigh, she looked up at the branches overhead. "You've taught me far too much, Lovingdon. I don't know how I shall ever be content with another."

"If he loves you, it will be even more satisfying."

"If he loves me *and* I love him. That's the secret to achieving both the physical and emotional release, isn't it? Without love, as marvelous as the sensations are, the entire experience is still rather empty."

Empty. An appropriate word. Had he not been feeling the same lately?

"I've upset you," he stated.

"No. I'm simply greedy. I want it all." Reaching down, she shook out her skirt. "I need to bathe before the evening."

An image of wet limbs flashed through his mind. He wanted to see her in the bath, he wanted to see her as he had no right to see her. Turning away, he strode over to where the horses chewed grass and shrubs. Grabbing the reins of her mare, he led the beast over to where Grace waited.

He placed his hands on her waist. Such a narrow waist. If he brought his wrists together his hands would span the width of it. If he were an artist, he would paint a slew of slender women. Her shape was elegant, refined, appealing. Leaning in, he took her mouth gently, lingering, capturing once more the feel and taste of her.

"Why did that seem like good-bye?" she asked, when he drew away.

"Because I can't distract you from your goal while we're here. No clandestine meetings, no wickedness. We're to focus on identifying the man who truly loves you."

He lifted her up onto the horse, watched as she maneuvered herself onto the sidesaddle. "I should probably arrive from another direction," he said.

"After chastising me earlier for riding alone? Besides, I believe we've made it perfectly clear that you are only interested in serving as guardian. No one would ever suspect that you've been naughty."

He supposed she was right. Where was the harm in his accompanying her home?

He'd slipped away from the others because he wanted time alone with Lady Grace Mabry, time to court her with no one to observe his attempts, time to convince her that she should accept his suit. But finding her was a challenge. She didn't seem to be in the residence, so he began searching the grounds.

To his everlasting disappointment, he saw her arriving at the stables with Lovingdon in tow.

Lovingdon who always seemed to be sniffing about, who appeared to be her unofficial protector.

He claimed to have no interest in marriage, but if he wasn't careful he was likely to be ensnared by it. It seemed he was forever managing to find time alone with Lady Grace. It was not to be tolerated.

She was the heiress with the largest dowry, a portion of which included land that bordered his own property. He would not be content to marry anyone else, and his own contentment mattered above all else.

He would have to redouble his efforts to convince her that they belonged together.

As she lounged in the copper tub, Grace could not help but reflect that her skin felt particularly sensitive. While she knew that she shouldn't allow Lovingdon to take such liberties, she couldn't deny that she relished the liberties taken. She yearned for his touch, his nearness, his kiss. She loved him, desperately. It was a pity she desired the same degree of love in return, that she couldn't be content to simply love.

Using her sponge, she rubbed it over her foot, between her toes. As lovely as it was, it didn't elicit the marvelous sensations that Lovingdon did. She imagined herself standing before him completely nude, while he ran his hands and mouth over her. In her fantasy, she had no scars for him to avoid.

She feared tonight's ball might be an exercise in futility. Shouldn't she crave the touch of any man she might be considering taking as a husband? Shouldn't she toss and turn at night with thoughts of his body riding hers? Shouldn't she want him to meet her in the shadows of a garden and have his way with her?

The gentlemen were all pleasant enough. Some of them she dearly liked. Some made her laugh. Some made her look forward to their next dance. But she couldn't imagine a single one of them grazing bare hands along her thigh or cupping her intimately. They would do that, of course. But thinking about it made breathing difficult, and not in the pleasant manner that Lovingdon had of taking her breath away.

This love business was such a complicated thing. She feared she might not figure it out until it was too late.

Dinner was turning out to be a dreadful affair, Lovingdon mused as he sat between two ladies who were determined to convince him that it was high time he placed himself back on the marriage market. He shouldn't have been surprised by the seating arrangements as Grace's mother was known for not giving a fig about ranking. She treated lord and commoner alike. So it was that Grace was surrounded by the most eligible of bachelors, while he was boxed in by innocent misses for whom he could generate little interest. Not that he could find any fault with them. They were pleasant to gaze upon, possessed sweet melodic voices, but they were too eager to please.

They weren't stubborn, opinionated, or determined to find love. They seemed in search of one thing—a husband and any lord would suffice for the role. Quite suddenly, it struck him that Grace had standards, that she wasn't simply in want of a husband, but something more, something with value, something that placed her above all the other ladies of her station. His admiration for her rose a notch.

She might have an odd way of going about gaining what she wanted, but by God she knew what she wanted.

Grinding his teeth, Lovingdon watched as she smiled at Somerdale, laughed with Vexley, and listened attentively to Bentley. Was she seriously considering one of them?

He tried to imagine each gentleman standing at the altar beside Grace, but brought himself up short when he envisioned their wedding night. They would do more than touch her as he had. They would know every aspect of her.

They would bring her joy and happiness that he couldn't. He wished that she had never come to him, that he had never realized the young girl he had consoled in the stables had become an enticing woman.

He did care about her, dammit, just not as she wished, not with his entire heart and soul. Those belonged to, would always belong to, Juliette.

He cared for Grace too much to place her second when she deserved to be some man's first.

Grace loved the first night because following dinner they held a ball that continued into the wee hours of the morning. The single ladies had rooms in the east wing, the bachelors in the west. Few of the mamas and papas showed, as the event had always been geared with the younger people in mind. It had begun when she was a child and her parents promised her and her brothers that they could bring their friends to share adventures for a few days during the Season.

Over the years, the adventures had changed. Sometimes she missed the games of her youth, when spending time with the boys was fun. Now it was almost a chore.

Although there was a room set aside for cards

and one for billiards, the ballroom was rather crowded. None of the rooms were for males only. Here the ladies played cards and billiards. Tomorrow some of them would go shooting.

The orchestra was almost finished warming up. She looked around for her first dance partner and spied him talking with Lovingdon. She was glad Drake hadn't sought out an excuse not to come. This had always been a family affair, and he was family, even if he was reluctant to admit it. She knew that he knew he was loved. He had no doubts there but had scars to remind him of his time on the streets, and she doubted he would ever be completely at home in these environs.

As she neared the two men, she thought they were the most handsome in the room. Drake had a roughness to him, a toughness that his evening clothes couldn't hide. In contrast, Lovingdon was elegant, aristocratic. Each man wore self-assurance like a second skin. They were complete opposites, one a lord of leisure, the other hardworking. But friendship bound them.

"Don't you two look handsome tonight?" she said in greeting.

Drake leaned down and kissed her cheek. "You look beautiful. I'm surprised some man hasn't snatched you up yet."

"It wasn't for want of trying, but you know me.

I was always hard to catch. Even when we played chase I could outrun the lads."

She turned to Lovingdon to find him studying her intently. He had always been attractive, but tonight he seemed more so. His dark blond hair was trimmed and styled, his face freshly shaven. He had lines formed by sorrow, but she could make out a few shaped by happiness. Sorrow always dug more deeply. His face contained character that it hadn't in his youth. He had gone through the fires of hell, and while she doubted he would see it as a compliment, to her, he had been forged into a rather remarkable man. He grieved deeply for those he loved; he kept their memories alive. He was keeping his word to help her find love, and she suspected he would assist Minerva as well.

The strains of the first waltz floated on the air.

"Drake, this dance is yours." She winked at Lovingdon. "You're next."

"Not as many suitors here?" Lovingdon asked.

"I have suitors aplenty but I always begin with my favorite gentlemen, so I etched you onto the card days ago."

"Rather confident that we'd be here," Lovingdon said.

"No, but I see no harm in sustaining hope that one's wishes will come true."

Drake offered his arm and led her onto the dance floor. She knew his habits, knew his reservations. Knew he would dance with her and then make his way to the card room or perhaps even the library to read. He thought he knew his place, but he didn't really have a clue.

"You know any of these ladies would be more than happy to dance with you," she told him.

"They're not for me, Grace. They never have been and they never will be," he said, discounting her words. "And you managed to get Lovingdon here, but don't think you've put him back together. That way lies heartache."

It was hardly fair that he wouldn't discuss his love life but seemed to believe it perfectly fine to discuss hers. "I'm well aware. He's adamant that he won't love again."

"But then you've always been a dreamer."

"I dream that someday you'll find love."

He laughed heartily, a deep, rich sound, and she wished the ladies of the Set could see him as she did. She thought of him as a brother too much to ever think of him as anything else, but she knew the goodness in him knew no bounds. Yet she also recognized there was darkness in him that could claim the same.

"Worry about yourself, Grace. My bloodline

coming to an end would be no loss, and I'm in no need of heirs."

"But you could use a wife. I've seen the way you live. You need someone to remind you to eat."

"I make out fine."

She wanted more than that for him, but she also knew he could be as stubborn as she. They might not have the same blood, but they had been raised in the same household, and they had some of the same traits.

When the dance ended, he escorted her to where Lovingdon waited. He was the only partner she wanted this evening, but she knew he would give her no more than a single dance. Still, it was better to have one dance than to have no dance at all.

She was aware of his gaze roaming over her as she neared, and when those amber eyes returned to meet her blue ones, they were smoldering with an intensity that heated her core. It couldn't have been more obvious that he desired her if he shouted it from atop the stairs. But in his case, desire was not love. He'd had women aplenty but only ever loved one. She wanted to see evidence that he loved her.

Just a little. That was all she would need.

He offered his arm, and she placed her hand on

it, relishing the firmness of his muscles bunched beneath her fingers.

"No lessons tonight," she said. "Don't teach me anything or demonstrate particular behaviors. Just dance with me to dance with me."

She peered over at him to find him watching her steadily. "I can't give you what you want."

"All I want is a dance," she assured him, wondering when their relationship had transformed into one where she could not be totally honest with him.

His eyes never leaving hers, he swept her into the fray of dancers. No words, no conversation to distract. She was aware of every aspect of him. The dark blond locks rebelling to fall over his brow. The smoothness of his jaw, which she wanted to scrape her lips over. The perfectly knotted cravat that she wanted to unknot. His bergamot scent that wafted toward her. The heat of his touch, the nearness of his body.

By all appearances, by all actions at the moment, he loved her. It had been one of his axioms.

He will look at you as though you are the only one in the room.

If he were anyone else, she would have thought, *He wants me not my dowry.* But she knew that her dowry was nothing to him.

And he wasn't anyone else. He was Lovingdon, haunted by his first love, by the woman he insisted would be his only love. She could not imagine an emotion so great that it dwarfed all others. Yet even as she thought it, somewhere in the back of her mind she heard, *Oh, but you can.*

She would always love him, but it didn't prevent her from loving another. Why could he not do the same?

She wasn't even aware of the music drifting into silence until he stopped moving. He tucked her arm into the crook of his elbow and they strolled leisurely toward the edge of the dance floor.

He won't be in a hurry to be rid of you.

All the signs pointed toward love, and yet—

I can't give you what you want.

His lessons had been for naught. He couldn't help her determine if a man truly loved her, because the signs could be misread, misinterpreted.

Trust your heart.

Hers was the heart of a fool.

Never taking his gaze from hers, he lifted her hand to his lips. The heat of his mouth seared the skin through her glove. She swallowed, licked her lips. His eyes darkened.

"Enjoy your next dance," he said, before releasing his hold on her and handing her off to Vexley.

She watched him walk off, then with determination turned to Vexley and smiled. She very much intended to enjoy the entire evening, Lovingdon be damned.

Standing in the gazebo, smoking a cheroot, Lovingdon looked out over the stream where the dappled moonlight danced over the water. The smoke he released momentarily clouded his vision. He wished it would cloud his mind.

He wanted Grace to find love, knew she wouldn't find it with him, but the acknowledgment didn't stop him from wanting her. He had watched her dance with one gentleman after another, and each gazed at her adoringly. He could hardly blame them. Her smile was the sweetest, her laughter warmed the soul. It was when he saw her slip into the garden with Somerdale that he decided he needed to leave, because his first inclination had been to follow them out and plant his fist in the center of the man's face.

He wasn't jealous, but merely being protective. She was wise, smart, able to look out for herself. He had given her enough warnings that she would not find herself forced into marriage by an over-zealous suitor.

Hadn't he taken Juliette for walks in the garden

at night whether the moon was full or absent, and behaved himself? A kiss on the back of her hand. Twice he leaned over for a kiss on the cheek. Once he had grazed his mouth across hers in much the same manner that Grace had described Somerdale's kiss. Innocent. Respectful. Boring as hell.

Only now did he realize how dull his courtship had been. He had loved Juliette. He held no doubt. He had been a boy on the cusp of manhood, eager to please her, terrified of frightening her with his passions, so he'd held them in check.

Why could he not do the same where Grace was concerned?

He caught the whiff of her rose and lavender fragrance before he heard her slippers crush leaves, before the floor of the gazebo vibrated as she stepped upon it. He felt her warmth as she neared. Out of the corner of his eye he saw her reach for his cheroot. She plucked it from his mouth, turned, leaned back against the railing and took a short puff. He was mesmerized watching the smoke escape through her slightly parted lips.

She extended the cheroot toward him. He took it, studied it. "Does your father know about your bad habits?"

"There are a good many things about me that my father doesn't know."

He wondered how many of those things were secrets kept from him? A lifetime of exploring her would never be enough. There would always be something new to learn, something new to relish. He couldn't travel that path. "Shouldn't you be inside dancing?"

"I've worn out three pairs of slippers. I've had enough of the ball. I think I've had enough of the Season."

He shifted his position until he was facing her squarely. "What do you mean by that?"

"If one of those gentlemen loves me, it doesn't matter, because I don't love him. I enjoy them. I enjoy them all. But my heart fails to speed up, my skin doesn't grow warm. I don't anticipate their nearness."

"That doesn't mean you won't come to love one of them."

"But it would be a passionless love."

And she so deserved a passionate love, a man who could not live without her. A man who woke up each morning and smiled because she was in his bed, a man for whom she was the sun and the moon.

Without looking at him, she held something toward him. He snatched the bottle from her. "You little minx. No glasses?"

In the light of the full moon he saw her slight smile. "I was attempting to escape from being so civilized."

"Well, you accomplished that." He removed the top from the bottle and offered it to her, not at all surprised when she took it. Too many shadows prevented him from observing the minute movements of her delicate throat as she swallowed, but he could see her faint skin washed by moonlight. His blood thrummed.

He retrieved the bottle from her and enjoyed several gulps, barely savoring the flavor of whiskey. She'd brought his preference, not hers, had known his preference. Juliette had never imbibed with him, nor smoked, nor used profanity. But then he'd kept all his vices on a short leash when she was alive. He hadn't wanted to offend her. He'd loved her, there was no denying that, but in being true to her had he been true to himself?

"You look as though you're deep into heavy thoughts," Grace said.

"Berating myself for failing to discover a man who loves you more than he loves your dowry."

"My father says I'm searching too hard. Perhaps I am."

She grabbed a beam, swung around and stepped through an opening onto the ground.

"Where are you going?" he asked.

"I want to walk along the stream."

"I smell the scent of rain on the air. You should head back to the manor if you're going anywhere." Taking another swallow of whiskey, he didn't want to admit his disappointment because she was leaving him already.

"You're hardly made of sugar," she called over her shoulder. "You won't melt if you get wet."

No, but he'd get chilled. So would she. Dammit. "Grace, you don't know what creatures are about."

"When did you become a coward, Lovingdon?" she taunted.

Blast her. He leapt off the gazebo and trudged after her, aware of the occasional raindrop pinging off him. "I'm a grown man, not a young boy in search of adventure."

"Are there adventures to be had here, do you think?"

Chuckling, he caught up to her. "Most assuredly. Especially if your father finds us out here. Rifle in tow, he'd no doubt hunt me down."

"He trusts you to behave, at least where I'm concerned."

"Yet you know that I don't always behave where you're concerned."

In spite of the gathering clouds, he could see her

smile in the moonlight. The rain began to fall in earnest. He needed to get her back. He didn't want to risk her catching her death. "I think you're out here trying to tempt me into wickedness again."

"It's crossed my mind that wickedness without love is better than no wickedness at all."

"I thought you valued love above all else. If you've been wicked, it'll be harder for him to love you."

At the water's edge she faced him. "Will it? If he truly loves me, shouldn't he love every aspect of me? That's what I want. A man who will love every aspect of me, even the imperfections."

"A woman who admits to imperfections, a rare find indeed."

She abruptly spun about, presenting her back to him, and he had the sense that perhaps she hadn't been teasing and that maybe he shouldn't have either. He moved up until he could see her profile and the tears glistening in her eyes.

"Grace?"

She shook her head. "There's something I haven't told you, something that's not talked about, and yet there are times when I feel this overwhelming need to shout about it."

"You can tell me."

She shook her head.

With one hand, he cradled her cheek. "Sweetheart, whatever it is—"

Lightning flashed, thunder crashed, the air reverberated, and frigid rain poured from the heavens.

Grace hunched her shoulders. Lovingdon tore off his jacket and draped it over her head to shelter her from the rain as much as possible. "Come along, we need to get back to the manor."

"There's an old crofter's cottage just beyond the trees. It's nearer."

He didn't argue as she began trudging away from the river, but worked to keep pace and keep his jacket over her. The wind picked up, slapping rain against them. Blast it! Where had this come from? A flash of lightning guided their steps. Another rumble of thunder cracked above them.

As they passed into a clearing, Lovingdon caught sight of the silhouette of a small building. It looked sturdy enough. As long as it had a sound roof, he'd be happy.

With a bit of fumbling, he found the latch, shoved open the door, and guided Grace inside.

"There's a lamp on the table just inside the doorway," she said, and he felt more than saw her moving away from him.

He found the table, realized he'd clung to the whiskey the entire time. Lightning arced through the sky, provided him with a glimpse of the items spread across the table. He set down the bottle and snatched up the box of matches before all grew dark. He struck a match, lit the lamp, and turned to the room, the only one in the dwelling. Grace was crouched before the empty fireplace. To his right was a bed, neatly made. As a matter of fact, everything appeared tidy. Drawings were pinned on walls around the room.

"It appears to be clean," he said.

"It's where I come to draw."

He glanced back at the bed.

"Sometimes late into the night," she explained, as though she knew he was confused by the out of place furniture. "Father had it redone for me a few years back."

He wanted to examine the drawings, especially the one that appeared to be a bunny with only one ear. He wondered if it was a sketch from her youth, as it seemed an odd choice for a woman. He remembered often seeing her, when she was younger, with sketchpad and pencil.

Crossing the distance separating them, he placed the lamp on the floor and crouched beside Grace. "And you have some firewood and kindling."

"The servants keep it tidy, as I never know when I might want to come here alone."

He worked diligently to get a fire going. "If I didn't know you so well, I would think you'd led us here on purpose."

"Only to escape the rain. I assure you that I'm well aware you'll never love me, and without love how can one *make* love?"

The fire caught and began to crackle. He wished he could make love to her, could give her what she wanted. He turned to find her simply sitting there, rocking back and forth. "You need to get out of those wet clothes. The fire is not going to provide you with enough warmth."

"I'll be fine."

"Humor me. Health is a fragile thing." Standing, he strode over to the bed and pulled off the quilt. "You can use this to cover yourself."

He walked back over and held the quilt up so it served as a curtain between them. "Come on now, Grace."

"I'm not going to disrobe in front of you."

"You're not in front of me. I can't see you."

"The fire will warm me."

"It'll warm you faster if you're not drenched, and I don't intend to stay in sodden clothes. You'll catch your death and I won't have that on my conscience."

"I'm not your responsibility."

She sneezed, sniffled. Blast her!

He crouched beside her. "Grace, don't be so stubborn. You're safe with me."

She was staring at the fire, refusing to look at him.

"I've seen plenty of women."

"Is that supposed to make me feel better?" she asked, and he could not mistake the pique in her voice or the way it made him want to smile.

"I'm not boasting, but merely pointing out that I'm skilled enough around women's clothing that we can do this without me seeing you at all."

He moved around behind her and began to work on the fastenings. She wiggled her shoulders. "No!"

She started to get up, and he wrapped his hand around her arm, bringing her back down. "You're pale, you have chill bumps that I can see, and your skin is like ice. Perhaps I'm overprotective, but by God, I'll not have you ill on my watch."

She studied him for a moment. He thought she might argue further. Instead, she nodded and presented her back to him. He quickly unfastened her dress and slipped the shoulders down her arms. He should have stopped there. He knew he should stop there. Instead he rubbed his palms briskly up and down her arms.

"How can you be so warm?" she asked.

"I have more meat on me." He moved away, stood, and lifted the blanket until it hid her from view. "Come along now. Discard the clothing."

He could hear her moving about, and fought like the devil not to imagine the bodice skimming down her torso, past her hips, her thighs—

The blanket was snatched from his fingers and she draped it around herself.

"There is little point to removing your wet clothes if you're going to get the blanket equally soaked." He knelt so he could glare at her on eye level, but she once again averted her gaze. He reached for the ribbons of her chemise. She shoved his hand away and it accidentally brushed over her breast.

Something wasn't right. It was too soft, too malleable.

"Grace—"

"Please leave me alone."

He should do as she asked. He'd never forced himself on a woman, but something was going on here. He retrieved the whiskey from the table where he'd left it earlier. "Here, drink this."

She upended the bottle as though her life depended on it. The blanket slid down, pooled at her hips. He could see the beginning of a scar, or perhaps it was the end. It peeked out above the lace of her chemise. To the side something else peeked out.

With his forefinger and thumb, he took hold of the rumpled linen. She grabbed his wrist. Holding her gaze, he saw the discomfort in hers. He was so accustomed to her confidence and boldness. He almost released his hold but realized that he had to know the truth.

She licked her lips, swallowed, gave the barest of nods. Slowly, ever so slowly, he pulled out the long strip of linen. Without it, her chemise appeared painfully empty on the left side.

Calmly, not wanting to startle her, taking the same sort of care that he took with a nervous filly, he tugged on the ribbon of her chemise.

"Lovingdon—"

"Shh." Cautiously, he untied the ribbon, then the next, and the next, the material parting. With great consideration, barely breathing, he moved aside the cloth to partially reveal one side, to reveal the thick rigid scars where once a left breast had been.

"Now you know why it is so important that he love me, for me."

Chapter 14

Grace had always expected to feel shame at this first moment when a man gazed upon her chest, but she saw no revulsion cross Lovingdon's features.

"What happened?" His voice was rough, scratchy.

"A malignancy."

He leapt to his feet as though she had lit a fire beneath his backside. He tore at his waistcoat, popping off buttons in his frenzy to get it off. His cravat came next. He slung it across the room. He unbuttoned his shirt, stopped and glowered at her. "Are you going to die?"

She heard the devastation, the pain so deep that she wanted to weep. She shook her head. "No, I shouldn't think so. If I weren't so slender, if I were not as flat as a plank of wood, I might not have noticed the growth for years, but I did notice and it was enlarging, so Dr. Graves said the best thing was to remove everything that might have a chance of becoming infected. He examines me every few months to make sure nothing else is amiss. You know how good he is."

Lovingdon glared at her. "Can he guarantee that you're all right, that you won't die?"

"We all die." Thunder sounded, the timing ominous, as though to punctuate her words. "You could walk outside and be struck by lightning. There are no guarantees. But Graves thinks it unlikely that I'll have to deal with it again."

Lovingdon strode around the room. She was surprised that he didn't go out into the rain.

"How could I not know that this happened to you?"

"The timing of it, I suppose." She licked her lips. "It was a little over two years ago. You were in the depths of grief and despair. And it's not as though we took out an advert. Mother and I went to the country, said we were taking a long holiday. I don't think anyone thought anything of it. She and I have always been close. Our going away together wasn't unusual. As I said by the river, it's not something that's shouted about. If people discuss it at all, it's in whispers."

She didn't know why she didn't cover herself up. Only she, Graves, her mother, and Felicity had ever seen her scars. That Lovingdon wasn't casting up his accounts gave her hope that perhaps another man might not be repelled either. He dropped down in front of her.

"I'm so sorry, Grace." He raised a hand, lowered it, lifted his gaze to hers. "I feel as though I should have done something."

"You're doing something now. Assisting me in finding love. I know if a man asks for my hand that I shall have to tell him, but I don't know exactly when I should, or how. I must know that he loves me. I must trust him implicitly. I don't want all of London to know. This is personal, private. And then I think, 'What should it matter?' Lady Sybil told me that Fitzsimmons only ever lifts the hem of her nightdress, that he never unbuttons it, never seems to care much about anything other than what's between her legs. So perhaps my husband would never know. If he's only interested in the lower portions—"

"If he loves you, Grace, he'll want to see all of you."

The problem with his honesty was that he told her things she'd rather not know. "I feared as much."

"You shouldn't fear it, because if he loves you, it won't matter."

"How can it not?"

"It won't." Gently, like a summer breeze wafting over a lake, he parted the material farther. "Is it painful?"

"Not very." She shook her head slightly. "Sometimes it pulls. It looks much worse than it is. Looks ghastly, actually."

"No . . . no." He lowered his gaze, then slowly began lowering his head. "If he loves you, he'll find every aspect of you beautiful."

But how could he? She didn't utter the words, fearful that he would think she was fishing for compliments. She didn't like being needy or unsure. She had always known her own mind. It was the minds of men that she didn't quite understand. Every time she thought she had them figured out, they surprised her.

Just as Lovingdon surprised the hell out of her now. He laid his lips against the ropy scars. She couldn't feel his touch, but she could see it, the light pressing that didn't smash his mouth. The gentleness of it, the reverence.

His mouth glided up until she felt the heat of it on her collarbone, then her neck. Then his lips were against hers, sipping at the corners. One of his hands came to the back of her head, holding her in place before his mouth smashed hers, his tongue urging her to part her lips, which she did gladly.

With a groan, he delved swiftly and deeply. She forgot about her scars, her imperfections, her fears of disappointing. All she knew was the hunger of his kiss, the urgency of their mating mouths.

He dragged his lips along the sensitive flesh just under her chin, his tongue tasting until he reached the shell of her ear. "Little Rose," he rasped, "never doubt that you're beautiful. I'm going to show you how beautiful."

With hardly any effort at all he lifted her into his arms and carried her to the bed. He laid her down gently. There was more darkness than light here, shadows providing a welcoming cover from his gaze. He walked away, and when he returned brought the glow of the lamp with him and set it on the table beside the bed.

"I'm not going to let you hide from me," he said.

"Lady Sybil says it's done in the dark."

"Lady Sybil is married to a buffoon."

Sitting on the edge of the bed, he took his fingers on a journey through her hair, discovering and removing the pins that had refused to take flight as she'd run to the cottage. He fanned out the strands.

They were relatively dry thanks to the protection of his jacket.

Folding his hands around her neck, he eased them down to her shoulders, then slid them down her arms, taking her chemise with them. She considered protesting, and yet when she saw his concentration, words failed her and she couldn't look away.

She saw anger at what she'd suffered; she saw sorrow, but she also saw wonder. The wonder stole her voice, her breath, her worries. During all the times when she envisioned revealing herself to a man, not once had she ever imagined that he would gaze on her with wonder reflected in his eyes.

When all her undergarments were gone, he retrieved the quilt he'd taken to the fireplace earlier and very gently dried whatever raindrops remained on her skin.

"I won't break, you know," she said.

His eyes met hers. "You are like blown glass, to be appreciated for your beauty, touched with care. Admired. So fair." He shifted his gaze down. "Except where you're red."

"It's not right for you to be able to look at all of me when I can see so little of you."

"You tempt me, Little Rose. If I remove my clothes, you won't leave here a virgin."

"I don't want to." Sitting up, she began unfastening the buttons on his shirt. "You tempt me as well."

When the last button was undone, he reached up and over his shoulders, grabbed the back of his shirt and pulled it over his head to unveil the smattering of hair on his chest and the sculpted muscles that revealed his life of debauchery included some sort of strenuous activities.

He was perfection, and he desired her.

She knew because she could see the bulge straining against his britches. His arousal.

Leaning in, he took her mouth tenderly, sweetly, exploring at his leisure as though he had never explored it before, as though the shape of it, the taste of it, were all new discoveries to be savored. It was only a kiss and yet it quite undid her.

He guided her back down to the pillows, then stood, and began giving the buttons of his trousers their freedom. One, two—

Her gaze shot up to his eyes, the smoldering depths, watching her as she watched him. By the time she dropped her gaze, his task was done, his clothes on the floor—

"Amazing how your body reacts when there is a woman in a bed—"

"It doesn't react this way for every woman I see in a bed. It's actually quite particular."

Stretching out beside her, he threaded his fingers through her hair. She heard thunder, or perhaps it was her own heart beating. The rain pounded the roof, creating a more intimate cocoon. When she had envisioned her first time with a man, she had not imagined this feeling of being whole and complete. He gazed down on her as though there were no imperfections, no scars. Through his eyes she felt remarkably lovely, not at all self-conscious, not at all wanting to cover up and hide.

As his mouth once again blanketed hers, he made her want to be bold, allowed her to be her true self, someone who had never retreated from adventure. What an adventure he was taking her on.

His mouth and hands explored while hers did the same. His skin was hot and slick to the touch, salty to the taste. His muscles coiled and undulated beneath her palms. He guided and encouraged her to touch him intimately, and the heat of him increased her fervor. They were like two flames, a conflagration dancing and writhing and generating more heat, building a bolder fire that ignited passion. She thought she might come away from this as little more than a cinder—

And then she realized that she would come away from this as beautiful hand-blown glass, shaped and molded with care, with precision, with love.

For surely only someone who loved her would devote so much attention to every aspect of her. He left no part of her unkissed, no part uncaressed.

He suckled her solitary breast and she nearly bucked off the bed with the pleasure of it. She threaded her fingers through his hair, held him there while his tongue lathed over the tiny pearl.

Then he skimmed his mouth over to the other side, bringing the sensations with him. They were phantom sensations, she thought, because he could only run his tongue over scars, but having a sense of what she should have felt, she felt it now.

Even if it was only in her mind, she didn't care, as he was creating other feelings elsewhere, across her hips, between her thighs, stroking, stroking, urging—

Pleasure escalated. He moved between her legs, wedging himself at her apex. She could feel him nudging at her entry. She skimmed her fingers over his damp chest, his breaths coming short and hard, his heart beating out a steady tattoo. Holding her gaze, he began inching himself in.

"Tell me if it hurts," he commanded.

As though she would, as though she would ruin this moment of their joining with complaints or whimpers. She'd endured much worse. He was slow, but determined, stretching her.

"You're so damned hot," he growled.

Fire, she thought, we're fire, shaping something beautiful and wonderful here.

He sighed with deep satisfaction. Her body curled and tightened around him. Yes, this was love, this melding that made it impossible to tell where she ended and he began.

He slid out, slipped back in. Short thrusts, hard thrusts, teasing ones, determined ones. All the while he caressed and kissed and whispered that she was beautiful, perfect, enticing.

Enticing. She liked it the best, because it meant he wanted her, wanted to be part of her. His tempo gained momentum, the deep thrusts dominated. Liquid sensations began swirling through her. Heating, cooling, taking shape into something that could not be denied.

She dug her fingers into his shoulders, scraped them down his back, curled them into his firm buttocks. They moved in unison as one.

Her sighs turned to cries as the pleasure intensified. Fire consumed her as the sensations exploded, ripping through her and then bringing her back, gasping, stunned, and utterly replete.

Above her, Lovingdon grunted, withdrew, and spilled his hot seed on her thigh. Breathing heavily, he bowed his head. She combed her fingers into his damp hair.

She never wanted to stop touching him, she never wanted them to leave this bed.

After cleaning her and himself up, Lovingdon lay on his side and trailed a finger along a scar, then circled it around her breast. He thought he'd always been there for her, but when she had needed him most, he was secluded in mourning, devastated, thinking that no one else had pain as great as his.

For the past two years he had convinced himself that he alone suffered. He had wrapped himself in a shroud of anguish. Breaking out of the tight cocoon was not turning him into something beautiful now, but perhaps it was making him stronger. Not that he would have ever willingly traded Juliette and Margaret for strength. He would have never let them go, but sometimes life didn't come with choices.

If Grace never found a man who loved her, who would appreciate her, he had wanted her to experience lovemaking at its finest. Two years of debauchery had taught him a great deal, and he'd wanted to share the lessons with her. At least that's what he told himself. In truth, thought and reasoning played no part in what had just transpired.

"I think Fitzsimmons is doing it wrong," she said quietly.

He peered into her eyes. "When you're in a man's bed, it's bad form to mention another man."

She smiled, the mischievous smile that always enthralled him. "I don't intend to make a habit of visiting different men's beds. Only my husband's. It's only that I think Sybil would have told me if she had experienced anything close to resembling what just transpired between us."

"Not all men care about the lady in their bed to such an extent."

"You care about me?"

"I do, very much, yes."

She studied him as though he hadn't said quite enough. He hoped his next words offered reassurance. "The storm has passed. It'll be light soon. We should get back to the manor so I can tidy up before asking your father for your hand in marriage."

She blinked, opened her mouth, closed it, furrowed her brow. "I beg your pardon?"

"I've compromised you, Grace. You can't possibly think that I'm going to shirk my responsibility here."

She quickly moved away from him, sat up, grabbed the quilt and covered herself from chin to toe. "Your responsibility?"

"Yes."

"Do you love me?"

"In a manner of speaking."

The fire in her blue eyes would melt glass. "A manner of speaking. Do give details on the manner, here."

"You know very well, as we've discussed it, I have limits regarding what I will allow myself to feel, especially in regard to—" He dropped his gaze to her chest.

"What does that look mean?"

He did not want to travel there. He did not. "You have no guarantee that the malignancy won't return. You can't guarantee that you'll survive another bout of it." He came up off the bed in a blind rage that took him a moment to get under control. The thought of her dying—he cared for her, yes. Losing her would be painful, but he would not allow her to own his heart and soul. If the disease came upon her again, he wouldn't be able to save her, just as he'd been unable to save Juliette. To lose Grace under those circumstances would send him straight to Bedlam.

He faced her. "You will be happy. And this between us"—he moved his hand back and forth between them—"it's good. We can make this work without the necessity of falling in love."

Staring at him, she shook her head. "I can't

make it work without falling in love. I won't. I deserve a man who cares if I die."

"I'll care. Of course I'll care. I just won't—"

"As much as you did when Juliette died."

"I can't go through that pain again. I won't."

"Go to the devil, Lovingdon." She came off the bed in a majestic sweep of bedclothes wrapped around her. She stood before him, her shoulders back, her chin level, a queen sorely disappointed in her subject. "Get dressed and get out. I'll see myself to the manor without you in tow when I'm good and ready."

"I'm not allowing you to traipse about unprotected."

"Good God, Lovingdon, I've traipsed about these grounds unprotected most of my life. I don't want you about. And don't you dare ask my father for my hand. I shan't marry you."

"You won't have a choice when I tell him what transpired here."

"You won't tell him." She turned her back on him.

He wanted to go to her, comfort her, but she was right. She deserved a man willing to give her his heart. He wasn't that man. He'd known all along he wasn't that man. It didn't stop him from admiring her, desiring her. But he would not force marriage on her.

In silence, he snatched up his clothes and hastily drew them on, barely bothering with the buttons on his shirt. With his waistcoat balled in his fist, he headed for the door. "I've left my jacket so you can at least have some protection from the early morning chill."

He opened the door.

"It was you," she called out softly. "You I fell in love with once. You who broke my heart at such a tender age. And now you've gone and done it again."

And with those simple words she eviscerated him.

She didn't know how long she sat in the cottage. Without looking back, he'd slammed the door in his wake. She didn't know why she'd confessed what she had.

Well, she certainly wasn't going to sit here all night feeling sorry for herself. She thought about trying to sketch. She had been working on a story told through pictures of a bunny who had lost an ear and feared no other rabbit would ever love him, because he was scarred and different. She thought she would have it published as a children's book, but at the moment she didn't care about the damn bunny.

She hurt too much to care about anything.

Why had she thought he would open his heart to her, that he would think for a single moment that he could have with her what he'd had with Juliette?

But at least for a few moments with him she'd felt beautiful again.

Somewhere a man existed who would love her, appreciate her, and find her beautiful. But her father had it right. She hadn't found love where she'd been searching for it. Perhaps the key was to stop searching.

She thought of the butterflies she'd chased as a girl, and how she never caught a single one. One afternoon she wanted to hold one so desperately that she'd run herself ragged, until she finally collapsed on the cool grass, breathing heavily, too exhausted to move. She'd felt it. The tiniest touch on the back of her hand. When she looked, she'd seen the orange and black wings, opening and closing in delicate rhythm. A butterfly was taking its rest near her thumb. She could have captured it with ease.

Instead she let it go. She had to do the same with Lovingdon. He'd had his love, short-lived but intense. He was content to live out the remainder of his life with the memory of it. Just as she had been with her singular butterfly. Some experiences were not meant to be repeated.

She'd been a fool for thinking otherwise. She would tell him so when next their paths crossed. She valued his friendship. It was enough. She didn't require more.

With a sigh, Grace stepped outside. The moon was hidden behind dark clouds and the rain had begun to fall again. She should delay, she thought, but was anxious to be home. Besides, she knew the path well.

She had taken but two steps when soft linen covered her mouth. Startled, she inhaled deeply, breathed in a familiar sweet fragrance that she associated with fear, with pain, with loss. Dr. Graves had used it as he prepared her for surgery.

She started to fight, tried to fight, but the drug was already taking effect. Her limbs were too heavy to move. Her knees began to buckle. She was aware of someone lifting her.

And then she was aware of nothing at all.

Chapter 15

Lovingdon stood at a window in the library gazing out on the thrashing rain. No outdoor activities today unless it involved building an ark.

"You wanted a word," Greystone reminded him.

Yes, he did. When Lovingdon entered the breakfast room it was filled to the gills, and for the first time ever he seriously studied every man there. Which one was right for Grace? Which one would truly love her as she deserved to be loved? Which would treat her better than he would?

Then his gaze fell on Grace's father and he'd known he needed to speak with the duke. He was allowing his daughter to run wild. Did he know she smoked a cheroot, drank rum, and slipped out of her room at all hours of the night? Did he know she cheated at cards? There were a thousand things about Grace that he wished to discuss with Greystone.

Now, he turned to face the man, who was casually leaning back in his chair. "I wish to ask for your blessing in marrying your daughter."

He was as surprised by the words as Greystone appeared to be. He didn't love Grace, refused to love her in the way a man loved a woman who encompassed the whole of his life, but he knew he could make her happy. And he'd compromised her, unforgivably.

He would convince her, one way or the other, that marriage to him was in her best interest. He would find a way to mend the heart he had broken.

Greystone tapped his finger on the arm of his chair. "I didn't even realize you were courting her."

"I suspect there are a good many things about your daughter of which you are unaware."

"Not as many as you might think. What do you offer her?"

Lovingdon was taken aback by the question. "You know me, you know my family well. You know what I offer. Impeccable lineage, title, wealth, lands—her dowry is not a consideration."

"What is?"

"I wasn't expecting a bloody inquisition."

Greystone stood. "So I gathered."

"She'll be happy. Of that I can promise you."

"I like you, Lovingdon, always have, but I can't give you my blessing on this matter."

"Why the hell not?"

"I think you know the answer to that."

The words were in his eyes, if not on his tongue. *Because you don't love her, you'll never love her as you did Juliette.*

The last thing Lovingdon had expected was a refusal. He could argue, he could insist, but he saw no point in it. "Then I bid you a good day."

With as much dignity as he could muster, he strode from the room. It shouldn't have mattered that his request had been denied. He preferred it, actually. He didn't have to feel guilty washing his hands of the entire matter. He didn't want a wife, especially one who might depart this earth before him. He couldn't go through that again. He had merely asked out of obligation.

But Lovingdon knew it was a poor reason indeed, and respected Greystone more for knowing it.

He needed to return to London and he wanted to let Grace know before he left. This assisting her in finding love was a colossal failure. In the process it also managed to ruin their friendship.

Damn it all to hell anyway.

He'd been a guest here often enough in his youth

that he was familiar with the family quarters, and he made his way to her bedchamber with no difficulty, but stood outside her door, trying to frame the words. He didn't want to hurt her any more than he already had, but neither could he pretend that all was right. She was the actress of their little group.

He considered simply walking in. After all, he had seen her in all her naked glory. There were no surprises left. But still there were privacy and boundaries. Just because she'd quivered in his arms didn't mean she'd be quivering with anticipation if he walked in. As a matter of fact, he rather suspected she might throw something at him.

He rapped lightly. And waited.

He looked up the hallway and down it. He didn't want to be caught here. If her father wasn't going to give his blessing, Lovingdon didn't want her reputation ruined. He rapped again. Pressed his ear to the door. No sound. She was sleeping.

He could come back later, but that would mean that he'd have to stay longer, possibly into the afternoon, and he preferred to be away as soon as possible. He released the latch, pushed open the door. It squeaked. He cringed.

Didn't the servants know to keep the hinges oiled?

He stepped into the room. The bed was made. Grace was obviously awake. He should have checked in the breakfast dining room first. He considered waiting here, but who knew how long she would be? Some gent might snag her and proceed to bore her to pieces in the parlor.

Returning to the hallway, he nearly smacked into her lady's maid. He straightened his spine and glared down at her as though it was perfectly fine for him to be exiting her mistress's bedchamber. "I'm in search of Lady Grace. Have you any notion where I might find her?"

"No, Your Grace. She didn't return to her rooms last night, so I assumed she was at her small cottage—although she doesn't usually go when company is about. When I saw the door ajar, I thought she was finally home. I'm thinking that I should probably alert His Grace to her absence."

"No need for that. I know where she is."

She obviously stayed in her cottage to sulk, although she'd never been one to sulk. Perhaps she just needed some guaranteed time alone.

Lovingdon returned to his room for a coat and hat, then struck out in the rain to retrieve her. He didn't know what he was going to say to her. As long as he'd known her, he never had any trouble at all speaking his mind, speaking to her. Even last night, when the sight of her scars, the knowledge of what she'd endured, should have left his tongue unable to move, he'd known what to say. He hadn't hesitated, hadn't thought through the words.

For the first time in two years he'd spoken without any thought, simply said what he'd needed to say, what he wanted her to hear. The stubborn, courageous, lovely girl she'd been had grown into a remarkable woman. She could have gone into seclusion, she could have hovered in corners. She could have stared out windows and wished upon stars for a different life. Instead she attended balls and soirees. She danced and laughed. She lived, God bless her. She lived.

While he was the one who had gone into seclusion. Not noticeably, of course. But he had withdrawn from life—until she brought him back into hers.

Juliette would have been disappointed in him, but no more so than he was in himself.

He strode past the gazebo, where everything had shifted and changed. If only he hadn't followed her—

If only she'd asked him sooner.

The rain pelted him, and he barely noticed as he approached the cottage. He still wasn't exactly certain what he would say to her. But he knew that when he laid eyes on her again, the right words would fall from his lips.

He arrived at the door, considered knocking, but in the end simply opened it and strode in.

Only to find it empty.

Unease skittered along his spine. If she wasn't at the manor, if she wasn't here, then where the deuce was she?

Rushing to the doorway, he glanced quickly around outside. Perhaps she just took a different path to the manor and they'd been as two ships passing in the night. That was probably it. She was no doubt there now, having a bath, or stretching out to sleep, or enjoying breakfast. Closing the door behind him, he started off—

Halted in his tracks.

Something caught his eye, in the mud, being battered by the rain. As he neared, he realized it was a bit of linen. The stuffing from her chemise? No, not nearly large enough.

Bending down, he picked it up and was assaulted by a sweet aroma that made him grow dizzy. Chloroform?

Bloody damned hell!

Grace was drifting out of slumber, languishing in a vague area where dreams were gossamer mists that hadn't yet faded. Rain pounded a roof, leather cooled her cheek, and a rocking motion threatened to ruin her appetite for breakfast. Her head was heavy. Her entire body was heavy, just as it had been after her surgery. Her mouth felt as though it had been stuffed with cotton. She couldn't swallow without discomfort.

"Would you like some water?"

Opening her eyes fully, she realized she was traveling in a coach. A man sat opposite her. "Vexley?" she croaked.

"Here." He extended a silver flask toward her.

She pushed herself into a sitting position. Dizziness assailed her. She took a moment to let it pass, before glaring at him. "What's going on here?"

"We're off to be married."

She stared at him. "I beg your pardon?"

"I have the special license here." He patted the left side of his chest. "We'll be at my estate by nightfall. When we reach the village, we'll make a quick stop by the church. The vicar owes me a favor. We'll exchange our vows, then off to my manor for our wedding night. We'll return to your father's estate on the morrow with the good news that you are now the Countess of Vexley."

She truly felt ill now, terribly, frightfully ill. Glancing out the coach window, all she could see was countryside and rain and dark clouds. "You can't possibly think that I'm going to exchange vows, that I will sign the registry—"

"Doesn't matter if you do or not. As I said, the vicar owes me a favor. He'll make certain all looks in order, even if it's not. With this little escapade and a night in my manor, you'll be ruined and have no choice except to accept me, and all this fluttering about from gentleman to gentleman that you've been doing will come to an end."

He was so damned smug, so haughty, so arrogant.

"I'm already ruined."

He narrowed his eyes at her, and she wondered why she'd never noticed before how terribly beady they looked when fully open. "Who?"

She met his gaze head on. She would not be ashamed of what had happened between her and Lovingdon. "It doesn't matter. It's done. Very recently, in fact. Should I become with child rather quickly, you'll never know whether it's yours or his."

"Lovingdon. Why else was he with you in that cottage? But it's of no consequence to me. I need your dowry. Rather desperately. Besides, the land that comes with you? A portion of it borders mine. I'm very keen to have it."

"You're mad if you think my father is going to hand over my dowry to a man who forced me into marriage and then forced himself upon my person."

He smiled, a horrid little ugly showing of teeth. "He loves you too much to see you do without. I'm certain we'll come to terms."

Oh, she doubted it very much but could see there was little point in arguing. If this marriage did take place, she suspected she would be a widow before the week was out. Her father, Drake, possibly Lovingdon, would see to it. They were all too familiar with the darker side of things to allow this travesty to stand.

The carriage suddenly lurched to a stop, tossing them both around. She regained her balance first, flung open the door and tumbled out into an immense amount of muck. She scrambled to her feet, but the mud clung to her skirt, her legs, her arms, weighing her down. If she was free of it, she had no doubt she could have outrun Vexley and climbed a tree to safety, one from which he wouldn't have been able to get her down. Instead, she slugged along, slow and clumsy, falling, shoving herself back up to stagger forward.

She felt a hand close firmly and possessively around her arm. Spun around, she found herself face-to-face with Vexley. Not only Vexley—

But a pistol.

She froze. The air backed up in her lungs.

"I'm most serious, Lady Grace. Don't force me to hurt you."

Then the realization dawned that if he shot her, he wouldn't have his bride. "If you kill me, you won't gain what you want."

"I have no intention of killing you, but merely slowing you down. I have no qualms marrying a woman who will walk with a limp for the remainder of her life." With his fingers biting into her arm, he dragged her back toward the coach, where the driver and footman were working diligently to rock the vehicle out of the mud.

As the rain soaked her, she fought not to feel despair. Surely someone would notice that she wasn't about, but would they notice in time? And how in God's name would they find her?

Haste. Haste was of the essence.

With urgency, Lovingdon galloped his horse alongside Drake's. From time to time the mud slowed them down, but they were determined to catch up with Vexley.

Lovingdon had returned to the manor, explained to Greystone his suspicions that he thought Grace might have been taken. Then they'd done a very discreet but incredibly quick accounting of the men present. Vexley was nowhere to be found. His carriage and driver were gone.

So Lovingdon and Drake had set out. While they could have asked others to join them, they thought it best to keep those aware of the situation to a small group in order to limit the damage to Grace's reputation. They were fortunate. Even with the rain, they discovered evidence of a carriage recently leaving. The direction of the ruts made sense. Vexley's ancestral estate. How many hours ahead of them was Vexley? How long had Grace been his captive? What might he have done to her during that time?

The rain was a blessing and a curse. It would slow Vexley, but it also slowed them. Not as much, though, Lovingdon was certain. His horse was surefooted and could lope across grassy ground when the roads were mired, while the coachman would have no choice except to stay on the path and slug through. The rain had to stop sometime, and when it did, Lovindgon would be able to push forward faster. But would he get there in time?

He didn't need much of an imagination to know what Vexley's plans were: Grace's ruination, a way to force her to become his countess. His countess when she deserved to be a duchess.

Lovingdon's heart pounded with the force of the hooves hitting the ground. It raced faster than the horse, and yet there were moments when it was unsuitably calm. He would not let Vexley have her, not for the long haul. If the man forced himself on Grace, he would castrate him, then kill him. He would probably do both anyway, regardless of the man's actions.

He just had to find him.

They rode, rode, rode. Through the rain and as night began to descend. They only stopped to rest their horses when absolutely necessary, and even then they trudged forward, horses in tow. He had to keep moving forward. Forward. Forward.

Dear God. Two years ago he'd stopped moving at all—

And then Grace with her schemes, her dodges, her cheating at cards, had started him moving again, reluctantly, slowly. He was squeaky and rusty, in need of oiling, and she had limbered him up, loosened him up. She had made him glad to get up in the morning, given him a reason to do so.

They were nearing Vexley Hall. In the distance he could make out some light, no doubt the village that resided within its shadow. On the other side of it—

A horse whinnied, screeched. Hearing Drake curse soundly, he glanced back to see that horse and rider had taken a tumble into the mud. He was torn. He needed to carry on, but he knew Grace would never forgive him if Drake was badly injured and he left him there to languish. He drew Beau up short and circled back.

The horse had regained its footing and was standing. Drake was kneeling beside it, examining a foreleg. He looked up as Lovingdon drew his own horse to a halt. "She's gone lame. Carry on. I'll catch up."

Lovingdon hesitated.

"I can't leave her," Drake said. "I'll walk her to the village, get a fresh horse there."

"Are you certain you're all right?"

"I will be once we have Grace back. Off with you."

Lovingdon urged his horse around and sent it back into a hard gallop. He knew the frantic pace was dangerous with the dark and the rain and the mud. But he was so near. It never occurred to him that he wouldn't find her. He just didn't know if he would do so in time to spare her Vexley's touch.

He reached the village but didn't bother to stop to make inquiries. Instead, he loped down the center of the road. Few people were about. He could hear merry-making in a tavern he passed. God, he could use a drink. After he had Grace back, they would all have a drink.

He was almost to the other side of the village when he spied the carriage. It had no markings but was a damned fine carriage for a villager to be driving about. He'd bet his life it belonged to someone of noble birth. It wasn't moving. No, it was quite still, positioned as it was in front of a path that led into a church.

"Weddings are supposed to take place in the morning, but not this early in the morning," Grace said. She wasn't quite sure of the hour but it had to be long past midnight. It had taken the driver and footman more than an hour to get the carriage out of the mud and on its way again. Then they'd gotten stuck three more times, before the driver slowed the horses' pace. She had been cold, damp, and miserable with the mud caking to her clothes. Vexley hadn't offered her his coat, only bits of cheese to eat and water to drink.

But he no longer recited poetry, as when they were on the picnic. He didn't speak to her of his unclaimed heart. After today's misadventures, she doubted he had one.

She supposed she should have been terrified, but she was more annoyed than anything else.

In long strides, his footsteps echoing off the rafters, Vexley paced in front of the altar. Only moments earlier he'd sent his driver to fetch the vicar.

"Vexley, rethink this mad scheme of yours," she told him.

"It's not a mad scheme. Do you know how many of my ancestors stole their brides? It's tradition in my family."

She thought perhaps he was striving to make light of his actions, but she saw no humor in it. Neither would her father. For a short while last night she had thought Lovingdon would stand as her champion, but he remained true to his word. He'd not love again.

He could recount every act of a man in love, but he had no heart to give. She envied Juliette to have been loved so much, to have the ability to hold onto Lovingdon's heart, even beyond the grave. Theirs was the sort of love she longed for, not this macabre travesty perpetuated by Vexley.

She glanced around surreptitiously. She had to find a means of escape. She didn't think asking for sanction would work, not if the vicar owed this man. The pistol was the problem, for even now Vexley had it in his coat pocket. He could retrieve it quickly and easily enough if she tried to run. He'd offered up a demonstration when they first arrived.

How could she have been so blind as to consider him a viable suitor? Who would have thought there was such a thing as a gentleman being too charming?

He wasn't at all like Lovingdon, who was not overly charming. He argued with her, got put out with her. He didn't seek to win her over with flowery words, but he'd managed to do it with honest ones. He was good and noble. As angry as she'd been at his reasons for marrying her, she couldn't deny that she admired his willingness to go into an arrangement that would bring him nothing but misery, to make amends for the fact that he'd compromised her. If only she could be content with that: duty instead of love.

If she had not run him off, she might not be here now.

Although it was equally likely that Vexley might have done him harm. She had long ago ceased to look back and wonder what if . . .

She heard footsteps echoing in the vestry and her heart began to race. The vicar.

Vexley grabbed her arm and pulled her to her feet. "Do as you're told and it'll all go very quickly."

"I do not know how to be any clearer, but I have no intention whatsoever of marrying you."

"You will, that I don't beat you. Make a fuss here and you will be black and blue for a week."

She needed to catch him off guard. Lowering her gaze, she tried to look as docile as possible. "Yes, my lord."

"Now where's that blasted vicar?"

The footsteps increased in tempo, moving quickly, growing louder, nearer. Vexley glanced back over his shoulder. Grace shot her fist straight up, aiming for his chin—

But he flung her aside before she could make direct contact. She merely grazed him as she stumbled and landed hard on the floor. She heard an animalistic growl, and a huge beast was flying through the air. It slammed into Vexley and took him down.

Not a beast. Lovingdon.

She watched as the two men struggled and rolled. Fists flew. Grunts echoed. She rushed to the altar and lifted a gold candlestick. The heft of it would do nicely. Turning back around, she saw that Lovingdon had gained the upper hand. He was on top, straddling Vexley.

Thunder boomed.

The gun. Oh, dear God, the gun.

Both men went still. Her ears rang. Candlestick poised, she approached cautiously. "Lovingdon?"

He rose slowly and delivered two quick punches to Vexley's nose. He struggled to stand. As he revealed his foe, she saw the blood on Vexley's chest. It was a horrid sight, but she felt no sympathy. Relief swamped her, and the candlestick clattered at her feet. She rushed to Lovingdon and threw her arms around him. He grunted.

"You're all right," she sobbed, tears welling in her eyes. "You're all right. I was so afraid—"

"I wouldn't have . . . let him . . . hurt you."

"I wasn't afraid for me, you silly man. I thought he'd hurt you."

He wrapped his arms around her. "You're safe."

"You saved me."

"I'm not a dragon slayer, Little Rose. I'm only a man."

She felt thick and warm liquid easing through her clothing. Vexley's blood. But why was it still so warm? Why was there so much of it on Lovingdon?

Pulling back, she saw the red blossoming over his shirt. "Oh, my dear God."

He gave her a sweet, sad smile as his fingers barely grazed her cheek. She could see the pain in his eyes. He dropped to all fours.

"Lovingdon!"

He slid the rest of the way to the floor. She fell to her knees, placed his head on her lap, and pressed a hand where the blood flowed. And then she screamed at the top of her lungs, "Help! Dear God, someone help!"

Chapter 16

⎯⎯⎯◦⎯⎯⎯

Grace sat in a chair beside the bed where Lovingdon lay as still as death. They were into the second night since his encounter with Vexley. After collapsing onto the floor, he'd not awoken. From time to time he mumbled incoherently. She wiped his fevered brow, held his clammy hand. It all seemed so futile.

Thank God for Drake. He'd found them at the church, and with the aid of the vicar and Vexley's driver, carried Lovingdon to an inn. He'd roused a constable to place Vexley in gaol until it was decided what to do with him, then secured a rested horse and fairly flew back to Mabry Manor to retrieve Dr. Graves.

Drake hadn't wanted to risk Lovingdon in a bouncing carriage over rutted and mud-slogged roads. He hadn't trusted the local physician, whom he'd thought in all likelihood was another of Vexley's men. He stayed only long enough to see the bleeding stanched and then left Grace in charge. She had thrown her father's name around to give weight to her words, and while many may not have heard of the Duke of Greystone, enough had that she was listened to. Or perhaps it was simply that she wouldn't tolerate not being obeyed.

Lovingdon had lost a good deal of blood before Graves took the scalpel to him to do what he could to repair the damage done. But she could tell by the expression on the physician's face that he didn't hold out much hope for Lovingdon returning to them as strong and bold as he'd been before the bullet struck him down.

Her family and Lovingdon's had taken over the inn. It was as quiet and somber as a church, and while people offered to relieve her, she wouldn't leave him, wouldn't give up these last minutes to be with him.

She wanted to hear his voice, just once more, to see his smile. She wanted to gaze into his eyes and know that he recognized her. She wanted to thank him for showing her that she could be beautiful, even with imperfections.

However had he borne it when Juliette was dying? And precious Margaret?

She understood now—with resounding clarity she wished she didn't possess—why he had broken. Her own heart felt as though it had turned to glass and at any moment would shatter beyond all recognition.

Somewhere a clock struck two. She was alone with this man whom she loved more than life. She wanted to beg, plead, cajole him into fighting—but his pain was so much more than physical. She understood that clearly now.

She pressed her lips to the back of his hand, a hand that had brought her pleasure and comfort and now brought her strength.

"What a silly chit I was. I thought love only mattered if I were loved in return, but I have learned that it is enough to love, and that one must love enough to care more for the other's happiness. I want nothing more than for you to be joyful and unburdened. So let go, my darling, go to Juliette. I know she awaits. Let go."

Let go. Juliette awaits.

Lovingdon was vaguely aware of the mantra urging him to let go, to release his hold on this aching body.

Yes, he needed to let go. He understood that now as he floated in oblivion. It was time, time to let go.

With a clarity born of deep memories, he envisioned Juliette as he'd loved her best, with her pale hair floating around her shoulders like gossamer moonbeams, of her blue eyes dancing with devilment. Her smile that welcomed and warmed.

And Margaret. Almost a mirrored reflection.

He loved them so damned much. But for the first time it didn't hurt to think of them. A kaleidoscope of memories washed through him, and each one lightened the weight of their passing. Why had he held the recollections at bay? Why had he thought they had the power to rip him apart, when in truth they were strong enough to lace him back together? So many wonderful moments. He wanted to hold them close, but they slipped through his fingers. They weren't solid. They were mist.

They didn't hold his hand. They didn't press warm lips to his knuckles. They didn't splash salty tears upon his skin.

Slowly, so very slowly, he cracked open his eyes. The room was dimly lit, but enough light escaped the lamp to cast a halo around Grace. She looked awful . . . and beautiful. With her eyes closed, she held his hand against her cheek. Her hair was a tangled mess. Her dress looked to be that of a servant. His last conscious memory was of her standing in the church. He vaguely remembered voices circling about him—Drake, Graves, his mother.

And Grace. Always Grace speaking to him.

"It's all right," she whispered now. "You can let go."

"I did."

Her eyes flew open and she stared at him as though he had risen from the dead. Perhaps he had. Dear God, he'd certainly felt dead these past two years. Until this marvelous woman had knocked on his bedchamber door. Until she challenged him and irritated him. Until she'd shown him what it was to want, to desire, to dream of something grand that would last a lifetime. Until she'd revealed profound courage and strength that far exceeded anything he'd ever possessed. She thought she needed someone who truly loved her because she believed herself imperfect, when in truth she was perfection. He'd known her when she was a girl but never truly known her as a woman—not until recently. Now she haunted him and occupied his thoughts.

"I let Juliette and Margaret go." His voice was rough, ragged, sounded strange to his ears.

Tears welled in her eyes. Because she hadn't released his hand, he had only to unfurl his fingers to touch her cheek. Her soft, damp cheek. "God help you, Grace, but I love you. I want to marry you. I need to marry you. I will marry you."

She shook her head. "You're delirious. You don't know what you're saying."

"I'm deliriously in love with you, and I do know what I'm saying." Sliding his hand around, he cupped the back of her neck. "I am too weak to sit up, however, so come lay down beside me."

She gave him some water first before nestling against his uninjured side. "I feared he'd killed you," she said softly, her hand curled on his chest.

"I feared it as well, and all I could think was that I hadn't had enough time with you. I want years with you, so many that we'll lose count."

"I don't know if I can promise you that, Lovingdon. We never know how much time we'll have."

He knew she was thinking of the malignancy, that it could return, that this time it could take her. The thought terrified him, but he wasn't going to hide from it, he wasn't going to deny himself time with her just because of what *might* happen. "Whatever time you have, Grace, whatever time either of us have, I want to spend it with you."

He heard a small sob, felt hot tears hit his skin.

"I thought you wanted a man who loves you," he teased.

Nodding, she lifted herself up on her elbow and skimmed her fingers along his jaw. "I love you. We shall be so happy together. But first we must get you well. I should fetch Dr. Graves so he can examine you."

"In a bit." His eyes began to grow heavy and he pulled her back down to him. "For now, just sleep. Sleep with me and never leave me until I am a crotchety old man."

He thought he heard her promise, but it hardly mattered. He would be grateful for whatever time he had with her. Be it a day, a month, a year. A moment.

He didn't know how long he slept, but when he awoke, light spilled in through the window. Grace was sleeping against his side. His arm was numb and would no doubt hurt like bloody hell when she left him, but like all hurts, it would subside, and she would soon be back in his arms. Tenderly, with his other hand, he brushed aside the strands of hair that partially hid her face. He was quite looking forward to all the mornings he would awaken to her in his bed.

Her nose twitched, she smiled, and slowly opened her eyes. So like her to be optimistic and smile before she saw what the day held.

"Good morning," he rasped.

" 'Morning."

"Not exactly how I envisioned our first morning together."

"You can't flirt with me just yet, not until Dr. Graves has seen you." Leaning up, she brushed a quick kiss across his lips, rolled out of bed, and with a tiny squeak came up short. "Father."

Lovingdon saw him now, standing near the foot of the bed, arms crossed. He didn't appear at all pleased to see that Lovingdon had survived. Or perhaps he merely looked as though he had grand plans for a painful death for the man who had taken his daughter into his bed without benefit of marriage. Even if nothing except innocence had transpired the night before.

Lovingdon struggled to sit up, fell back against the pillows. He supposed an inch was better than none. "I know you refused to give us your blessing when I asked for it, but I intend to marry your daughter with or without it."

Grace jerked her head around. "You asked for his blessing?"

He nodded. "The morning after . . . the night that we argued."

She looked at her father. "And you didn't give it?"

"I didn't give any of them my blessing."

Grace blinked, stared. "Any of them?"

Greystone looked at the ceiling. "Hmm. Yes. I think there were twenty-two, twenty-three, who asked for your hand in marriage."

"You denied them all?" Grace asked.

The duke looked unabashed. "You wanted love, sweetheart. I knew to a man who truly loved you that it wouldn't matter whether I gave my blessing." His gaze came back to bear on Lovingdon. "Seems I was right." His brow puckered. "Although I didn't take a man of Vexley's ilk into consideration."

"He asked for my hand in marriage?" Grace asked.

"He cornered me at the ball. He seemed to take my response civilly enough. I misjudged him."

"I think we all did," Lovingdon said, once again feeling his strength draining.

"I'll fetch Graves," Greystone said. He began to walk out.

Grace rushed after him and wound her arms around his neck. "Thank you, Papa. Thank you for your blessing."

"Be happy, sweetheart. Be very happy."

Grace turned, strode back to the bed, sat on its edge and took Lovingdon's hand.

He threaded his fingers through hers. "You will be happy."

She smiled. "I know."

Chapter 17

As Grace sat at her vanity while Felicity pinned her hair, she gave her gaze freedom to wander over to the red vase filled with her favorite flowers—red roses. They had arrived first thing that morning with a missive.

> *Because they're your favorite, you should have them today.*
> —*L*

Her heart had done a little somersault. It had been six weeks since the Midsummer Eve's ball. Lovingdon's wound had healed. When he needed fresh air, he had invited her for an open carriage ride through the park. As he'd grown stronger, they walked.

And talked. They spoke of everything. Their

upcoming wedding. The trip they would take to Paris. All the exhibits they would see.

While rumors concerning what exactly had transpired following her family's country ball were scarce, everyone was well aware that the Earl of Vexley was persona non grata in the eyes of London's most powerful families. He'd lost his membership at Dodger's. No woman with any dowry welcomed his courtship and he courted no woman who had no dowry. He was seen about London sporting two black eyes and a broken nose. As he had taken to mumbling when he spoke, many thought he might have a broken jaw.

They were right.

Grace knew the nose was the result of Lovingdon's punches in the church, and she suspected that Vexley's broken jaw was the result of Drake spending a little time with him in gaol. As a lord of the realm, Vexley had neatly sidestepped arrest for abducting her and shooting Lovingdon. He'd claimed self-defense on the latter charge, asserting he was convinced Lovingdon meant to kill him. Considering the murderous rage she'd seen on Lovingdon's face when he flung himself at Vexley, she suspected the earl's assumption was correct. But with the other families delivering their own messages to Vexley—and no doubt additional blows—she was convinced he'd suffered enough. He was ostracized. She doubted he'd ever regain his place in Society, and was rather embarrassed to admit she'd ever found him charming.

Her attention wandered again to the red roses and the vase that held them. She would have them delivered to her new home so they were waiting for her when she arrived this evening. The other glass pieces were already there, as were most of her belongings.

Today she was going to become a wife, but more than that, she was going to marry a man who loved her, imperfections and all.

When her hair was done, she stepped into her wedding gown of lace and pearls. Felicity gently padded the left side. Grace knew that Lovingdon wouldn't care if it was flat on one side but she liked the symmetry, and on this day, at least, she was vain enough to care.

Carefully, she placed the pearls at her neck, pearls her mother had given her, pearls given to her mother by the man she believed to be her father. Grace sometimes found it difficult to believe the life her mother had led, the life that had brought her here to capture the heart of a duke.

Now she possessed her own duke's heart.

She had no doubts that Lovingdon loved her.

Even if he hadn't known her favorite flower, she had no doubts where his affections lay. It was strange to think that she once doubted her ability to gauge love, but Lovingdon had told her to trust her heart, that it would know. By Jove, but he was right about that.

Flowers, listening, gazing into her eyes, touching her, small but important things he had cited as examples—Lovingdon did them all, without thought or artifice. He didn't need her dowry, but apparently what he did need was her love. He possessed it in abundance.

A rap sounded on her door all of three seconds before her mother opened it. She smiled. "Don't you look beautiful?"

"I feel beautiful. He makes me feel beautiful."

"As well he should. Are you ready to be off to St. George's?"

"I've never been more ready for anything in my life."

Lovingdon stood at the front of the church, Drake and Avendale beside him, while he waited for Grace. He didn't want to think of Juliette, and in fact could only vaguely recall the last time he had stood here. He'd been so much younger, more boy than man, filled with promise and promises.

He was more tempered now, not quite so eager or brash. More cautious about life. More determined to never take Grace for granted. His wound was healed. He was as fit as ever. He'd need that fitness tonight. While he had been with Grace since the night he rescued her from Vexley, he'd had very few moments alone with her—a kiss here, another one there, but nothing beyond that. He ached to touch all of her again, to sink his body into hers, to know her again as he'd known her in the little cottage, but not quite the same. There would be a deepness and richness to their lovemaking this time. He'd once thought that he loved nothing more than being nestled between a woman's thighs. But now he knew he loved nothing more than being nestled between hers.

The organ began to play, and he looked up the aisle to see her maid of honor and bridesmaid leading the way: Lady Ophelia and then Minerva. Minnie winked at him and smiled. He wondered how much longer it would be before she was a bride.

The music rose in crescendo, and he turned his attention toward the back of the church. With her arm tucked around her father's, Grace glided up the aisle, taking his breath. The hair she had once despised was the most colorful part about her. She was a vision in white, a gossamer veil covering her face. Such a silly bit of frippery that would prevent him from gazing on her fully. Then she was near enough that he could inhale her lavender and rose scent. The rose was a little heavier, as she held a bouquet of red roses.

Yes, he'd known her favorite flower. He'd always known, from the moment he'd likened her to a red rose and she gave him a gap-toothed grin. He'd known her all of her life, had so many memories of her growing up. It still astounded him to realize that he had managed to overlook her blossoming into the woman he once promised her she'd become.

What a fortunate man he was that her suitors had not seen beyond the dowry, did not recognize the beauty that he did.

When the Duke of Greystone turned her over to his keeping, Lovingdon felt a tightness in his chest. The responsibility, the fears, the doubts, they were all there. That he would make promises he could not keep. He'd done that once before.

But then Grace smiled at him, and he saw the determination and the understanding in her eyes. She had been forged by her own fires and was stronger because of them. She'd not require that he watch over her, but watch over her he would.

He listened intently as she recited her vows, then he recited his with a sure voice. When he was told he could kiss the bride, he lifted her veil to find her blue eyes fastened on him.

"You never looked away from me," she said in wonder.

"That's because I'm in love with you." He lowered his mouth to hers, wishing hundreds of people weren't about.

Soon, very soon, he would have her all to himself.

Chapter 18

Grace waltzed with the first man she had ever loved: her father.

While it was not customary for the bride and groom to attend the evening ball usually held on the day of their wedding, she'd wanted one more dance with her father, and her husband had been inclined to indulge her whim. She suspected he would do quite a bit of indulging over the coming years.

While the orchestra played, she and her father were the only ones on the dance floor. He moved with ease, as he had no worries about stumbling into anyone. He was tall and handsome, and she could easily understand why he had swept her mother off her feet. She hoped he still had enough vision remaining that he could see her joyous smile and the sparkle in her eyes. She had never known such happiness. And she knew it was only the beginning.

"You're beautiful," he said, "so much like your mother on the day I married her."

She could not have received a compliment that would have pleased her more, but she knew the truth of it. "Love does that to a person, I hear."

Grinning, he bowed his head in acknowledgment. "It does indeed."

"You should know that as Lovingdon has no need for my dowry, we're going to use the land to establish a sanctuary where women can heal when faced with surgeries about which people will never speak. They can confide in each other, draw comfort and strength from similar tribulations. We're going to place the money that comes with the dowry into a trust fund to cover the expenses of the upkeep and servants."

"I suspect even if Lovingdon were in need of funds, he would still allow you to do with your dowry as you pleased. He loves you, Grace. For him, the dowry was never a consideration."

"I know." She couldn't seem to stop herself from smiling broadly. "I'm the most fortunate woman on earth."

"I may be a bit biased, but I say he's the fortunate one."

Out of the corner of her eye she watched as Lovingdon led her mother into the dance area and swept her across the floor. She and her mother did favor each other. She hoped that she would still have an opportunity to dance with Lovingdon when her hair had faded and lines created by years of joy creased her face.

Lovingdon caught her gaze, and with smooth yet swift movements managed to change dance partners. The Duke and Duchess of Greystone now waltzed together, while Grace waltzed with the man she loved.

"I do believe this is the longest song I've ever heard," he grumbled.

"I asked them to play it twice, without stopping. Thank you for delaying the start of our wedding trip so that I could dance with my father. It means a great deal to me to have a final waltz with him."

"I love you too much to deny you anything, Little Rose."

Her heart somersaulted, once, twice, thrice. She would never tire of him saying the words, and it seemed he wouldn't tire of saying them. He never missed an opportunity to remind her that to him she was everything.

The music drifted into silence. He brought her gloved hand to his lips and held her gaze. "I would very much like to take my wife home now."

His wife. She was his wife. She could hardly fathom it. She nodded. "I should very much like for my husband to take me home."

As they journeyed in his coach through the dark London streets, Lovingdon kissed Grace sweetly, gently, and she knew that he was holding his passion in check. She also knew she had no reason to be nervous, and yet she was, just a bit. While he'd been healing, they'd shared an occasional kiss but nothing more. Tonight they would finally be alone, but more than that they were allowed to be alone. His restraint made her worry that perhaps the hunger of their previous encounters had been a result of doing things they shouldn't. Now they were legal. Now she was his wife, and she couldn't help but wonder if he viewed her differently.

While she viewed him quite the same. She could hardly wait to be in bed with him. She could look at him to her heart's content. Touch him, snuggle against him.

The coach came to a halt. A footman opened the door. Lovingdon leaped out. When she leaned into the doorway, he slid an arm around her, lifted her out, and quickly placed his other arm beneath her legs. She wound her arms around his neck.

"What are you doing?" she asked.

"Carrying my wife."

"But your injury—"

"Is completely healed."

She nestled her head against his shoulder and protested halfheartedly, "Whatever will the servants think?"

"That the Duke of Lovingdon loves his wife to distraction."

He climbed the steps. Another footman opened the door, and Lovingdon carried her into the foyer. She'd expected him to put her down there, but he continued up the wide sweeping stairs to the upper floor.

He stopped before the door to his bedchamber, and she thought of the long-ago night when she had knocked on it. She couldn't help but wonder if a secretive part of her had wished then that she would end up here.

"You need to take me to my chamber so I can prepare myself for you," she told him.

He grinned broadly at her, and she couldn't help but believe that she had managed to put joy back into his life. "I'll see to preparing you."

"But I bought a lovely lace nightdress to wear for you."

"Why bother putting it on when I'll only tear it off you?"

With a light laugh, she tightened her arms around him. "I feared as my husband, you might get all proper on me."

"Because I only kissed you in the carriage? I've been anticipating this night too much to ruin it on the journey here. I want you in my bed." His eyes darkened. "Open the door."

Leaning over, she released the latch and he kicked the door open. As he carried her in, she was assailed by a faint familiar scent.

"I smell paint," she told him.

"Yes, I had some work done. I was hoping it would all air out by now."

She glanced around. "But your walls are all papered."

"The ceiling isn't."

Glancing up, she released a bubble of laughter. "The nymphs!"

Gone were the voluptuous maidens who had greeted her before. These vixens were slender and long-limbed, every one of them. Their red hair—the exact shade as hers—cascaded wildly around them.

"Oh, Lovingdon." She planted her mouth on his, kissing him deeply and passionately. She was vaguely aware of him walking, then carrying her down to the bed. Without breaking from the kiss, he stretched out beside her, cradled her face with one hand, and began to ravish her mouth with all the enthusiasm she'd hoped for. She didn't know if he could have done anything that would have pleased her more.

But then his hot mouth trailed along her throat, and she realized that everything he gave her was going to please her.

"You like them?" he murmured against her skin.

"Very much so."

Raising himself on an elbow, he began plucking the pins from her hair. "It was rather fascinating to watch as Leo transformed what was there into what I desired."

"In spite of being up in years, he's a remarkable artist." She was familiar with him as he'd done several portraits of her family.

"He is indeed. I would lie here at night in torment because my favorite nymph wasn't in my bed. Now you're here, and I intend to make you very glad that you are."

He rolled out of bed, brought her to her feet, and turned her so she was facing away from him. He went to work on her lacings, his mouth following the path as skin was revealed. His hands made short work of the tasks, and in no time at all, her clothes were piled on the floor. Cupping his palms over her shoulders, he slowly turned her.

It wasn't fair that he remained clothed, but she couldn't quite bring herself to reach for him, not when he was studying her as he was. He lowered his gaze, and she fought not to hide herself from him. Lovingdon loved her. He'd seen her scars. They weren't a surprise.

Finally, he slid his hands down until one cradled her breast and the other flattened against her scars.

"These terrify me, you know," he said quietly, "because of what they could portend."

"Don't think about that."

He lifted his gaze to hers, and she was taken aback to see the thin veil of tears. "I also find them remarkably beautiful because they are part of you, your strength, your courage. I don't know that I'm worthy of you, Grace, because I have neither your strength nor your courage. But I swear that you will never find a man who loves you more than I do."

Leaning in, he pressed his lips to the corner of her mouth before sliding his mouth over to cover hers. The kiss was deep, hungry. It reached into her soul, caused everything inside her to curl inward like a rose closing up for the night, and then sensations blossomed like petals unfurling.

Tearing his mouth from hers, he trailed it along her throat, her collarbone, nibbling, licking, teasing.

"I want your clothes off," she breathed on a heady rush.

Stepping back, he held out his arms and grinned. "I'm all yours to do with as you please."

Her fingers were not as nimble as his as she worked to remove his clothing, but she took great pleasure in revealing him inch by inch until his clothes were resting on the floor beside hers. She flattened her palm on the puckered scar at his side.

"I always thought scars were hideous things, but I was wrong. You have these because you saved me. You have them because you lived. To me, they are quite beautiful."

Cradling her face between his hands, he tilted up her chin until she held his gaze. "Nothing, no one is as beautiful as you."

His mouth blanketed hers as he carried her down to the bed. She loved the feel of his silken skin against hers.

Once again, he began to take his lips on a sojourn along her throat. "I love the length of your neck," he rasped. "Truth be told, I love the entire length of you." He closed his hand over her breast. "I love the way you fit within my palm." Kneading her flesh gently, he leaned over and kissed her scars.

She loved that he didn't avoid any inch of her,

that he relished every part of her. She had so hoped to find a man who would appreciate each aspect of her, and Lovingdon did. Just as she appreciated all of him. She ran her hands over his shoulders, through his dark golden locks. She skimmed her fingers over his jaw.

He moved lower, leaving a hot trail of kisses along her stomach. Lower still. Then he adjusted himself so he was at her feet and she couldn't reach him at all. But when she protested, he simply said, "Patience."

After massaging her feet, he ran his hands up her legs. "I love your long legs. I want them wrapped around me."

She crooked a finger at him. "Then come back up here."

"Not yet."

He kissed his way along her calves, one then the other. He lingered at her knees, before giving attention to the inside of her thighs, again one side then the other. He kissed all of her, every inch, front and back, over and under. She felt very much like the coin he so often rolled over his fingers. Constantly being touched, constantly moving.

But she couldn't simply receive. She had to give as well.

She began following his lead: caressing, tasting,

exploring the peaks and the valleys, the flat plains. He was firm muscle, hot skin. He was perfection, scars and all.

Sensations became all-encompassing. Their breathing grew harsher, their bodies slick. There was no rush and yet there was a hunger that couldn't be denied. Suddenly it wasn't enough to be a tangle of limbs. She needed more and based on the tightness of his jaw, she knew he did as well.

Opening herself to him, she welcomed him, relishing his fullness as he sank into her. She would never have to resist again, never have to curb her passion, her desires.

Nuzzling her neck, he said, "You feel so good. So good."

Bringing her legs up, she wrapped them around him and squeezed. He groaned, before proceeding to ravish her mouth. Every sensation was more intense, every aspect of their coming together was richer.

Because he loves me, she thought. Because I love him.

He possessed her heart, her body, her soul.

He began rocking against her, slowly at first, increasing his tempo as she urged him on with her cries. Scraping her fingers over his back, she wondered how it was possible that so many different sensations could be spiraling through her at the same time. They consumed her, just as he did.

The feel of his mouth on her skin, the caress of his hands, his growls, his arms tightening around her—all served to increase her pleasure as it rose to a fevered pitch.

They moved in unison, touching, kissing. He whispered sweet endearments, and she responded in kind. She wanted to give as much as he gave her, wanted him to take all she had to offer.

Undulating waves of pleasure began coursing through her, taking her ever higher. Beneath her fingers, his sinewy muscles bunched and bulged.

"Come with me, Grace," he urged.

And she did. She followed him into a realm where there was nothing except sensations, where her body sang, her heart soared, and her soul rejoiced.

Breathing heavily, he buried his face in the curve of her neck. They lay there replete and exhausted. She thought she might never move again.

It was long moments before he rose up on his elbows and gazed down on her. With his fingers, he moved aside the damp strands of her hair.

"I hope you didn't find that an empty experience."

She laughed with abandon. "I most certainly did not."

"Good. I didn't either. Now, I have something wicked in mind that involves brandy. Are you up for it?"

She was the one who made use of the brandy, dripping droplets on his chest, then lapping them up like a greedy little cat, purring as she did so, a vibration in her throat that sent pleasure coursing through him.

He wondered why he ever thought he had the strength to deny his love for her. Why he had denied it, why he hadn't embraced it sooner. She made life fun again, laughing and teasing him in bed. She was open to whatever manner he might devise to bring her pleasure. She was willing to learn all she could about bringing pleasure to him.

Not that he needed much. Kissing her, touching her, being buried inside her was enough. Sometimes he thought the heat generated between them would scald them both—but all it did was leave them breathless and anxious to rekindle the fire.

He nudged his wife over until she was straddling his hips. Then he plowed his hands into her hair and brought her mouth down to his. She tasted of brandy mingled with him, yet underneath it all was her own flavoring, so sweet. A man could never have enough of it, could never fill up on it.

Her luscious kiss could bring him to his knees if he wasn't already prone.

She wasn't timid, she didn't hold back. Her tongue parried with his on equal terms. He would not compare her to what he'd had before except to acknowledge that she was unlike anything he'd ever known. He hadn't been able to keep up with her when she was younger. He hoped to God he could keep up with her now.

Tearing his mouth from hers, he dragged it along her silken throat. "I love you."

She smiled, dropping her head back to give him easier access. "I adore you."

"Then come to me."

He lifted her up, settled her down, feeling her heat envelop him as she sheathed him. She felt marvelous. So tight, so molten. God, she was like a furnace.

She rocked against him, rode him. Unbashful, unrepentant, unapologetic. She was wildly beautiful when passion caught hold of her. Her blue eyes dazzled, her skin flushed, her hair danced around her like living flames. Red and copper.

His rose. A bud who had unfurled into something rare and precious.

She was his, as he was hers. For whatever time they had. He would relish every moment. He didn't fear losing her. He feared wasting moments that they could have shared. She would no doubt grow tired of his constant attentions.

He cupped her breast. It barely filled his palm, but it was enough. Gently, he kneaded, his thumb circling the pearl of her nipple. She looked down on him. With his free hand, he cradled the back of her neck and brought her down.

"I love you," he rasped again before taking her mouth. He should not be this hungry for her again, and yet he was. She stirred something deep inside him that had never been touched. Odd for a man who had loved as deeply as he had to discover that there were depths yet to be explored.

Breaking off the kiss, she pushed herself up, pressing her palms to his chest, leveraging herself, riding him with wild abandon. The pleasure built. Her cries echoed around him, her spine arched, and she threw her head back.

"Gorgeous," he rasped, just before his orgasm shook him to the core.

She sprawled across him. He draped his arms over her, holding her near, while his heart settled into a normal rhythm, a rhythm that beat for her.

Grace awoke to an empty bed, something she'd not expected. It was still night. The clock on the mantel indicated that it was a bit past two. Reaching out, she touched the rumpled sheets where Lovingdon had lain. They were cool.

Slipping off the mattress, she donned her night-dress, but didn't bother with the wrap at the foot of the bed. She wanted her husband.

She found him in the library, standing in front of the life-size portrait of his wife. It was no longer above the fireplace but perched in front of it. She didn't resent it, knowing that Juliette and Margaret had shaped him, would always be part of him. But something inside her twisted. She'd hoped that at least on their wedding night it would be only the two of them in this house, in his bed. It seemed they could not escape the memories or the ghost of his previous life.

Lovingdon glanced over his shoulder. He hadn't bothered to straighten his hair, mussed from her fingers. She wanted to muss it some more. "Grace?"

"I'm sorry. I didn't mean to disturb you."

"Come here, sweetheart."

She hesitated, knowing she was being silly to feel as though she were intruding. This was her home now, their home. She forced herself to move forward. When she was close enough, he took her hand and drew her in against his warm solid body.

"I didn't expect to find you gone from our bed," she said quietly.

"I was just saying good-bye to Juliette."

She looked up at him. His gaze wasn't on the portrait, but on her.

"When I was unconscious, fevered, in pain, I kept hearing this strong, determined voice urging me to let go, of life I think."

She nodded. "I wanted you to be happy."

"But if I let go of life, it meant releasing you, and I could not find the strength to do that. So I let go of Juliette. I am not the man who fell in love with her. Nor am I the man with whom she fell in love." Turning, he cradled her face. "I am the man who fell in love with you. God knows I didn't want to love you. I think losing you would kill me—but the thought of not having some days and nights with you because of my own cowardice . . . I could not live with myself if I missed out on a single moment with you." He kissed her then, gently, sweetly.

She understood what he was telling her. She was right for him, perfect for him. He had changed, and she loved the man he was now. She loved everything about him.

When they broke apart, she could have sworn that the smile on the portrait seemed softer, warmer.

"I'm going to put a portrait of her and Margaret in my study, so I don't forget them. The rest are going into storage. You are my life now."

As much as she relished his words, she couldn't be so selfish. "I don't want you to forget them."

"I shan't forget them; I couldn't if I tried, but it is time for me to begin anew." He lifted her into his arms and began carrying her from the room.

"I love you, Lovingdon," she said against his neck.

"When I'm done with you, in an hour or so, you're going to love me just a little bit more."

She laughed. "What have you in mind, my wicked duke?"

He smiled at her, and she realized that she already loved him just a little bit more.

Epilogue

From the Journal of the Duke of Lovingdon

In my lifetime I loved two women. I cannot say which I loved more because I was a very different man when I loved each of them. And I loved each of them differently.

I began adulthood with Juliette.

When my life comes to a close, it shall be with Grace at my side.

She blessed me with an heir, a spare, and a daughter. While I know that a father should not have favorites, I must admit my ginger-haired little girl wrapped herself around my heart the first time she wound her small hand around my finger. Watching Lavinia grow into womanhood was one of the most joyous, yet bittersweet aspects of my life. She resembled Margaret not at all, but there were times when I watched her that I could not help but mourn my first daughter.

Being as strong-willed as her mother, Lavinia did not serve as a substitute for Margaret.

Just as Grace did not serve as a replacement for Juliette.

When she was forty, Grace exhibited signs of another malignancy, and Graves did what needed to be done to ensure that she not yet leave me. She had once asked of me, "Is it not better to hold someone for a short span of time rather than not to have held them at all?"

During the agonizing hours while I waited for him to assure me that she would be well, I came to accept with startling clarity the truth of her words. All the moments we'd shared—I would not have given up a single one of them in order to spare myself the sorrow of losing her.

Holding her for a short time was indeed preferable to never having had the pleasure of holding her at all.

But this time the Fates were kind, and they allowed me to hold awhile longer that which I treasured above all else.

We are up into our years now. I see no signs that we shall be parting anytime soon.

My darling Grace wished only to marry a man who loved her. She met with astonishing success in that regard. For I loved her yesterday, I love her today, and I shall love her for all eternity.

Whether or not the Fates are kind.

Author's Note

The beauty in writing fiction is the license I have to change facts so they match what is needed for the story.

Public awareness of breast cancer is a recent phenomenon, which is why only Grace's parents knew of her condition. Unfortunately, the mores of Victorian times made it something of which to be ashamed, but in quiet corners I'm certain Grace encouraged women to pay attention to their bodies.

By this time in history a good many physicians had begun removing lymph nodes when they performed mastectomies. As anyone who has read the Scoundrels of St. James series knows, Dr. William Graves was ahead of his time when it came to caring for his patients. While I didn't go into the details of his treatment for Grace, rest assured he took all measures known at the time to ensure she lived a long life.

The beauty in writing romance fiction is the license I have to ensure my couples always have their happy ending. Lovingdon and Grace are no exception. They lived long, joy-filled lives.

I enjoyed sharing their story with you and look forward to sharing Drake's next.

Warmly,
Lorraine

Next month, don't miss these exciting
new love stories only from
Avon Books

Moonlight on My Mind by Jennifer McQuiston
Months ago, Julianne Baxter wrongly implicated
Patrick, the new Earl of Haversham, in his older
brother's death. Now, convinced of his innocence, she's
tracked him to Scotland. But a clandestine wedding
may be the only way to save her reputation—and his
neck from the hangman's noose.

Between the Devil and Ian Eversea by Julie Anne Long
The moment American heiress Titania "Tansy" Danforth
arrives in England she cuts a swath through Sussex,
enslaving hearts and stealing beaux. But Ian Eversea, the
only man who fascinates her, couldn't be less interested.
Eversea never dreams the real Tansy—vulnerable, brave,
and achingly sensual—will tempt him beyond
endurance.

Wallflower Gone Wild by Maya Rodale
Lady Olivia Archer's marriage prospects are so bleak
that her parents have betrothed her to Phinneas Cole, a
stranger with a dire reputation. If he wants a biddable
bride, perhaps Olivia can frighten him off by breaking
every ladylike rule. Soon the newly provocative Olivia
discovers there's nothing so appealing as a fiancé who's
mad, bad, and dangerously seductive . . .

REL 0314

Give in to your Impulses!

These unforgettable stories only take a second to buy and give you hours of reading pleasure!

Go to *www.AvonImpulse.com* and see what we have to offer.

Available wherever e-books are sold.

AVONIMPULSE